Gordon Goodwin, Arthur Henry Bullen

The Poems of William Browne of Tavistock

Volume 1

Gordon Goodwin, Arthur Henry Bullen

The Poems of William Browne of Tavistock
Volume 1

ISBN/EAN: 9783744770248

Printed in Europe, USA, Canada, Australia, Japan

Cover: Foto ©Andreas Hilbeck / pixelio.de

More available books at **www.hansebooks.com**

The Muses' Library.

The Muses' Library.

POEMS

OF

WILLIAM BROWNE

VOL. I.

BRITANNIA'S
Pastorals.
Lond: print: for Geo: Norton. dwell: at Temple barr. W. Hole f.

THE POEMS OF
WILLIAM BROWNE

OF TAVISTOCK:

EDITED BY GORDON GOODWIN,

WITH AN INTRODUCTION

BY A. H. BULLEN.

VOL. I.

<table>
<tr><td>LONDON:</td><td>NEW YORK:</td></tr>
<tr><td>LAWRENCE & BULLEN,</td><td>CHARLES SCRIBNER'S SONS,</td></tr>
<tr><td>16 HENRIETTA STREET, W.C</td><td>743 & 745 BROADWAY.</td></tr>
<tr><td>1894.</td><td>1894.</td></tr>
</table>

LONDON:
PRINTED BY WOODFALL AND KINDER,
70 TO 76 LONG ACRE, W.C.

CONTENTS.

	PAGE
Editor's Note	ix
Introduction	xiii
Britannia's Pastorals. Books I. and II.	1

EDITOR'S NOTE.

—

In the present edition of Browne's poems the text has been revised by a careful collation of the original editions and all known manuscripts. The more important various readings are given in the notes at the end of the second volume.

The first book of *Britannia's Pastorals* appeared in folio, without any date on the curiously-engraved title-page, but the address to the reader is dated 18th June, 1613, and the volume was entered in the Stationers' Registers on the ensuing 15th November. The second book followed in 1616. The two books were reissued in an octavo volume in 1625. The third book of the *Pastorals* was not published in the poet's lifetime; but Beriah Botfield, while engaged in collecting materials for his

work on cathedral libraries, discovered a manu
script copy of it in the library of Salisbury
Cathedral. It is a neatly-written manuscript,
bound up at the end of a copy of the folio
edition of the first two books (1613–16), which
appears to have belonged to one Richard
Charles. Preceding it are two leaves, roughly
written and with many corrections and erasures,
containing the elegy on Thomas Manwood (the
fourth eclogue of *The Shepherd's Pipe*), and
three short poems, which are now printed for
the first time. In the printed portion of the
volume are several manuscript emendations.
The MS., so far as it related to the *Pastorals*,
was printed for the Percy Society in 1852, under
the editorship of T. Crofton Croker, and it has
since been reprinted in Mr. W. Carew Hazlitt's
collective edition of Browne's works (2 vols.
1868–69).

The Shepherd's Pipe appeared in 1614, small
8vo. It contains seven eclogues by Browne, to
which are appended eclogues by Christopher
Brooke, George Wither, and John Davies of
Hereford. A reprint of it was included in *The
Works of Master George Wither* (1620).

The Inner Temple Masque, written to be
represented by the members of that society on

the 13th January, 1614–15, was first printed in Thomas Davies's edition of Browne's poems (3 vols. 1772), from a manuscript in the library of Emmanuel College, Cambridge. Another manuscript copy is in the possession of Mr. H. Chandos Pole-Gell, of Hopton Hall, Wirksworth, and has been kindly lent for collation.

Among the Lansdowne MSS. (No. 777) in the British Museum is a collection of poems by Browne, dated 1650, but apparently made a few years earlier, which was first printed by Sir Samuel Egerton Brydges at the Lee Priory Press in 1815, and reprinted in 1869 by Mr. Hazlitt. Another middle seventeenth-century MS. in the library of Trinity College, Dublin, contains two poems by Browne—the epitaph on Anne Prideaux (six lines), and that on the Countess of Pembroke (twelve lines), both of which, however, are in the Lansdowne MS.

Browne's elegy on Henry, Prince of Wales, his earliest publication, was printed in 1613, with an elegy by Christopher Brooke, in a small quarto of seventeen leaves, entitled *Two Elegies, consecrated to the never-dying Memory of the most worthily admired, most heartily loved, and generally bewailed Prince, Henry Prince of Wales.* There is a manuscript copy of this elegy in the Bodleian Library. It was afterwards introduced, in a somewhat altered form, into the fifth song of the first book of *Britannia's Pastorals*.

I have derived considerable assistance from the previous labours of Mr. Hazlitt : his commentary contains much that is suggestive ; while the topographical and other notes of his Devonshire correspondent, Mr. John Shelly, have but one fault—they are too few.

GORDON GOODWIN.

INTRODUCTION.

INTRODUCTION.

WILLIAM BROWNE was a modest unassuming
spirit, but he flushed with honest pride when he
reflected on the worthiness of his native Devonshire. In the Third Song of the Second Book
of *Britannia's Pastorals*, he writes :—

> Show me who can so many crystal rills,
> Such sweet-cloth'd vallies or aspiring hills;
> Such wood-ground, pastures, quarries, wealthy mines ;
> Such rocks in whom the diamond fairly shines.

If for beauty and fertility Devonshire might be
matched, yet where could be found such another
race of sea-ruling men as Grenville, Davis,
Gilbert, Drake, Hawkins, and

>   thousands more
> That by their power made the Devonian shore
> Mock the proud Tagus?

He sadly contrasted the stirring days of
Elizabeth with the pusillanimous reign of

James I.   In a passage of striking picturesque-
ness, he describes how the old ships that had
repelled the Armada, and had harassed the
Spaniard. on every sea, now lay rotting in
harbour :

> And on their masts, where oft the ship-boy stood,
> Or silver trumpet charm'd the brackish flood,
> Some wearied crow is set.

Once these ships had sailed into the Devon
ports laden with the harvests snatched from
Spain, but now

> Upon their hatches, where half-pikes were borne,
> In every chink rise stems of bearded corn :
> Mocking our idle times that so have wrought us,
> Or putting us in mind what once they brought us.

It is pleasant to know that the old poet who
sang so heartily the praises of Devon is yet
beloved * on the banks of the Tavy and the
Plym.

Tavistock was Browne's native place, and he
was born not later than 1591.   No record of
his baptism is extant, as the Tavistock registers
do not begin before 1640.   He was a son of

* Articles on Browne are in the Transactions of the
Devonshire Association, vol. vi, 532, and vol. xix, 219–
237.

Thomas Browne of Tavistock, who is supposed
by Prince (*Worthies of Devon*) to have belonged
to the knightly family of the Brownes of
Browne's Ilash in the parish of Langtree, near
Great Torrington, Devonshire, a branch of the
Brownes of Betchworth Castle in Surrey.*
From Tavistock Grammar-school he passed
" about the beginning of the reign of James I."
(Wood's *Fasti*) to Exeter College, Oxford.
Leaving the University without a degree, he
entered Clifford's Inn, whence he migrated in
November 1611 to the Inner Temple.† On
18th April, 1615, a William Browne was
appointed pursuivant to the Court of Wards
and Liveries ; but we cannot be confident‡ that
it was the poet who received the appointment,
for there were two other William Brownes at

* The pedigree on the following page was given by
Sir Egerton Brydges from Harl. MS. 6164, before the
collection of Browne's miscellaneous poems issued from
the Lee Priory Press in 1815.

† He was admitted to the Inner Temple on 1st March,
1611-12 (not 1612-13, as stated by Mr. Hazlitt). George
Glapthorne, who became a surety for him on his
admission, was the elder brother of Henry Glapthorne
the dramatist.

‡ It is worth noting that the poet's friend Sir Benjamin
Rudyard was appointed Surveyor of this Court in 1618.

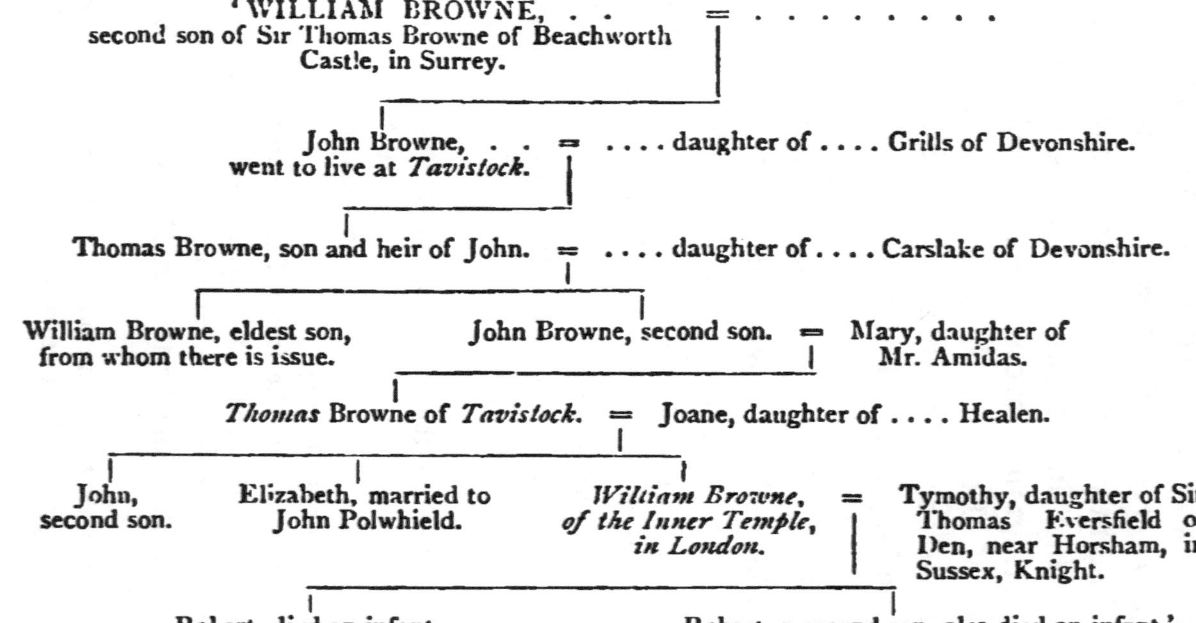

[Brydges was not aware that Timothy Eversfield was the poet's *second* wife,—a fact discovered by Mr. Gordon Goodwin.]

thè Inner Temple—one from Chichester, and one from Walcott, Northants (*Students of the Inner Temple*, 1571–1625, pp. 32, 57).

Browne was twice married. His first wife appears to have died in 1614. Among his miscellaneous poems in Lansdowne MS. 777 (first printed by Brydges) is the following epitaph :—

In Obitum M S, X° Maij, 1614.

May ! be thou never grac'd with birds that sing,
　　　Nor Flora's pride !
In thee all flowers and roses spring,
　　　Mine only died.

The letters " M S " may well stand for " Maritæ Suæ." In the same collection is an undated epitaph "On his Wife"; it is immediately preceded by " My own Epitaph," which is subscribed " Wm. Browne, 1614." His second wife was Timothy, daughter of Sir Thomas Eversfield, Kt., of Denne in the parish of Horsham, Sussex. The series of Sonnets (II, 217–225) headed " Cælia " was evidently addressed to this lady. From the epistle beginning " Dear soul, the time is come and we must part " (II, 228-9) it may be gathered that the engagement was protracted,—

Seven summers now are fully spent and gone,
Since first I lov'd, lov'd you, and you alone.

Browne's friend Michael Drayton wooed a
lady for thirty years, and the marriage never
took place after all. Browne began to pay his
addresses to Miss Eversfield in 1615 (see *An
Epistle*, II, 234-6) ; and at length, after thirteen
years' courtship, they were married at Horsham
on 24th December, 1628. Two sons were born
of the marriage, but died in infancy.* Sir
Thomas Eversfield, in his will proved on 25th
October, 1616, wished his three unmarried
daughters—Timothy, Joyce, and Bridget—to
have such portions as his wife should think fit
to be raised out of his lease of Tilgate, and he
named one thousand marks apiece as being a
suitable sum. Lady Eversfield appears to have
paid Timothy's dowry in full, as her will (made
in October 1640) concludes with this emphatic
declaration :—" I owe my son Browne not one
farthing of my daughter's portion for use nor
yet principal."†

* 1. Robert, baptized at Horsham on 27th September,
1629, died soon afterwards; 2. Robert, baptized on
20th March, 1630-1, buried on 22nd of the following
March.

† Lady Eversfield thus mentions Mrs. Browne in her
will :—" I give to my daughter Browne for a remembrance, to whom I have already given a portion, more
now, twenty shillings to make her a ring to wear for

Browne dedicated the First Book of *Britannia's Pastorals*, n. d. [1613], and *The Shepherd's Pipe*, 1614, to Lord Zouch, who had been President of Wales, and was afterwards (1615) Warden of the Cinque Ports. Selden contributed laudatory verses in Greek, Latin, and English; Michael Drayton, Christopher Brooke, and others added their commendations. The Second Book of *Britannia's Pastorals*, 1616, was dedicated to that famous patron of poets, himself a poet, William Herbert, third Earl of Pembroke. Among those who prefixed complimentary verses were John Davies of Hereford, George Wither, and Ben Jonson. One of the contributors, John Morgan of the Inner Temple, delicately expressed the hope that Browne would receive some tangible token of the Earl's esteem :—

> And may thy early strains affect the ear
> Of that rare Lord, who judge and guerdon can
> The richer gifts which do advantage man.

Browne owed much to the Herberts ; and his

my sake, and my seal ring, and my velvet gown and white petticoat, my gold coif and crosscloth to it."—For this extract I am indebted to Mr. Gordon Goodwin, whose researches have supplied whatever additions I have been able to make to Browne's family history.

monument of gratitude—the noble epitaph* on " Sidney's sister, Pembroke's mother "—will endure to the end of time.

At the beginning of 1624 Browne returned to Exeter College as tutor to Hon. Robert Dormer,† afterwards Earl of Carnarvon. The Matriculation Book contains the entry—" 30 April 1624, William Browne, son of Thomas Browne, gentleman, of Tavistock, matriculated, age 33." On 25th August of the same year he obtained permission to be created Master of Arts, and the degree was conferred on 16th November. In the public register of the University he was styled " vir omni humana literarum et bonarum artium cognitione instructus." By the members of his college he was held in high admiration. Beloe possessed a copy of the 1625 edition of *Britannia's Pastorals*, containing MS. commendatory poems, evidently written to accompany the Third Book (*circ.* 1635), which was prepared for publication, but was left unpublished. These

* This epitaph is commonly assigned (without authority) to Ben Jonson. The evidence in favour of Browne's claim is convincing. See note, vol. ii, p. 350.

† Dormer contributed Latin elegiacs on the death of James I. to the Oxford collection of " Parentalia, ' 1625, to which Browne also contributed.

poems in almost every instance bear the signatures of members of Exeter College ; their merit is slender, but they testify strongly to the affectionate esteem which Browne had won for himself. Sometimes we find his name coupled with the name of his dear friend Michael Drayton.* In 1629 Samuel Austin, a Cornishman who had been educated at Exeter College, dedicated a sacred poem, " Urania," to " my ever-honoured friends, those most refined wits and favourers of most exquisite learning, Mr. M. Drayton, Mr. Will. Browne, and my most ingenious kinsman, Mr. Andrew Pollexfen." Young Abraham Holland, a son of Philemon Holland, addressed a copy of verses (preserved in Ashmole MS. 36) to " my honest father Mr.

* In his delightful Epistle to Henry Reynolds of Poets and Poesy (1627), Drayton spoke with cordial warmth of the friendship that he bore to Browne :—

" Then the two Beaumonts and my Browne arose,
My dear companions whom I freely chose
My bosom friends, and in their several ways
Rightly born poets, and in these last days
Men of much note and no less nobler parts,
Such as have freely told to me their hearts
As I have mine to them."

One of his ep.stles was addressed to Browne.

Michael Drayton and my new yet loved friend
Mr. Will. Browne."

Anthony à Wood states that, after acting as
tutor to Robert Dormer, Browne was received
into the family of the Herberts at Wilton, where
"he got wealth and purchased an estate."
Browne may have been temporarily in the
service of the Herberts (as Samuel Daniel had
been in earlier days), but it is hard to believe
the latter part of Wood's statement. He seems
to have acquired in some way a modest compe-
tence, which secured him immunity from the
troubles that weighed so heavily on men of
letters. In Surrey, round Betchworth and
Dorking, his family had been long established.
He married in 1628, as we have seen, a knight's
daughter at Horsham, who brought him a
portion. With the patronage of the Herberts
and the Dormers, and with such money as he
received with his wife, he was able to "rub on,"
though he may not have "got wealth and purchased an estate." After his second marriage
he appears to have settled in the neighbourhood
of Dorking. In Ashmole MS. 830 is preserved
the following letter (first printed by Mr. Hazlitt),
which he addressed in November, 1640, to Sir
Benjamin Rudyard :—

To Sir Benjamin Rudyard.

Sir,—I beseech you to pardon my interposing your most serious affairs with the remembrance of my service. The cause requires it, and every man who knows I have the honour to be known by you would think me stupid in not congratulating what every one thinks he hath a share in. I mean your late speech in Parliament, wherein they believe the spirit which inspired the Reformation and the genius which dictated the Magna Charta possessed you. In my poor cell and sequestration from all business, I bless God and pray for more such members in the Commonwealth; and could you but hear (as it is pity but you should) what I do, it would add some years to your honoured hairs. Believe it, Sir, you have given such a maintenance to that repute which your former deportment had begotten that it will need no other livelihood than a chronicle, which I hope our ensuing age will not see it want for. I have now done. 'Tis Sunday night: when I have prayed for my honoured lord the Lord Chamberlain,* my good lord and master the Earl of Carnarvon, and for you and your good proceedings, I hope I shall wake with the same thoughts again, and be ever

Your most obliged servant,

Wm. Browne.

Dorking, Nov. 29, 1640.

* Philip Herbert, fourth Earl of Pembroke. He was father-in-law to the Earl of Carnarvon (Robert Dormer). In the Civil Wars he sided with the Parliament; his son-in-law fell, fighting for the King, at the first battle of Newbury (20th Sept., 1643).

The speech to which the letter refers was delivered before the Long Parliament early in November. It dealt freely with the subject of public grievances, urging that evil counsellors should be removed from the King.

William Browne died in or before 1645. Administration of his estate was granted (in the Prerogative Court of Canterbury) to his widow, Timothy Browne, on 6th November, 1645.* In the Act† he is described as "late of Dorking, in the county of Surrey, Esquire." There is no trace of his death or burial in the Dorking register, and the Horsham register has been searched in vain. It is possible that he was buried at Tavistock. The Tavistock register, under date 27th March, 1643, has an entry— " William Browne was buried." No portrait of the poet is known. Prince says that he had a great mind in a little body,—a conventional expression.

---

* His estate was again administered in May 1662, by which time his widow was presumably dead. The Act Book for that year is lost, so that the name of the person to whom this second administration was granted cannot be ascertained.

† Administration Acts afford no clue to the actual date of death. Wood surmised that Browne died in 1645.

The bulk of William Browne's poetry was composed in youth and early manhood. He states that the First Book of *Britannia's Pastorals* was written before he had reached his twentieth year :—

> O how, methinks, the imps of Mneme bring
> Dews of invention from the sacred spring !
> Here could I spend that spring of poesy
> Which not twice ten suns have bestow'd on me.

The story of the *Pastorals*, if story there be, is naught ; it would be a hopeless task to attempt to give an intelligible summary of the adventures of Celand, Marina, and the others. But the dallying diffuseness of the poem constitutes no small part of its charm. Horace Walpole threw out the suggestion that somebody should issue a series of " Lounging Books "—books that one can take up, without fatigue, at odd moments. I fear that his nice critical judgment would not have included William Browne in the series ; but to the lovers of our old poets *Britannia's Pastorals* will always be a favourite lounging book. They know that, at whatever page they open, they have not far to travel before they find entertainment. In the Third Song of the Second Book there is a description of a delightful grove, perfumed with " odoriferous buds and herbs of price," where fruits hang in gallant clusters from the trees, and birds tune their notes to the music of running water ; so fair a pleasaunce

that you are fain
Where last you walk'd to turn and walk again.

A generous reader might apply that description to Browne's poetry ; he might urge that the breezes which blew down those leafy alleys and over those trim parterres were not more grateful than the fragrance exhaled from the *Pastorals*, that the brooks and birds babble and twitter in the printed page not less blithely than in that western Paradise.

What so pleasant as to read of May-games, true-love knots, and shepherds piping in the shade? of pixies and fairy-circles? of rustic bridals and junketings? of angling, hunting the squirrel, nut-gathering? Of such-like subjects William Browne treats, singing like the shepherd in the *Arcadia* as though he would never grow old. He was a happy poet. It was his good fortune to grow up among wholesome surroundings, whose gracious influences sank into his spirit. He loved the hills and dales round Tavistock, and lovingly described them in his verse. Frequently he indulges in descriptions of sunrise and sunset ; they leave no vivid impression, but charm the reader by their quiet beauty. It cannot be denied that his fondness for simple, homely images sometimes led him into sheer fatuity ;* and candid admirers must also admit that, despite his study of simplicity, he could not refrain from hunting (as the manner was) after far-fetched outrageous conceits.

Browne had nothing of that restless energy which inspired the old dramatists ; he was all for pastoral contentment. Assuredly he was not a great poet, but he was a true poet, and a modest. In the Fourth Song of the Second Book he tells of the pleasure that he took in writing his poetry, and manfully declares that his free-born Muse shall never stoop to servile

---

* No excuse can be offered for such a passage as the following (Book 1, Song 3) :—

> " As when some boy trying the somersault,
> Stands on his head, and feet, as he did lie
> To kick against earth's spangled canopy ;
> When seeing that his heels are of such weight,
> That he cannot obtain their purpos'd height,
> Leaves any more to strive ; and thus doth say,
> What now I cannot do, another day
> May well effect : it cannot be denied
> I show'd a will to act, because I tried."

flattery.   He cultivated poetry for its own sake,
and not for what it might bring of advantage or
reward :—

> In this case I, as oft as I will choose,
> Hug sweet content by my retired Muse,
> And in a study find as much to please
> As others in the greatest palaces.

Sidney and Spenser, whom he regarded as his
masters, he held in highest veneration. Among
his friends were Ben Jonson, Chapman (" the
learned shepherd of fair Hitchin hill "), " well-
languaged Daniel," Christopher Brooke, John
Davies of Hereford, and Wither. In the
Second Song of the Second Book he passes
these poets in review, and eulogizes each in
turn. The praise that he bestowed on con-
temporary poets was by them amply repaid ;
and with poets of a later age Browne has found
favour. In Mr. Huth's library is preserved a
copy of the folio edition of *Britannia's Pastorals*,
containing MS. annotations stated to be in the
handwriting of Milton (who may possibly have
taken some hints for *Comus* from Browne's
Inner Temple Masque). Henry Vaughan, in
his praises of the river Usk, borrowed from
the Second Song of the First Book of the
Pastorals. Keats, who chose a motto from

the *Pastorals* for one of his early poems, was much under Browne's influence at the beginning of his glorious career, but quickly passed to regions of fancy far removed from the ken of the earlier poet. Mrs. Browning did not omit to introduce Browne in her *Vision of the Poets.*

Browne was not only a poet, but a scholar and antiquary,—the friend of Selden. At the beginning of the *Pastorals* he refers (in a marginal note) to an MS. copy of William of Malmesbury "in the hands of my learned friend M. Selden." In *The Shepherd's Pipe* he printed from MS. a poem of Hoccleve, and announced "As this shall please, I may be drawn to publish the rest of his works, being all perfect in my hands." Seemingly the public of those days had no anxiety to see Hoccleve's works collected : the project fell through. A curious passage occurs in Nathaniel Carpenter's[*] *Geography delineated forth in two Bookes*, 1625 (pp. 263-4) :—" Many inferiour faculties are yet left, wherein our Devon hath displaied her abilities as well as in the former, as in Philosophers, Historians, Oratours and Poets, the blazoning

---

[*] Carpenter was a fellow of Exeter College. He dedicated his *Geography* to William, Earl of Pembroke.

of whom to the life, especially the last, I had rather leave to my worthy friend Mr. W. Browne, who, as hee hath already honoured his countrie in his elegant and sweet *Pastoralls*, so questionles will easily bee intreated a little farther to grace it by drawing out the line of his Poeticke Auncesters, beginning in Josephus Iscanus and ending in himselfe." Probably Carpenter threw out this suggestion at a venture, for there is no evidence to show that Browne had any intention of collecting materials for Lives of the Poets of Devonshire.*

The Two Books of *Pastorals*, the Eclogues in *The Shepherd's Pipe*, and some contributions to the 1614 edition of *England's Helicon*, contain all the poetry that Browne published. He left in MS. a Third Book of *Pastorals*, the *Inner Temple Masque*, and some miscellaneous poems. Among the miscellaneous pieces are the excellent bacchanalian song "Now that the spring hath filled our veins,"† and the

---

* Anthony à Wood and others, garbling Carpenter's words, have represented that Browne was engaged on a History of English Poetry.

† It was popular in the xviith century, though no early printed copy is extant. In *Poor Robin's Almanac*, 1699, it is mentioned as a well-known song :—" Now [June]

famous ballad " Lydford Journey." Browne lived in an age of song-writing, and at times he could sing with the best. Some charming songs, notably " Shall I tell you whom I love ? " and " Venus by Adonis' side," are scattered through the *Pastorals*, and there are good lyrical passages in the *Masque*.

In 1647 appeared a translation from the French of M. Le Roy, Sieur de Gomberville,— *The History of Polexander. Done into English by William Browne, Gent. For the Right Honourable Philip, Earle of Pembroke and Montgomery, &c.* London, printed by Tho : Harper for Thomas Walkley, fol. It is to be noted that Walkley was the publisher of the 1620 edition of *The Shepherd's Pipe.* The translation (a holiday task of slender interest) was issued without dedication or preface. Probably the translator may be identified with the author of the *Pastorals*, for we hear of no other William Browne who was connected with the Pembroke family. A copy of the French original is in the library at Wilton, but not of the English translation.

is the time when Farmers shear their Sheep . . . and yet for all this, the old Song is in force still, and ever will be,

' Shear Sheep that have 'em cry we still.' "

Whether his be the translation or not, the poet was dead when *Polexander* appeared. His early years were passed in the delightful town of Tavistock; he spent much time at Wilton, the home of the Herberts; and he died in, or near, Dorking. Tavistock,—Wilton, —Dorking.   Surely few poets have had a more tranquil journey to the Elysian Fields.

A. H. BULLEN.

16, Henrietta Street,
Covent Garden, London.
September, 1893.

BRITANNIA'S PASTORALS

VOL. 1.

TO

*The no less Ennobled by Virtue, than Ancient
in Nobility, the Right Honourable*

EDWARD,

Lord Zouch, St. Maur, and Cantelupe,

*and one of His Majesty's Most Honourable
Privy Council.*

Honour's bright ray,
More highly crown'd with virtue than with years,
Pardon a rustic Muse that thus appears
In shepherd's grey,
Entreating your attention to a lay
Fitting a sylvan bower, not courtly trains;
Such choicer ears,
Should have Apollo's priests, not Pan's rude swains.
But if the music of contented plains
A thought uprears
For your approvement of that part she bears,
When time (that embryons to perfection brings)

B 2

Hath taught her strains

May better boast their being from the spring
Where brave heroës' worths the Sisters sing :

(In lines whose reigns

In spite of Envy and her restless pains
Be unconfin'd as blest eternity :)

The vales shall ring

Thy honour'd name, and every song shall be
A pyramis built to thy memory.

Your Honour's

W. Browne.

TO THE READER.

The times are swoll'n so big with nicer wits,
That nought sounds good but what Opinion strikes
Censure with Judgment seld[a] together sits ;
And now the man more than the matter likes.

The great rewardress of a poet's pen,
Fame, is by those so clogg'd she seldom flies ;
The Muses sitting on the graves of men,
Singing that Virtue lives and never dies,

• Seld, seldom.

Are chas'd away by the malignant tongues
Of such, by whom Detraction is ador'd :
Hence grows the want of ever-living songs,
With which our isle was whilom[a] bravely stor'd.

If such a basilisk dart down his eye
(Impoison'd with the dregs of utmost hate),
To kill the first blooms of my poesy,
It is his worst, and makes me fortunate.
    Kind wits I vail[b] to, but to fools precise
    I am as confident as they are nice.

From the Inner Temple, June the 18th, 1613.

W. B.

[a] *Whilom*, formerly.
[b] *Vail to*, submit, defer to.

IN BUCOLICA G. BROUN.

Quod per secessus rustici otia licuit, ad Amic. & Bon.
Lit. amantiss.

ANACREONTICUM.

Κάλλος σὸν, Κυθέρεια,
Σὸν, Κούραι Διὸς, ἦθος
Ἐμνήστευσαν, Ἰλερμέ·
Τῇ συμπράξαν Ἐρῶτες·
Ταῖς σὺν Παλλάδι Φοῖβος·
Τῆς Μοῦσαι προκατῆρχον·
Ταῖς σὺ δοῦλος ὑπαρχεις·
Τῆς οὐμήν ἀεκούσης.

Ὦ γάρ ἐστ' ἀνέραστος
Ψυχή Ἔννεα τῆνον
Φεύγουσ'· αὐτῷ ἔπονται
Ὅς προστύσσετ' Ἐρῶτας.
Μούσαις κ' Ἀφρογενείῃ
Προῦπτον τοῦτο πέλεσκε.
Νόσσαξ ἀμφοτερῆσιν
Οὗτως ἐσσὶ φίλιστος.

Ad Amoris Numina.

QUIN vostrum Paphie, Anteros, Erôsque
Ut regnum capiat mali quid, absit !
Venus, per Syrium nimis venustum !
Amplexus teneros, pares, suaves
Psyches, per, tibi, basiationum
Eros quantum erat ! & per Anterotis

Felices animas ! periclitanti
Obtestor, dubiæque consulatis
Rei vostræ ! Miserûm magis favete
Languori, miserûm favete amantum,
Divi, cordolio ! Quod est amatum
Ictu propitii ferite pectus !
Ictus quin fit ab aurea sagitta !
Ortas spe placita fovete flammas !
Ortis quin similes parate flammas !
Suas gnaviter ambiant* Neæras !
Et cautim laciant suos Neæræ !
Dextras sternuite adprobationes !
Adsuctis detur osculum labellis !
Et junctis detur osculum salivis !
Tui nectaris adde, Diva,* quinctam.
Conturbet tremulæ libido linguæ,
Ne quis basia* fascinare possit !
Morsus mutua temperet voluptas !
Dormitis, nimiumque defuistis
Procis, atque adamantinis puellis.
Isthæc prospiciens tibi, Cupido,
Audax admonui. Tuas Apollo,
Deusque, Arcadiæ, Minerva, & Hermes
Supplantant Veneres. Murinus arcum
Tendit, quin jaculis tua pharetra
Surreptis petimur. Camena texit
Cantu dædala, blandulum Aphrodites
Cestum, & insidias plicat. Minervæ
Buxus, Mercurii chelys, cicuta

* Amica. Do-
mina (nostro
idiomate
amatorio,
Mistress)
& Neæra sunt
uti synonyma
Prudentio,
ante alios,
Peri Steph.
hymn. 12. &
alicubi. v.
si placet &
Jos. Scalig.
ad 3. Tibulli.

* Horat.
Carm. 1. od.
13.

* Ne scilicet
quis permu-
meret, Fini-
tus n. &
notus nume-
rus fascino,
apud Vete-
res, obnoxi-
us. Idque in
Basiis obser-
vatum ha-
bes ap. Catul.
carm. 5 & 7.

Fauni, dulce melos canunt.   Erota,
En, ollm* docuit, plagas Eroti
Jam tendit, Juvenis, Poëta, Pastor,
Isthaec prospiciens tibi, Cupido,
Audax admonui.   Fave, Cupido.

> * Amor à
> Pastore omne
> genus Mu-
> sices ollm
> edoctus.
> Bion Idyll. 3.

By the Same.

So much a stranger my severer Muse
Is not to love-strains, or a shepward's[a] reed,
But that she knows some rites of Phœbus' dues,
Of Pan, of Pallas, and her Sisters' meed.
Read and commend she durst these tun'd essays
Of him that loves her.   (She hath ever found
Her studies as one circle.)   Next she prays
His readers be with rose and myrtle crown'd !
No willow touch them !   As his bays* are free
From wrong of bolts, so may their chaplets be.

J. SELDEN, Juris C.

> * Bays (fair
> Readers) be-
> ing the mate-
> rials of Poets'
> Garlands (as
> myrtle and
> roses are for
> enjoying lov-
> ers, and the
> fruitless wil-
> low for them
> which your
> inconstancy
> too oft makes
> most un-
> happy) are
> supposed not
> subject to
> any hurt of
> Jupiter's
> thunderbolts.
> as other trees
> are.

To his Friend the Author.

Drive forth thy flock, young pastor, to that plain
Where our old shepherds wont their flocks to feed ;
To those clear walks where many a skilful swain
To'ards the calm ev'ning tun'd his pleasant reed.

* *Shepward*, shepherd.

Those, to the Muses once so sacred, downs,
As no rude foot might there presume to stand :
(Now made the way of the unworthiest clowns,
Digg'd and plough'd up with each unhallowed hand)
If possible thou canst redeem those places,
Where, by the brim of many a silver spring,
The learned maidens and delightful graces
Often have sat to hear our shepherds sing :
Where on those pines, the neighb'ring groves among
(Now utterly neglected in these days),
Our garlands, pipes, and cornamutes[a] were hung,
The monuments of our deserved praise.
So may thy sheep like,[b] so thy lambs increase,
And from the wolf feed ever safe and free !
So may'st thou thrive, among the learned prease,[c]
As thou young shepherd art belov'd of me !

MICHAEL DRAYTON.

To his ingenious and worthy Friend the Author.

HE that will tune his oaten-pipe aright
To great Apollo's harp ; he that will write
A living poem, must have many years,
And settled judgment 'mongst his equal peers,

[a] *Cornamutes*, rustic instruments blown like the bagpipe.
[b] *Like*, thrive.
[c] *Prease*, press or crowd.

In well-rigg'd bark to steer his doubtful course ;
Lest secret, rocky envy, or the source
Of frothy, but sky-tow'ring arrogance,
Or fleeting, sandy vulgar-censure chance
To leave him shipwreck'd on the desert main,
Imploring aged Neptune's help in vain.
The younger cygnet, even at best, doth tear
With his harsh squealings the melodious ear :
It is the old and dying swan that sings
Notes worthy life, worthy the Thespian springs.
But thou art young ; and yet thy voice as sweet,
Thy verse as smooth, composure as discreet
As any swan's whose tuneful notes are spent
On Thames his banks ; which makes me confident,
He knows no music, hath nor ears, nor tongue,
That not commends a voice so sweet, so young.

On him ; a Pastoral Ode to his fairest Shepherdess.

SYREN more than earthly fair,
Sweetly break the yielding air ;
Sing on Albion's whitest rocks ;
Sing ; whilst Willy to his flocks
Deftly tunes his various reed.
Sing ; and he, whilst younglings feed,
Answer shall thy best of singing,
With his rural music bringing

Equal pleasure ; and requite
Music's sweets with like delight.
What though Willy's songs be plain ?
Sweet they be : for he's a swain
Made of purer mould than earth.
Him did Nature from his birth,
And the Muses single out,
For a second Colin Clout.[a]
Tityrus[b] made him a singer :
Pan him taught his pipe to finger :
Numbers, curious ears to please,
Learn'd he of Philisides.[c]
Kala[d] loves him : and the lasses
Point at him as by he passes,
Wishing never tongue that's bad
Censure may so blithe a lad.
Therefore well can he requite
Music's sweets with like delight :
Sing then, break the yielding air
Syren more than earthly fair.

EDWARD HEYWARD,

è So. Int. Templ.

[a] *Colin Clout* is the pastoral name which Spenser adopted for himself.

[b] *Tityrus*, Virgil.

[c] *Philisides*, one of the poetical names of Sir Philip Sidney, invented by himself, and evidently formed from portions of the two names, *Philip* and *Sidney*.

[d] *Kala*, a shepherdess in Sidney's *Arcadia*.

To his Friend the Author upon his Poem.

THIS plant is knotless that puts forth these leaves,
Upon whose branches I his praise do sing :
Fruitful the ground, whose verdure it receives
From fertile Nature, and the learned Spring.
In zeal to good known, but unpractis'd ill,
Chaste in his thoughts, though in his youthful prime,
He writes of past'ral love with nectar'd quill,
And offers up his first fruits unto Time.
Receive them (Time) and in thy border place them
Among thy various flowers of poesy ;
No envy blast, nor ignorance deface them,
But keep them fresh in fairest memory !
   And, when from Daphne's tree he plucks more bays,
   His Shepherd's Pipe may chant more heav'nly lays.

CHRISTOPHER BROOKE.

ANAGRAMMA.

Guilielmus Browne.   Ne vulgo Librum ejus.

SI vulgus gustare tuo velis apta palato ;
I, pete vulgares, ac aliunde, dapes.
Nil vulgare sapit liber hic ; hinc vulgus abesto :
Non nisi delicias hæc tibi mensa dabit.

FR : DYNNE,
è So. Int. Templ.

To his Friend the Author.

ON (jolly lad) and hie thee to the field
Among the best swains that the valleys yield ;
Go boldly, and in presence of them all,
 Proceed a shepherd with this Pastoral.
Let Pan, and all his rural train attending,
From stately mountains to the plains descending,
Salute this Pastor with their kind embraces,
And entertain him to their holy places.
Let all the nymphs of hills and dales together
Kiss him for earnest of his welcome thither :
Crown him with garlands of the choicest flowers,
And make him ever dwell within their bowers :
For well I wot in all the plains around,
There are but few such shepherds to be found,
That can such learned lays and ditties frame,
Or aptly fit their tunes unto the same.
And let them all (if this young swain should die)
Tune all their reeds to sing his memory.

THO. GARDINER,

è So. Int. Templ

To the Author.

HAD I beheld thy Muse upon the stage,
A poesy in fashion with this age ;
Or had I seen, when first I view'd thy task,
An active wit dance in a satyr's mask,

I should in those have prais'd thy wit and art,
But not thy ground, a poem's better part :
Which being the perfect'st image of the brain,
Not fram'd to any base end, but to gain
True approbation of the artist's worth,
When to an open view he sets it forth,
Judiciously he strives no less t'adorn
By a choice subject than a curious form :
Well hast thou then pass'd o'er all other rhyme,
And in a Pastoral spent thy leisure's time :
Where fruit so fair, and field so fruitful is,
That hard it is to judge whether in this
The substance or the fashion more excel,
So precious is the gem, and wrought so well.
Thus rest thou prais'd of me, fruit, field, gem, art,
Do claim much praise to equal such desert.

W. FERRAR,
è So. Med. Templ.

To the Author.

FRIEND, I'll not err in blazing of thy worth ;
This work in truest terms will set it forth :
In these few lines the all I do intend,
Is but to show that I have such a friend.

FR : OULDE,
è S. In. Templ.

BRITANNIA'S PASTORALS.

THE FIRST SONG.

THE ARGUMENT.

Marina's love, yclep'd* the fair,
Celand's disdain, and her despair.
Are the first wings my Muse puts on
To reach the sacred Helicon.

I THAT whilere near Tavy's* straggling spring
Unto my seely sheep did use to sing,
And play'd to please myself on rustic reed,
Nor sought for bay (the learned shepherd's meed),

*.—*Ycleped*, called.   2.—*Seely*, simple.

* Tavy is a river, having his head in Dartmoor in Devon, some few miles from Mary Tavy, and falls southward into Tamar: out of the same moor riseth, running northward, another, called Tau: which by the way the rather I speak of, because in the printed Malmesbury degest. Pontific. lib. 2, fol. 146, you read, "Est in Domnonia cænobium monachorum juxta Tau fluvium, quod Tavistok vocatur:" whereas upon Tau stands (near the north side of the shire) Tawstock, being no remnants of a monastery: so that you must there read, "Juxta Taui Fluvium," as in a manuscript copy of Malmesbury (the form of the hand assuring Malmesbury's time) belonging to the Abbey of S. Augustine in Canterbury I have seen, in the hands of my very learned friend M. Selden.

But as a swain unkent fed on the plains,   5
And made the Echo umpire of my strains :
Am drawn by time (although the weak'st of many)
To sing those lays as yet unsung of any.
What need I tune the swains of Thessaly ?
Or, bootless, add to them of Arcadie ?   10
No, fair Arcadia cannot be completer ;
My praise may lessen, but not make thee greater.
My Muse for lofty pitches shall not roam,
But homely pipen of her native home ;
And to the swains, love rural minstrelsy ;   15
Thus, dear Britannia, will I sing of thee.
   High on the plains of that renowned isle,
Which all men Beauty's garden-plot enstyle,
A shepherd dwelt, whom Fortune had made rich
With all the gifts that silly men bewitch.   20
Near him a shepherdess for beauty's store
Unparallel'd of any age before.
Within those breasts her face a flame did move,
Which never knew before what 'twas to love,   [25
Dazzling each shepherd's sight that view'd her eyes :
And as the Persians did idolatrize
Unto the sun : they thought that Cynthia's light
Might well be spar'd where she appear'd in night.
And as when many to the goal do run,
The prize is given never but to one :   30
So first, and only Celandine was led,

5.—Unkent, unknown, for unkenned.

Of Destiny's and Heaven much favoured,
To gain this beauty, which I here do offer
To memory : his pains (who would not proffer   [35
Pains for such pleasures?) were not great nor much,
But that his labour's recompense was such
As countervailed all : for she, whose passion,
(And passion oft is love,) whose inclination
Bent all her course to him-wards, let him know
He was the elm whereby her vine did grow :   40
Yea, told him, when his tongue began this task,
She knew not to deny when he would ask.
Finding his suit as quickly got as mov'd,
Celandine, in his thoughts not well approv'd
What none could disallow, his love grew feign'd, 45
And what he once affected now disdain'd.
But fair Marina (for so was she call'd)
Having in Celandine her love install'd,
Affected so this faithless shepherd's boy,
That she was rapt beyond degree of joy.   50
Briefly, she could not live one hour without him,
And thought no joy like theirs that liv'd about him.
   This variable shepherd for a while
Did Nature's jewel by his craft beguile :
And still the perfecter her love did grow,   55
His did appear more counterfeit in show.
Which she perceiving that his flame did slake,
And lov'd her only for his trophy's sake :
" For he that's stuffed with a faithless tumour,
Loves only for his lust and for his humour : "   60

And that he often in his merry fit
Would say, his good came ere he hop'd for it:
His thoughts for other subjects being press'd,
Esteeming that as nought which he possess'd:
"For what is gotten but with little pain,   65
As little grief we take to lose again."
Well-minded Marine grieving, thought it strange
That her ingrateful swain did seek for change.
Still by degrees her cares grew to the full,
Joys to the wane, heartrending grief did pull   70
Her from herself, and she abandon'd all
To cries and tears, fruits of a funeral;
Running the mountains, fields, by wat'ry springs,
Filling each cave with woful echoings;
Making in thousand places her complaint,   75
And uttering to the trees what her tears meant.
"For griefs conceal'd (proceeding from desire)
Consume the more, as doth a close-pent fire."
Whilst that the day's sole eye doth gild the seas
In his day's journey to th' Antipodes,   80
And all the time the jetty-charioteer
Hurls her black mantle through our hemisphere,
Under the covert of a sprouting pine
She sits and grieves for faithless Celandine.
Beginning thus: Alas! and must it be   85
That Love which thus torments and troubles me
In settling it, so small advice hath lent
To make me captive, where enfranchisement
Cannot be gotten? nor where, like a slave,

The office due to faithful prisoners, have?   90
Oh cruel Celandine, why shouldst thou hate
Her, who to love thee, was ordain'd by Fate!
Should I not follow thee, and sacrifice
My wretched life to thy betraying eyes?
Aye me! of all my most unhappy lot;   95
What others would, thou may'st, and yet wilt not.
Have I rejected those that me ador'd,
To be of him, whom I adore, abhorr'd?
And pass'd by others' tears, to make election
Of one, that should so pass-by my affection?   100
I have: and see the heav'nly powers intend
" To punish sinners in what they offend."
Maybe he takes delight to see in me
The burning rage of hellish jealousy;
Tries if in fury any love appears;   105
And bathes his joy within my flood of tears.
But if he lov'd to soil my spotless soul,
And me amongst deceived maids enrol,
To publish to the world my open shame: [110
Then, heart, take freedom; hence, accursed flame;
And, as queen-regent, in my heart shall move
" Disdain, that only over-ruleth Love:"
By this infranchis'd sure my thoughts shall be,
And in the same sort love, as thou lov'st me.
But what? or can I cancel or unbind   115
That which my heart hath seal'd and love hath sign'd?
No, no, grief doth deceive me more each hour;
" For, who so truly loves, hath not that power."

I wrong to say so since of all 'tis known,
" Who yields to love doth leave to be her own." 120
But what avails my living thus apart ?
Can I forget him ? or out of my heart
Can tears expulse his image ? surely no.
" We well may fly the place, but not the woe :
Love's fire is of a nature which by turns   125
Consumes in presence, and in absence burns."
And knowing this : aye me ! unhappy wight !
What means is left to help me in this plight ?
And from that peevish shooting, hood-wink'd elf,
To repossess my love, my heart, myself?   130
Only this help I find, which I elect :
Since what my life nor can nor will effect,
My ruin shall : and by it, I shall find,
" Death cures (when all helps fail) the grieved mind."
And welcome here (than Love a better guest),   135
That of all labours art the only rest :
Whilst thus I live, all things discomfort give,
The life is sure a death wherein I live :
Save life and death do differ in this one,
That life hath ever cares, and death hath none.   140
But if that he (disdainful swain) should know
That for his love I wrought my overthrow ;
Will he not glory in't ? and from my death
Draw more delights, and give new joys their breath ?
Admit he do, yet better 'tis that I   145

120.—*Leave*, cease.   123.—*Expulse*, expel.

Render myself to Death than misery.
I cannot live, thus barred from his sight,
Nor yet endure, in presence, any wight
Should love him but myself.   O Reason's eye,
How art thou blinded with vild jealousy !   150
And is it thus ?   Then which shall have my blood,
Or certain ruin, or uncertain good ?
Why do I doubt ?   Are we not still advis'd
"That certainty in all things best is priz'd ? "
Then, if a certain end can help my moan,   155
"Know Death hath certainty, but Life hath none."
    Here is a mount, whose top seems to despise
The far inferior vale that under lies :
Who like a great man rais'd aloft by fate,
Measures his height by others' mean estate :   160
Near to whose foot there glides a silver flood.
Falling from hence, I'll climb unto my good,
And by it finish Love and Reason's strife,
And end my misery as well as life.
But as a coward's heartener in war,   165
The stirring drum, keeps lesser noise from far :
So seem the murmuring waves tell in mine ear
That guiltless blood was never spilled there.
Then stay a while ; the beasts that haunt those springs,
Of whom I hear the fearful bellowings,   170
May do that deed (as moved by my cry),
Whereby my soul, as spotless ivory,

150.—*Vild*, vile.   165.—*Heartener*, an encourager.

May turn from whence it came, and, freed from hence,
Be unpolluted of that foul offence.
But why protract I time? death is no stranger: 175
" And generous spirits never fear for danger:
Death is a thing most natural to us,
And fear doth only make it odious."
As when to seek her food abroad doth rove
The Nuncius of peace, the seely dove,   180
Two sharp-set hawks do her on each side hem,
And she knows not which way to fly from them:
Or like a ship, that tossed to and fro
With wind and tide; the wind doth sternly blow,
And drives her to the main, the tide comes sore   185
And hurls her back again towards the shore;
And since her ballast and her sails do lack,
One brings her out, the other beats her back;
Till one of them increasing more his shocks,
Hurls her to shore, and rends her on the rocks: 190
So stood she long, 'twixt love and reason toss'd,
Until despair (who where it comes rules most)
Won her to throw herself, to meet with death,
From off the rock into the flood beneath.
The waves that were above when as she fell,   195
For fear flew back again into their well,
Doubting ensuing times on them would frown,
That they so rare a beauty help'd to drown.
Her fall, in grief, did make the stream so roar,

180.—*Nuncius*, messenger.   180.—*Seely*, simple.

That sullen murmurings fill'd all the shore.   200
    A shepherd (near this flood that fed his sheep,
Who at this chance left grazing and did weep)
Having so sad an object for his eyes,
Left pipe and flock, and in the water flies,
To save a jewel, which was never sent   205
To be possess'd by one sole element :
But such a work Nature dispos'd and gave,
Where all the elements concordance have.
He took her in his arms, for pity cried,
And brought her to the river's further side :   210
Yea, and he sought by all his art and pain,
To bring her likewise to herself again :
While she that by her fall was senseless left,
And almost in the waves had life bereft,
Lay long, as if her sweet immortal spirit   215
Was fled some other palace to inherit.
    But as clear Phœbus, when some foggy cloud
His brightness from the world a while doth shroud,
Doth by degrees begin to show his light
Unto the view : or, as the queen of night,   220
In her increasing horns, doth rounder grow,
Till full and perfect she appear in show :
Such order in this maid the shepherd spies,
When she began to show the world her eyes.   [225
Who (thinking now that she had pass'd death's dream,
Occasion'd by her fall into the stream,

202.—*Chance*, mishap.

And that hell's ferryman did then deliver
Her to the other side th' infernal river)
Said to the swain : O Charon, I am bound
More to thy kindness than all else that round   230
Come thronging to thy boat : thou hast pass'd over
The woful'st maid that e'er these shades did cover.
But, prithee, ferryman, direct my spright
Where that black river runs that Lethe hight,
That I of it (as other ghosts) may drink,   235
And never of the world, or love, more think.
The swain perceiving by her words ill sorted,
That she was wholly from herself transported,
And fearing lest those often idle fits
Might clean expel her uncollected wits :   240
Fair nymph (said he), the powers above deny
So fair a beauty should so quickly die.
The heavens unto the world have made a loan,
And must for you have interest, three for one.   [245
Call back your thoughts o'ercast with dolour's night ;
Do you not see the day, the heavens, the light ?
Do you not know in Pluto's darksome place
The light of heaven did never show his face ?
Do not your pulses beat ? y'are warm, have breath,
Your sense is rapt with fear, but not with death. 250
I am not Charon, nor of Pluto's host ;
Nor is there flesh and blood found in a ghost ;
But as you see, a seely shepherd's swain,

234.—*Hight*, called.

Who though my mere revenues be the train
Of milk-white sheep, yet am I joy'd as much   255
In saving you (O, who would not save such?),
As ever was the wand'ring youth of Greece,
That brought from Colchos home the golden fleece.
     The never-too-much-praised fair Marine,
Hearing those words, believ'd her ears and eyne: 260
And knew how she escaped had the flood
By means of this young swain that near her stood.
Whereat for grief she 'gan again to faint,
Redoubling thus her cries and sad complaint:
Alas! and is that likewise barr'd from me,   265
Which for all persons else lies ever free?
Will life, nor death, nor ought abridge my pain?
But live still dying, die to live again?
Then most unhappy I! which find most sure,
The wound of love neglected is past cure.   270
Most cruel god of love (if such there be),
That still to my desires art contrary!
Why should I not in reason this obtain,
That as I love, I may be lov'd again?
Alas! with thee too, Nature plays her parts,   275
That fram'd so great a discord 'tween two hearts:
One flies, and always doth in hate persever;
The other follows, and in love grows ever.
Why dost thou not extinguish clean this flame,
And place't on him that best deserves the same? 280
Why had not I affected some kind youth,
Whose every word had been the word of truth?

Who might have had to love, and lov'd to have,
So true a heart as I to Celand gave.
For Psyche's love ! if beauty gave thee birth,   285
Or if thou hast attractive power on earth,
Dame Venus' sweetest child, requite this love.
Or fate yield means my soul may hence remove !
Once seeing in a spring her drowned eyes,
O cruel beauty, cause of this (she cries),   290
Mother of Love (my joy's most fatal knife),
That work'st her death, by whom thyself hast life !
      The youthful swain that heard this loving saint
So oftentimes to pour forth such complaint,
Within his heart such true affection prais'd,   295
And did perceive kind love and pity rais'd
His mind to sighs ; yea, beauty forced this,
That all her grief he thought was likewise his.
And having brought her what his lodge affords,
Sometime he wept with her, sometime with words 300
Would seek to comfort ; when, alas ! poor elf,
He needed then a comforter himself.
Daily whole troops of grief unto him came
For her who languish'd of another flame.
If that she sigh'd, he thought him lov'd of her,   305
When 'twas another sail her wind did stir :
But had her sighs and tears been for this boy,
Her sorrow had been less, and more her joy.
Long time in grief he hid his love-made pains,
And did attend her walks in woods and plains :   310
Bearing a fuel, which her sun-like eyes

Enflam'd, and made his heart the sacrifice :
Yet he, sad swain, to show it did not dare ;
And she, lest he should love, nigh died for fear.
She, ever-wailing, blam'd the powers above,   315
That night nor day give any rest to love.
He prais'd the heavens in silence, oft was mute,
And thought with tears and sighs to win his suit.
    Once in the shade, when she by sleep repos'd,
And her clear eyes 'twixt her fair lids enclos'd,   320
The shepherd swain began to hate and curse
That day unfortunate, which was the nurse
Of all his sorrows.   He had given breath
And life to her which was his cause of death.
O Æsop's snake, that thirstest for his blood,   325
From whom thyself receiv'd'st a certain good.
Thus oftentimes unto himself alone
Would he recount his grief, utter his moan ;
And after much debating, did resolve
Rather his grandame Earth should clean involve 330
His pining body, ere he would make known
To her, what tares love in his breast had sown.
Yea, he would say when grief for speech hath
        cried,
"'Tis better never ask than be denied."
    But as the queen of rivers, fairest Thames,   335
That for her buildings other floods enflames
With greatest envy ; or the Nymph of Kent,

337.—*Nymph of Kent*, the River Medway.

That stateliest ships to sea hath ever sent ;
Some baser groom, for lucre's hellish course,
Her channel having stopp'd, kept back her source, 340
(Fill'd with disdain) doth swell above her mounds,
And overfloweth all the neighb'ring grounds,
Angry she tears up all that stops her way,
And with more violence runs to the sea :
So the kind shepherd's grief (which long up-pent 345
Grew more in power, and longer in extent)
Forth of his heart more violently thrust,
And all his vow'd intentions quickly burst.
Marina, hearing sighs, to him drew near,
And did entreat his cause of grief to hear ;   350
But had she known her beauty was the sting
That caused all that instant sorrowing,
Silence in bands her tongue had stronger kept,
And sh'ad not ask'd for what the shepherd wept.
  The swain first, of all times, this best did think 355
To show his love, whilst on the river's brink
They sat alone, then thought, he next would move
      her
With sighs and tears (true tokens of a lover) ;
And since she knew what help from him she found
When in the river she had else been drown'd,   360
He thinketh sure she cannot but grant this,
To give relief to him by whom she is ;
By this incited, said : Whom I adore,

339.—*Groom,* fellow.

Sole mistress of my heart, I thee implore,
Do not in bondage hold my freedom long.   365
And since I life or death hold from your tongue,
Suffer my heart to love ; yea, dare to hope
To get that good of love's intended scope.
Grant I may praise that light in you I see,
And dying to myself, may live in thee.   370
Fair nymph, surcease this death-alluring languish,
So rare a beauty was not born for anguish.
Why shouldst thou care for him that cares not for thee ?
Yea, most unworthy wight, seems to abhor thee.
And if he be as you do here paint forth him,   375
He thinks you, best of beauties, are not worth him ;
That all the joys of love will not quite cost
For all lov'd freedom which by it is lost.
Within his heart such self-opinion dwells,
That his conceit in this he thinks excels ;   380
Accounting women's beauties sugar'd baits,
That never catch but fools with their deceits.
" Who of himself harbours so vain a thought,
Truly to love could never yet be brought."
Then love that heart where lies no faithless seed, 385
That never wore dissimulation's weed :
Who doth account all beauties of the spring,
That jocund summer days are ushering,
As foils to yours. But if this cannot move
Your mind to pity, nor your heart to love,   390

371.—*Surcease*, cease.

Yet, sweetest, grant me love to quench that flame,
Which burns you now.   Expel his worthless name,
Clean root him out by me, and in his place
Let him inhabit that will run a race
More true in love.   It may be for your rest.   395
And when he sees her, who did love him best,
Possessed by another, he will rate
The much of good he lost, when 'tis too late:
" For what is in our powers we little deem,
And things possess'd by others best esteem."   400
If all this gain you not a shepherd's wife,
Yet give not death to him which gave you life.
  Marine the fair, hearing his wooing tale,
Perceived well what wall his thoughts did scale ;
And answer'd thus : I pray, Sir Swain, what boot 405
Is it to me to pluck up by the root
My former love, and in his place to sow
As ill a seed, for anything I know ?
Rather 'gainst thee I mortal hate retain,
That seek'st to plant in me new cares, new pain. 410
Alas ! th'hast kept my soul from death's sweet bands
To give me over to a tyrant's hands,
Who on his racks will torture by his power
This weaken'd, harmless body, every hour.
Be you the judge, and see if reason's laws   415
Give recompense of favour for this cause.
You from the streams of death brought life on shore ;
Releas'd one pain to give me ten times more.
For love's sake, let my thoughts in this be free ;

Object no more your hapless saving me :   420
That obligation which you think should bind,
Doth still increase more hatred in my mind.
Yea, I do think more thanks to him were due
That would bereave my life than unto you.

The thunder-stricken swain lean'd to a tree,   425
As void of sense as weeping Niobe ;
Making his tears the instruments to woo her,
The sea wherein his love should swim unto her :
And, could there flow from his two-headed font,
As great a flood as is the Hellespont,   430
Within that deep he would as willing wander
To meet his Hero, as did e'er Leander.
Meanwhile the nymph withdrew herself aside,
And to a grove at hand her steps applied.

With that sad sigh (O ! had he never seen,   435
His heart in better case had ever been)
Against his heart, against the stream he went,
With this resolve, and with a full intent,
When of that stream he had discovered
The fount, the well-spring, or the bubbling head, 440
He there would sit, and with the well-drop vie,
That it before his eyes would first run dry.
But then he thought the god* that haunts that lake,
The spoiling of his spring would not well take ;
And therefore leaving soon the crystal flood,   445
Did take his way unto the nearest wood :

*Deæ sane,
i. Nymphæ,
plerumque
fontibus &
fluviis præ-
sunt apud
poetas, quæ,
Ephydriades,
& Naiades
dictæ : ve-
rum & nobis
tamen deum
præficere (sic
Alpheum Ty-
berinum, &
Rhenum, &
id genus alios
divos legi-
mus) haud
illicitum.

420.—*Object*, urge.

Seating himself within a darksome cave,
(Such places heavy Saturnists do crave,)
Where yet the gladsome day was never seen,
Nor Phœbus' piercing beams had ever been,   450
Fit for the synod house of those fell legions,
That walk the mountains and Silvanus' regions ;
Where Tragedy might have her full scope given,
From men['s] aspects, and from the view of heaven.
Within the same some crannies did deliver   455
Into the midst thereof a pretty river ;
The nymph whereof came by out of the veins
Of our first mother, having late ta'en pains
In scouring of her channel all the way,
From where it first began to leave the sea :   460
And in her labour thus far now had gone,
When coming through the cave, she heard that one
Spake thus : If I do in my death persever,
Pity may that effect which love could never.
By this she can conjecture 'twas some swain,   465
Who overladen by a maid's disdain,
Had here (as fittest) chosen out a place
Where he might give a period to the race
Of his loath'd life : which she (for pity's sake)
Minding to hinder, div'd into her lake,   470
And hasten'd where the ever-teeming Earth
Unto her current gives a wishèd birth ;
And by her new-deliver'd river's side,

448.-- *Saturnists*, persons supposed to be under the influence
of the planet Saturn, which tended to make men morose.

Upon a bank of flow'rs, had soon espied   [475
Remond, young Remond, that full well could sing,
And tune his pipe at Pan's birth carolling ;
Who for his nimble leaping, sweetest lays,
A laurel garland wore on holy-days ;
In framing of whose hand Dame Nature swore
There never was his like, nor should be more ;   480
Whose locks (ensnaring nets) were like the rays
Wherewith the sun doth diaper the seas,
Which, if they had been cut and hung upon
The snow-white cliffs of fertile Albion,
Would have allured more to be their winner,   485
Than all the diamonds* that are hidden in her.
Him she accosted thus : Swain of the Wreath,
Thou art not placed only here to breathe ;
But Nature in thy framing shows to me
Thou shouldst to others as she did to thee,   490
Do good ; and surely I myself persuade,
Thou never wert for evil action made.
In heaven's consistory 'twas decreed
That choicest fruit should come from choicest seed ;
In baser vessels we do ever put   495
Basest materials, do never shut
Those jewels most in estimation set,
But in some curious costly cabinet.
If I may judge by th' outward shape alone,

* Julium Cæsarem, spe Margaritarum Britanniam petisse, scribit Sueton. in Jul. cap. 47. & ex iis Thoracem factum Veneri genetrici dicåsse. Plin. Hist. Nat. 9, ca. 35. De Margaritis verò nostris consulas Camden. in Cornub. & Somerset.

482.—*Diaper*, variegate.
493.—*Consistory*, an ecclesiastical court ; hence, a solemn assembly.

Within, all virtues have convention :   500
" For 't gives most lustre unto Virtue's feature,
When she appears cloth'd in a goodly creature."
Half way the hill, near to those aged trees,
Whose insides are as hives for lab'ring bees,
(As who should say, before their roots were dead, 505
For good work's sake and alms they harboured
Those whom nought else did cover but the skies :)
A path, untrodden but of beasts, there lies,
Directing to a cave in yonder glade,
Where all this forest's citizens for shade   510
At noon-time come, and are the first, I think,
That (running through that cave) my waters drink :
Within this rock there sits a woful wight,
As void of comfort as that cave of light ;
And as I wot, occasion'd by the frowns   515
Of some coy shepherdess that haunts these downs.
This I do know (whos'ever wrought his care)
He is a man nigh treading to despair.
Then hie thee thither, since 'tis charity
To save a man ; leave here thy flock with me :   520
For whilst thou sav'st him from the Stygian bay,
I'll keep thy lambkins from all beasts of prey.
The nearness of the danger (in his thought)
As it doth ever, more compassion wrought :
So that, with reverence to the nymph, he went   525
With wingèd speed, and hasten'd to prevent
Th' untimely seizure of the greedy grave.
Breathless, at last, he came into the cave,

Where, by a sigh directed to the man,
To comfort him he in this sort began :   530
Shepherd, all hail ! what mean these plaints ? this
          cave
(Th' image of death, true portrait of the grave)
Why dost frequent ? and wail thee underground
From whence there never yet was pity found ?
Come forth, and show thyself unto the light,   535
Thy grief to me.   If there be ought that might
Give any ease unto thy troubled mind,
We joy as much to give, as thou to find.
The love-sick swain replied : Remond, thou art
The man alone to whom I would impart   540
My woes more willing than to any swain,
That lives and feeds his sheep upon the plain.
But vain it is, and 'twould increase my woes
By their relation, or to thee or those
That cannot remedy.   Let it suffice,   545
No fond distrust of thee makes me precise
To show my grief.   Leave me then, and forego
This cave more sad since I have made it so.
Here tears broke forth, and Remond 'gan anew
With such entreaties, earnest to pursue   550
His former suit, that he (though hardly) wan
The shepherd to disclose, and thus began :
Know briefly, Remond, then, a heavenly face,
Nature's idea, and perfection's grace,
Within my breast hath kindled such a fire,   555
That doth consume all things, except desire ;

Which daily doth increase, though always burning,
And I want tears, but lack no cause of mourning.
" For he whom love under his colours draws,
May often want th' effect, but ne'er the cause."   560
Quoth th' other, have thy stars malign been such,
That their predominations sway so much
Over the rest, that with a mild aspect
The lives and loves of shepherds do affect ?
Then do I think there is some greater hand,   565
Which thy endeavours still doth countermand :
Wherefore I wish thee quench the flame, thus mov'd,
" And never love except thou be belov'd.
For such an humour every woman seizeth,   [570
She loves not him that plaineth, but that pleaseth.
When much thou lovest, most disdain comes on
            thee ;
And when thou think'st to hold her, she flies from
            thee :
She follow'd, flies ; she fled from follows post,
And loveth best where she is hated most.
'Tis ever noted both in maids and wives,   575
Their hearts and tongues are never relatives.
Hearts full of holes (so elder shepherds sain)
Are apter to receive than to retain."
Whose crafts and wiles did I intend to show,
This day would not permit me time, I know :   580
The day's swift horses would their course have run,

573.—*Post*, post-haste as we should say.

And div'd themselves within the ocean,
Ere I should have performed half my task,
Striving their crafty subtleties t'unmask.
And, gentle swain, some counsel take of me;   585
Love not still where thou may'st; love, who loves
        thee;
Draw to the courteous, fly thy love's abhorrer, ·
" And if she be not for thee, be not for her."
If that she still be wavering, will away,   [590
Why shouldst thou strive to hold that will not stay?
This maxim reason never can confute,
" Better to live by loss than die by suit."
If to some other love she is inclin'd,
Time will at length clean root that from her mind.
Time will extinct love's flames, his hell-like
        flashes,   595
And like a burning brand consume 't to ashes.
Yet may'st thou still attend, but not importune:
" Who seeks oft misseth, sleepers light on fortune,"
Yea, and on women too.   "Thus doltish sots
Have Fate and fairest women for their lots.   600
Favour and pity wait on patience:"
And hatred oft attendeth violence.
If thou wilt get desire whence love hath pawn'd it,
Believe me, take thy time, but ne'er demand it.
Women, as well as men, retain desire;   605
But can dissemble, more than men, their fire.
Be never caught with looks, nor self-wrought rumour;
Nor by a quaint disguise, nor singing humour.

Those outside shows are toys which outwards snare,
But virtue lodg'd within is only fair.   610
If thou hast seen the beauty of our nation,
And find'st her have no love, have thou no passion :
But seek thou further ; other places sure
May yield a face as fair, a love more pure :
Leave, O then leave, fond swain, this idle course, 615
For Love's a god no mortal wight can force.
    Thus Remond said, and saw the fair Marine
Plac'd near a spring, whose waters crystalline
Did in their murmurings bear a part, and plain'd
That one so true, so fair, should be disdain'd :   620
Whilst in her cries, that fill'd the vale along,
Still Celand was the burthen of her song.
The stranger shepherd left the other swain,
To give attendance to his fleecy train ;
Who, in departing from him, let him know,   625
That yonder was his freedom's overthrow,
Who sat bewailing (as he late had done)
That love by true affection was not won.
This fully known, Remond came to the maid,
And after some few words, (her tears allay'd,)   630
Began to blame her rigour, call'd her cruel,
To follow hate, and fly love's chiefest jewel.
    Fair, do not blame him that he thus is mov'd ;
For women sure were made to be belov'd.
If beauty wanting lovers long should stay,   635
It like an house undwelt in would decay :
When in the heart if it have taken place

Time cannot blot, nor crooked age deface.
The adamant and beauty we discover
To be alike ; for beauty draws a lover,   640
The adamant his iron.   Do not blame
His loving then, but that which caus'd the same.
Whoso is lov'd, doth glory so to be :
The more your lovers, more your victory.   [645
Know, if you stand on faith, most women's loathing,
'Tis but a word, a character of nothing.
Admit it somewhat, if what we call constance
Within a heart hath long time residence,
And in a woman, she becomes alone
Fair to herself, but foul to every one.   650
If in a man it once have taken place,
He is a fool, or dotes, or wants a face
To win a woman, and I think it be
No virtue, but a mere necessity.
Heaven's powers deny it ! Swain (quoth she) have
          done,   655
Strive not to bring that in derision,
Which whosoe'er detracts in setting forth,
Doth truly derogate from his own worth.
It is a thing which heaven to all hath lent
To be their virtue's chiefest ornament :   660
Which whoso wants is well compar'd to these
False tables wrought by Alcibiades,

639.—*Adamant*, the magnet : the loadstone.
647.—*Constance*, constancy.

Which noted well of all were found t' have been
Most fair without but most deform'd within.
Then, shepherd, know, that I intend to be   665
As true to one as he is false to me.
    To one? (quoth he) why so? Maids pleasure take
To see a thousand languish for their sake :
Women desire for lovers of each sort,
And why not you? Th' amorous swain for sport ; 670
The lad that drives the greatest flock to field
Will buskins, gloves, and other fancies yield ;
The gallant swain will save you from the jaws
Of ravenous bears, and from the lions' paws.
Believe what I propound ; do many choose ;   675
" The least herb in the field serves for some use."
    Nothing persuaded, nor assuag'd by this,
Was fairest Marine, or her heaviness :
But pray'd the shepherd, as he e'er did hope
His silly sheep should fearless have the scope   680
Of all the shadows that the trees do lend,
From reynard's stealth, when Titan doth ascend,
And run his midway course, to leave her there,
And to his bleating charge again repair.
He condescended ; left her by the brook,   685
And to the swain and 's sheep himself betook.
    He gone, she with herself thus 'gan to sain :
Alas ! poor Marine, think'st thou to attain
His love by sitting here ? or can the fire

685.—*Condescended*, agreed.

Be quench'd with wood? can we allay desire   690
By wanting what's desired?   O that breath,
The cause of life, should be the cause of death !
That who is shipwreck'd on love's hidden shelf,
Doth live to others, dies unto herself.
Why might not I attempt by death as yet   695
To gain that freedom which I could not get,
Being hinder'd heretofore?   A time as free,
A place as fit offers itself to me,
Whose seed of ill is grown to such a height,
That makes the earth groan to support his weight. 700
Whoso is lull'd asleep with Midas' treasures,
And only fears by death to lose life's pleasures ;
Let them fear death : but since my fault is such,
And only fault, that I have lov'd too much,
On joys of life why should I stand?   For those   705
Which I ne'er had I surely cannot lose.
Admit a while I to these thoughts consented,
" Death can be but deferred, not prevented."
Then raging with delay, her tears that fell
Usher'd her way, and she into a well   710
Straightways leapt after.   " O ! how desperation
Attends upon the mind enthrall'd to passion ! "
   The fall of her did make the god below,
Starting, to wonder whence that noise should grow ;
Whether some ruder clown in spite did fling   715
A lamb, untimely fall'n, into his spring :

693.—*Shelf*, rock.   716.—*Untimely fall'n*, stillborn.

And if it were, he solemnly then swore
His spring should flow some other way : no more
Should it in wanton manner e'er be seen
To writhe in knots, or give a gown of green   720
Unto their meadows, nor be seen to play,
Nor drive the rushy mills that in his way
The shepherds made ; but rather for their lot,
Send them red waters that their sheep should rot ;
And with such moorish springs embrace their field, 725
That it should nought but moss and rushes yield.
Upon each hillock, where the merry boy
Sits piping in the shades his notes of joy,
He'd show his anger by some flood at hand,
And turn the same into a running sand.   730
Upon the oak, the plum-tree, and the holm,
The stock-dove and the blackbird should not come,
Whose muting on those trees do make to grow
Rots-curing hyphear,* and the mistletoe.   [735
Nor shall this help their sheep, whose stomach fails,
By tying knots of wool near to their tails :
But as the place next to the knot doth die,
So shall it all the body mortify.
Thus spake the god : but when as in the water [740
The corps came sinking down, he spied the matter,
And catching softly in his arms the maid,
He brought her up, and having gently laid

* Hyphear ad saginanda pecora utilius : omnino autem satum nullo modo nascitur, nec nisi per alvum avium redditum, maximè palumbis ac turdis. Plin. Hist. Nat. 16. cap. 93. Hinc illud vetus verbum turdus sibi malum cæcat.

731.—*Holm*, the holly.
733.—*Muting*, dropping dung (of birds).
734.—*Hyphear*, the Latin name for mistletoe.

Her on his bank, did presently command
Those waters in her to come forth : at hand
They straight came gushing out, and did contest 745
Which chiefly should obey their god's behest.
This done, her then pale lips he straight held ope,
And from his silver hair let fall a drop
Into her mouth of such an excellence,
That call'd back life which griev'd to part from
        thence,   750
Being for troth assur'd that than this one,
She ne'er possess'd a fairer mansion.
Then did the god her body forwards sleep,
And cast her for a while into a sleep ;
Sitting still by her did his full view take   755
Of Nature's masterpiece.   Here for her sake,
My pipe in silence as of right shall mourn,
Till from the wat'ring we again return.

        753.—*Sleep*, to lay down lengthways.

THE SECOND SONG.

***

THE ARGUMENT.

Oblivion's spring, and Dory's love,
With fair Marina's rape, first move
Mine oaten pipe, which after sings
The birth of two renowned springs.

***

Now till the sun shall leave us to our rest,
And Cynthia have her brother's place possess'd,
I shall go on : and first in diff'ring stripe,
The flood-god's speech thus tune on oaten pipe.
    Or mortal, or a power above,   5
    Enrag'd by fury, or by love,
    Or both, I know not ; such a deed
    Thou wouldst effected, that I bleed
    To think thereon : alas ! poor elf,
    What, grown a traitor to thyself?   10
    This face, this hair, this hand so pure
    Were not ordain'd for nothing, sure.
    Nor was it meant so sweet a breath

3.—*Stripe*, measure.

Should be expos'd by such a death ;
But rather in some lover's breast   15
Be given up, the place that best
Befits a lover yield his soul.
Nor should those mortals e'er control
The gods, that in their wisdom sage
Appointed have what pilgrimage   20
Each one should run : and why should men
Abridge the journey set by them ?
But much I wonder any wight
If he did turn his outward sight
Into his inward, dar'd to act   25
Her death, whose body is compact
Of all the beauties ever Nature
Laid up in store for earthly creature.
No savage beast can be so cruel
To rob the earth of such a jewel.   30
Rather the stately unicorn
Would in his breast enraged scorn,
That maids committed to his charge
By any beast in forest large
Should so be wronged.   Satyrs rude   35
Durst not attempt, or e'er intrude
With such a mind the flow'ry balks
Where harmless virgins have their walks.
Would she be won with me to stay,
My waters should bring from the sea   40

37.—*Balks*, a ridge of land left by the plough in plough-
ing.

The coral red, as tribute due,
And roundest pearls of Orient hue :
Or in the richer veins of ground
Should seek for her the diamond.
And whereas now unto my spring   45
They nothing else but gravel bring,
They should within a mine of gold
In piercing manner long time hold,
And having it to dust well wrought,
By them it hither should be brought ;   50
With which I'll pave and overspread
My bottom, where her foot shall tread.
The best of fishes in my flood
Shall give themselves to be her food.
The trout, the dace, the pike, the bream,   55
The eel, that loves the troubled stream,
The miller's thumb, the hiding loach,
The perch, the ever-nibbling roach,
The shoats with whom is Tavy fraught,
The foolish gudgeon, quickly caught,   60
And last the little minnow-fish,
Whose chief delight in gravel is.
   In right she cannot me despise
Because so low mine empire lies.
For I could tell how Nature's store   65
Of majesty appeareth more
In waters than in all the rest

59.—*Shoats*, or shotes, a kind of trout.

Of elements.   It seem'd her best
To give the waves most strength and power :
For they do swallow and devour   70
The earth ; the waters quench and kill
The flames of fire : and mounting still
Up in the air, are seen to be
As challenging a seignorie
Within the heavens, and to be one   75
That should have like dominion.
They be a ceiling and a floor
Of clouds, caus'd by the vapours' store
Arising from them, vital spirit
By which all things their life inherit   80
From them is stopped, kept asunder.
And what's the reason else of thunder,
Of lightning's flashes all about,
That with such violence break out,
Causing such troubles and such jars,   85
As with itself the world had wars?
And can there anything appear
More wonderful than in the air
Congealed waters oft to spy
Continuing pendant in the sky?   90
Till falling down in hail or snow,
They make those mortal wights below
To run, and ever help desire
From his foe element the fire,

74.—*Seignorie*, domain.

Which fearing then to come abroad,   95
Within doors maketh his abode ;
Or falling down ofttime in rain,
Doth give green liveries to the plain,
Make[s] shepherds' lambs fit for the dish,
And giveth nutriment to fish ;   100
Which nourisheth all things of worth
The earth produceth and brings forth ;
And therefore well considering
The nature of it in each thing :
As when the teeming earth doth grow   105
So hard, that none can plough nor sow,
Her breast it doth so mollify,
That it not only comes to be
More easy for the share and ox,
But that in harvest times the shocks   110
Of Ceres' hanging eared corn
Doth fill the hovel and the barn.
To trees and plants I comfort give,
By me they fructify and live :
For first ascending from beneath   115
Into the sky, with lively breath,
I thence am furnish'd, and bestow
The same on herbs that are below.
So that by this each one may see
I cause them spring and multiply.   120
Who seeth this can do no less,
Than of his own accord confess,
That notwithstanding all the strength

The earth enjoys in breadth and length,
She is beholding to each stream,   125
And hath received all from them.
Her love to him she then must give
By whom herself doth chiefly live.
This being spoken by this water's god,
He straightway in his hand did take his rod,   130
And struck it on his bank, wherewith the flood
Did such a roaring make within the wood,
That straight the nymph* who then sat on her shore,
Knew there was somewhat to be done in store :
And therefore hasting to her brother's spring   135
She spied what caus'd the waters' echoing.
Saw where fair Marine fast asleep did lie,
Whilst that the god still viewing her sat by :
Who when he saw his sister nymph draw near,
He thus 'gan tune his voice unto her ear :   140
    My fairest sister (for we come
    Both from the swelling Thetis' womb)
    The reason why of late I strook
    My ruling wand upon my brook,
    Was for this purpose : Late this maid   145
    Which on my bank asleep is laid,
    Was by herself or other wight
    Cast in my spring, and did affright
    With her late fall the fish that take
    Their chiefest pleasure in my lake :   150
    Of all the fry within my deep,
    None durst out of their dwellings peep.

** The watery nymph that spoke to Remond.*

E 2

The trout within the weeds did scud,
The eel him hid within the mud.
Yea, from this fear I was not free :   155
For as I musing sat to see
How that the pretty pebbles round
Came with my spring from underground,
And how the waters issuing
Did make them dance about my spring ;   160
The noise thereof did me appall :
That starting upward therewithal,
I in my arms her body caught,
And both to light and life her brought :
Then cast her in a sleep you see.   165
But, brother, to the cause (quoth she)
Why by your raging waters wild
Am I here called?   Thetis' child,
Replied the god, for thee I sent,
That when her time of sleep is spent,   170
I may commit her to thy gage,
Since women best know women's rage.
Meanwhile, fair nymph, accompany
My spring with thy sweet harmony ;
And we will make her soul to take   175
Some pleasure, which is said to wake,
Although the body hath his rest.
She gave consent, and each of them address'd
Unto their part.   The wat'ry nymph did sing

171.—*Gage*, here used in the sense of "temporary keeping."

In manner of a pretty questioning :   180
The god made answer to what she propounded,
Whilst from the spring a pleasant music sounded,
Making each shrub in silence to adore them,
Taking their subject from what lay before them.

Nymph. What's that, compact of earth, infus'd with
      air ;   185
  A certain made full with uncertainties ;
  Sway'd by the motion of each several sphere ;
  Who's fed with nought but infelicities ;
    Endures nor heat nor cold ; is like a swan,
    That this hour sings, next dies ?   190
                 God. It is a man.

Nymph. What's he, born to be sick, so always dying,
  That's guided by inevitable fate ;
  That comes in weeping, and that goes out crying ;
  Whose calendar of woes is still in date ;   195
    Whose life's a bubble, and in length a span ;
    A concert still in discords ?
                 God. 'Tis a man.

Nymph. What's he, whose thoughts are still quell'd
      in th' event,
  Though ne'er so lawful, by an opposite,   200
  Hath all things fleeting, nothing permanent,
  And at his ears wears still a parasite :

Hath friends in wealth, or wealthy friends, who can
In want prove mere illusions?

God. 'Tis a man.   205

Nymph. What's he, that what he is not strives to
   seem ;
That doth support an Atlas-weight of care ;
That of an outward good doth best esteem,
And looketh not within how solid they are ;
   That doth not virtuous, but the richest scan, 210
   Learning and worth by wealth?

God. It is a man.

Nymph. What's that possessor, which of good makes
   bad ;
And what is worst, makes choice still for the best ;
That grieveth most to think of what he had,   215
And of his chiefest loss accounteth least ;
   That doth not what he ought, but what he can ;
   Whose fancy's ever boundless ?

God. 'Tis a man.

Nymph. But what is it wherein Dame Nature wrought
   The best of works, the only frame of Heaven ;[220
And having long to find a present sought,
Wherein the world's whole beauty might be given,
   She did resolve in it all arts to summon,
   To join with Nature's framing?   225

God. 'Tis this woman.

Nymph. If beauty be a thing to be admired,
  And if admiring draw to it affection,
  And what we do affect is most desired,
  What wight is he to love denies subjection ?   230
    And can his thoughts within himself confine ?

the gods. As Hesiod, ὅτι πάντες Ὀλύμπια δώματ' ἔχοντες Δῶρον ἐδώρησαν.

Marine that waking lay, said : Celandine.
He is the man that hates which some admire ;
He is the wight that loathes whom most desire ;
'Tis only he to love denies subjecting,   235
And but himself, thinks none is worth affecting.
Unhappy me the while, accurs'd my fate,
That Nature gives no love where she gave hate.
The wat'ry rulers then perceived plain,
Nipp'd with the winter of love's frost, disdain,   240
This nonpareil of beauty had been led
To do an act which Envy pitied :
Therefore in pity did confer together
What physic best might cure this burning fever.
At last found out that in a grove below,   245
Where shadowing sycamores past number grow,
A fountain takes his journey to the main,
Whose liquor's nature was so sovereign
(Like to the wondrous well and famous spring,
Which in Bœotia* hath his issuing),   250
That whoso of it doth but only taste,
All former memory from him doth waste ;
Not changing any other work of Nature,
But doth endow the drinker with a feature

* Pliny writes of two springs rising in Bœotia, the first helping memory, called μνήμη : the latter causing oblivion, called λήθη.

More lovely.   Fair Medea took from hence   255
Some of this water, by whose quintessence
Æson from age came back to youth.   This known,
The god thus spake :

             Nymph, be thine own,
And after mine.   This goddess here
(For she's no less) will bring thee where   260
Thou shalt acknowledge springs have do[n]e
As much for thee as any one.
Which ended, and thou gotten free,
If thou wilt come and live with me,
No shepherd's daughter, nor his wife,   265
Shall boast them of a better life.
Meanwhile I leave thy thoughts at large,
Thy body to my sister's charge ;
Whilst I into my spring do dive
To see that they do not deprive   270
The meadows near, which much do thirst,
Thus heated by the sun.   May first
(Quoth Marine) swains give lambs to thee ;
And may thy flood have seignorie
Of all floods else, and to thy fame   275
Meet greater springs, yet keep thy name.
May never evet nor the toad
Within thy banks make their abode !
Taking thy journey from the sea,

274.—*Seignorie*, lordship, dominion.
277.—*Evet*, or hibit, the Devonshire name of the newt.

May'st thou ne'er happen in thy way   280
On nitre or on brimstone mine,
To spoil thy taste ! this spring of thine
Let it of nothing taste but earth,
And salt conceived, in their birth
Be ever fresh !   Let no man dare   285
To spoil thy fish, make lock or ware ;
But on thy margent still let dwell
Those flowers which have the sweetest smell.
And let the dust upon thy strand
Become like Tagus' golden sand.   290
Let as much good betide to thee,
As thou hast favour show'd to me.

Thus said, in gentle paces they remove,
And hasten'd onward to the shady grove,
Where both arriv'd ; and having found the rock, 295
Saw how this precious water it did lock.
As he whom avarice possesseth most,
Drawn by necessity unto his cost,
Doth drop by piecemeal down his prison'd gold,
And seems unwilling to let go his hold :   300
So the strong rock the water long time stops,
And by degrees lets it fall down in drops.
Like hoarding housewives that do mould their food,
And keep from others what doth them no good.
　　The drops within a cistern fell of stone,   305
Which fram'd by Nature, Art had never one

286.—*Ware*, weir

Half part so curious.   Many spells then using,
The water's nymph 'twixt Marine's lips infusing
Part of this water, she might straight perceive
How soon her troubled thoughts began to leave 310
Her love-swoll'n breast ; and that her inward flame
Was clean assuaged, and the very name
Of Celandine forgotten ; did scarce know
If there were such a thing as love or no.
And sighing, therewithal threw in the air   315
All former love, all sorrow, all despair ;
And all the former causes of her moan
Did therewith bury in oblivion.
Then must'ring up her thoughts, grown vagabonds,
Press'd to relieve her inward bleeding wounds,   320
She had as quickly all things past forgotten,
As men do monarchs that in earth lie rotten.
As one new born she seem'd, so all-discerning,
" Though things long learn'd are the long'st unlearn-
          ing."
Then walk'd they to a grove but near at hand,   325
Where fiery Titan had but small command,
Because the leaves, conspiring, kept his beams,
For fear of hurting (when he's in extremes)
The under-flowers, which did enrich the ground
With sweeter scents than in Arabia found.   330
The earth doth yield (which they through pores
          exhale)
Earth's best of odours, th'aromatical :
Like to that smell which oft our sense descries

Within a field which long unploughed lies,
Somewhat before the setting of the sun ;   335
And where the rainbow in the horizon
Doth pitch her tips : or as when in the prime,
The earth being troubled with a drought long time,
The hand of Heaven his spongy clouds doth strain,
And throws into her lap a shower of rain :   340
She sendeth up (conceived from the sun)
A sweet perfume and exhalation.
Not all the ointments brought from Delos' Isle,
Nor from the confines of seven-headed Nile,
Nor that brought whence Phœnicians have abodes, 345
Nor Cyprus' wild vine-flowers, nor that of Rhodes,
Nor roses' oil from Naples, Capua,
Saffron confected in Cilicia,
Nor that of quinces, nor of marjoram,
That ever from the Isle of Coös came;   350
Nor these, nor any else, though ne'er so rare,
Could with this place for sweetest smells compare.
There stood the elm, whose shade so mildly dim
Doth nourish all that groweth under him ;
Cypress that like pyramids run topping,   355
And hurt the least of any by their dropping ;
The alder, whose fat shadow nourisheth,
Each plant set near to him long flourisheth ;
The heavy-headed plane-tree, by whose shade
The grass grows thickest, men are fresher made ; 360

337.—*Prime*, spring.
348.—*Confected*, prepared as sweetmeats.

The oak, that best endures the thunder-shocks ;
The everlasting eben, cedar, box ;
The olive that in wainscot never cleaves ;
The amorous vine, which in the elm still weaves ;
The lotus, juniper, where worms ne'er enter ;   365
The pine, with whom men through the ocean venter ;
The warlike yew, by which (more than the lance)
The strong-arm'd English spirits conquer'd France.
Amongst the rest the tamarisk there stood,
For housewives' besoms only known most good ; 370
The cold-place-loving birch, and service-tree ;
The walnut loving vales, and mulberry ;
The maple, ash, that do delight in fountains
Which have their currents by the sides of mountains ;
The laurel, myrtle, ivy, date, which hold   375
Their leaves all winter, be it ne'er so cold ;
The fir, that oftentimes doth rosin drop ;
The beech, that scales the welkin with his top ;
All these, and thousand more within this grove,
By all the industry of Nature strove   380
To frame an harbour that might keep within it
The best of beauties that the world hath in it.
     Here ent'ring, at the entrance of which shroud,
The sun, half angry, hid him in a cloud,
As raging that a grove should from his sight   385
Lock up a beauty whence himself had light,

369.—*Tamarisk*, a shrub growing freely on the south coast
of England. *See* Note.
371.—*Service-tree*, the wild pear-tree.

The flowers pull'd in their heads as being 'sham'd
Their beauties by the others were defam'd.
　Near to this wood there lay a pleasant mead,
Where fairies often did their measures tread,　　390
Which in the meadow made such circles g[r]een,
As if with garlands it had crowned been,
Or like the circle where the signs we track,
And learned shepherds call't the Zodiac :
Within one of these rounds was to be seen　　395
A hillock rise, where oft the fairy-queen
At twilight sat, and did command her elves
To pinch those maids that had not swept their
　　　　　shelves ;
And further, if by maidens' oversight
Within doors water were not brought at night ;　400
Or if they spread no table, set no bread,
They should have nips from toe unto the head ;
And for the maid that had perform'd each thing,
She in the water-pail bade leave a ring.
　Upon this hill there sat a lovely swain,　　405
As if that Nature thought it great disdain
That he should (so through her his genius told him)
Take equal place with swains, since she did hold him
Her chiefest work, and therefore thought it fit
That with inferiors he should never sit.　　410
Narcissus' change sure Ovid clean mistook,
He died not looking in a crystal brook,
But (as those which in emulation gaze)
He pin'd to death by looking on this face.

When he stood fishing by some river's brim,   415
The fish would leap, more for a sight of him
Than for the fly.   The eagle, highest bred,
Was taking him once up for Ganymede.
The shag-hair'd satyrs, and the tripping fawns,
With all the troop that frolic on the lawns,   420
Would come and gaze on him, as who should say
They had not seen his like this many a day.
Yea, Venus knew no difference 'twixt these twain,
Save Adon was a hunter, this a swain.
The wood's sweet quiristers from spray to spray   425
Would hop them nearer him, and then there stay :
Each joying greatly from his little heart
That they with his sweet reed might bear a part.
This was the boy (the poets did mistake)
To whom bright Cynthia so much love did make ; 430
And promis'd for his love no scornful eyes
Should ever see her more in horned guise :
But she at his command would as of duty
Become as full of light as he of beauty.
Lucina at his birth for midwife stuck ;   435
And Cytherea nurs'd and gave him suck,
Who to that end, once dove-drawn from the sea,
Her full paps dropp'd, whence came the milky-way.
And as when Plato did i' th' cradle thrive,
Bees to his lips brought honey from their hive :   440
So to this boy they came, I know not whether

425.—*Quiristers*, choristers.

They brought, or from his lips did honey gather.
The wood-nymphs oftentimes would busied be,
And pluck for him the blushing strawberry,
Making of them a bracelet on a bent,   445
Which for a favour to this swain they sent.
Sitting in shades, the sun would oft by skips
Steal through the boughs, and seize upon his lips.
The chiefest cause the sun did condescend
To Phaeton's request was to this end,   450
That whilst the other did his horses rein,
He might slide from his sphere and court this swain,
Whose sparkling eyes vied lustre with the stars,
The truest centre of all circulars.
In brief, if any man in skill were able   455
To finish up Apelles' half-done table,
This boy (the man left out) were fittest sure ·
To be the pattern of that portraiture.
    Piping he sat, as merry as his look,
And by him lay his bottle and his hook.   460
His buskins (edg'd with silver) were of silk,
Which held a leg more white than morning's milk.
Those buskins he had got and brought away
For dancing best upon the revel day.
His oaten reed did yield forth such sweet notes,   465
Joined in concert with the birds' shrill throats,

445.—*Bent*, a long coarse grass.
449.—*Condescend*, consent.
456.—*Table*, a picture of Aphrodite.

That equaliz'd the harmony of spheres,
A music that would ravish choicest ears.
Long look'd they on, (who would not long look on,
That such an object had to look upon?)   470
Till at the last the nymph did Marine send
To ask the nearest way whereby to wend
To those fair walks where sprung Marina's ill,
Whilst she would stay : Marine obey'd her will,
And hasten'd towards him (who would not do so, 475
That such a pretty journey had to go?)
Sweetly she came, and with a modest blush,
Gave him the day, and then accosted thus :

    Fairest of men, that (whilst thy flock doth feed)
Sitt'st sweetly piping on thine oaten reed   480
Upon this little berry (some ycleep
A hillock) void of care, as are thy sheep
Devoid of spots, and sure on all this green
A fairer flock as yet was never seen :
Do me this favour (men should favour maids)   485
That whatsoever path directly leads,
And void of danger, thou to me do show,
That by it to the Marish I might go.
Marriage ! (quoth he) mistaking what she said,
Nature's perfection : thou most fairest maid,   490
(If any fairer than the fairest may be)
Come sit thee down by me ; know, lovely lady,

481.—*Berry*, barrow, or mound. Berry, Berry-Head, Berry
Pomeroy, all in Devonshire, are perhaps instances of its use.
488.—*Marish*, marsh.

Love is the readiest way: if ta'en aright,
You may attain thereto full long ere night.
The maiden thinking he of marish spoke,   495
And not of marriage, straightway did invoke,
And pray'd the shepherds' god might always keep
Him from all danger, and from wolves his sheep.
Wishing withal that in the prime of spring
Each sheep he had two lambs might yearly bring. 500
But yet (quoth she) arede, good gentle swain,
If in the dale below, or on yond plain;
Or is the village situate in a grove,
Through which my way lies, and ycleeped Love?
Nor on yond plain, nor in this neighbouring wood;
Nor in the dale where glides the silver flood;   [505
But like a beacon on a hill so high,
That every one may see 't which passeth by,
Is Love yplac'd : there's nothing can it hide,
Although of you as yet 'tis unespied.   510
But on which hill (quoth she) pray tell me true?
Why here (quoth he) it sits and talks to you.
And are you Love (quoth she?) fond swain, adieu,
You guide me wrong, my way lies not by you.
Though not your way, yet you may lie by me :   515
Nymph, with a shepherd thou as merrily
May'st love and live, as with the greatest lord.
"Greatness doth never most content afford."
I love thee only, not affect world's pelf;

501.—*Arede*, explain.

"She is not lov'd that's lov'd not for herself."   520
How many shepherds' daughters, who in duty
To griping fathers have enthrall'd their beauty,
To wait upon the gout, to walk when pleases
Old January halt.   O that diseases   [525
Should link with youth !   She that hath such a mate
Is like two twins born both incorporate :
Th' one living, th' other dead : the living twin
Must needs be slain through noisomeness of him
He carrieth with him : such are their estates,
Who merely marry wealth and not their mates.   530
    As ebbing waters freely slide away
To pay their tribute to the raging sea ;
When meeting with the flood they jostle stout,
Whether the one shall in, or th' other out :   [535
Till the strong flood new power of waves doth bring,
And drives the river back into his spring :
So Marine's words off'ring to take their course,
By Love then ent'ring, were kept back, and force
To it, his sweet face, eyes, and tongue assign'd,
And threw them back again into her mind.   540
" How hard it is to leave and not to do
That which by nature we are prone unto !
We hardly can (alas why not ?) discuss,
When Nature hath decreed it must be thus.
It is a maxim held of all, known plain :   545
Thrust Nature off with forks, she'll turn again."
    Blithe Doridon (so men this shepherd hight)
Seeing his goddess in a silent plight,

("Love often makes the speech's organs mute,")
Began again thus to renew his suit :   550
   If by my words your silence hath been such,
Faith I am sorry I have spoke so much.
Bar I those lips? fit to be th' utt'rers when
The heavens would parley with the chief of men ;
Fit to direct (a tongue all hearts convinces)   555
When best of scribes writes to the best of princes.
Were mine like yours, of choicest words completest,
"I'd show how grief's a thing weighs down the
      greatest ;
The best of forms (who knows not) grief doth taint it,
The skilfull'st pencil never yet could paint it ; " 560
And reason good, since no man yet could find
What figure represents a grieved mind.
Methinks a troubled thought is thus express'd,
To be a chaos rude and indigest :
Where all do rule, and yet none bears chief sway: 565
Check'd only by a power that's more than they.
This do I speak, since to this every lover
That thus doth love, is thus still given over.
If that you say you will not, cannot love :   [570
Oh heavens ! for what cause then do you here move?
Are you not fram'd of that expertest mould
For whom all in this round concordance hold ?
Or are you framed of some other fashion,
And have a form and heart, but yet no passion ?

572.—*Round*, globe, world.

It cannot be : for then unto what end   575
Did the best workman this great work intend ?
Not that by minds' commerce, and joint estate,
The world's continuers still should propagate ?
Yea, if that Reason (regent of the senses)
Have but a part amongst your excellences,   580
She'll tell you what you call Virginity,
Is fitly liken'd to a barren tree ;
Which when the gard'ner on it pains bestows,
To graft an imp thereon, in time it grows
To such perfection that it yearly brings   585
As goodly fruit as any tree that springs.
Believe me, maiden, vow no chastity :
For maidens but imperfect creatures be.

  Alas, poor boy (quoth Marine), have the Fates
Exempted no degrees ? are no estates   590
Free from Love's rage ? Be rul'd, unhappy swain ;
Call back thy spirits, and recollect again
Thy vagrant wits.   I tell thee for a truth
" Love is a siren that doth shipwreck youth."
Be well advis'd ; thou entertain'st a guest   595
That is the harbinger of all unrest :
Which like the viper's young, that lick the earth,
Eat out the breeder's womb to get a birth.

  Faith (quoth the boy), I know there cannot be
Danger in loving or enjoying thee.   600
For what cause were things made and called good,

584.—*Imp*, shoot.

But to be loved ?   If you understood
The birds that prattle here, you would know then,
As birds woo birds, maids should be woo'd of men.
But I want power to woo, since what was mine   605
Is fled, and lie as vassals at your shrine :
And since what's mine is yours, let that same move,
Although in me you see nought worthy love.
Marine about to speak, forth of a sling
(Fortune to all misfortunes plies her wing   610
More quick and speedy) came a sharpen'd flint,
Which in the fair boy's neck made such a dint,
That crimson blood came streaming from the wound,
And he fell down into a deadly swound.
The blood ran all along where it did fall,   615
And could not find a place of burial :
But where it came, it there congealed stood,
As if the Earth loath'd to drink guiltless blood.
   Gold-hair'd Apollo, Muses' sacred king,
Whose praise in Delphos' Isle doth ever ring,   620
Physic's first founder, whose art's excellence
Extracted Nature's chiefest quintessence,
Unwilling that a thing of such a worth
Should so be lost, straight sent a dragon forth
To fetch this blood, and he perform'd the same : 625
And now apothecaries give it name,
From him that fetch'd it—(doctors know it good
In physic's use)—and call it dragon's blood.
Some of the blood by chance did downward fall,
And by a vein got to a mineral,   630

Whence came a red : decayed dames infuse it
With Venice ceruse, and for painting use it.
Marine astonish'd (most unhappy maid),
O'ercome with fear, and at the view afraid,
Fell down into a trance, eyes lost their sight,   635
Which being open made all darkness light.
Her blood ran to her heart, or life to feed,
Or loathing to behold so vile a deed.

And as when winter doth the earth array
In silver suit, and when the night and day   640
Are in dissension, night locks up the ground,
Which by the help of day is oft unbound,
A shepherd's boy with bow and shafts address'd,
Ranging the fields, having once pierc'd the breast
Of some poor fowl, doth with the blow straight rush
To catch the bird lies panting in the bush :   [645
So rush'd this striker in, up Marine took,
And hasten'd with her to a near-hand brook.
Old shepherds sain (old shepherds sooth have sain)
Two rivers* took their issue from the main,   650
Both near together, and each bent his race,
Which of them both should first behold the face
Of radiant Phœbus : one of them in gliding
Chanc'd on a vein where nitre had abiding :
The other, loathing that her purer wave   655
Should be defil'd with that the nitre gave,

* An expression of the natures of two rivers rising near together, and differing in their tastes and manner of running.

632.—*Venice ceruse*, white-lead, used by ladies for painting their faces and bosoms.

Fled fast away, the other follow'd fast,
Till both been in a rock ymet at last.
As seemed best, the rock did first deliver
Out of his hollow sides the purer river,   660
(As if it taught those men in honour clad
To help the virtuous and suppress the bad,)
Which gotten loose, did softly glide away.
As men from earth, to earth; from sea, to sea;
So rivers run: and that from whence both came 665
Takes what she gave: waves, earth: but leaves a
          name.
As waters have their course, and in their place
Succeeding streams will out, so is man's race:
The name doth still survive, and cannot die,
Until the channels stop, or spring grow dry.   670
   As I have seen upon a bridal day
Full many maids clad in their best array,
In honour of the bride come with their flaskets
Fill'd full with flowers: others in wicker-baskets
Bring from the marish rushes to o'erspread   675
The ground whereon to church the lovers tread;
Whilst that the quaintest youth of all the plain
Ushers their way with many a piping strain:
So, as in joy, at this fair river's birth,
Triton came up a channel with his mirth,   680

673.—*Flaskets*, clothes-baskets.
675.—*Marish*, marsh.
677.—*Quaintest*, neat, elegant, or ingenious.

And call'd the neighb'ring nymphs each in her turn
To pour their pretty rivulets from their urn.
To wait upon this new-deliver'd spring,
Some running through the meadows, with them bring
Cowslip and mint : and 'tis another's lot   685
To light upon some gard'ner's curious knot,
Whence she upon her breast (love's sweet repose)
Doth bring the queen of flowers, the English rose.
Some from the fen bring reeds, wild-thyme from
          downs ;
Some from a grove the bay that poets crowns ;   690
Some from an aged rock the moss hath torn,
And leaves him naked unto winter's storm ;
Another from her banks (in mere goodwill)
Brings nutriment for fish, the camomile.
Thus all bring somewhat, and do overspread   695
The way the spring unto the sea doth tread.
    This while the flood which yet the rock up-pent,
And suffer'd not with jocund merriment
To tread rounds in his spring, came rushing forth,
As angry that his waves (he thought) of worth   700
Should not have liberty, nor help the prime.
And as some ruder swain composing rhyme,
Spends many a grey goose-quill unto the handle,
Buries within his socket many a candle,
Blots paper by the quire, and dries up ink,   705

686.—*Knot*, garden plat.
691.—*An aged rock*, etc. *See* Note.

As Xerxes' army did whole rivers drink,
Hoping thereby his name his work should raise
That it should live until the last of days :
Which finished, he boldly doth address
Him and his works to undergo the press ;   710
When lo (O Fate !) his work not seeming fit
To walk in equipage with better wit,
Is kept from light, there gnawn by moths and worms,
At which he frets : right so this river storms :
But broken forth ; as Tavy creeps upon   715
The western vales of fertile Albion,
Here dashes roughly on an aged rock,
That his intended passage doth up-lock ;
There intricately 'mongst the woods doth wander,
Losing himself in many a wry meander :   720
Here amorously bent, clips some fair mead ;
And then dispers'd in rills, doth measures tread
Upon her bosom 'mongst her flow'ry ranks :
There in another place bears down the banks
Of some day-labouring wretch : here meets a rill, 725
And with their forces join'd cuts out a mill
Into an island, then in jocund guise
Surveys his conquest, lauds his enterprise :
Here digs a cave at some high mountain's foot :
There undermines an oak, tears up his root :   730
Thence rushing to some country-farm at hand,
Breaks o'er the yeoman's mounds, sweeps from his land

712.—*To walk in equipage,* etc. *See* Note.
729.—*Here digs a cave,* etc. *See* Note.

His harvest hope of wheat, of rye, or pease :
And makes that channel which was shepherd's lease :
Here, as our wicked age doth sacrilege,   735
Helps down an abbey, then a natural bridge
By creeping underground he frameth out,
As who should say he either went about
To right the wrong he did, or hid his face,
For having done a deed so vile and base :   740
So ran this river on, and did bestir
Himself to find his fellow-traveller.

But th' other fearing lest her noise might show
What path she took, which way her streams did flow :
As some wayfaring man strays thro' a wood,   745
Where beasts of prey, thirsting for human blood,
Lurk in their dens, he softly list'ning goes,
Not trusting to his heels, treads on his toes ;
Dreads every noise he hears, thinks each small bush
To be a beast that would upon him rush ;   750
Feareth to die, and yet his wind doth smother ;
Now leaves this path, takes that, then to another :
Such was her course.   This feared to be found,
The other not to find, swells o'er each mound,
Roars, rages, foams, against a mountain dashes,   755
And in recoil makes meadows standing plashes :
Yet finds not what he seeks in all his way,
But in despair runs headlong to the sea.

734.—*Lease*, pasture.
736.—*Helps down an abbey*, etc. *See* Note.
756.—*Plashes*, pools.

This was the cause them by tradition taught,
Why one flood ran so fast, th' other so soft,   760
Both from one head.   Unto the rougher stream,
(Crown'd by that meadow's flow'ry diadem,
Where Doridon lay hurt) the cruel swain
Hurries the shepherdess, where having lain
Her in a boat like the cannows of Inde,   765
Some silly trough of wood, or some tree's rind,
Puts from the shore, and leaves the weeping strand,
Intends an act by water, which the land
Abhorr'd to bolster ; yea, the guiltless earth
Loath'd to be midwife to so vile a birth :   770
Which to relate I am enforc'd to wrong
The modest blushes of my maiden-song.
Then each fair nymph whom Nature doth endow
With beauty's cheek, crown'd with   a shamefast
          brow ;
Whose well-tun'd ears, chaste-object-loving eyne 775
Ne'er heard nor saw the works of Aretine ;*
Who ne'er came on the Cytherean shelf,
But is as true as Chastity itself ;
Where hated Impudence ne'er set her seed ;
Where lust lies not veil'd in a virgin's weed :   780

* An ob-
scene Italian
poet.

765.—*Cannows*, canoes.
769.—*Bolster*, support.
777.—*Cytherean shelf*, Cythera, a very rocky island lying off
the south-eastern extremity of Laconia, represented in the
Greek and Latin poets as one of the favourite residences of
Aphrodite.

Let her withdraw.   Let each young shepherdling
Walk by, or stop his ear, the whilst I sing.
　　But ye, whose blood, like kids upon a plain,
Doth skip and dance lavoltas in each vein ;   [785
Whose breasts are swoll'n with the venerean game,
And warm yourselves at lust's alluring flame ;
Who dare to act as much as men dare think,
And wallowing lie within a sensual sink ;
Whose feigned gestures do entrap our youth
With an apparency of simple truth ;   790
Insatiate gulfs, in your defective part
By Art help Nature, and by Nature, Art:
Lend me your ears, and I will touch a string
Shall lull your sense asleep the while I sing.
　　But stay : methinks I hear something in me   795
That bids me keep the bounds of modesty ;
Says, " Each man's voice to that is quickly mov'd
Which of himself is best of all belov'd ;
By utt'ring what thou know'st less glory's got,
Than by concealing what thou knowest not."   800
If so, I yield to it, and set my rest
Rather to lose the bad than wrong the best.
My maiden-Muse flies the lascivious swains,
And scorns to soil her lines with lustful strains ;
Will not dilate (nor on her forehead bear   805
Immodesty's abhorred character)

784.—*Lavoltas*, romping waltzes.
801.—*Set my rest*, am determined, a metaphor from the once
fashionable game of primero.

His shameless pryings, his undecent doings,
His curious searches, his respectless wooings;
How that he saw—But what ?   I dare not break it,
You safer may conceive than I dare speak it.   810
Yet verily had he not thought her dead,
Sh'ad lost, ne'er to be found, her maidenhead.
  The rougher stream, loathing a thing compacted
Of so great shame should on his flood be acted,
(According to our times not well allow'd   815
In others what he in himself avow'd)
Bent hard his forehead, furrow'd up his face,
And danger led the way the boat did trace.
And as within a landskip that doth stand
Wrought by the pencil of some curious hand,   820
We may descry, here meadow, there a wood ;
Here standing ponds, and there a running flood ;
Here on some mount a house of pleasure vanted,
Where once the roaring cannon had been planted ;
There on a hill a swain pipes out the day,   825
Out-braving all the quiristers of May ;
A huntsman here follows his cry of hounds,
Driving the hare along the fallow grounds,
Whilst one at hand seeming the sport t' allow,   [830
Follows the hounds and careless leaves the plough ;
There in another place some high-rais'd land,
In pride bears out her breasts unto the strand ;

823.—*Vanted*, made an ostentatious display.
826.—*Quiristers*, choristers, constantly used for birds.

Here stands a bridge, and there a conduit head ;
Here round a Maypole some the measures tread ;
There boys the truant play and leave their book ; 835
Here stands an angler with a baited hook ;
There for a stag one lurks within a bough ;
Here sits a maiden milking of her cow ;
There on a goodly plain (by time thrown down)
Lies buried in his dust some ancient town),   840
Who now invillaged there's only seen
In his vast ruins what his state had been ;
And of all these in shadows so express'd
Make the beholders' eyes to take no rest :
So for the swain the flood did mean to him   845
To show in Nature (not by Art to limn)
A tempest's rage : his furious waters threat,
Some on this shore, some on the other beat.
Here stands a mountain where was once a dale ;
There where a mountain stood is now a vale.   850
Here flows a billow, there another meets ;
Each, on each side the skiff, unkindly greets.
The waters underneath 'gan upward move,
Wond'ring what stratagems were wrought above :
Billows that miss'd the boat still onward thrust, 855
And on the cliffs, as swoll'n with anger, burst.
All these, and more, in substance so express'd,
Made the beholder's thoughts to take no rest.
Horror in triumph rid upon the waves ;
And all the Furies from their gloomy caves   860
Came hovering o'er the boat, summon'd each sense

Before the fearful bar of conscience ;
Were guilty all, and all condemned were
To undergo their horrors with despair.
    What Muse ? what Power ? or what thrice sacred
        herse,   865
That lives immortal in a well-tun'd verse,
Can lend me such a sight that I might see
A guilty conscience' true anatomy ;
That well-kept register wherein is writ
All ills men do, all goodness they omit ?   ··870
His pallid fears, his sorrows, his affrightings ;
His late-wish'd had-I-wists, remorseful bitings ;
His many tortures, his heartrending pain ;
How were his griefs composed in one chain,
And he by it let down into the seas,   875
Or through the centre to th' Antipodes ?
He might change climates, or be barr'd Heaven's
        face ;
Yet find no salve, nor ever change his case.
Fears, sorrows, tortures, sad affrights, nor any, [880
Like to the conscience sting, though thrice as many ;
Yet all these torments by the swain were borne,
Whilst Death's grim visage lay upon the storm.
    But as when some kind nurse doth long time keep
Her pretty baby at suck, whom fall'n asleep
She lays down in his cradle, stints his cry   885
With many a sweet and pleasing lullaby ;
Whilst the sweet child, not troubled with the shock,
As sweetly slumbers, as his nurse doth rock :

So lay the maid, th' amazed swain sat weeping,
And Death in her was dispossess'd by sleeping.   890
The roaring voice of winds, the billows' raves,
 Nor all the mutt'ring of the sullen waves
Could once disquiet, or her slumber stir;
But lull'd her more asleep than waken'd her.
Such are their states whose souls from foul offence 895
Enthroned sit in spotless innocence.
Where rest my Muse; till (jolly shepherds' swains)
Next morn with pearls of dew bedecks our plains
We'll fold our flocks, then in fit time go on
To tune mine oaten pipe for Doridon.   900

THE THIRD SONG.

———

THE ARGUMENT.

The shepherd's swain here singing on,
Tells of the cure of Doridon :
And then unto the waters' falls
Chanteth the rustic Pastorals.

———

Now had the sun, in golden chariot hurl'd,
Twice bid good-morrow to the nether world ;
And Cynthia, in her orb and perfect round,
Twice view'd the shadows of the upper ground ;
Twice had the day-star usher'd forth the light ;   5
And twice the evening-star proclaim'd the night ;
Ere once the sweet-fac'd boy (now all forlorn)
Came with his pipe to resalute the morn.
  When grac'd by time (unhappy time the while)
The cruel swain (who ere knew swain so vile ?)   10
Had struck the lad, in came the wat'ry nymph
To raise from sound poor Doridon (the imp

1.—*Hurl'd,* wheeled.   12.—*Sound,* swoon.
  12.—*Imp,* a graft or shoot inserted into a tree, used meta-
phorically for offspring, a child.

Whom Nature seem'd to have selected forth
To be ingrafted on some stock of worth ;)
And the maid help, but since "to dooms of Fate 15
Succour, though ne'er so soon, comes still too late,"
She rais'd the youth, then with her arms enrings him,
And so with words of hope she homewards brings
     him.
   At door expecting him his mother sat,
Wond'ring her boy should stay from her so late ; 20
Framing for him unto herself excuses,
And with such thoughts gladly herself abuses :
As that her son, since day grew old and weak,
Stay'd with the maids to run at barley-break ;
Or that he cours'd a park with females fraught, 25
Which would not run except they might be caught ;
Or in the thickets laid some wily snare
To take the rabbit or the purblind hare ;
Or taught his dog to catch the climbing kid :
Thus shepherds do, and thus she thought he did. 30
" In things expected meeting with delay,
Though there be none, we frame some cause of stay."
And so did she (as she who doth not so ?)
Conjecture Time unwing'd he came so slow.
But Doridon drew near, so did her grief : 35
" Ill-luck, for speed, of all things else is chief."
* Homer.   For as the blind man* sung, " Time so provides,
That Joy goes still on foot, and Sorrow rides."

24 and 25.—*Barley-break*, and *Course-a-park*, country games.

Now when she saw (a woful sight) her son,
Her hopes then fail'd her, and her cries begun   40
To utter such a plaint, that scarce another,
Like this, ere came from any love-sick mother.
   If man hath done this, Heaven, why mad'st thou
      men ?
Not to deface thee in thy children,
But by the work the workman to adore ;   45
Framing that something which was nought before.
Aye me, unhappy wretch ! if that in things
Which are as we (save title) men fear kings,
That be their postures to the life limn'd on
Some wood as frail as they, or cut in stone,   50
" 'Tis death to stab : why then should earthly things
Dare to deface his form who formed kings ?
When the world was but in his infancy,
Revenge, desires unjust, vile jealousy,
Hate, envy, murder, all these six then reign'd,   55
When but their half of men the world contain'd :
Yet but in part of these, those ruled then.
When now as many vices live as men.
Live they ? yes, live, I fear, to kill my son,
With whom my joys, my love, my hopes are done. 60
   Cease, quoth the water's nymph, that led the swain ;
Though 'tis each mother's cause thus to complain,
Yet "abstinence in things we must profess
Which Nature fram'd for need, not for excess."
   Since the least blood, drawn from the lesser part 65
Of any child, comes from the mother's heart,

We cannot choose but grieve, except that we
Should be more senseless than the senseless tree,
Replied his mother.   Do but cut the limb
Of any tree, the trunk will weep for him :   70
Rend the cold sycamore's* thin bark in two,
His name and tears would say, So love should do.
" That mother is all flint (than beasts less good)
Which drops no water when her child streams blood."
      At this the wounded boy fell on his knee,   75
Mother, kind mother (said) weep not for me.
Why, I am well.   Indeed I am : if you
Cease not to weep, my wound will bleed anew.
When I was promis'd first the light's fruition,
You oft have told me, 'twas on this condition,   80
That I should hold it with like rent and pain
As others do, and one time leave 't again.
Then, dearest mother, leave, oh leave to wail,
" Time will effect where tears can nought avail."
      Herewith Marinda taking up her son,   85
Her hope, her love, her joy, her Doridon,
She thank'd the nymph for her kind succour lent,
Who straight tripp'd to her wat'ry regiment.
      Down in a dell (where in that month* whose fame
Grows greater by the man who gave it name,   90
Stands many a well-pil'd cock of short sweet hay
That feeds the husband's neat each winter's day)

* Alluding to our English pronunciation and indifferent orthography.

* July took his name from Julius Cæsar.

83.—*Leave*, cease.
92. —*Husband's neat*, farmer's oxen.

A mountain had his foot, and 'gan to rise
In stately height to parley with the skies.
And yet as blaming his own lofty gait,   95
Weighing the fickle props in things of state,
His head began to droop, and downwards bending,
Knock'd on that breast which gave it birth and
   ending :
And lies so with an hollow hanging vaut,
As when some boy trying the somersault,   100
Stands on his head, and feet, as he did lie
To kick against earth's spangled canopy ;
When seeing that his heels are of such weight,
That he cannot obtain their purpos'd height,
Leaves any more to strive ; and thus doth say,   105
What now I cannot do, another day
May well effect : it cannot be denied
I show'd a will to act, because I tried :
The Scornfull-hill men call'd him, who did scorn
So to be call'd, by reason he had borne   110
No hate to greatness, but a mind to be
The slave of greatness through humility :
For had his mother Nature thought it meet,
He meekly bowing would have kiss'd her feet.
 Under the hollow hanging of this hill   115
There was a cave cut out by Nature's skill :
Or else it seem'd the mount did open 's breast,
That all might see what thoughts he there possess'd.

99.—*Vaut*, vault.   105.—*Leaves*, ceases.

Whose gloomy entrance was environ'd round   [120
With shrubs that cloy ill husbands' meadow-ground :
The thick-grown hawthorn and the binding briar,
The holly that out-dares cold winter's ire :
Who all entwin'd, each limb with limb did deal,
That scarce a glimpse of light could inward steal.
An uncouth place, fit for an uncouth mind,   125
That is as heavy as that cave is blind.
Here liv'd a man his hoary hairs call'd old,
Upon whose front time many years had told ;
Who, since Dame Nature in him feeble grew,
And he unapt to give the world ought new,   130
The secret power of herbs that grow on mould,
Sought out, to cherish and relieve the old.

   Hither Marinda all in haste came running,
And with her tears desir'd the old man's cunning ;
When this good man (as goodness still is prest   135
At all assays to help a wight distress'd)
As glad and willing was to ease her son,
As she would ever joy to see it done ;
And giving her a salve in leaves up-bound,
And she directed how to cure the wound,   140
With thanks, made homewards (longing still to see
Th' effect of this good hermit's surgery).
There carefully, her son laid on a bed
(Enriched with the blood he on it shed),

135.—*Still*, constantly.   *Prest*, ready.
136.—*Assays*, essays, trials.

She washes, dresses, binds his wound (yet sore)   145
That griev'd it could weep blood for him no more.
   Now had the glorious sun ta'en up his inn,
And all the lamps of heav'n enlighten'd been ;
Within the gloomy shades of some thick spring
Sad Philomel 'gan on the hawthorn sing   150
(Whilst every beast at rest was lowly laid),
The outrage done upon a silly maid.
All things were hush'd ; each bird slept on his bough ;
And night gave rest to him day tir'd at plough ;
Each   beast,   each   bird,   and   each   day-toiling
         wight   155
Receiv'd the comfort of the silent night ;
Free from the gripes of sorrow every one,
Except poor Philomel and Doridon ;
She on a thorn sings sweet though sighing strains ;
He on a couch more soft, more sad complains ;   160
Whose in-pent thoughts him long time having pain'd,
He sighing, wept, and weeping thus complain'd :
   Sweet Philomela (then he heard her sing),
I do not envy thy sweet carolling,
But do admire thee that each even and morrow   165
Canst carelessly thus sing away thy sorrow.
Would I could do so too ! and ever be
In all my woes still imitating thee :
But I may not attain to that, for then
Such most unhappy, miserable men   170

147.—*Inn,* lodging.   149.—*Spring,* wood.

Would strive with Heaven, and imitate the sun,
Whose golden beams in exhalation,
Though drawn from fens, or other grounds impure,
Turn all to fructifying nouriture ;
When we draw nothing by our sun-like eyes,   175
That ever turns to mirth, but miseries.
Would I had never seen, except that she
Who made me wish so, love to look on me.
Had Colin Clout yet liv'd (but he is gone),
That best on earth could tune a lover's moan,   180
Whose sadder tones enforc'd the rocks to weep,
And laid the greatest griefs in quiet sleep :
Who when he sung (as I would do to mine)
His truest loves to his fair Rosaline,
Entic'd each shepherd's ear to hear him play,   185
And rapt with wonder, thus admiring say :
Thrice happy plains (if plains thrice happy may be)
Where such a shepherd pipes to such a lady.
Who made the lasses long to sit down near him ;
And woo'd the rivers from their springs to hear
        him.   190
Heaven rest thy soul (if so a swain may pray)
And as thy works live here, live there for aye.
Meanwhile (unhappy) I shall still complain
Love's cruel wounding of a seely swain.
   Two nights thus pass'd : the lily-handed Morn 195
Saw Phœbus stealing dew from Ceres' corn.

179.—*Colin Clout*, Spenser.

The mounting lark (day's herald) got on wing,
Bidding each bird choose out his bough and sing.
*The lofty treble sung the little wren ;
Robin the mean, that best of all loves men ;   200
The nightingale the tenor, and the thrush
The counter-tenor sweetly in a bush.
And that the music might be full in parts,
Birds from the groves flew with right willing hearts ;
But (as it seem'd) they thought (as do the swains,   205
Which tune their pipes on sack'd Hibernia's plains)
There should some droning part be, therefore will'd
Some bird to fly into a neighb'ring field,
In embassy unto the King of Bees,
To aid his partners on the flowers and trees   210
Who, condescending, gladly flew along
To bear the bass to his well-tuned song.
The crow was willing they should be beholding
For his deep voice, but being hoarse with scolding,
He thus lends aid ; upon an oak doth climb,   215
And nodding with his head, so keepeth time.
   O true delight, enharbouring the breasts
Of those sweet creatures with the plumy crests.
Had Nature unto man such simpl'ess given,
He would, like birds, be far more near to heaven.   220
But Doridon well knew (who knows no less ?)
" Man's compounds have o'erthrown his simpleness."

* A description of a musical concert of birds.

211.—*Condescending*, agreeing.

Noontide the Morn had woo'd, and she 'gan yield,
When Doridon (made ready for the field)
Goes sadly forth (a woful shepherd's lad)   225
Drowned in tears, his mind with grief yclad,
To ope his fold and let his lambkins out,
(Full jolly flock they seem'd, a well-fleec'd rout)
Which gently walk'd before, he sadly pacing,   [230
Both guides and follows them towards their grazing.
When from a grove the wood-nymphs held full dear,
Two heavenly voices did entreat his ear,
And did compel his longing eyes to see
What happy wight enjoy'd such harmony ;
Which joined with five more, and so made
        seven,   235
Would parallel in mirth the spheres of heaven.
To have a sight at first he would not press,
For fear to interrupt such happiness ;
But kept aloof the thick-grown shrubs among,
Yet so as he might hear this wooing song :   240

F. Fie, shepherd's swain, why sit'st thou all alone,
        Whilst other lads are sporting on the leys ?
R. Joy may have company, but grief hath none :
        Where pleasure never came, sports cannot please.
F. Yet may you please to grace our this day's
        sport,   245
        Though not an actor, yet a looker-on.

228.—*Rout,* company.   242.—*Leys,* leas or pastures.

R. A looker-on, indeed ! so swains of sort,
Cast low, take joy to look whence they are thrown?
    R. Seek joy and find it.
    F. Grief doth not mind it.   250

Both.

Then both agree in one,
    Sorrow doth hate
    To have a mate ;
" True grief is still alone."

F. Sad swain, arede (if that a maid may ask)   255
What cause so great effects of grief hath
    wrought ?
R. Alas ! Love is not hid, it wears no mask ;
To view 'tis by the face conceiv'd and brought.
F. The cause I grant : the causer is not learn'd :
Your speech I do entreat about this task.   260
R. If that my heart were seen, 'twould be discern'd ;
And Fida's name found graven on the cask.
    F. Hath Love young Remond moved?
    R. 'Tis Fida that is loved.

Both.

Although 'tis said that no men   265
    Will with their hearts,

255.—*Arede*, explain.   262.—*Cask*, casket.

Or goods' chief parts
Trust either seas or women.

F. How may a maiden be assur'd of love,
    Since falsehood late in every swain excelleth ? 270
R. When protestations·fail, time may approve
    Where true affection lives, where falsehood
        dwelleth.
F. The truest cause elects a judge as true :
    Fie, how my sighing my much loving telleth.
R. Your love is fix'd in one whose heart to you 275
    Shall be as constancy, which ne'er rebelleth.
      F. None other shall have grace.
      R. None else in my heart place.

Both.

Go, shepherds' swains and wive all,
    For love and kings   280
    Are two like things
Admitting no co-rival.

As when some malefactor judg'd to die
For his offence, his execution nigh,
Casteth his sight on states unlike to his,   285
And weighs his ill by others' happiness :
So Doridon thought every state to be
Further from him, more near felicity.
    O blessed sight, where such concordance meets,

Where truth with truth, and love with liking
    greets.   290
Had (quoth the swain) the Fates giv'n me some
    measure
Of true delight's inestimable treasure,
I had been fortunate : but now so weak
My bankrupt heart will be enforc'd to break.
Sweet love, that draws on earth a yoke so even ; 295
Sweet life, that imitates the bliss of heaven ;
Sweet death they needs must have, who so unite
That two distinct make one hermaphrodite :
Sweet love, sweet life, sweet death, that so do meet
On earth ; in death, in heaven be ever sweet !   300
Let all good wishes ever wait upon you,
And happiness as handmaid tending on you.
Your loves within one centre meeting have !
One hour your deaths, your corps possess one
    grave !   [305
Your names still green, (thus doth a swain implore)
Till time and memory shall be no more !
    Herewith the couple hand-in-hand arose,
And took the way which to the sheep-walk goes.
And whilst that Doridon their gait look'd on,
His dog disclos'd him, rushing forth upon   310
A well-fed deer, that trips it o'er the mead
As nimbly as the wench did whilom tread

312.—*The wench*, Camilla, one of the swift-footed huntresses
of Diana (Virgil, *Æneid*, vii. 803, etc.).

On Ceres' dangling ears, or shaft let go
By some fair nymph that bears Diana's bow.
When turning head, he not a foot would stir,   315
Scorning the barking of a shepherd's cur :
So should all swains as little weigh their spite,
Who at their songs do bawl, but dare not bite.
   Remond, that by the dog the master knew,
Came back, and angry bade him to pursue.   320
Dory (quoth he), if your ill-tutor'd dog
Have nought of awe, then let him have a clog.
Do you not know this seely timorous deer,
(As usual to his kind) hunted whilere
The sun not ten degrees got in the signs,   325
Since to our maids, here gathering columbines,
She weeping came, and with her head low laid
In Fida's lap, did humbly beg for aid.
Whereat unto the hounds they gave a check,
And saving her, might spy about her neck   330
A collar hanging, and (as yet is seen)
These words in gold wrought on a ground of green :
" Maidens, since 'tis decreed a maid shall have me,
Keep me till he shall kill me that must save me."
But whence she came, or who the words concern, 335
We neither know nor can of any learn.
Upon a pallat she doth lie at night,
Near Fida's bed, nor will she from her sight :
Upon her walks she all the day attends,

337.—*Pallat*, straw bed.

And by her side she trips where'er she wends.   340
   Remond (replied the swain) if I have wrong'd
Fida in ought which unto her belong'd,
I sorrow for't, and truly do protest,
As yet I never heard speech of this beast :
Nor was it with my will ; or if it were,   345
Is it not lawful we should chase the deer,
That breaking our enclosures every morn
Are found at feed upon our crop of corn ?
Yet had I known this deer, I had not wrong'd
Fida in ought which unto her belong'd.   350
   I think no less, quoth Remond ; but, I pray,
Whither walks Doridon this holy-day ?
Come drive your sheep to their appointed feeding,
And make you one at this our merry meeting.
Full many a shepherd with his lovely lass   355
Sit telling tales upon the clover grass.
There is the merry shepherd of the Hole,
Thenot, Piers, Nilkin, Duddy, Hobbinoll,
Alexis, Silvan, Teddy of the Glen,
Rowly and Perigot here by the Fen,   360
With many more (I cannot reckon all)
That meet to solemnize this festival.
   I grieve not at their mirth, said Doridon :
Yet had there been of feasts not any one
Appointed or commanded, you will say,   365
" Where there's content 'tis ever holy-day."
   Leave further talk (quoth Remond) let's be gone,
I'll help you with your sheep, the time draws on.

Fida will call the hind, and come with us.
    Thus went they on, and Remond did discuss   370
Their cause of meeting, till they won with pacing
The circuit chosen for the maidens' tracing.
It was a roundel seated on a plain,
That stood as sentinel unto the main,
Environ'd round with trees and many an arbour, 375
Wherein melodious birds did nightly harbour,
And on a bough within the quick'ning spring,
Would be a-teaching of their young to sing;
Whose pleasing notes the tired swain have made
To steal a nap at noontide in the shade.   380
Nature herself did there in triumph ride,
And made that place the ground of all her pride.
Whose various flow'rs deceiv'd the rasher eye
In taking them for curious tapestry.
A silver spring forth of a rock did fall,   385
That in a drought did serve to water all.
Upon the edges of a grassy bank
A tuft of trees grew circling in a rank,
As if they seem'd their sports to gaze upon,
Or stood as guard against the wind and sun.   390
So fair, so fresh, so green, so sweet a ground
The piercing eyes of Heaven yet never found.
Here Doridon all ready met doth see,
(Oh, who would not at such a meeting be?)

372.—*Tracing*, dancing.
373.—*Roundel*, a round space of ground.

Where he might doubt, who gave to other grace, 395
Whether the place the maids, or maids the place.
Here 'gan the reed and merry bagpipe play,
Shrill as a thrush upon a morn of May,
(A rural music for an heavenly train)
And every shepherdess danc'd with her swain.   400
   As when some gale of wind doth nimbly take
A fair white lock of wool, and with it make
Some pretty driving; here it sweeps the plain;
There stays, here hops, there mounts, and turns
       again;
Yet all so quick, that none so soon can say   405
That now it stops, or leaps, or turns away:
So was their dancing: none look'd thereupon,
But thought their several motions to be one.
   A crooked measure was their first election,
Because all crooked tends to best perfection.   410
And as I ween this often bowing measure
Was chiefly framed for the women's pleasure.
Though like the rib, they crooked are and bending,
Yet to the best of forms they aim their ending.
Next in an (I) their measure made a rest,   415
Showing when love is plainest it is best.
Then in a (Y) which thus doth love commend,
Making of two at first, one in the end.
And lastly closing in a round do enter,
Placing the lusty shepherds in the centre: 420
About the swains they dancing seem'd to roll,
As other planets round the heav'nly pole,

Who by their sweet aspèct or chiding frown,
Could raise a shepherd up, or cast him down.
Thus were they circled till a swain came near,   425
And sent this song unto each shepherd's ear :
The note and voice so sweet, that for such mirth
The gods would leave the heavens, and dwell on earth.

    Happy are you so enclosed ;
    May the maids be still disposed   430
      In their gestures and their dances,
    So to grace you with entwining,
    That Envy wish in such combining,
      Fortune's smile with happy chances.

    Here it seems as if the Graces   435
    Measur'd out the plain in traces,
      In a shepherdess disguising.
    Are the spheres so nimbly turning ?
    Wand'ring lamps in heaven burning,
      To the eye so much enticing ?   440

Yes, Heaven means to take these thither,
And add one joy to see both dance together.

    Gentle nymphs, be not refusing,
    Love's neglect is time's abusing,
      They and beauty are but lent you,   445
    Take the one and keep the other :
    Love keeps fresh what age doth smother :
      Beauty gone you will repent you.

'Twill be said when yee haue proued,
Neuer Swaines more truely loued:
O then flye all nice behauiour.
Pitty faine would (as her dutie)
Be attending still on beautie
Let her not be out of fauour.

Disdaine is now so much rewarded,
That Pitty weepes since shee is vnregarded.

The measure and the Song here being ended :
Each Swaine his thoughts thus to his Loue commended.

The first presents his *Dogge,* with these:

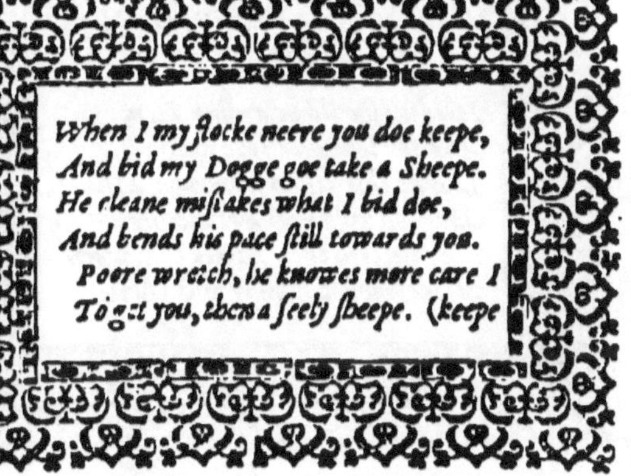

The second, his *Pipe,* with these:

The third, a paire of *Gloues*, thus:

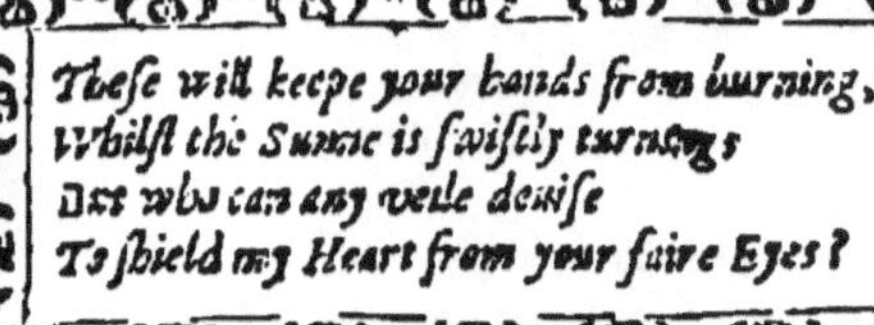

The fourth, an *Anagram.*

MAIDEN
AIDMEN.

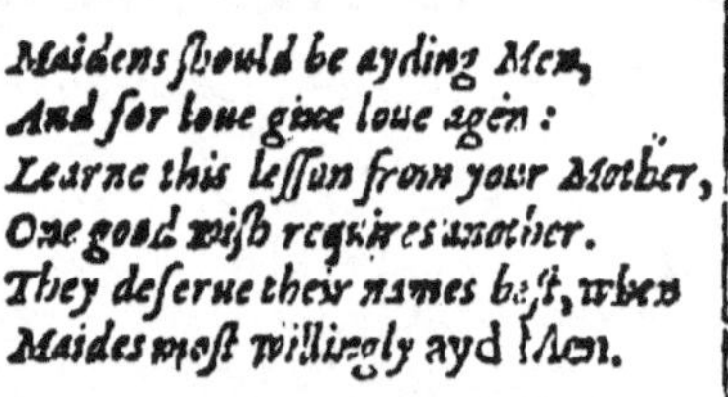

The sift, a *Ring*, with a Picture in a Iewell on it.

The sixt, a *Nosegay* of Roses, with
a Nettle in it.

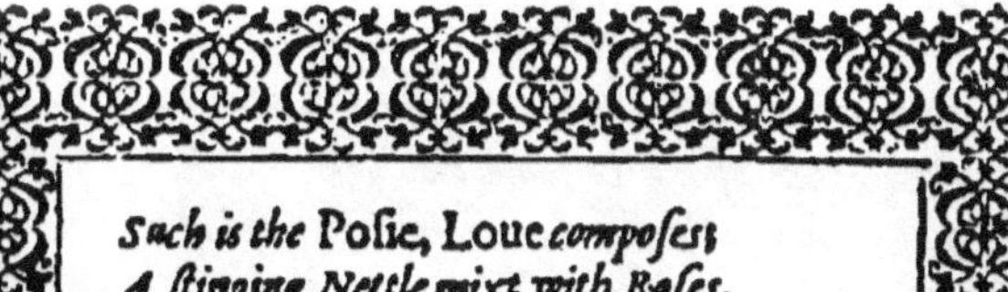

The seauenth, a *Girdle.*

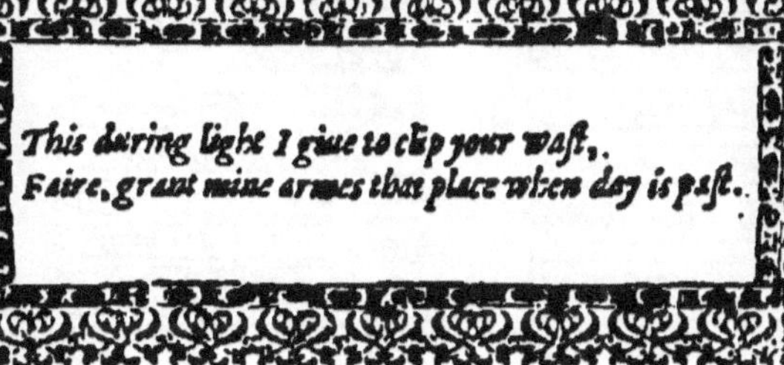

The Eighth

You haue the substance, and I liue
But by the shadowe which you giue,
Substance and shadowe, both are due,
And giuen of me to none but you
Then whence is life but from that part
Which is possessor of the hart.

The Nymph

The Hooke of right belongs to you, for when I take but seeke Sheepe, yo still take Men

The Tenth

O, mickle maiden best of any
Of our plaines though thrice as many
Vnto to loue, and leaue denying.
Endles knotts lett lifes be tyeing.
Such a face, so fyne a feature
IR indeed fairest sweetest creature
Neuer yet was found her longing
O then lett my plaints be moouing.
Trust a shepheard if it will I meane't.
Truth is best when shee is plainest.
I loue not with verses contesting:
Faith is faith without protesting.
Time y' all thinges doth inherit
Renders each desert his merrit.
If y' faile in me, as nee man
Doubtles tyme nere wonne a woman

Maidens still should be relentinge.
And once flinty, still repentinge.
Youth with youth is best combyned.
Each one with his like is twynned
Beauty should have beauteous tyringe
Euer y' hope easeth pyninge
Vnto you whome Nature dresses
Needs no combe to smooth yo' tresses.
This way yt may doe his dutie
In yo' locks to shade your beautie
Doe see, and to loue be turninge
Else each hart it will be burninge.

The Eleaventh

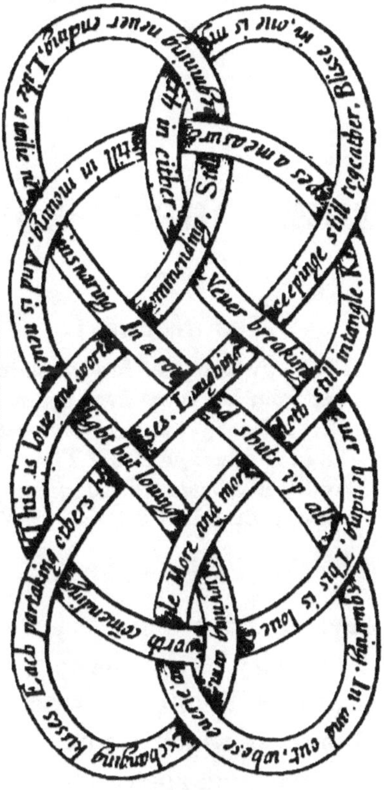

The Twelfth

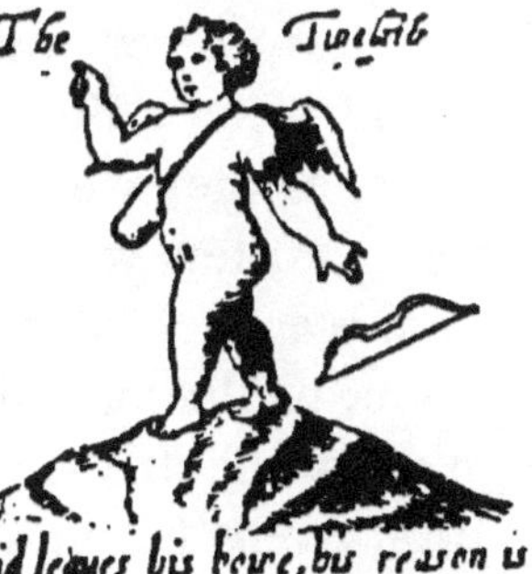

See Cupid leaues his bowe, his reason is
Because your eyes wounde when his shafts doe misse

THE FOURTH SONG.

THE ARGUMENT.

Fida's distress, the hind is slain,
Yet from her ruins lives again.
Riot's description next I rhyme;
Then Aletheia, and old Time:
And lastly, from this song I go,
¯aving describ'd the Vale of Woe.

HAPPY ye days of old, when every waste
Was like a Sanctuary to the chaste;
When incests, rapes, adulteries, were not known;
All pure as blossoms which are newly blown.
Maids were as free from spots, and soils within,   5
As most unblemish'd in the outward skin.
Men every plain and cottage did afford,
As smooth in deeds, as they were fair of word.
Maidens with men as sisters with their brothers,   [10
And men with maids convers'd as with their mothers;
Free from suspicion, or the rage of blood.
Strife only reign'd, for all striv'd to be good.
    But then as little wrens but newly fledge,

First, by their nests hop up and down the hedge ;
Then one from bough to bough gets up a tree :   15
His fellow noting his agility,
Thinks he as well may venture as the other,
So flushing from one spray unto another,
Gets to the top, and then embolden'd flies,
Unto an height past ken of human eyes :   20
So time brought worse, men first desir'd to talk ;
Then canie suspect ; and then a private walk ;
Then by consent appointed times of meeting,
Where most securely each might kiss his sweeting ;
Lastly, with lusts their panting breasts so swell,   25
They came to—— But to what I blush to tell,
And enter'd thus, rapes used were of all,
Incest, adultery, held as venial :
The certainty in doubtful balance rests,
If beasts did learn of men, or men of beasts.   30
Had they not learn'd of man who was their king,
So to insult upon an underling,
They civilly had spent their lives' gradation,
As meek and mild as in their first creation ;
Nor had th' infections of infected minds   35
So alter'd nature, and disorder'd kinds,
Fida had been less wretched, I more glad,
That so true love so true a progress had.
　　When Remond left her (Remond then unkind)
Fida went down the dale to seek the hind ;   40

18.—*Flushing*, flying out suddenly.

And found her taking soil within a flood :
Whom when she call'd straight follow'd to the wood.
Fida, then wearied, sought the cooling shade,
And found an arbour by the shepherds made
To frolic in (when Sol did hottest shine)   45
With cates which were far cleanlier than fine ;
For in those days men never us'd to feed
So much for pleasure as they did for need.
Enriching then the arbour down she sat her ;
Where many a busy bee came flying at her :   50
Thinking when she for air her breasts discloses,
That there had grown some tuft of damask roses,
And that her azure veins which then did swell,
Were conduit-pipes brought from a living well ;
Whose liquor might the world enjoy for money,   55
Bees would be bankrupt ; none would care for honey
The hind lay still without (poor silly creature,
How like a woman art thou fram'd by Nature ?
Timorous, apt to tears, wily in running,
Caught best when force is intermix'd with cunning) 60
Lying thus distant, different chances meet them,
And with a fearful object Fate doth greet them.

Description
of Riot.   Something appear'd, which seem'd, far off, a man
In stature, habit, gait, proportion :
But when their eyes their objects' masters were,   65
And it for stricter censure came more near,
By all his properties one might well guess,
Than of a man, he sure had nothing less.

41.—*Taking soil,* a term in hunting for taking water.

For verily since old Deucalion's flood,
Earth's slime did ne'er produce a viler brood.   70
Upon the various earth's embroidered gown
There is a weed upon whose head grows down ;
Sow-thistle 'tis yclept, whose downy wreath,
If any one can blow off at a breath,
We deem her for a maid : such was his hair,   75
Ready to shed at any stirring air.
His ears were strucken deaf when he came nigh,
To hear the widow's or the orphan's cry ;
His eyes encircled with a bloody chain,
With poring in the blood of bodies slain ;   80
His mouth exceeding wide, from whence did fly
Vollies of execrable blasphemy,
Banning the heavens, and he that rideth on them,
Dar'd vengeance to the teeth to fall upon him :
Like Scythian wolves, or men* of wit bereaven,   85   * Men of
Which howl and shoot against the lights of heaven.   Scirum shoot
                                                     against the
His hands (if hands they were) like some dead stars.
          corse,
With digging up his buried ancestors ;
Making his father's tomb and sacred shrine
The trough wherein the hog-herd fed his swine.   90
And as that beast hath legs (which shepherds fear,
Yclept a badger, which our lambs doth tear)
One long, the other short, that when he runs
Upon the plains, he halts ; but when he wons

94.— *Wons*, dwells.

On craggy rocks, or steepy hills, we see   95
None runs more swift, nor easier than he :
Such legs the monster had, one sinew shrunk,
That in the plains he reel'd, as being drunk ;
And halted in the paths to virtue tending,
And therefore never durst be that way bending :   100
But when he came on carved monuments,
Spiring colosses, and high-raised rents,
He pass'd them o'er, quick, as the Eastern wind
Sweeps through a meadow ; or a nimble hind,
Or satyr on a lawn, or skipping roe,   105
Or well-wing'd shaft forth of a Parthian bow.
His body made (still in consumptions rife)
A miserable prison for a life.

Riot he hight ; whom some curs'd fiend did raise,
When like a chaos were the nights and days :   110
Got and brought up in the Cimmerian clime,
Where sun nor moon, nor days, nor nights do time :
As who should say, they scorn'd to show their faces
To such a fiend should seek to spoil the Graces.

At sight whereof Fida, nigh drown'd in fear,   115
Was clean dismay'd when he approached near ;
Nor durst she call the deer, nor whistling wind her,
Fearing her noise might make the monster find her ;

102.—*Rents*, fissures, crevices.
111.—*Cimmerian clime*, a land described by Homer (*Odyssey*,
xi. 14) as being beyond the ocean-stream, plunged in darkness,
and unblest by the rays of the sun.
117.—*Wind her*, make her turn.

Who slyly came, for he had cunning learn'd him,
And seiz'd upon the hind ere she discern'd him.   120
Oh, how she striv'd and struggl'd ; every nerve
Is press'd at all assays a life to serve :
Yet soon we lose what we might longer keep
Were not prevention commonly asleep.
Maids, of this monster's brood be fearful all ;   125
What to the hind may hap to you befall.
Who with her feet held up instead of hands,
And tears which pity from the rock commands,
She sighs, and shrieks, and weeps, and looks upon
      him :   [130
Alas ! she sobs, and many a groan throws on him ;
With plaints which might abate a tyrant's knife
She begs for pardon, and entreats for life.
The hollow caves resound her moanings near it,
That heart was flint which did not grieve to hear it ;
The high-topp'd firs which on that mountain keep, 135
Have ever since that time been seen to weep.
The owl till then, 'tis thought, full well could sing,
And tune her voice to every bubbling spring :
But when she heard those plaints, then forth she yode
Out of the covert of an ivy tod,   140
And hollowing for aid, so strain'd her throat,
That since she clean forgot her former note.
A little robin sitting on a tree,
In doleful notes bewail'd her tragedy.

139.— *Yode*, went.

An asp, who thought him stout, could not dissemble,
But show'd his fear, and yet is seen to tremble.   [145
Yet Cruelty was deaf, and had no sight
In ought which might gainsay the appetite :
But with his teeth rending her throat asunder,
Besprinkl'd with her blood the green grass under, 150
And gormandizing on her flesh and blood,
He, vomiting, returned to the wood.
  Riot but newly gone, as strange a vision,
Though far more heavenly, came in apparition.
As that Arabian bird (whom all admire)   155
Her exequies prepar'd and funeral fire,
Burnt in a flame conceived from the sun,
And nourished with slips of cinnamon,
Out of her ashes hath a second birth,
And flies abroad, a wonderment on earth :   160
So from the ruins of this mangled creature
Arose so fair and so divine a feature,
That Envy for her heart would dote upon her;
Heaven could not choose but be enamour'd on her :
Were I a star, and she a second sphere,   165
I'd leave the other, and be fixed there.
Had fair Arachne wrought this maiden's hair,
When she with Pallas did for skill compare,
Minerva's work had never been esteem'd,
But this had been more rare and highly deem'd ; 170
Yet gladly now she would reverse her doom,
Weaving this hair within a spider's loom.
Upon her forehead, as in glory, sat

Descrip-
tion of Truth.

Mercy and Majesty, for wond'ring at,
As pure and simple as Albania's snow,   175
Or milk-white swans which stem the streams of Po :
Like to some goodly foreland, bearing out
Her hair, the tufts which fring'd the shore about.
And lest the man which sought those coasts might slip,
Her eyes like stars did serve to guide the ship.   180
Upon her front (heaven's fairest promontory)
Delineated was th' authentic story
Of those elect, whose sheep at first began
To nibble by the springs of Canaan :
Out of whose sacred loins (brought by the stem   185
Of that sweet singer of Jerusalem)
Came the best Shepherd ever flocks did keep,
Who yielded up his life to save his sheep.
  O thou Eterne ! by whom all beings move,
Giving the springs beneath, and springs above ; 190
Whose finger doth this universe sustain,
Bringing the former and the latter rain ;
Who dost with plenty meads and pastures fill,
By drops distill'd like dew on Hermon hill :
Pardon a silly swain, who (far unable   195
In that which is so rare, so admirable)
Dares on an oaten pipe thus meanly sing
Her praise immense, worthy a silver string.
And thou which through the desert and the deep,
Didst lead thy chosen like a flock of sheep :   200
As sometime by a star thou guided'st them,
Which fed upon the plains of Bethlehem ;

So by thy sacred Spirit direct my quill,
When I shall sing ought of thy holy hill,
That times to come, when they my rhymes rehearse, 205
May wonder at me, and admire my verse :
For who but one rapt in celestial fire,
Can by his Muse to such a pitch aspire,
That from aloft he might behold and tell
Her worth, whereon an iron pen might dwell ?   210
 When she was born, Nature in sport began
To learn the cunning of an artisan,
And did vermilion with a white compose,
To mock·herself and paint a damask rose.
But scorning Nature unto Art should seek,   215
She spilt her colours on this maiden's cheek.
Her mouth the gate from whence all goodness came,
Of power to give the dead a living name.
Her words embalmed in so sweet a breath,   [220
That made them triumph both on Time and Death ;
Whose fragrant sweets, since the chameleon knew,
And tasted of, he to this humour grew,
Left other elements, held this so rare,
That since he never feeds on ought but air.
 O had I Virgil's verse, or Tully's tongue,   225
Or raping numbers like the Thracian's song,
I have a theme would make the rocks to dance,
And surly beasts that through the desert prance,
Hie from their caves, and every gloomy den,

226.—*Raping*, ravishing. *The Thracian*, Orpheus.

To wonder at the excellence of men.   230
Nay, they would think their states for ever rais'd,
But once to look on one so highly prais'd.
 Out of whose maiden breasts (which sweetly rise)
The seers suck'd their hidden prophecies :
And told that for her love in times to come,   235
Many should seek the crown of martyrdom,
By fire, by sword, by tortures, dungeons, chains,
By stripes, by famine, and a world of pains ;
Yet constant still remain (to her they lov'd)
Like Sion Mount, that cannot be remov'd.   240
Proportion on her arms and hands recorded,
The world for her no fitter place afforded.
Praise her who list, he still shall be her debtor :
For Art ne'er feign'd, nor Nature fram'd a better.
 As when a holy father hath began   245
To offer sacrifice to mighty Pan,
Doth the request of every swain assume,
To scale the welkin in a sacred fume
Made by a widow'd turtle's loving mate,
Or lambkin, or some kid immaculate,   250
The off'ring heaves aloft, with both his hands,
Which all adore that near the altar stands :
So was her heavenly body comely rais'd
On two fair columns ; those that Ovid prais'd
In Julia's borrow'd name, compar'd with these,   255
Were crabs to apples of th' Hesperides ;

255.—*Julia's borrow'd name*, Corinna.

Or stump-foot Vulcan in comparison
With all the height of true perfection.
   Nature was here so lavish of her store,
That she bestow'd until she had no more ;   260
Whose treasure being weaken'd (by this dame)
She thrusts into the world so many lame.
   The highest synod of the glorious sky
(I heard a wood-nymph sing) sent Mercury
To take a survey of the fairest faces,   265
And to describe to them all women's graces ;
Who long time wand'ring in a serious quest,
Noting what parts by Beauty were possess'd :
At last he saw this maid, then thinking fit
To end his journey, here, nil-ultra, writ.   270
   Fida in adoration kiss'd her knee,
And thus bespake : Hail glorious Deity !
(If such thou art, and who can deem you less?)
Whether thou reign'st queen of the wilderness,
Or art that goddess ('tis unknown to me)   275
Which from the ocean draws her pettigree :
Or one of those, who by the mossy banks
Of drizzling Helicon, in airy ranks
Tread roundelays upon the silver sands,
Whilst shaggy satyrs, tripping o'er the strands,   280
Stand still at gaze, and yield their senses thralls
To the sweet cadence of your madrigals :
Or of the fairy troop which nimbly play,

276.—*Pettigree*, pedigree.

And by the springs dance out the summer's day,
Teaching the little birds to build their nests,   285
And in their singing how to keepen rests ;
Or one of those who, watching where a spring
Out of our Grandame Earth hath issuing,
With your attractive music woo the stream
(As men by fairies led, fall'n in a dream)   290
To follow you, which sweetly trilling wanders
In many mazes, intricate meanders ;
Till at the last, to mock th' enamour'd rill,
Ye bend your traces up some shady hill ;
And laugh to see the wave no further tread ;   295
But in a chafe run foaming on his head,
Being enforc'd a channel new to frame,
Leaving the other destitute of name.
If thou be one of these, or all, or more,
Succour a seely maid, that doth implore   300
Aid, on a bended heart, unfeign'd and meek,
As true as blushes of a maiden cheek.
    Maiden, arise, replied the new-born maid :
" Pure Innocence the senseless stones will aid."
Nor of the fairy troop, nor Muses nine,   305
Nor am I Venus, nor of Proserpine :
But daughter to a lusty aged swain,
That cuts the green tufts off th' enamell'd plain ;
And with his scythe hath many a summer shorn
The plough'd-lands lab'ring with a crop of corn ; 310
Who from the cloud-clipt mountain by his stroke   Descrip-
Fells down the lofty pine, the cedar, oak :   tion of Time.

He opes the flood-gates as occasion is,
Sometimes on that man's land, sometimes on this.
When Verulam, a stately nymph of yore,   315
Did use to deck herself on Isis' shore,
One morn (among the rest) as there she stood,
Saw the pure channel all besmear'd with blood ;
Inquiring for the cause, one did impart,
Those drops came from her holy Alban's heart ;   320
Herewith in grief, she 'gan entreat my sire,
That Isis' stream, which yearly did attire
Those gallant fields in changeable array,
Might turn her course and run some other way,
Lest that her waves might wash away the guilt   325
From off their hands which Alban's blood had
          spilt :
He condescended, and the nimble wave
Her fish no more within that channel drave :
But as a witness left the crimson gore
To stain the earth, as they their hands before.   330
He had a being ere there was a birth,
And shall not cease until the sea and earth,
And what they both contain, shall cease to be,
Nothing confines him but eternity.
By him the names of good men ever live,   335
Which short-liv'd men unto oblivion give :
And in forgetfulness he lets him fall,
That is no other man than natural :

327.—*Condescended*, agreed.

'Tis he alone that rightly can discover
Who is the true, and who the feigned lover.   340
In summer's heat, when any swain to sleep
Doth more addict himself than to his sheep ;
And whilst the leaden god sits on his eyes,
If any of his fold or strays or dies,
And to the waking swain it be unknown,   345
Whether his sheep be dead, or stray'd, or stol'n ;
To meet my sire he bends his course in pain,
Either where some high hill surveys the plain ;
Or takes his step toward the flow'ry valleys,
Where Zephyr with the cowslip hourly dallies ;   350
Or to the groves, where birds from heat or weather,
Sit sweetly tuning of their notes together ;
Or to a mead a wanton river dresses
With richest collars of her turning esses ;
Or where the shepherds sit old stories telling,   355
Chronos, my sire, hath no set place of dwelling ;
But if the shepherd meet the aged swain,
He tells him of his sheep, or shows them slain.
So great a gift the sacred Powers of heaven
(Above all others) to my sire have given,   360
That the abhorred stratagems of night,
Lurking in caverns from the glorious light,
By him (perforce) are from their dungeons hurl'd,
And show'd as monsters to the wond'ring world.
What mariner is he sailing upon   365
The wat'ry desert-clipping Albion,
Hears not the billows in their dances roar,

Answer'd by echoes from the neighbour shore?
To whose accord the maids trip from the downs,
And rivers dancing come, ycrown'd with towns,   370
All singing forth the victories of Time
Upon the monsters of the Western clime,
Whose horrid, damned, bloody plots would bring
Confusion on the laureate poet's king,
Whose hell-fed hearts devis'd how never more   375
A swan might singing sit on Isis' shore :
But croaking ravens, and the screech-owl's cry,
The fit musicians for a tragedy,
Should evermore be heard about her strand,
To fright all passengers from that sad land.   380
　　Long summer's days I on his worth might spend,
And yet begin again when I would end.
All ages since the first age first begun,
Ere they could know his worth their age was done :
Whose absence all the treasury of earth   385
Cannot buy out.   From far-fam'd Tagus' birth,
Not all the golden gravel he treads over,
One minute past, that minute can recover.
I am his only child (he hath no other),
Clept Aletheia, born without a mother :   390
Poor Aletheia, long despis'd of all,
Scarce Charity would lend an hospital
To give my month's cold watching one night's rest,
But in my room took in the miser's chest.

390.—*Aletheia*, Greek 'Aλήθεια, truth.

In winter's time, when hardly fed the flocks,   395
And icicles hung dangling on the rocks ;
When Hyems bound the floods in silver chains,
And hoary frosts had candied all the plains ;
When every barn rung with the threshing flails,
And shepherds' boys for cold 'gan blow their nails: 400
Wearied with toil in seeking out some one
That had a spark of true devotion,
It was my chance (chance only helpeth need)
To find an house ybuilt for holy deed,
With goodly architect, and cloisters wide,   405
With groves and walks along a river's side ;
The place itself afforded admiration,
And every spray a theme of contemplation.
But (woe is me !) when knocking at the gate,
I 'gan entreat an enterance thereat :   410
The porter ask'd my name : I told ; he swell'd,
And bade me thence : wherewith in grief repell'd,
I sought for shelter to a ruin'd house,
Harb'ring the weasel, and the dust-bred mouse ;
And others none, except the two-kind bat,   415
Which all the day there melancholy sat :
Here sat I down, with wind and rain ybeat ;
Grief fed my mind, and did my body eat.
Yet Idleness I saw (lam'd with the gout)
Had entrance when poor Truth was kept without. 420
There saw I Drunkenness with dropsies swoll'n ;

415.—*Two-kind bat*, *i.e.* half-bird and half-mouse.

And pamper'd Lust, that many a night had stol'n
Over the abbey-wall when gates were lock'd,
To be in Venus' wanton bosom rock'd :
And Gluttony, that surfeiting had been,   425
Knock at the gate and straightway taken in ;
Sadly I sat, and sighing, griev'd to see
Their happiness, my infelicity.
At last came Envy by, who, having spied
Where I was sadly seated, inward hied,   430
And to the convent eagerly she cries,
Why sit you here, when with these ears and eyes
I heard and saw a strumpet dares to say
She is the true fair Aletheia,
Which you have boasted long to live among you, 435
Yet suffer not a peevish girl to wrong you?
With this provok'd, all rose, and in a rout
Ran to the gate, strove who should first get out,
Bade me begone, and then (in terms uncivil)
Did call me counterfeit, witch, hag, whore, devil ; 440
Then like a strumpet drove me from their cells,
With tinkling pans, and with the noise of bells.
And he that lov'd me, or but moan'd my case,
Had heaps of firebrands banded at his face.
    Thus beaten thence (distress'd, forsaken wight) 445
Enforc'd in fields to sleep, or wake all night ;
A silly sheep, seeing me straying by,
Forsook the shrub where once she meant to lie ;

437.—*Rout*, crowd.

As if she in her kind (unhurting elf)
Did bid me take such lodging as herself: 450
Gladly I took the place the sheep had given,
Uncanopied of anything but heaven.
Where, nigh benumb'd with cold, with grief fre-
        quented,
Unto the silent night I thus lamented :
   Fair Cynthia, if, from thy silver throne,   455
Thou ever lent'st an ear to virgin's moan !
Or in thy monthly course one minute stay'd
Thy palfreys' trot, to hear a wretched maid !
Pull in their reins, and lend thine ear to me,
Forlorn, forsaken, cloth'd in misery :   460
But if a woe hath never woo'd thine ear,
To stop those coursers in their full career;
But as stone-hearted men, uncharitable,
Pass careless by the poor, when men less able
Hold not the needy's help in long suspense,   465
But in their hands pour their benevolence.
O ! if thou be so hard to stop thine ears,
When stars in pity drop down from their spheres,
Yet for a while in gloomy veil of night,   .
Enshroud the pale beams of thy borrow'd light ! 470
O ! never once discourage Goodness (lending
One glimpse of light) to see Misfortune spending
Her utmost rage on Truth, despis'd, distress'd,
Unhappy, unrelieved, yet undress'd !
Where is the heart at Virtue's suff'ring grieveth? 475
Where is the eye that, pitying, relieveth ?

Where is the hand that still the hungry feedeth?
Where is the ear that the decrepit steedeth?
That heart, that hand, that ear, or else that eye,
Giveth, relieveth, feeds, steeds Misery?   480
O Earth ! produce me one of all thy store
Enjoys ; and be vain-glorious no more.
　By this had chanticleer, the village clock,
Bidden the goodwife for her maids to knock ;
And the swart ploughman for his breakfast stay'd, 485
That he might till those lands were fallow laid :
The hills and valleys here and there resound
With the re-echoes of the deep-mouth'd hound.
Each shepherd's daughter, with her cleanly peal,
Was come afield to milk the morning's meal,   490
And ere the sun had climb'd the eastern hills,
To gild the mutt'ring bourns and pretty rills,
Before the lab'ring bee had left the hive,
And nimble fishes which in rivers dive,
Began to leap, and catch the drowned fly,   495
I rose from rest, not in felicity.
Seeking the place of Charity's resort,
Unware I happen'd on a prince's court ;
Where, meeting Greatness, I requir'd relief,
(O happy undelay'd) she said in brief,   500
To small effect thine oratory tends,

478.—*Steedeth*, assists.
485.—*Swart*, sunburnt.
489.—*Peal*, pail.

How can I keep thee and so many friends?
If of my household I should make thee one,
Farewell my servant, Adulation :
I know she will not stay when thou art there :   505
But seek some great man's service otherwhere.
Darkness and light, summer and winter's weather
May be at once, ere you two live together.
Thus with a nod she left me cloth'd in woe.

    Thence to the city once I thought to go,   510
But somewhat in my mind this thought had thrown,
It was a place wherein I was not known.
And therefore went unto these homely towns,
Sweetly environ'd with the daisied downs.

    Upon a stream washing a village end   515
A mill is plac'd, that never difference kenn'd
'Twixt days for work, and holy-tides for rest,
But always wrought and ground the neighbours' grist.
Before the door I saw the miller walking,
And other two (his neighbours) with him talking :   520
One of them was a weaver, and the other
The village tailor, and his trusty brother.
To them I came, and thus my suit began :
Content, the riches of a country-man,
Attend your actions, be more happy still   525
Than I am hapless ! and as yonder mill,
Though in his turning it obey the stream,
Yet by the headstrong torrent from his beam
Is unremov'd, and till the wheel be tore,
It daily toils ; then rests, and works no more :   530

Truth en-
treats suc-
cour from a
miller, a
tailor, and a
weaver.

So in life's motion may you never be
(Though sway'd with griefs) o'erborne with misery.
    With that the miller, laughing, brush'd his clothes,
Then swore by Cock and other dunghill oaths,
I greatly was to blame that durst so wade   535
Into the knowledge of the wheelwright's trade.
Ay, neighbour quoth the tailor (then he bent
His pace to me, spruce like a Jack of Lent)
Your judgment is not seam-rent when you spend it,
Nor is it botching, for I cannot mend it.   540
And, maiden, let me tell you in displeasure,
You must not press the cloth you cannot measure :
But let your steps be stitch'd to Wisdom's chalking,
And cast presumptuous shreds out of your walking.
The weaver said, Fie, wench ! yourself you wrong,
Thus to let slip the shuttle of your tongue ;   [545
For mark me well, yea, mark me well, I say,
I see you work your speech's web astray.
    Sad to the soul, o'erlaid with idle words,
O Heaven ! quoth I, where is the place affords 550
A friend to help, or any heart that ru'th
The most dejected hopes of wronged Truth ?
Truth ! quoth the miller, plainly for our parts,
I and the weaver hate thee with our hearts :
The strifes you raise I will not now discuss,   555

    534.—*Cock*, a vulgar corruption of the name of God.
    538.—*Jack of Lent*, a stuffed puppet which was thrown at
during Lent : hence a term of reproach.
    551.—*Ru'th*, rueth, pities.

Between our honest customers and us :
But get you gone, for sure you may despair
Of comfort here, seek it some otherwhere.
Maid (quoth the tailor) we no succour owe you,
For as I guess here's none of us doth know you :   560
Nor my remembrance any thought can seize
That I have ever seen you in my days.
Seen you? nay, therein confident I am ;
Nay, till this time I never heard your name,
Excepting once, and by this token chief,   565
My neighbour at that instant call'd me thief.
By this you see you are unknown among us,
We cannot help you, though your stay may wrong us.
  Thus went I on, and further went in woe :
For as shrill-sounding Fame, that's never slow,   570
Grows in her going, and increaseth more,
Where she is now, than where she was before :
So Grief (that never healthy, ever sick,
That froward scholar to arithmetic,
Who doth division and subtraction fly,   575
And chiefly learns to add and multiply)
In longest journeys hath the strongest strength,
And is at hand, suppress'd, unquail'd at length.
  Between two hills, the highest Phœbus sees
Gallantly crown'd with large sky-kissing trees,   580
Under whose shade the humble valleys lay ;
And wild boars from their dens their gambols play :
There lay a gravell'd walk o'ergrown with green,
Where neither tract of man nor beast was seen.

Descrip-
tion of a
solitary vale.

And as the ploughman, when the land he tills,   585
Throws up the fruitful earth in ridged hills,
Between whose chevron form he leaves a balk ;
So 'twixt those hills had Nature fram'd this walk,
Not over-dark, nor light, in angles bending,
And like the gliding of a snake, descending ;   590
All hush'd and silent as the mid of night ;
No chatt'ring pie, nor crow appear'd in sight ;
But further in I heard the turtle-dove
Singing sad dirges on her lifeless love.
Birds that compassion from the rocks could bring, 595
Had only license in that place to sing :
Whose doleful notes the melancholy cat
Close in a hollow tree sat wond'ring at.
And trees that on the hill-side comely grew,
When any little blast of Æol blew,   600
Did nod their curled heads, as they would be
The judges to approve their melody.
   Just half the way this solitary grove,
A crystal spring from either hill-side strove,   [605
Which of them first should woo the meeker ground,
And makes the pebbles dance unto their sound.
But as when children having leave to play,
And near their master's eye sport out the day,
(Beyond condition) in their childish toys
Oft vex their tutor with too great a noise,   610

587.—*Chevron*, zigzag.
587.—*Balk*, a bank or ridge of land left by the plough.

And make him send some servant out of door,
To cease their clamour, lest they play no more :
So when the pretty rill a place espies,
Where with the pebbles she would wantonize,
And that her upper stream so much doth wrong
        her   615
To drive her thence, and let her play no longer ;
If she with too loud mutt'ring ran away,
As being much incens'd to leave her play,
A western, mild and pretty whispering gale
Came dallying with the leaves along the dale,   620
And seem'd as with the water it did chide,
Because it ran so long unpacified :
Yea, and methought it bade her leave that coil,
Or he would choke her up with leaves and soil :
Whereat the riv'let in my mind did weep,   625
And hurl'd her head into a silent deep.
   Now he that guides the chariot of the sun,
Upon th' ecliptic circle had so run,
That his brass-hoof'd fire-breathing horses wan
The stately height of the meridian :   630
And the day-lab'ring man (who all the morn
Had from the quarry with his pickaxe torn
A large well-squared stone, which he would cut
To serve his stile, or for some water-shut)
Seeing the sun preparing to decline,   635
Took out his bag, and sat him down to dine :

      623.—*Coil*, tumult, bustle.
      635.—*Water-shut*, a floodgate, dam.

When by a sliding, yet not steep descent,
I gain'd a place, ne'er poet did invent
The like for sorrow ; not in all this round
A fitter seat for passion can be found.   640
    As when a dainty fount, and crystal spring,
Got newly from the earth's imprisoning,
And ready prest some channel clear to win,
Is round his rise by rocks immured in,
And from the thirsty earth would be withheld,   645
Till to the cistern top the waves have swell'd,
But that a careful hind the well hath found,
As he walks sadly through his parched ground ;
Whose patience suff'ring not his land to stay
Until the water o'er the cistern play,   650
He gets a pickaxe, and with blows so stout
Digs on the rock, that all the groves about
Resound his stroke, and still the rock doth charge,
Till he hath made a hole both long and large,
Whereby the waters from their prison run   655
To close earth's gaping wounds made by the sun :
So through these high-rais'd hills, embracing round
This shady, sad, and solitary ground,
Some power (respecting one whose heavy moan
Requir'd a place to sit and weep alone)   660
Had cut a path, whereby the grieved wight
Might freely take the comfort of this site.
About the edges of whose roundly form

643.—*Ready prest*, ready and eager.

In order grew such trees as do adorn
The sable hearse, and sad forsaken mate,   665
And trees whose tears their loss commiserate.
Such are the cypress, and the weeping myrrh,
The dropping amber, and the refin'd fir,
The bleeding vine, the wat'ry sycamore,
And willow for the forlorn paramour;   670
In comely distance : underneath whose shade
Most neat in rudeness Nature arbours made :
Some had a light, some so obscure a seat,
Would entertain a suff'rance ne'er so great :
Where grieved wights sat (as I after found,   675
Whose heavy hearts the height of sorrow crown'd)
Wailing in saddest tunes the dooms of Fate
On men by virtue cleeped fortunate.

    The first note that I heard I soon was won
To think the sighs of fair Endymion ;   680
The subject of whose mournful heavy lay
Was his declining with fair Cynthia.

    Next him a great man sat, in woe no less ;
Tears were but barren shadows to express
The substance of his grief, and therefore stood   685
Distilling from his heart red streams of blood :
He was a swain whom all the Graces kiss'd,

679.—*The first note*, etc., referring to Sir Walter Raleigh,
who was for some time in disgrace at Court.
    682.—*Cynthia*, Queen Elizabeth.
    683.—*A great man*, Robert Devereux, second Earl of Essex.
See Note.

VOL. I.   K

A brave, heroic, worthy martialist :
Yet on the downs he oftentimes was seen
To draw the merry maidens of the green   690
With his sweet voice : once, as he sat alone,
He sung the outrage of the lazy drone
Upon the lab'ring bee, in strains so rare,
That all the flitting pinionists of air
Attentive sat, and in their kinds did long   695
To learn some note from his well-timed song.
    Exiled Naso (from whose golden pen
The Muses did distil delights for men)
Thus sang of Cephalus (whose name was worn
Within the bosom of the blushing Morn :)   700
He had a dart was never set on wing,
But Death flew with it : he could never fling,
But life fled from the place where stuck the head.
A hunter's frolic life in woods he led
In separation from his yoked mate,   705
Whose beauty, once, he valued at a rate
Beyond Aurora's cheek, when she (in pride)
Promis'd their offspring should be deified ;
Procris she hight ; who (seeking to restore
Herself that happiness she had before)   710
Unto the green wood wends, omits no pain
Might bring her to her lord's embrace again :
But Fate thus cross'd her, coming where he lay
Wearied with hunting all a summer's day,

688.—*Martialist*, a soldier.
694.—*Pinionists*, winged creatures, birds.

He somewhat heard within the thicket rush, 715
And deeming it some beast hid in a bush,
Raised himself, then set on wing a dart,
Which took a sad rest in the restless heart
Of his chaste wife ; who with a bleeding breast
Left love and life and slept in endless rest. 720
With Procris' heavy fate this shepherd's wrong
Might be compar'd, and ask as sad a song.
   In th' autumn of his youth and manhood's spring,
Desert (grown now a most dejected thing)
Won him the favour of a royal maid, 725
Who with Diana's nymphs in forests stray'd,
And liv'd a huntress' life, exempt from fear.
She once encounter'd with a surly bear,
Near to a crystal fountain's flowery brink :
Heat brought them thither both, and both would
       drink, 730
When from her golden quiver she took forth
A dart, above the rest esteem'd for worth,
And sent it to his side : the gaping wound
Gave purple streams to cool the parched ground. [735
Whereat he gnash'd his teeth, storm'd his hurt limb,
Yielded the earth what it denied him :
Yet sunk not there, but (wrapt in horror) hied
Unto his hellish cave, despair'd and died.
   After the bear's just death the quick'ning sun
Had twice six times about the zodiac run, 740

728.—*A surly bear*, Robert Dudley, Earl of Leicester, in
allusion probably to his arms, a bear and ragged staff.

And (as respectless) never cast an eye
Upon the night-enveil'd Cimmerii,
When this brave swain, approved valorous,
In opposition of a tyrannous
And bloody savage being long time gone,   745
Quelling his rage with faithless Gerion,
Returned from the stratagems of wars,
Enriched with his quail'd foes' bootless scars,
To see the clear eyes of his dearest love,
And that her skill in herbs might help remove   750
The freshing of a wound which he had got
In her defence by Envy's poison'd shot,
And coming through a grove wherein his fair
Lay with her breasts display'd to take the air,
His rushing through the boughs made her arise, 755
And dreading some wild beast's rude enterprise,
Directs towards the noise a sharpen'd dart,
That reach'd the life of his undaunted heart,
Which when she knew, twice twenty moons nigh
          spent
In tears for him, and died in languishment.   760
    Within an arbour shadow'd with a vine,
Mixed with rosemary and eglantine,
A shepherdess was set, as fair as young,
Whose praise full many a shepherd whilom sung,
Who on an altar fair had to her name,   765
In consecration, many an anagram :

742.—*Cimmerii. See* Note at p. 108.
746.—*Gerion,* Philip II., King of Spain. *See* Note.

And when with sugar'd strains they strove to raise
Worth to a garland of immortal bays,
She as the learned'st maid was chose by them,
Her flaxen hair crown'd with an anadem,   770
To judge who best deserv'd, for she could fit
The height of praise unto the height of wit.
But, well-a-day ! those happy times were gone :
Millions admit a small subtraction.

  And as the year hath first his jocund spring,   775
Wherein the leaves, to birds' sweet carolling,
Dance with the wind ; then sees the summer's day
Perfect the embryon blossom of each spray ;
Next cometh autumn, when the threshed sheaf
Loseth his grain, and every tree his leaf ;   780
Lastly, cold winter's rage, with many a storm,
Threats the proud pines which Ida's top adorn,
And makes the sap leave succourless the shoot,
Shrinking to comfort his decaying root :
Or as a quaint musician being won   785
To run a point of sweet division,
Gets by degrees unto the highest key ;
Then, with like order, falleth in his play
Into a deeper tone ; and lastly, throws
His period in a diapason close :   790
So every human thing terrestrial,

  770.—*Anadem*, garland.
  785.—*Quaint*, skilled.
  786.—*Division*, rapid passage.
  790.—*Diapason close*, a close with the interval of an octave.

His utmost height attain'd, bends to his fall.
And as a comely youth, in fairest age,
Enamour'd on a maid, whose parentage
Had Fate adorn'd, as Nature deck'd her eye,   795
Might at a beck command a monarchy,
But poor and fair could never yet bewitch
A miser's mind, preferring foul and rich,
And therefore, as a king's heart left behind,
When as his corps are borne to be enshrin'd,   800
(His parents' will, a law) like that dead corse,
Leaving his heart, is brought unto his horse,
Carried unto a place that can impart
No secret embassy unto his heart,
Climbs some proud hill, whose stately eminence 805
Vassals the fruitful vale's circumference :
From whence, no sooner can his lights descry
The place enriched by his mistress' eye,
But some thick cloud his happy prospect blends,
And he in sorrow rais'd, in tears descends :   810
So this sad nymph (whom all commiserate)
Once pac'd the hill of greatness and of state,
And got the top ; but when she 'gan address
Her sight, from thence to see true happiness,
Fate interpos'd an envious cloud of fears,   815
And she withdrew into this vale of tears,
Where Sorrow so enthrall'd best Virtue's jewel,
Stones check'd Grief's hardness, call'd her too, too
        cruel.
A stream of tears upon her fair cheeks flows,

As morning dew upon the damask rose,   820
Or crystal glass veiling vermilion,
Or drops of milk on the carnation :
She sang and wept (O ye sea-binding cleeves,
Yield tributary drops, for Virtue grieves !)
And to the period of her sad sweet key   825
Intwinn'd her case with chaste Penelope.
But see, the drizzling south my mournful strain
Answers in weeping drops of quick'ning rain ;
And since this day we can no further go,
Restless I rest within this vale of woe,   830
Until the modest Morn on Earth's vast zone
The ever gladsome Day shall re-enthrone.

823.—*Cleeves*, cliffs

THE FIFTH SONG.

***

THE ARGUMENT.

In notes that rocks to pity move,
Idya* sings her buried love :
And from her horn of plenty gives
Comfort to Truth, whom none relieves.
Repentance' house next calls me on,
With Riot's true conversion :
Leaving Amintas' love to Truth
To be the theme the Muse ensu'th.

***

HERE full of April, veil'd with Sorrow's wing,
For lovely lays, I dreary dirges sing.
Whoso hath seen young lads (to sport themselves)
Run in a low ebb to the sandy shelves ;
Where seriously they work in digging wells,
Or building childish sorts of cockle-shells ;
Or liquid water each to other bandy ;
Or with the pebbles play at handy-dandy,

---

* *Idya*, the pastoral name of England.
4.—*Shelves*, rocks.
8.—*Handy-dandy*, a game played by two children.

Till unawares the tide hath clos'd them round,
And they must wade it through or else be drown'd : 10
May (if unto my pipe he listen well)
My Muse' distress with theirs soon parallel.
For where I whilom sung the loves of swains,
And woo'd the crystal currents of the plains,
Teaching the birds to love, whilst every tree   15
Gave his attention to my melody :
Fate now (as envying my too-happy theme)
Hath round begirt my song with Sorrow's stream,
Which till my Muse wade through and get on shore,
My grief-swoll'n soul can sing of love no more.   20
    But turn we now (yet not without remorse)
To heavenly Aletheia's sad discourse,
That did from Fida's eyes salt tears exhale,
When thus she show'd the solitary vale.
    Just in the midst this joy-forsaken ground   25
A hillock stood, with springs embraced round,
(And with a crystal ring did seem to marry
Themselves to this small Isle sad-solitary,)
Upon whose breast, which trembled as it ran,
Rode the fair downy-silver-coated swan :   30
And on the banks each cypress bow'd his head,
To hear the swan sing her own epiced.*
    As when the gallant youth which live upon
The western downs of lovely Albion,
Meeting, some festival to solemnize,   35
Choose out two, skill'd in wrestling exercise,
Who strongly, at the wrist or collar cling,

> * A funeral song before the corpse be interred.

Whilst arm-in-arm the people make a ring :
So did the water round this Isle enlink,
And so the trees grew on the water's brink ;   40
Waters their streams about the Island scatter
And trees perform'd as much unto the water :
Under whose shade the nightingale would bring
Her chirping young, and teach them how to sing.
The woods' most sad musicians thither hie,   45
As it had been the Sylvians' Castalie,
And warbled forth such elegiac strains,
That struck the winds dumb ; and the motley plains
Were fill'd with envy that such shady places
Held all the world's delights in their embraces.   50
  O how (methinks) the imps of Mneme bring
Dews of invention from their sacred spring !
Here could I spend that spring of poesy,
Which not twice ten suns have bestow'd on me ;
And tell the world the Muses' love appears   55
In nonag'd youth as in the length of years.
But ere my Muse erected have the frame,
Wherein t' enshrine an unknown shepherd's name,
She many a grove, and other woods must tread,   [60
More hills, more dales, more founts must be display'd,
More meadows, rocks, and from them all elect
Matter befitting such an architect.
  As children on a play-day leave the schools,

48.—*Motley*, various-coloured.
51.—*Imps*, offspring.   *Mneme*, Greek μνήμη, memory.
56.—*Nonag'd youth*, not of full age.

And gladly run unto the swimming pools ;
Or in the thickets, all with nettles stung,   65
Rush to despoil some sweet thrush of her young ;
Or with their hats (for fish) lade in a brook
Withouten pain ; but when the Morn doth look
Out of the Eastern gates, a snail would faster
Glide to the schools, than they unto their master : 70
So when before I sung the songs of birds,
Whilst every moment sweeten'd lines affords,
I pip'd devoid of pain, but now I come
Unto my task, my Muse is stricken dumb.
My blubb'ring pen her sable tears lets fall   75
In characters right hieroglyphical,
And mixing with my tears are ready turning
My late white paper to a weed of mourning ;
Or ink and paper strive how to impart
My words, the weeds they wore, within my heart : 80
Or else the blots unwilling are my rhymes
And their sad cause should live till after-times ;
Fearing if men their subject should descry,
They forthwith would dissolve in tears and die.

   Upon the Island's craggy rising hill   85
A quadrant ran, wherein by artless skill,
At every corner Nature did erect
A column rude, yet void of all defect :
Whereon a marble lay.   The thick-grown briar,
And prickled hawthorn (woven all entire)   90
Together clung, and barr'd the gladsome light
From any entrance, fitting only night.

No way to it but one, steep and obscure,
The stairs of rugged stone, seldom in ure,
All overgrown with moss, as Nature sat   95
To entertain Grief with a cloth of state.
   Hardly unto the top I had ascended,
But that the trees (siding the steps) befriended
My weary limbs, who bowing down their arms
Gave hold unto my hands to 'scape from harms : 100
Which evermore are ready, still present
Our feet, in climbing places eminent.
Before the door (to hinder Phœbus' view)
A shady box-tree grasped with a yew,
As in the place' behalf they menac'd war   105
Against the radiance of each sparkling star.
And on their barks (which Time had nigh deprav'd)
These lines (it seem'd) had been of old engrav'd :
" This place was fram'd of yore to be possess'd
By one which sometime hath been happiest."   110
   Lovely Idya, the most beauteous
Of all the darlings of Oceanus,
Hesperia's envy and the Western pride,
Whose party-coloured garment Nature dy'd
In more eye-pleasing hues, with richer grain,   115
Than Iris' bow attending April's rain ;
Whose lily white inshaded with the rose
Had that man seen who sung th' Eneidos,
Dido had in oblivion slept, and she

94.—*Ure*, use.

Had given his Muse her best eternity.   120
Had brave Atrides, who did erst employ
His force to mix his dead with those of Troy,
Been proffer'd for a truce her feigned peace
Helen had stay'd, and that had gone to Greece :
The   Phrygian   soil   had   not   been   drunk   with
          blood,   125
Achilles longer breath'd, and Troy yet stood :
The prince of poets had not sung his story,
My friend had lost his ever-living glory.
   But as a snowy Swan, who many a day
On Tamar's swelling breasts hath had her play,   130
For further pleasure doth assay to swim
My native Tavy, or the sandy Plim ;
And on the panting billows bravely rides,
Whilst country-lasses, walking on the sides,
Admire her beauty, and with clapping hands,   135
Would force her leave the stream, and tread the sands,
When she, regardless, swims to th' other edge,
Until an envious briar, or tangling sedge,
Despoils her plumes ; or else a sharpen'd beam
Pierceth her breast, and on the bloody stream   140
She pants for life : so whilom rode this maid
On streams of worldly bliss, more rich array'd
With Earth's delight than thought could put in ure
To glut the senses of an epicure.

   128.—*My friend*, George Chapman, translator of Homer's
poems.
   130.—The old editions read " his play."

Whilst neighb'ring kings upon their frontiers stood,
And offer'd for her dower huge seas of blood :   [145
And perjur'd Gerion to win her rent
The Indian rocks for gold, and bootless spent
Almost his patrimony for her sake,
Yet nothing like respected as the Drake   150
That scour'd her channels, and destroy'd the weed
Which spoil'd her fishers' nets and fishes' breed.
At last her truest love she threw upon
A royal youth, whose like, whose paragon,
Heaven never lent the Earth : so great a spirit   155
The world could not contain, nor kingdoms merit :
And therefore Jove did with the saints enthrone him,
And left his lady nought but tears to moan him.
   Within this place (as woful as my verse)
She with her crystal founts bedew'd his hearse ;   160
Inveiled with a sable weed she sat,
Singing this song which stones dissolved at.

WHAT time the world, clad in a mourning-robe,
A stage made for a woful tragedy ;
When showers of tears from the celestial globe   165
Bewail'd the fate of sea-lov'd Britany ;
When sighs as frequent were as various sights,
When Hope lay bed-rid, and all pleasures dying,

150.—*The Drake*, Sir Francis Drake.
154.—*A royal youth*, Henry, Prince of Wales. *See* Note.

When Envy wept,
And Comfort slept,   170

When Cruelty itself sat almost crying,
Nought being heard but what the mind affrights;
  When Autumn had disrob'd the Summer's pride,
  Then England's honour, Europe's wonder, died.

O saddest strain that e'er the Muses sung !   175
A text of woe for Grief to comment on;
Tears, sighs, and sobs, give passage to my tongue,
Or I shall spend you till the last is gone.
Which done, my heart in flames of burning love
(Wanting his moisture) shall to cinders turn;   180

But first, by me
Bequeathed be

To strew the place wherein his sacred urn
Shall be enclos'd : this might in many move
  The like effect : who would not do it when   185
  No grave befits him but the hearts of men ?

That man whose mass of sorrows hath been such,
That by their weight laid on each several part,
His fountains are so dry, he but as much
As one poor drop hath left to ease his heart;   190
Why should he keep it ? since the time doth call,
That he ne'er better can bestow it in ;

If so he fears
That others' tears

In greater number, greatest prizes win ;   195
Know none gives more than he which giveth all.
  Then he which hath but one poor tear in store,
  O let him spend that drop, and weep no more.

Why flows not Helicon beyond her strands?
Is Henry dead, and do the Muses sleep ?   200
Alas ! I see each one amazed stands ;
" Shallow fords mutter, silent are the deep."
Fain would they tell their griefs, but know not
          where ;
All are so full, nought can augment their store :
            Then how should they   205
            Their griefs display
To men so cloy'd, they fain would hear no more,
Though blaming those whose plaints they cannot
          hear ?
  And with this wish their passions I allow,
  May that Muse never speak that's silent now ! 210

Is Henry dead ? alas ! and do I live
To sing a screech-owl's note that he is dead?
If any one a fitter theme can give,
Come, give it now, or never to be read.
But let him see it do of horror taste,   215
Anguish, destruction : could it rend in sunder
            With fearful groans
            The senseless stones,

Yet should we hardly be enforc'd to wonder,
Our former griefs would so exceed their last.   220
   Time cannot make our sorrows ought completer ;
   Nor add one grief to make our mourning greater.

England was ne'er engirt with waves till now ;
Till now it held part with the Continent.
Aye me ! some one in pity show me how   225
I might in doleful numbers so lament,
That any one which lov'd him, hated me,
Might dearly love me for lamenting him.
         Alas ! my plaint
         In such constraint   230
Breaks forth in rage, that though my passions swim,
Yet are they drowned ere they landed be :
   Imperfect lines ! O happy ! were I hurl'd
   And cut from life as England from the world.

O happier had we been ! if we had been   235
Never made happy by enjoying thee !
Where hath the glorious eye of heaven seen
A spectacle of greater misery ?
Time, turn thy course, and bring again the spring ;
Break Nature's laws ; search the records of old, 240
        If aught befell
        Might parallel
Sad Britain's case : weep, rocks, and Heaven behold
What seas of sorrow she is plunged in,

Where storms of woe so mainly have beset her,   245
She hath no place for worse, nor hope for better.

Britain was whilom known (by more than fame)
To be one of the Islands Fortunate.
What frantic man would give her now that name,
Lying so rueful and disconsolate ?   250
Hath not her wat'ry zone in murmuring
Fill'd every shore with echoes of her cry?
   Yes, Thetis raves,
   And bids her waves
Bring all the nymphs within her emperie   255
To be assistant in her sorrowing.
 See where they sadly sit on Isis' shore,
 And rend their hairs as they would joy no more.

Isis, the glory of the Western world,
When our heroë (honour'd Essex) died,   260
Strucken with wonder, back again she hurl'd,
And fill'd her banks with an unwonted tide :
As if she stood in doubt, if it were so,
And for the certainty had turn'd her way.
   Why do not now   265
   Her waves reflow ?
Poor nymph, her sorrows will not let her stay ;
Or flies to tell the world her country's woe ;
 Or cares not to come back, perhaps, as showing
 Our tears should make the flood, not her reflow-
   ing.   270

Sometimes a tyrant held the reins of Rome,
Wishing to all the city but one head,
That all at once might undergo his doom,
And by one blow from life be severed.
Fate   wish'd   the   like   on   England,   and   'twas
       given :   275
  O miserable men, enthrall'd to Fate !)
       Whose heavy hand
       That never scann'd
The misery of kingdoms ruinate,
Minding to leave her of all joys bereaven,   280
  With one sad blow (alas ! can worser fall ?)
  Hath given this little Isle her funeral.

O come, ye blessed imps of Memory,
Erect a new Parnassus on his grave !
There tune your voices to an elegy,   285
The saddest note that e'er Apollo gave.
Let every accent make the stander-by
Keep time unto your song with dropping tears,
       Till drops that fell
       Have made a well   290
To swallow him which still unmoved hears !
And though myself prove senseless of your cry,
  Yet gladly should my light of life grow dim,
  To be entomb'd in tears are wept for him.

283.—*Imps*, children.

When last he sicken'd, then we first began   295
To tread the labyrinth of woe about :
And by degrees we further inward ran,
Having his thread of life to guide us out.
But Destiny no sooner saw us enter
Sad Sorrow's maze, immured up in night,   300
            (Where nothing dwells
            But cries and yells
Thrown from the hearts of men depriv'd of light,)
When we were almost come into the centre,
    Fate (cruelly) to bar our joys returning,   305
    Cut off our thread, and left us all in mourning.

    If you have seen at foot of some brave hill
Two springs arise, and delicately trill
In gentle chidings through an humble dale,
Where tufty daisies nod at every gale,   310
And on the banks a swain, with laurel crown'd,
Marrying his sweet notes with their silver sound ;
When as the spongy clouds swoll'n big with water,
Throw their conception on the world's theatre,
Down from the hills the rained waters roar,   315
Whilst every leaf drops to augment their store ;
Grumbling the stones fall o'er each other's back,
Rending the green turfs with their cataract,*
And through the meadows run with such a noise,
That taking from the swain the fountain's voice, 320
Enforce him leave their margent, and alone

* A fall of
waters from
a very high
place.

Couple his base pipe with their baser tone :
Know (Shepherdess) that so I lent an ear
To those sad wights whose plaints I told whilere ;
But when this goodly lady 'gan address   325
Her heavenly voice to sweeten heaviness,
It drown'd the rest, as torrents little springs ;
And strucken mute at her great sorrowings,
Lay still and wonder'd at her piteous moan,
Wept at her griefs, and did forget their own,   330
Whilst I attentive sat, and did impart
Tears when they wanted drops, and from a heart,
As high in sorrow as e'er creature wore,
Lent thrilling groans to such as had no more.
    Had wise Ulysses (who regardless flung   335
Along the ocean when the sirens sung)
Pass'd by and seen her on the sea-torn cleeves
Wail her lost love (while Neptune's wat'ry thieves
Durst not approach for rocks :) to see her face
He would have hazarded his Grecian race, ·   340
Thrust headlong to the shore, and to her eyes
Offer'd his vessel as a sacrifice.
Or had the sirens on a neighbour shore
Heard in what raping notes she did deplore
Her buried glory, they had left their shelves,   345
And to come near her would have drown'd them-
        selves.

Aletheia to
Fida.

335.—*Flung*, hastened.   337.—*Cleeves*, cliffs.
        344.—*Raping*, ravishing.

Now silence lock'd the organs of that voice
Whereat each merry sylvan wont rejoice,
When with a bended knee to her I came,
And did impart my grief and hated name.   350
But first a pardon begg'd, if that my cause
So much constrain'd me as to break the laws
Of her wish'd sequestration, or ask'd bread
(To save a life) from her whose life was dead;
But lawless famine, self-consuming hunger,   355
Alas! compell'd me : had I stayed longer,
My weaken'd limbs had been my want's forc'd meed,
And I had fed on that I could not feed.
When she (compassionate) to my sad moan
Did lend a sigh, and stole it from her own;   360
And (woful lady wreck'd on hapless shelf)
Yielded me comfort, yet had none herself:
Told how she knew me well since I had been
As chiefest consort of the Fairy Queen.
O happy Queen! for ever, ever praise   365
Dwell on thy tomb; the period of all days
Only seal up thy fame; and as thy birth
Enrich'd thy temples on the fading earth,
So have thy virtues crown'd thy blessed soul,
Where the first Mover with his words control;   370
As with a girdle the huge ocean binds;
Gathers into his fist the nimble winds;
Stops the bright courser in his hot career;

366.—*O happy Queen*, Elizabeth.

Commands the moon twelve courses in a year :
Live thou with him in endless bliss, while we   375
Admire all virtues in admiring thee.
   Thou, thou, the fautress of the learned Well ;
Thou nursing mother of God's Israel ;
Thou, for whose loving truth, the heavens rains
Sweet mel and manna on our flow'ry plains ;   380
Thou, by whose hand the sacred Trine did bring
Us out of bonds, from bloody Bonnering.
Ye suckling babes, for ever bless that name
Releas'd your burning in your mothers' flame !
Thrice-blessed   maiden,   by   whose   hand   was
      given   385
Free liberty to taste the food of Heaven.
Never forget her (Albion's lovely daughters)
Which led you to the springs of living waters !
And if my Muse her glory fail to sing,
May to my mouth my tongue for ever cling !   390
   Herewith (at hand) taking her horn of plenty   Idya
Fill'd with the choice of every orchard's dainty,   cherisheth
As pears, plums, apples, the sweet raspis-berry,   Aletheia.
The quince, the apricock, the blushing cherry,
The mulberry (his black from Thisbe taking),   395
The cluster'd filbert, grapes oft merry-making.
(This fruitful horn th' immortal ladies fill'd
With all the pleasures that rough forests yield,

377.—*Fautress*, patroness.   381.—*Trine*, Trinity.
382.—*Bonnering.* *See* Note.   395.—*Thisbe.* See Note.

And gave Idya, with a further blessing,
That thence, as from a garden, without dressing 400
She these should ever have, and never want
Store, from an orchard without tree or plant.)
With a right willing hand she gave me hence
The stomach's comforter, the pleasing quince ;
And for the chiefest cherisher she lent   405
The royal thistle's milky nourishment.
   Here stay'd I long ; but when to see Aurora
Kiss the perfum'd cheeks of dainty Flora,
Without the vale I trod one lovely morn,
With true intention of a quick return,   410
An unexpected chance strove to defer
My going back, and all the love of her.
But, maiden, see the day is waxen old,
And 'gins to shut in with the marigold.
The neatherd's kine do bellow in the yard ;   415
And dairy maidens, for the milk prepar'd,
Are drawing at the udder ; long ere now
The ploughman hath unyok'd his team from plough.
My transformation to a fearful hind
Shall to unfold a fitter season find.   420
Meanwhile yond palace, whose brave turrets' tops
Over the stately wood survey the copse,
Promis'th (if sought) a wished place of rest,
Till Sol our hemisphere have repossess'd.
   Now must my Muse afford a strain to Riot,   425

419.—*Fearful*, timid.

Who, almost kill'd with his luxurious diet,
Lay eating grass (as dogs) within a wood,
So to disgorge the undigested food.
By whom fair Aletheia pass'd along
With Fida, queen of every shepherd's song,   430
By them unseen (for he securely lay
Under the thick of many a leaved spray)
And through the levell'd meadows gently threw
Their neatest feet, wash'd with refreshing dew,
Where he durst not approach, but on the edge   435
Of th' hilly wood, in covert of a hedge,
Went onward with them, trod with them in paces,
And far off much admir'd their forms and graces.
Into the plains at last he headlong venter'd ;
But they the hill had got and palace enter'd.   440
    When, like a valiant, well-resolved man,
Seeking new paths i' th' pathless ocean,
Unto the shores of monster-breeding Nile,
Or through the North to the unpeopled Thyle,
Where, from the equinoctial of the spring   445
To that of autumn, Titan's golden ring
Is never off ; and till the spring again
In gloomy darkness all the shores remain :
Or if he furrow up the briny sea
To cast his anchors in the frozen bay   450

444.—*Thyle*, or rather Thule, the name given by Greek and
Roman geographers to a land situated to the North of Britain,
which they held to be the most northerly portion of Europe—
indeed of the known world.

Of woody Norway, who hath ever fed
Her people more with scaly fish than bread,
Though rattling mounts of ice thrust at his helm,
And by their fall still threaten to o'erwhelm
His little vessel, and though Winter throw   455
(What age should on their heads) white caps of snow ;
Strives to congeal his blood ; he cares not for't,
But arm'd in mind, gets his intended port :
   So Riot, though full many doubts arise
Whose unknown ends might grasp his enterprise, 460
Climbs towards the palace, and with gait demure,
With hanging head, a voice as feigning pure,
With torn and ragged coat, his hairy legs
Bloody, as scratch'd with briars, he entrance begs.
   Remembrance sat as portress of this gate :   465
A lady always musing as she sat,
Except when sometime suddenly she rose,
And with a back-bent eye, at length, she throws
Her hands to heaven ; and in a wond'ring guise,
Star'd on each object with her fixed eyes :   470
As some wayfaring man passing a wood,
Whose waving top hath long a sea-mark stood,
Goes jogging on, and in his mind nought hath,
But how the primrose finely strew the path,
Or sweetest violets lay down their heads   475
At some tree's root on mossy feather-beds,
Until his heel receives an adder's sting,
Whereat he starts, and back his head doth fling.
   She never mark'd the suit he did prefer,

But (careless) let him pass along by her.   480
  So on he went into a spacious court,
All trodden bare with multitudes' resort ;
At th' end whereof a second gate appears,
The fabric show'd full many thousand years,
Whose postern-key that time a lady kept,   485
Her eyes all swoll'n as if she seldom slept,
And would by fits her golden tresses tear,
And strive to stop her breath with her own hair.
Her lily hand (not to be lik'd by Art)
A pair of pincers held ; wherewith her heart   490
Was hardly grasped, while the piled stones
Re-echoed her lamentable groans.
  Here at this gate the custom long had been
When any sought to be admitted in,
Remorse thus us'd them, ere they had the key,   495
And all these torments felt, pass'd on their way.
  When Riot came, the lady's pains nigh done,
She pass'd the gate ; and then Remorse begun
To fetter Riot in strong iron chains,
And doubting much his patience in the pains :   500
As when a smith and 's man, lame Vulcan's fellows,
Call'd from the anvil or the puffing bellows,
To clap a well-wrought shoe, for more than pay,
Upon a stubborn nag of Galloway,
Or unback'd jennet, or a Flanders mare,   505
That at the forge stand snuffing of the air ;

505.—*Jennet*, a small Spanish horse.

The swarty smith spits in his buckhorn fist,
And bids his man bring out the five-fold twist,
His shackles, shacklocks, hampers, gyves and chains,
His linked bolts ; and with no little pains   510
These make him fast ; and lest all these should falter,
Unto a post with some six-doubled halter
He binds his head ; yet all are of the least
To curb the fury of the headstrong beast ;
When, if a carrier's jade he brought unto him,   515
His man can hold his foot whilst he can shoe him :
Remorse was so enforc'd to bind him stronger,
Because his faults requir'd infliction longer
Than any sin-press'd wight which many a day
Since Judas hung himself had pass'd that way.   520
    When all the cruel torments he had borne,
Galled with chains, and on the rack nigh torn,
Pinching with glowing pincers his own heart,
All lame and restless, full of wounds and smart,
He to the postern creeps, so inward hies,   525
And from the gate a two-fold path descries,
One leading up a hill, Repentance' way,
And (as more worthy) on the right hand lay :
The other headlong, steep, and liken'd well
Unto the path which tendeth down to hell :   530
All steps that thither went show'd no returning,
The port to pains, and to eternal mourning ;

507.—*Swarty*, grimy.
509.—*Shacklocks* locks for fetters.

Where certain Death liv'd, in an ebon chair,
The soul's black homicide, meagre Despair,
Had his abode : there 'gainst the craggy rocks   535
Some dash'd their brains out with relentless knocks ;
Others on trees (O most accursed elves !)
Are fastening knots, so to undo themselves.
Here one in sin, not daring to appear
At Mercy's seat with one repentant tear,   540
Within his breast was lancing of an eye,
That unto God it might for vengeance cry ;
There from a rock a wretch but newly fell,
All torn in pieces, to go whole to hell.
Here with a sleepy potion one thinks fit   545
To grasp with Death, but would not know of it ;
There in a pool two men their lives expire,
And die in water to revive in fire.
Here hangs the blood upon the guiltless stones ;
There worms consume the flesh of human bones. 550
Here lies an arm ; a leg there ; here a head ;
Without other limbs of men unburied,
Scatt'ring the ground, and as regardless hurl'd,
As they at virtue spurned in the world.
   Fie, hapless wretch ! O thou, whose graces sterv-
         ing,   555
Measur'st God's mercy by thine own deserving ;
Which cri'st (distrustful of the power of Heaven)
" My sins are greater than can be forgiven ; "
Which still are ready to " curse God and die "
At every stripe of worldly misery :   560

O learn thou, in whose breasts the dragon lurks,
God's mercy ever is o'er all his works.
Know he is pitiful, apt to forgive ;
Would not a sinner's death, but that he live.
O ever, ever rest upon that word .   565
Which doth assure thee, though his two-edg'd sword
Be drawn in justice 'gainst thy sinful soul,
To separate the rotten from the whole ;
Yet if a sacrifice of prayer be sent him,
He will not strike ; or, if he strike, repent him. 570
Let none despair : for cursed Judas' sin
Was not so much in yielding up the King
Of life to death, as when he thereupon
Wholly despair'd of God's remission.
   Riot, long doubting stood which way were
      best   575
To lead his steps : at last, preferring rest
(As foolishly he thought) before the pain
Was to be past ere he could well attain
The high-built palace, 'gan adventure on
That path which led to all confusion,   580
When suddenly a voice as sweet as clear,
With words divine began entice his ear :
Whereat, as in a rapture, on the ground
He prostrate lay, and all his senses found
A time of rest ; only that faculty   585
Which never can be seen, nor ever die,
That in the essence of an endless nature
Doth sympathize with the All-good Creator,

That only wak'd which cannot be interr'd
And from a heavenly choir this ditty heard.   590

Vain man, do not mistrust
    Of heaven winning ;
Nor (though the most unjust)
    Despair for sinning.
God will be seen his sentence changing,   595
If he behold thee wicked ways estranging.

Climb up where pleasures dwell
    In flow'ry alleys ;
And taste the living well
    That decks the valleys.   600
Fair Metanoia is attending
To crown thee with those joys which know no ending.

Herewith on leaden wings sleep from him flew,
When on his arm he rose, and sadly threw
Shrill acclamations ; while an hollow cave,   605
Or hanging hill, or heaven an answer gave.
O sacred essence, light'ning me this hour !
How may I lightly style thy great Power? *Echo.*
    Power.

Power ? but of whence ? under the green-wood spray,
Or liv'st in heav'n ? say.   *Echo.* In heavens aye.   610

601.—*Metanoia*, Greek μετάνοια, repentance.

In heavens aye I tell.   May I it obtain
By alms, by fasting, prayer, by pain? *Echo.* By pain.
Show me the pain, 't shall be undergone :
I to mine end will still go on.   *Echo.* Go on.
But whither? On ! Show me the place, the time. 615
What if the mountain I do climb? *Echo.* Do ; climb.
Is that the way to joys which still endure ?
O bid my soul of it be sure !   *Echo.* Be sure.
Then thus assured, do I climb the hill.   [620
Heaven be my guide in this thy will.   *Echo.* I will.

    As when a maid taught from her mother wing
To tune her voice unto a silver string,
When she should run, she rests, rests when should
        run,
And ends her lesson having now begun :
Now misseth she her stop, then in her song,   625
And doing of her best she still is wrong,
Begins again, and yet again strikes false,
Then in a chafe forsakes her virginals,
And yet within an hour she tries anew,
That with her daily pains (Art's chiefest due)   630
She gains that charming skill ; and can no less
Tame the fierce walkers of the wilderness,
Than that Oeagrin harpist, for whose lay

628.—*Virginals*, the more usual name for the keyed musical
instrument, the virginal, with one string, jack and quill to each
note : it was the precursor of the harpsichord.
    633.—*Oeagrin Harpist*, Orpheus, according to some accounts,
the son of Oeagrus and Clio or Polyhymnia.

Tigers with hunger pin'd and left their prey :
So Riot, when he 'gan to climb the hill,   635
Here maketh haste and there long standeth still,
Now getteth up a step, then falls again,
Yet not despairing all his nerves doth strain
To clamber up anew, then slide his feet,
And down he comes : but gives not over yet,   640
For (with the maid) he hopes a time will be
When merit shall be link'd with industry.
   Now as an angler melancholy standing
Upon a green bank yielding room for landing,
A wriggling yellow worm thrust on his hook,   645
Now in the midst he throws, then in a nook :
Here pulls his line, there throws it in again,
Mendeth his cork and bait, but all in vain,
He long stands viewing of the curled stream ;
At last a hungry pike, or well-grown bream   650
Snatch at the worm, and hasting fast away,
He knowing it a fish of stubborn sway,
Pulls up his rod, but soft, as having skill,
Wherewith the hook fast holds the fish's gill ;
Then all his line he freely yieldeth him,   655
Whilst furiously all up and down doth swim
Th' insnared fish, here on the top doth scud,
There underneath the banks, then in the mud,
And with his frantic fits so scares the shoal,
That each one takes his hide, or starting hole :   660
By this the pike, clean wearied, underneath
A willow lies. and pants (if fishes breathe)

Wherewith the angler gently pulls him to him,
And lest his haste might happen to undo him,
Lays down his rod, then takes his line in hand,   665
And by degrees getting the fish to land,
Walks to another pool : at length is winner
Of such a dish as serves him for his dinner :
So when the climber half the way had got,
Musing he stood, and busily 'gan plot   670
How (since the mount did always steeper tend)
He might with steps secure his journey end.
At last (as wand'ring boys to gather nuts)
A hooked pole he from a hazel cuts ;
Now throws it here, then there to take some hold, 675
But bootless and in vain, the rocky mould
Admits no cranny where his hazel hook
Might promise him a step, till in a nook
Somewhat above his reach he hath espied
A little oak, and having often tried   680
To catch a bough with standing on his toe,
Or leaping up, yet not prevailing so,
He rolls a stone towards the little tree,
Then gets upon it, fastens warily
His pole unto a bough, and at his drawing   685
The early-rising crow with clam'rous cawing,
Leaving the green bough, flies about the rock,
Whilst twenty twenty couples to him flock :
And now within his reach the thin leaves wave,
With one hand only then he holds his stave,   690
And with the other grasping first the leaves,

A pretty bough he in his fist receives ;
Then to his girdle making fast the hook,
His other hand another bough hath took ;
His first, a third, and that, another gives,   695
To bring him to the place where his root lives.
Then, as a nimble squirrel from the wood,
Ranging the hedges for his filberd-food,
Sits peartly on a bough his brown nuts cracking,
And from the shell the sweet white kernel taking, 700
Till with their crooks and bags a sort of boys,
To share with him, come with so great a noise,
That he is forc'd to leave a nut nigh broke,
And for his life leap to a neighbour oak,
Thence to a beech, thence to a row of ashes ;   705
Whilst through the quagmires, and red water plashes,
The boys run dabbling thorough thick and thin ;
One tears his hose, another breaks his shin,
This, torn and tatter'd, hath with much ado
Got by the briars ; and that hath lost his shoe ;   710
This drops his band ; that headlong falls for haste ;
Another cries behind for being last ;
With sticks and stones, and many a sounding holloa,
The little fool, with no small sport, they follow,
Whilst he, from tree to tree, from spray to spray, 715
Gets to the wood, and hides him in his dray :

699.—*Peartly*, briskly.
701.—*Sort*, set or company.
706.—*Plashes*, pools.
716.—*Dray*, a squirrel's nest.

Such shift made Riot ere he could get up,
And so from bough to bough he won the top,
Though hindrances, for ever coming there,
Were often thrust upon him by Despair.   720
    Now at his feet the stately mountain lay,
And with a gladsome eye he 'gan survey
What perils he had trod on since the time
His weary feet and arms assayed to climb.
When with a humble voice, withouten fear,   725
Though he look'd wild and overgrown with hair,
A gentle nymph, in russet coarse array,
Comes and directs him onward in his way.

First, brings she him into a goodly hall,
Fair, yet not beautified with mineral: 730
But in a careless art and artless care
Made loose neglect more lovely far than rare.
Upon the floor ypav'd with marble slate,
With sack-cloth cloth'd, many in ashes sat ;
And round about the walls for many years   735
Hung crystal vials of repentant tears ;
And books of vows, and many a heavenly deed
Lay ready open for each one to read.
Some were immured up in little sheds,
There to contemplate heaven, and bid their beads ;
Others with garments thin of camel's hair,   [740
With head, and arms, and legs, and feet all bare,
Were singing hymns to the Eternal Sage,
For safe returning from their pilgrimage ;
Some with a whip their pamper'd bodies beat ;   745

Others in fasting live, and seldom eat :
But as those trees which do in India grow
And call'd of elder swains full long ago
The sun and moon's fair trees, full goodly dight,
And ten times ten feet challenging their height,   750
Having no help to overlook brave towers,
From cool refreshing dew, or drizzling showers,
When as the earth, as oftentimes is seen,
Is interpos'd 'twixt Sol and Night's pale queen ;
Or when the moon eclipseth Titan's light,   755
The trees all comfortless robb'd of their sight
Weep liquid drops, which plentifully shoot
Along the outward bark down to the root,
And by their own shed tears they ever flourish,
So their own sorrows, their own joys do nourish : 760
And so within this place full many a wight
Did make his tears his food both day and night,
And had it g[r]anted from th' Almighty great
To swim through them unto his mercy-seat.
Fair Metanoia in a chair of earth,   765
With count'nance sad, yet sadness promis'd mirth,
Sat veil'd in coarsest weeds of camel's hair,
Enriching poverty ; yet never fair
Was like to her, nor since the world begun
A lovelier lady kiss'd the glorious sun.   770
For her the god of thunder, mighty, great,
Whose footstool is the earth, and heaven his seat,
Unto a man who from his crying birth
Went on still shunning what he carried, earth,

When he could walk no further for his grave,   775
Nor could step over, but he there must have
A seat to rest, when he would fain go on,
But age in every nerve, in every bone
Forbad his passage : for her sake hath Heaven
Fill'd up the grave, and made his path so even   780
That fifteen courses had the bright steeds run,
(And he was weary) ere his course was done.
For scorning her the courts of kings which throw
A proud rais'd pinnacle to rest the crow,
And on a plain outbrave a neighbour rock   785
In stout resistance of a tempest's shock,
For her contempt Heaven, raining his disasters,
Have made those towers but piles to burn their
          masters.
    To her the lowly nymph (Humblessa hight)
Brought as her office this deformed wight ;   790
To whom the lady courteous semblance shows,
And pitying his estate in sacred thewes,
And letters worthily ycleep'd divine,
Resolv'd t' instruct him : but her discipline
She knew of true effect would surely miss,   795
Except she first his metamorphosis
Should clean exile : and knowing that his birth
Was to inherit reason, though on earth
Some witch had thus transform'd him, by her skill,
Expert in changing, even the very will,   800

792.—*Thewes*, manners.

In few days' labours with continual prayer,
(A sacrifice transcends the buxom air)
His grisly shape, his foul deformed feature,
His horrid looks, worse than a savage creature,
By Metanoia's hand from heaven, began   805
Receive their sentence of divorce from man.
 And as a lovely maiden, pure and chaste,
With naked iv'ry neck, and gown unlac'd,
Within her chamber, when the day is fled,
Makes poor her garments to enrich her bed :   810
First, puts she off her lily-silken gown,
That shrieks for sorrow as she lays it down;
And with her arms graceth a waistcoat fine,
Embracing her as it would ne'er untwine.
Her flaxen hair, ensnaring all beholders,   815
She next permits to wave about her shoulders,
And though she cast it back, the silken slips
Still forward steal and hang upon her lips :
Whereat she sweetly angry, with her laces
Binds up the wanton locks in curious traces,   820
Whilst (twisting with her joints) each hair long
          lingers,
As loth to be enchain'd but with her fingers.
Then on her head a dressing like a crown ;
Her breasts all bare, her kirtle slipping down,
And all things off (which rightly ever be   825
Call'd the foul-fair marks of our misery)

 802.—*Buxom*, yielding, in which sense it is constantly used
by Spenser.

Except her last, which enviously doth seize her,
Lest any eye partake with it in pleasure,
Prepares for sweetest rest, while sylvans greet her,
And longingly the down bed swells to meet her : 830
So by degrees his shape all brutish vild,
Fell from him (as loose skin from some young child)
In lieu whereof a man-like shape appears,
And gallant youth scarce skill'd in twenty years,
So fair, so fresh, so young, so admirable   835
In every part, that since I am not able
In words to show his picture, gentle swains,
Recall the praises in my former strains ;
And know if they have graced any limb,
I only lent it those, but stole 't from him.   840
    Had that chaste Roman dame beheld his face,
Ere the proud king possess'd her husband's place,
Her thoughts had been adulterate, and this stain
Had won her greater fame had she been slain.
The lark that many morns herself makes merry 845
With the shrill chanting of her teery-lerry,
(Before he was transform'd) would leave the skies,
And hover o'er him to behold his eyes.
Upon an oaten pipe well could he play,
For when he fed his flock upon the lay   850
Maidens to hear him from the plains came tripping,

831.—*Vild*, vile.
846.—*Teery-lerry*, more usually tirra-lirra, borrowed from
the French tire-lire.
850.—*Lay*, ley, lea.

And birds from bough to bough full nimbly skipping ;
His flock (then happy flock) would leave to feed,
And stand amaz'd to listen to his reed ;
Lions and tigers, with each beast of game,   855
With hearing him were many times made tame ;
Brave trees and flowers would towards him be bend-
     ing,
And none that heard him wish'd his song an ending :
Maids, lions, birds, flocks, trees, each flower, each
     spring
Were wrapt with wonder when he used to sing. 860
So fair a person to describe to men
Requires a curious pencil, not a pen.
   Him Metanoia clad in seemly wise
(Not after our corrupted age's guise,
Where gaudy weeds lend splendour to the limb, 865
While that his clothes receiv'd their grace from him),
Then to a garden set with rarest flowers,
With pleasant fountains stor'd and shady bowers,
She leads him by the hand, and in the groves,
Where thousand pretty birds sung to their loves, 870
And thousand thousand blossoms (from their stalks)
Mild Zephyrus threw down to paint the walks :
Where yet the wild boar never durst appear :
Here Fida (ever to kind Raymond dear)
Met them, and show'd where Aletheia lay,   875
The fairest maid that ever bless'd the day.
Sweetly she lay, and cool'd her lily hands
Within a spring that threw up golden sands :

As if it would entice her to persever
In living there, and grace the banks for ever.   880
    To her Amintas (Riot now no more)
Came, and saluted : never man before
More bless'd, nor like this kiss hath been another
But when two dangling cherries kiss'd each other :
Nor ever beauties, like, met at such closes,   885
But in the kisses of two damask roses.
O how the flowers (press'd with their treadings on
        them)
Strove to cast up their heads to look upon them !
How jealously the buds that so had seen them
Sent forth the sweetest smells to step between
        them,   890
As fearing the perfume lodg'd in their powers
Once known of them, they might neglect the flowers.
How often wish'd Amintas with his heart,
His ruddy lips from hers might never part ;
And that the heavens this gift were them bequeath-
        ing,   895
To feed on nothing but each other's breathing !
    A truer love the Muses never sung,
Nor happier names e'er grac'd a golden tongue.
O ! they are better fitting his sweet stripe,
Who on the banks of Ancor tun'd his pipe :   900

899.—*Stripe*, strain or measure.
900.—*Ancor*, or Anker, the river intersecting Hartshill in
Warwickshire, the birthplace of Michael Drayton.

Or rather for that learned swain whose lays
Divinest Homer crown'd with deathless bays :
Or any one sent from the sacred Well
Inheriting the soul of Astrophel :
These, these in golden lines might write this story,
And make these loves their own eternal glory : [905
Whilst I, a swain as weak in years as skill,
Should in the valley hear them on the hill.
Yet when my sheep have at their cistern been,
And I have brought them back to shear the green,
To miss an idle hour, and not for meed,   [910
With choicest relish shall mine oaten reed
Record their worths : and though in accents rare
I miss the glory of a charming air,
My Muse may one day make the courtly swains 915
Enamour'd on the music of the plains,
And as upon a hill she bravely sings,
Teach humble dales to weep in crystal springs.

901.—*That learned swain,* George Chapman, the translator
of Homer's poems.

904.—*Astrophel,* a poetical name given by Spenser and his
contemporaries to Sir Philip Sidney.

BRITANNIA'S PASTORALS.

The second Booke.

HORAT.

Carmine Dij superi placantur, carmine Manes.

LONDON:
Printed by THOMAS SNODHAM for GEORGE
NORTON, and are to be sold at the signe of
the Red Bull without Temple-barre.
1616.

TO

The truly Noble and Learned

WILLIAM, EARL OF PEMBROKE,

Lord Chamberlain to His Majesty, &c.

Not that the gift, great Lord, deserves your hand,
Held ever worth the rarest works of men,
Offer I this ; but since in all our land
None can more rightly claim a poet's pen :
That noble blood and virtue truly known,
Which circular in you united run,
Makes you each good, and every good your own,
If it can hold in what my Muse hath done.
But weak and lowly are these tuned lays,
Yet though but weak to win fair Memory,
You may improve them, and your gracing raise ;
For things are priz'd as their possessors be.
   If for such favour they have worthless striven,
   Since love the cause was, be that love forgiven !

Your Honour

W. BROWNE.

INGENIOUS swain! that highly dost adorn
Clear Tavy! on whose brink we both were born!
Just praise in me would ne'er be thought to move
From thy sole worth, but from my partial love.
Wherefore I will not do thee so much wrong,
As by such mixture to allay thy song.
But while kind strangers rightly praise each grace
Of thy chaste Muse, I (from the happy place
That brought thee forth, and thinks it not unfit
To boast now that it erst bred such a wit)
Would only have it known I much rejoice
To hear such matters sung by such a voice.

JOHN GLANVILL.

To his Friend Mr. Browne.

ALL that do read thy works, and see thy face,
Where scarce a hair grows up thy chin to grace,
Do greatly wonder how so youthful years
Could frame a work where so much worth appears.

VOL. I.   N

To hear how thou describ'st a tree, a dale,
A grove, a green, a solitary vale,
The evening showers, and the morning gleams,
The golden mountains, and the silver streams,
How smooth thy verse is, and how sweet thy rhymes,
How sage, and yet how pleasant are thy lines ;
   What more or less can there be said by men,
   But, Muses rule thy hand, and guide thy pen.

THO. WENMAN,

è Societate Inter. Templi.

To his worthily-affected Friend Mr. W. Browne.

AWAKE, sad Muse, and thou my sadder spright,
Made so by Time, but more by Fortune's spite ;
   Awake, and hie us to the green ;
     There shall be seen
   The quaintest lad of all the time
     For neater rhyme :
   Whose free and unaffected strains
     Take all the swains
   That are not rude and ignorant,
     Or Envy want.

And Envy, lest its hate discover'd be,
A courtly love and friendship offers thee :
   The shepherdesses, blithe and fair,
     For thee despair.

And whosoe'er depends on Pan
Holds him a man
Beyond themselves (if not compare),
He is so rare,
So innocent in all his ways
As in his lays.
He masters no low soul who hopes to please
The nephew[a] of the brave Philisides.

Another to the same.

WERE all men's envies fix'd in one man's looks,
That monster that would prey on safest Fame,
Durst not once check at thine, nor at thy name :
So he who men can read as well as books
    Attest thy lines ; thus tried, they show to us
    As Scæva's shield,[b] thyself Emeritus.

W. HERBERT.

*To my Browne, yet brightest swain
That woons,[c] or haunts or hill or plain.*

Poeta nascitur.

PIPE on, sweet swain, till joy, in bliss, sleep waking ;
Hermes, it seems, to thee, of all the swains,

[a] *The nephew*, etc., William, Earl of Pembroke, to whom the book is dedicated.
[b] *Scæva's shield*, transfixed in a hundred and twenty places at the battle of Dyrrhachium.
[c] *Woons*, wons, dwells.

Hath lent his pipe and art : for thou art making
With   sweet   notes   (noted)   heav'n   of   hills   and
          plains !
Nay, if as thou begin'st, thou dost hold on,
The total earth thine Arcadie will be,
And Neptune's monarchy thy Helicon ;
So all in both will make a god of thee,
To whom they will exhibit sacrifice
Of richest love and praise ; and envious swains
(Charm'd with thine accents) shall thy notes agnize[a]
To reach above great Pan's in all thy strains.
Then ply this vein, for it may well contain
The richest morals under poorest shroud ;
And sith in thee the past'ral spirit doth reign,
On such wit's-treasures let it sit abrood,
Till it hath hatch'd such numbers as may buy
The rarest fame that e'er enriched air ;
Or fann'd the way fair to eternity,
To which unsoil'd thy glory shall repair !
Where (with the gods that in fair stars do dwell,
When thou shalt, blazing, in a star abide)
Thou shalt be styl'd the shepherds' star to tell
Them many mysteries and be their guide.
  Thus do I spur thee on with sharpest praise,
To use thy gifts of Nature and of skill,
To double-gild Apollo's brows and bays,
Yet make great Nature Art's true sov'reign still.

* *Agnize*, acknowledge.

So Fame shall ever say, to thy renown,
The shepherd's-star, or bright'st in sky, is Browne !

The true lover of thine

Art and Nature,

JOHN DAVIES of Heref.

*Ad Illustrissimum Juvenem Gulielmum Browne
Generosum, in Operis sui Tomum secun-
dum Carmen gratulatorium.*

SCRIPTA priùs vidi, legi, digitoque notavi
  Carminis istius singula verba meo.
Ex scriptis sparsim quærebam carpere dicta,
  Omnia sed par est, aut ego nulla notem.
Filia si fuerit facies hæc nacta sororis,
  Laudator prolis solus & Author eris :
Hæc nondum visi qui flagrat amore libelli
  Prænarrat scriptis omnia certa tuis.

CAROLUS CROKE.

To my noble Friend the Author.

A PERFECT pen itself will ever praise.
So pipes our shepherd in his roundelays,
That who could judge of Music's sweetest strain,
Would swear thy Muse were in a heavenly vein.

A work of worth shows what the workman is :
When as the fault that may be found amiss,
(To such at least as have judicious eyes)
Nor in the work, nor yet the workman lies.
Well worthy thou to wear the laurel wreath :
When from thy breast these blessed thoughts do
   breathe,
That in thy gracious lines such grace do give,
It makes thee everlastingly to live.
 Thy words well·couch'd, thy sweet invention show
 A perfect poet that could place them so.

UNTON CROKE,

è Societate Inter. Templi.

To the Author.

THAT privilege which others claim,
 To flatter with their friends,
With thee, friend, shall not be mine aim ;
 My verse so much pretends.
The general umpire of best wit
 In this will speak thy fame.
The Muses' minions, as they sit,
 Will still confirm the same :
Let me sing him that merits best ;
 Let others scrape for fashion ;
Their buzzing prate thy worth will jest,
 And slight such commendation.

ANTH. VINCENT.

To his worthy Friend Mr. W. Browne, on his Book.

THAT poets are not bred so, but so born,
Thy Muse it proves; for in her age's morn
She hath struck Envy dumb, and charm'd the love
Of ev'ry Muse whose birth the skies approve.
Go on; I know thou art too good to fear.
And may thy early strains affect the ear
Of that rare Lord, who judge and guerdon can
The richer gifts which do advantage man!

JOHN MORGAN,

è Societate Inter. Templi.

To his Friend the Author.

SOMETIMES, dear friend, I make thy book my meat,
And then I judge 'tis honey that I eat.
Sometimes my drink it is, and then I think
It is Apollo's nectar, and no drink.
And being hurt in mind, I keep in store
Thy book, a precious balsam for the sore.
  'Tis honey, nectar, balsam most divine :
  Or one word for them all; my friend, 'tis thine.

THO. HEYGATE,

è Societate Inter. Templi.

To his Friend the Author.

IF antique swains wan such immortal praise,
Though they alone with their melodious lays
Did only charm the woods and flow'ry lawns,
Satyrs, and floods, and stones, and hairy fawns :
How much, brave youth, to thy due worth belongs,
That charm'st not them but men with thy sweet
       songs?

AUGUSTUS CÆSAR,

è Societate Inter. Templi.

To the Author.

'TIS known I scorn to flatter, or commend,
What merits not applause, though in my friend ;
Which by my censure should now more appear,
Were this not full as good as thou art dear :
But since thou couldst not (erring) make it so,
That I might my impartial humour show
By finding fault ; nor one of these friends tell
How to show love so ill, that I as well
Might paint out mine : I feel an envious touch,
And tell thee, swain, that at thy fame I grutch,[a]
Wishing the art that makes this poem shine,
And this thy work (wert not thou wronged) mine.

    [a] *Grutch*, grumble.

For when detraction shall forgotten be,
This will continue to eternize thee ;
And if hereafter any busy wit
Should, wronging thy conceit, miscensure it,
Though seeming learn'd or wise : here he shall see,
'Tis prais'd by wiser and more learn'd than he.

G. WITHER.

To Mr. Browne.

WERE there a thought so strange as to deny
That happy bays do some men's births adorn,
Thy work alone might serve to justify,
That poets are not made so, but so born.
How could thy plumes thus soon have soar'd thus
      high,
Hadst thou not laurel in thy cradle worn?
  Thy birth o'ertook thy youth : and it doth make
  Thy youth (herein) thine elders overtake.

W. B.

To my truly belov'd Friend M. Browne, on his Pastorals.

SOME men, of books or friends not speaking right,
May hurt them more with praise than foes with
      spite.
But I have seen thy work. and I know thee :
And, if thou list thyse'f, what thou canst be.

For though but early in these paths thou tread,
I find thee write most worthy to be read.
It must be thine own judgment yet that sends
This thy work forth: that judgment mine commends.
And, where the most read books, on authors' fames,
Or, like our money-brokers, take up names
On credit, and are cozen'd ; see that thou,
By off'ring not more sureties than enow,
Hold thine own worth unbroke, which is so good
Upon th' Exchange of Letters, as I would
More of our writers would, like thee, not swell
With the how much they set forth, but th' how well.

BEN. JONSON.

BRITANNIA'S PASTORALS.

THE SECOND BOOK.

THE FIRST SONG.

Marina's freedom now I sing,
And of her new endangering :
Of Famine's Cave, and then th' abuse
Tow'rds buried Colin* and his Muse.

As when a mariner, accounted lost,
Upon the wat'ry Desert long time tost,
In Summer's parching heat, in Winter's cold,
In tempests great, in dangers manifold,
Is by a fav'ring wind drawn up the mast,   5
Whence he descries his native soil at last,
For whose glad sight he gets the hatches under,
And to the ocean tells his joy in thunder,

* *Colin*, Edmund Spenser.

(Shaking those barnacles into the sea,
At once that in the womb and cradle lay)   10
When suddenly the still inconstant wind
Masters before, that did attend behind,
And grows so violent that he is fain
Command the pilot stand to sea again,
Lest want of sea-room in a channel straight,   15
Or casting anchor might cast o'er his freight :
    Thus, gentle Muse, it happens in my song :
A journey, tedious for a strength so young,
I undertook by silver-seeming floods,
Past gloomy bottoms and high-waving woods,   20
Climb'd mountains where the wanton kidling dallies,
Then with soft steps enseal'd the meeken'd valleys,
In quest of memory : and had possest
A pleasant garden for a welcome rest
No sooner, than a hundred themes come on,   25
And hale my bark anew for Helicon.
    Thrice-sacred Powers ! (if sacred Powers there be
Whose mild aspect engyrland Poesy)
Ye happy sisters of the learned Spring,
Whose heavenly notes the woods are ravishing !   30
Brave Thespian maidens, at whose charming lays
Each moss-thrumb'd mountain bends, each current
            plays !
Pierian singers ! O ye blessed Muses !

28.—*Engyrland*, encircle.
32.—*Moss-thrumb'd*, knitted over with moss.

Who as a gem too dear the world refuses !
Whose truest lovers never clip with age,   35
O be propitious in my pilgrimage !
Dwell on my lines ! and till the last sand fall,
  Run hand in hand with my weak Pastoral !
Cause every coupling cadence flow in blisses,
And fill the world with envy of such kisses.   40
Make all the rarest beauties of our clime,
That deign a sweet look on my younger rhyme,
To linger on each line's enticing graces,
As on their lovers' lips and chaste embraces !   [45
    Through rolling trenches of self-drowning waves,
Where stormy gusts throw up untimely graves,
By billows whose white foam show'd angry minds
For not out-roaring all the high-rais'd winds,
Into the ever-drinking thirsty sea
By rocks that under water hidden lay   50
To shipwreck passengers, (so in some den
Thieves bent to robb'ry watch wayfaring men,)
Fairest Marina, whom I whilom sung,
In all this tempest, violent though long,
Without all sense of danger lay asleep :   55
Till tossed where the still inconstant deep,
With widespread arms, stood ready for the tender
Of daily tribute that the swoll'n floods render
Into her chequer ; whence, as worthy kings,
She helps the wants of thousand lesser springs :   60

35.— *Clip*, embrace.

Here wax'd the winds dumb, shut up in their caves ;
As still as midnight were the sullen waves ;
And Neptune's silver ever-shaking breast
As smooth as when the halcyon builds her nest.
None other wrinkles on his face were seen   65
Than on a fertile mead, or sportive green,
Where never ploughshare ripp'd his mother's womb
To give an aged seed a living tomb ;
Nor blinded mole the batt'ning earth e'er stirr'd ;
Nor boys made pitfalls for the hungry bird.   70
The whistling reeds upon the waters' side
Shot up their sharp heads in a stately pride ;
And not a binding osier bow'd his head,
But on his root him bravely carried.
No dandling leaf play'd with the subtile air,   75
So smooth the sea was, and the sky so fair.

   Now with his hands, instead of broad-palm'd oars,
The swain attempts to get the shell-strew'd shores,
And with continual lading making way.
Thrust the small boat into as fair a bay   80
As ever merchant wish'd might be the road
Wherein to ease his sea-torn vessel's load.
It was an island, hugg'd in Neptune's arms,
As tend'ring it against all foreign harms,
And Mona hight : so amiably fair,   85
So rich in soil, so healthful in her air,

64.—*Halcyon*, kingfisher.
69.—*Batt'ning*, thriving, fertile.

So quick in her increase, (each dewy night
Yielding that ground as green, as fresh of plight
As 'twas the day before, whereon then fed
Of gallant steers full many a thousand head)   90
So deck'd with floods, so pleasant in her groves,
So full of well-fleec'd flocks and fatten'd droves ;
That the brave issue of the Trojan line,
Whose worths, like diamonds, yet in darkness shine ;
Whose deeds were sung by learned bards as high, 95
In raptures of immortal poesy,
As any nations, since the Grecian lads
Were famous made by Homer's Iliads :
Those brave heroic spirits, 'twixt one another,
Proverbially call Mona Cambria's mother. *   100   * Mon Mam
Kumbry.
Yet Cambria is a land from whence have come
Worthies well worth the race of Ilium ;
Whose true desert of praise could my Muse touch,
I should be proud that I had done so much.
And though of mighty Brute I cannot boast,   105
Yet doth our warlike strong Devonian coast
Resound his worth, since on her wave-worn strand
He and his Trojans first set foot on land,
Struck sail, and anchor cast on Totnes'* shore,
Though now no ship can ride there any more.   110
    In th' island's road the swain now moors his boat
Unto a willow, lest it outwards float,
And with a rude embracement taking up
The maid, more fair than she* that fill'd the cup
Of the great thunderer, wounding with her eyes 115

* Petunt
Classem
omnibus
bonis onus-
tam. pros-
peris ventis
mare sul-
cantes in
Totenesio
littore felici-
ter applica-
runt. Galf.
Monum.
* Hebe.

More hearts than all the troops of deities,
He wades to shore, and sets her on the sand,
That gently yielded when her foot should land ;
Where bubbling waters through the pebbles fleet,
As if they strove to kiss her slender feet.   120
   Whilst like a wretch, whose cursed hand hath ta'en
The sacred relics from a holy fane,
Feeling the hand of Heaven (enforcing wonder)
In his return, in dreadful cracks of thunder,
Within a bush his sacrilege hath left,   125
And thinks his punishment freed with the theft :
So fled the swain from one ; had Neptune spied
At half an ebb he would have forc'd the tide
To swell anew, whereon his car should sweep,
Deck'd with the riches of th' unsounded deep,   130
And he from thence would with all state on shore,
To woo this beauty, and to woo no more.
   Divine Electra (of the sisters seven
That beautify the glorious orb of heaven)
When Ilium's stately towers serv'd as one light   135
To guide the ravisher in ugly night
Unto her virgin beds, withdrew her face,
And never would look down on human race
Till this maid's birth ; since when some power hath
                won her
By often fits to shine as gazing on her.   140
Grim Saturn's son, the dread Olympic Jove,

122.—*Fane*, temple.
133.—*The sisters seven*, the seven Pleiades.

That dark'd three days to frolic with his love,
Had he in Alcmen's stead clipp'd this fair wight,
The world had slept in everlasting night.
For whose sake only (had she lived then)   145
Deucalion's flood had never rag'd on men;
Nor Phaeton perform'd his father's duty,
For fear to rob the world of such a beauty:
In whose due praise a learned quill might spend
Hours, days, months, years, and never make an end.

   What wretch inhuman, or what wilder blood, [150
Suck'd in a desert from a tiger's brood,
Could leave her so disconsolate? but one
Bred in the wastes of frost-bit Calydon;
For had his veins been heat with milder air,   155
He had not wrong'd so foul a maid so fair.

   Sing on, sweet Muse, and whilst I feed mine eyes
Upon a jewel and unvalued prize,
As bright a star, a dame, as fair, as chaste,
As eye beheld, or shall, till Nature's last,   160
Charm her quick senses, and with raptures sweet
Make her affection with your cadence meet!
And if her graceful tongue admire one strain,
It is the best reward my pipe would gain.
In lieu whereof, in laurel-worthy rhymes   165
Her love shall live until the end of times,
And spite of age the last of days shall see
Her name embalm'd in sacred poesy.

158.—*Unvalued*, priceless.

Sadly alone upon the aged rocks,
Whom Thetis grac'd in washing oft their locks   170
Of branching samphire, sat the maid o'ertaken
With sighs and tears, unfortunate, forsaken,
And with a voice that floods from rocks would borrow,
She thus both wept and sung her notes of sorrow:

  If Heaven be deaf and will not hear my cries,   175
But adds new days to add new miseries ;
Hear then, ye troubled waves and flitting gales,
That cool the bosoms of the fruitful vales !
Lend, one, a flood of tears, the other, wind,
To weep and sigh that Heaven is so unkind !   180
But if ye will not spare of all your store
One tear or sigh unto a wretch so poor ;
Yet as ye travel on this spacious round,
Through forests, mountains, or the lawny ground,
If't hap you see a maid weep forth her woe,   185
As I have done, O bid her as ye go
Not lavish tears ! for when her own are gone,
The world is flinty and will lend her none.
If this be eke deni'd, O hearken then,
Each hollow vaulted rock and crooked den !   190
And if within your sides one Echo be,
Let her begin to rue my destiny !
And in your clefts her plainings do not smother,
But let that Echo teach it to another !   [195
Till round the world in sounding coombe and plain,

183.—*Round*, globe.   195.—*Coombe*, valley.

The last of them tell it the first again :
Of my sad fate so shall they never lin,
But where one ends, another still begin.
Wretch that I am, my words I vainly waste ;
Echo of all woes only speaks the last ;   200
And that's enough : for should she utter all,
As at Medusa's head, each heart would fall
Into a flinty substance, and repine
At no one grief except as great as mine.
No careful nurse would wet her watchful eye,   205
When any pang should gripe her infantry,
Nor though to Nature it obedience gave,
And kneel'd to do her homage in the grave,
Would she lament her suckling from her torn ;
'Scaping by death those torments I have borne.   210
   This sigh'd, she wept, low leaning on her hand,
Her briny tears down raining on the sand,
Which seen by them that sport it in the seas
On dolphins' backs, the fair Nereides,
They came on shore, and slily as they fell   215
Convey'd each tear into an oyster-shell,
And by some power that did affect the girls,
Transform'd those liquid drops to orient pearls,
And strew'd them on the shore : for whose rich prize
In winged pines the Roman colonies   220

197.—*Lin*, cease.
206.—*Infantry*, children.
220.—*Pines*, ships.

Flung through the deep abyss to our white rocks
For gems to deck their ladies' golden locks:
Who valu'd them as highly in their kinds
As those the sunburnt Æthiopian finds.

   Long on the shore distress'd Marina lay: 225
For he that opes the pleasant sweets of May,
Beyond the noonstead so far drove his team,
That harvest folks, with curds and clouted cream,
With cheese and butter, cakes, and cates enow,
That are the yeoman's from the yoke or cow,   230
On sheaves of corn were at their noonshun's close,
Whilst [by] them merrily the bagpipe goes :
Ere from her hand she lifted up her head,
Where all the Graces then inhabited.
When casting round her over-drowned eyes,   235
(So have I seen a gem of mickle price
Roll in a scallop-shell with water fill'd)
She, on a marble rock at hand beheld,
In characters deep cut with iron stroke,   [240
A shepherd's moan, which, read by her, thus spoke :

Glide soft, ye silver floods,
  And every spring:
Within the shady woods
  Let no bird sing !
Nor from the grove a turtle-dove   245
Be seen to couple with her love ;

227.—*Noonstead*, period of noon.
231.—*Noonshun*, luncheon.

But silence on each dale and mountain dwell,
Whilst Willy bids his friend and joy farewell.

But (of great Thetis' train)
Ye mermaids fair,   250
That on the shores do plain
Your sea-green hair,
As ye in trammels knit your locks,
Weep ye ; and so enforce the rocks
In heavy murmurs through the broad shores tell 255
How Willy bade his friend and joy farewell.

Cease, cease, ye murd'ring winds,
To move a wave ;
But if with troubled minds
You seek his grave ;   260
Know 'tis as various as yourselves,
Now in the deep, then on the shelves,
His coffin toss'd by fish and surges fell,
Whilst Willy weeps and bids all joy farewell.

Had he Arion-like   265
Been judg'd to drown,
He on his lute could strike
So rare a sowne,

251.—*Plain*, make smooth.
262.—*Shelves*, rocks.
268.—*Sowne*, sound.

A thousand dolphins would have come
And jointly strive to bring him home.   270
But he on shipboard died, by sickness fell,
Since when his Willy bade all joy farewell.

    Great Neptune, hear a swain !
      His coffin take,
    And with a golden chain   275
      For pity make
It fast unto a rock near land !
Where ev'ry calmy morn I'll stand,
And ere one sheep out of my fold I tell,
Sad Willy's pipe shall bid his friend farewell.   280

Ah heavy shepherd, whosoe'er thou be,
Quoth fair Marina, I do pity thee :
For who by death is in a true friend cross'd,
Till he be earth, he half himself hath lost.
More happy deem I thee, lamented swain,   285
Whose body lies among the scaly train,
Since I shall never think that thou canst die,
Whilst Willy lives, or any poetry :
For well it seems in versing he hath skill,
And though he, aided from the sacred hill,   290
To thee with him no equal life can give,
Yet by his pen thou may'st for ever live.
With this a beam of sudden brightness flies
Upon her face, so dazzling her clear eyes,
That neither flower nor grass which by her grew 295

She could discern cloth'd in their perfect hue.
For as a wag, to sport with such as pass,
Taking the sunbeams in a looking-glass,
Conveys the ray into the eyes of one
Who, blinded, either stumbles at a stone,   300
Or as he dazzled walks the peopled streets,
Is ready justling every man he meets :
So then Apollo did in glory cast
His bright beams on a rock with gold enchas'd,
And thence the swift reflection of their light   305
Blinded those eyes, the chiefest stars of night.
When straight a thick-swoll'n cloud (as if it sought
In beauty's mind to have a thankful thought)
Inveil'd the lustre of great Titan's car,
And she beheld from whence she sat, not far,   310
Cut on a high-brow'd rock, inlaid with gold,
This epitaph, and read it, thus enroll'd :

In depth of waves long hath Alexis slept,
So choicest jewels are the closest kept ;
Whose death the land had seen, but it appears   315
To countervail his loss men wanted tears.
So here he lies, whose dirge each mermaid sings,
For whom the clouds weep rain, the Earth her springs.

Her eyes these lines acquainted with her mind
Had scarcely made, when o'er the hill behind   320
She heard a woman cry : " Ah well-a-day,
What shall I do ? Go home, or fly, or stay ? "

Admir'd Marina rose, and with a pace
As graceful as the goddesses did trace
O'er stately Ida when fond Paris' doom   325
Kindled the fire should mighty Troy entomb,
She went to aid the woman in distress,
(True beauty never was found merciless)
Yet durst she not go nigh lest, being spied,
Some villain's outrage that might then betide, 330
For ought she knew, unto the crying maid,
Might grasp with her : by thickets which array'd
The high sea-bounding hill so near she went,
She saw what wight made such loud dreriment.
Loud? yes : sung right : for since the azure sky 335
Imprison'd first the world, a mortal's cry
With greater clangour nevei pierc'd the air.
  A wight she was so far from being fair ;
None could be foul esteem'd compar'd with her.
  Describing foulness, pardon if I err,   340
Ye shepherds' daughters, and ye gentle swains !
My Muse would gladly chant more lovely strains :
Yet since on miry grounds she trod, for doubt
Of sinking, all in haste, thus wades she out.
As when great Neptune in his height of pride   345
The inland creeks fills with a high spring-tide,
Great shoals of fish among the oysters hie,
Which by a quick ebb on the shores left dry,

325.—*Doom*, judgment.
334.—*Dreriment*, lamentation.

The fishes yawn, the oysters gapen wide :
So broad her mouth was.   As she stood and cried, 350
She tore her elvish knots of hair, as black
And full of dust as any collier's sack.
Her eyes, unlike, were like her body right,
Squint and misshapen, one dun, t'other white.
   As in a picture limn'd unto the life,   355
Or carved by a curious workman's knife,
If twenty men at once should come to see
The great effects of untir'd industry,
Each sev'rally would think the picture's eye
Was fix'd on him and on no stander-by :   360
So as she bawling was upon the bank,
If twice five hundred men stood on a rank,
Her ill face towards them, every one would say,
She looks on me ; when she another way
Had cast her eyes, as on some rock or tree,   365
And on no one of all that company.
Her nose (O crooked nose !) her mouth o'erhung,
As it would be directed by her tongue :
Her forehead such, as one might near avow   [370
Some ploughman there had lately been at plough.
Her face so scorch'd was, and so vild it shows,
As on a pear-tree she had scar'd the crows.
Within a tanner's fat I oft have eyed
(That three moons there had lain) a large ox-hide
In liquor mix'd with strongest bark (for gain)   375

351.—*Elvish knots*, elf-locks, tangled hair.
373.—*Fat*, vat.

Yet had not ta'en one-half so deep a stain
As had her skin, and that as hard well-nigh
As any brawns long harden'd in the sty.
Her shoulders such, as I have often seen
A silly cottage on a village green   380
Might change his corner-posts, in good behoof,
For four such under-proppers to his roof.
Housewives, go hire her, if you yearly gave
A lambkin more than use, you that might save
In washing-beetles, for her hands would pass   385
To serve that purpose, though you daily wash.
For other hidden parts thus much I say ;
As ballad-mongers on a market-day
Taking their stand, one (with as harsh a noise
As ever cart-wheel made) squeaks the sad choice 390
Of Tom the Miller with a golden thumb,
Who, cross'd in love, ran mad and deaf and dumb ;
Half part he chants, and will not sing it out,
But thus he speaks to his attentive rout :
Thus much for love I warbled from my breast,   395
And, gentle friends, for money take the rest :
So speak I to the over-longing ear,
That would the rest of her description hear,
Much have I sung for love, the rest (not common)
Martial will show for coin in 's crabbed woman. 400

378.—*Brawns*, hogs.
380.—*Silly*, simple, humble.
385.—*Washing-beetles*, or batlets, instruments with which
washers beat their coarse clothes.

If e'er you saw a pedant 'gin prepare
To speak some graceful speech to master mayor,
And being bashful, with a quaking doubt
That in his eloquence he may be out,
He oft steps forth, as oft turns back again ;   405
And long 'tis ere he ope his learned vein :
Think so Marina stood : for now she thought
To venture forth, then some conjecture wrought
Her to be jealous left this ugly wight,   [410
Since like a witch she look'd, through spells of night
Might make her body thrall that yet was free
To all the foul intents of witchery :
This drew her back again.   At last she broke
Through all fond doubts, went to her, and bespoke
In gentle manner thus : Good day, good maid ;   415
With that her cry she on a sudden stay'd,
And rubb'd her squint eyes with her mighty fist
But as a miller, having ground his grist,
Lets down his flood-gates with a speedy fall,
And quarring up the passage therewithal,   420
The waters swell in spleen, and never stay
Till by some cleft they find another way :
So when her tears were stopp'd from either eye
Her singults, blubb'rings seem'd to make them fly
Out at her oyster-mouth and nosethrils wide.   425
Can there (quoth fair Marina) e'er betide

414.—*Fond*, foolish.
420.—*Quarring*, closing.   424.—*Singults*, sobs.
425.—*Nosethrils*, nostrils.

In these sweet groves a wench so great a wrong,
That should enforce a cry so loud, so long?
On these delightful plains how can there be
So much as heard the name of villainy?   430
Except when shepherds in their gladsome fit
Sing hymns to Pan that they are free from it.
   But show me, what hath caus'd thy grievous yell?
As late (quoth she) I went to yonder well,
(You cannot see it here ; that grove doth cover   435
With his thick boughs his little channel over)
To fetch some water, as I use, to dress
My master's supper (you may think of flesh ;
But well I wot he tasteth no such dish)
Of rotchets, whitings, or such common fish,   440
That with his net he drags into his boat :
Among the flags below there stands his cote,
A simple one, thatch'd o'er with reed and broom ;
It hath a kitchen and a several room
For each of us.—But this is nought : you flee,   445
Replied Marine, I prithee answer me
To what I question'd. Do but hear me first,
Answer'd the hag. He is a man so curst,
Although I toil at home, and serve his swine,
Yet scarce allows he me whereon to dine :   450
In summer time on blackberries I live,
On crabs and haws, and what wild forests give :
In winter's cold, barefoot, I run to seek

440.—*Rotchets*, piper-fish.   442.—*Cote*, cottage.

For oysters and small winkles in each creek,
Whereon I feed, and on the meagre slone.   455
But if he home return and find me gone,
I still am sure to feel his heavy hand.
Alas and wealaway, since now I stand
In such a plight : for if I seek his door
He'll beat me ten times worse than e'er before.   460
What hast thou done ? (yet ask'd Marina) say?
I with my pitcher lately took my way
(As late I said) to thilk same shaded spring,
Fill'd it, and homewards, rais'd my voice to sing ;
But in my back return, I (hapless) spied   465
A tree of cherries wild, and them I eyed
With such a longing that unwares my foot
Got underneath a hollow-growing root ;
Carrying my pot as maids use on their heads,
I fell with it, and broke it all to shreds.   470
This is my grief, this is my cause of moan.
And if some kind wight go not to atone
My surly master with me, wretched maid,
I shall be beaten dead.   Be not afraid,
Said sweet Marina, hasten thee before ;   475
I'll come to make thy peace : for since I sore
Do hunger, and at home thou hast small cheer,
(Need and supply grow far off, seldom near,)
To yonder grove I'll go to taste the spring,
And see what it affords for nourishing.   480

455.—*Slone*, sloe.   463.—*Thilk*, that.

Thus parted they.   And sad Marina blest
'The hour she met the maid, who did invest
Her in assured hope she once should see
Her flock again and drive them merrily
To their flower-decked lair, and tread the shores 485
Of pleasant Albion through the well-pois'd oars
Of the poor fisherman that dwelt thereby.
    But as a man who in a lottery
Hath ventur'd of his coin, ere he have ought,
Thinks this or that shall with his prize be bought, 490
And so enrich'd, march with the better rank,
When suddenly he's call'd, and all is blank :
To chaste Marina so doth Fortune prove,
" Statesmen and she are never firm in love."
    No sooner had Marina got the wood,   495
But as the trees she nearly search'd for food,
A villain lean as any rake appears,
That look'd, as pinch'd with famine, Egypt's years,
Worn out and wasted to the pithless bone,
As one that had a long consumption.   500
His rusty teeth (forsaken of his lips
As they had serv'd with want two 'prenticeships)
Did through his pallid cheek and lankest skin
Bewray what number were enrank'd within.
His greedy eyes deep sunk into his head,   505
Which with a rough hair was o'ercovered.
How many bones made up this starved wight

496.—*Nearly*, narrowly.

Was soon perceiv'd ; a man of dimmest sight
Apparently might see them knit, and tell
How all his veins and every sinew fell.   510
His belly inwards drawn, his bowels press'd,
His unfill'd skin hung dangling on his breast,
His feeble knees with pain enough uphold
That pined carcase, casten in a mould
Cut out by Death's grim form. If small legs wan 515
Ever the title of a gentleman,
His did acquire it.   In his flesh pull'd down
As he had liv'd in a beleaguer'd town,
Where plenty had so long estranged been
That men most worthy note in grief were seen   520
(Though they rejoic'd to have attain'd such meat)
Of rats and half-tann'd hides with stomachs great
Gladly to feed : and where a nurse, most vild,
Drunk her own milk, and starv'd her crying child.
Yet he through want of food not thus became :   525
But Nature first decreed, that as the flame
Is never seen to fly his nourishment,
But all consumes : and still the more is lent
The more it covets : and as all the floods,
Down trenching from small groves and greater
          woods,   530
The vast insatiate sea doth still devour,
And yet his thirst not quenched by their power :
So ever should befall this starved wight,

530.—*Down trenching*, flowing down through made channels.

The more his viands more his appetite.
Whate'er the deeps bring forth, or earth, or air,   535
He ravine should, and want in greatest fare.
And what a city twice seven years would serve,
He should devour, and yet be like to starve.
A wretch so empty, that if e'er there be
In Nature found the least vacuity,   540
'Twill be in him.   The grave to Ceres' store ;
A cannibal to lab'rers old and poor ;
A sponge-like dropsy, drinking till it burst ;
The sickness term'd the wolf, vild and accurs'd ;
In some respects like th' art of alchemy,   545
That thrives least when it long'st doth multiply.
Limos he cleeped was : whose long-nail'd paw
Seizing Marina, and his sharp-fang'd jaw
(The strongest part he had) fix'd in her weeds,   [550
He forc'd her thence, through thickets and high reeds,
Towards his cave.   Her fate the swift winds rue,
And round the grove in heavy murmurs flew.
The limbs of trees that, as in love with either,
In close embracements long had liv'd together,
Rubb'd each on other, and in shrieks did show   555
The winds had mov'd more partners of their woe.
Old and decayed stocks that long time spent
Upon their arms their roots' chief nourishment,
And that drawn dry, as freely did impart
Their boughs a-feeding on their father's heart,   560

547.—*Limos.* the Greek word for famine.

Yet by respectless imps when all was gone,
Pithless and sapless, naked left alone,
Their hollow trunks, fill'd with their neighbours'
       moans,
Sent from a thousand vents ten thousand groans.
All birds flew from the wood, as they had been   565
Scar'd with a strong bolt rattling 'mong the treen.
   Limos with his sweet theft full slily rushes
Through sharp-hook'd brambles, thorns, and tangling
       bushes,
Whose tenters sticking in her garments sought,
Poor shrubs, to help her, but availing nought,   570
As angry (best intents miss'd best proceeding)
They scratch'd his face and legs, clear water bleed-
       ing.
Not greater haste a fearful school-boy makes
Out of an orchard whence by stealth he takes
A churlish farmer's plums, sweet pears or grapes, 575
Than Limos did, as from the thick he 'scapes
Down to the shore.   Where resting him a space,
Restless Marina 'gan entreat for grace
Of one whose knowing it as desp'rate stood,
As where each day to get supply of food.   580
   O ! had she thirsty such entreaty made
At some high rock, proud of his evening shade,
He would have burst in two, and from his veins,
For her avail, upon the under plains

      569.—*Tenters*, prickles

A hundred springs a hundred ways should swim, 585
To show her tears enforced floods from him.
Had such an oratress been heard to plead
For fair Polyxena, the murth'rer's head
Had been her pardon, and so 'scap'd that shock,
Which made her lover's tomb her dying block.   590
Not an enraged lion, surly, wood ;
No tiger reft her young, nor savage brood ;
No, not the foaming boar, that durst approve
Loveless to leave the mighty Queen of Love,
But her sad plaints their uncouth walks among   595
Spent in sweet numbers from her golden tongue,
So much their great hearts would in softness steep,
They at her foot would grovelling lie and weep.
Yet now (alas !) nor words, nor floods of tears
Did ought avail.   The belly hath no ears.   600
    As I have known a man loath meet with gain
That carrieth in his front least show of pain,
Who for his victuals all his raiment pledges,
Whose stacks for firing are his neighbours' hedges,
From whence returning with a burden great,   605
Wearied, on some green bank he takes his seat,
But fearful (as still theft is in his stay)
Gets quickly up, and hasteth fast away :

588.—*Murth'rer's head*, that of Paris, who treacherously
slew Achilles, the lover of Polyxena.
591.—*Wood*, mad or wild.
593.—*The foaming boar*, etc., alluding to Adonis, beloved
of Venus, who met his death while hunting a boar.
595.—*Uncouth*, unfrequented.

So Limos sooner eased than yrested
Was up and through the reeds (as much molested 610
As in the brakes) who lovingly combine,
And for her aid together twist and twine ;
Now manacling his hands, then on his legs
Like fetters hang the under-growing segs :
And had his teeth not been of strongest hold,   615
He there had left his prey.   Fates uncontroll'd
Denied so great a bliss to plants or men,
And lent him strength to bring her to his den.
    West, in Apollo's course to Tagus' stream,
Crown'd with a silver-circling diadem   620
Of wet exhaled mists, there stood a pile
Of aged rocks (torn from the neighbour isle
And girt with waves) against whose naked breast
The surges tilted, on his snowy crest
The tow'ring falcon whilom built, and kings   625
Strove for that aerie, on whose scaling wings
Monarchs in gold refin'd as much would lay
As might a month their army royal pay.
Brave birds they were, whose quick, self-less'ning kin
Still won the girlonds from the peregrine.*   630 * A falcon
Not Cerna Isle in Afric's silver main,   differing from
Nor lustful-bloody-Tereus' Thracian strain,   the falcon-
Nor any other lording of the air,   gentle.
Durst with this aerie for their wing compare.

614.—*Segs*, sedges.
630.—*Girlonds*, garlands.
631.—*Cerna Isle*, Mauritius.

About his sides a thousand sea-gulls bred,   635
The mevy and the halcyon famosed
For colours rare, and for the peaceful seas
Round the Sicilian coast, her brooding days.
Puffins (as thick as starlings in a fen)   [640
Were fetch'd from thence : there sat the pewet hen,
And in the clefts the martin built his nest.
But those by this curs'd caitiff dispossess'd
Of roost and nest, the least ; of life, the most :
All left that place, and sought a safer coast.
Instead of them the caterpillar haunts,   645
And cankerworm among the tender plants,
That here and there in nooks and corners grew
Of cormorants and locusts not a few ;
The cramming raven, and a hundred more
Devouring creatures ; yet when from the shore   650
Limos came wading (as he easily might
Except at high tides) all would take their flight,
Or hide themselves in some deep hole or other,
Lest one devourer should devour another.
    Near to the shore that border'd on the rock   655
No merry swain was seen to feed his flock,
No lusty neatherd thither drove his kine,
Nor boorish hogherd fed his rooting swine :
A stony ground it was, sweet herbage fail'd :
Nought there but weeds, which Limos, strongly
      nail'd,   660

636.—*Mevy*, sea-mew.   *Halcyon*, kingfisher.   *Famosed*, celebrated.

Tore from their mother's breast to stuff his maw.
No crab-tree bore his load, nor thorn his haw.
As in a forest well complete with deer
We see the hollies, ashes, everywhere
Robb'd of their clothing by the browsing game : 665
So near the rock all trees where'er you came,
To cold December's wrath stood void of bark.
Here danc'd no nymph, no early-rising lark
Sung up the ploughman and his drowsy mate :
All round the rock['s] barren and desolate.   670
    In midst of that huge pile was Limos' cave,*
Full large and round, wherein a miller's knave
Might for his horse and quern have room at will :
Where was out-drawn by some enforced skill
What mighty conquests were achiev'd by him.   675
First stood the siege of great Jerusalem,
Within whose triple wall and sacred city—
(Weep, ye stone-hearted men ! oh, read and pity !
'Tis Sion's cause invokes your briny tears :
Can any dry eye be when she appears   680
As I must sing her? oh, if such there be,
Fly, fly th' abode of men ! and hasten thee
Into the desert, some high mountain under,
Or at thee boys will hiss, and old men wonder)—
Here sits a mother weeping, pale and wan,   685
With fixed eyes, whose hopeless thoughts seem'd
        ran

> * The de-
> scription of
> the Cave of
> Famine.

672.—*Knave*, servant.   673.—*Quern*, mill.

How (since for many days no food she tasted,
Her meal, her oil consum'd, all spent, all wasted)
For one poor day she might attain supply,
And desp'rate of aught else, sit, pine, and die.   690
At last her mind meets with her tender child
That in the cradle lay (of osiers wild),
Which taken in her arms, she gives the teat,
From whence the little wretch with labour great
Not one poor drop can suck : whereat she, wood, 695
Cries out, O Heaven ! are all the founts of food
Exhausted quite ? and must my infant young
Be fed with shoes ? yet wanting those ere long,
Feed on itself?   No, first the room that gave
Him soul and life shall be his timeless grave :   700
My dugs, thy best relief, through griping hunger
Flow now no more, my babe ; then since no
          longer
By me thou canst be fed, nor any other,
Be thou the nurse and feed thy dying mother.
Then in another place she straight appears,   705
Seething her suckling in her scalding tears.
From whence not far the painter made her stand
Tearing his sod flesh with her cruel hand
In gobbets which she ate.   O cursed womb,
That to thyself art both the grave and tomb.   710
    A little sweet lad, there, seems to entreat
With held up hands his famish'd sire for meat,
Who wanting aught to give his hoped joy
But throbs and sighs ; the over-hungry boy,

For some poor bit in dark nooks making quest,   715
His satchel finds, which grows a gladsome feast
To him and both his parents.   Then, next day
He chews the points wherewith he us'd to play :
Devouring last his books of every kind,
They fed his body which should feed his mind :   720
But when his satchel, points, books all were gone,
Before his sire he droops, and dies anon.
    In height of art then had the workman done,
A pious, zealous, most religious son,
Who on the enemy excursion made,   725
And spite of danger strongly did invade
Their victuals' convoy, bringing from them home
Dri'd figs, dates, almonds, and such fruits as come
To the beleag'ring foe, and sates the want
Therewith of those who from a tender plant   730
Bred him a man for arms : thus oft he went,
And stork-like sought his parents' nourishment,
Till fates decreed he on the Roman spears
Should give his blood for them who gave him
              theirs.
A million of such throes did Famine bring   735
Upon the city of the mighty king,
Till, as her people, all her buildings rare
Consum'd themselves and dimm'd the lightsome air.
    Near this the curious pencil did express
A large and solitary wilderness,   740
Whose high well-limned oaks in growing show'd
As they would ease strong Atlas of his load :

Here underneath a tree in heavy plight,
Her bread and pot of water wasted quite,
Egyptian Hagar, nipp'd with hunger fell,   745
Sat robb'd of hope : her infant Ishmael,
Far from her being laid, full sadly seem'd
To cry for meat, his cry she naught esteem'd,
But kept her still, and turn'd her face away,
Knowing all means were bootless to assay   750
In such a desert ; and since now they must
Sleep their eternal sleep, and cleave to dust,
She chose apart to grasp one death alone,
Rather than by her babe a million.

Then Eresichthon's case in Ovid's song   755
Was portrayed out ; and many more along
The insides of the cave, which were descried
By many loop-holes round on every side.

These fair Marina view'd, left all alone,
The cave fast shut, Limos for pillage gone ;   760
Near the wash'd shore 'mong roots and breers and
        thorns,
A bullock finds, who delving with his horns
The hurtless earth (the while his tough hoof tore
The yielding turf) in furious rage he bore
His head among the boughs that held it round,   765
While with his bellows all the shores resound :

755.—*Eresichthon*, a son of Triopas, who cut down trees in
a grove sacred to Demeter, for which he was punished by the
goddess with fearful hunger.

761.—*Breers*, briars.

Him Limos kill'd, and hal'd with no small pain
Unto the rock ; fed well ; then goes again :
Which serv'd Marina fit, for had his food   [770
Fail'd him, her veins had fail'd their dearest blood.
  Now great Hyperion left his golden throne
That on the dancing waves in glory shone,
For whose declining on the western shore
The oriental hills black mantles wore,
And thence apace the gentle twilight fled,   775
That had from hideous caverns ushered
All-drowsy Night, who in a car of jet,
By steeds of iron-grey, which mainly sweat
Moist drops on all the world, drawn through the sky,
The helps of darkness waited orderly.   780
First thick clouds rose from all the liquid plains ;
Then mists from marishes, and grounds whose veins
Were conduit-pipes to many a crystal spring ;
From standing pools and fens were following
Unhealthy fogs ; each river, every rill   785
Sent up their vapours to attend her will
These pitchy curtains drew 'twixt earth and heaven.
And as Night's chariot through the air was driven,
Clamour grew dumb, unheard was shepherd's song,
And silence girt the woods ; no warbling tongue 790
Talk'd to the Echo ; satyrs broke their dance,
And all the upper world lay in a trance.
Only the curled streams soft chidings kept ;

782.—*Marishes*, marshes.

And little gales that from the green leaf swept
Dry summer's dust, in fearful whisp'rings stirr'd,   795
As loath to waken any singing bird.
   Darkness no less than blind Cimmerian
Of Famine's cave the full possession wan,
Where lay the shepherdess inwrapt with night,
The wished garment of a mournful wight.   800
Here silken slumbers and refreshing sleep
Were seldom found ; with quiet minds those keep,
Not with disturbed thoughts ; the beds of kings
Are never press'd by them, sweet rest enrings
The tired body of the swarty clown,   805
And oft'ner lies on flocks than softest down.
   Twice had the cock crown, and in cities strong
The bellman's doleful noise and careful song
Told men, whose watchful eyes no slumber hent,
What store of hours theft-guilty night had spent. 810
Yet had not Morpheus with this maiden bcen,
As fearing Limos, whose impetuous teen
Kept gentle rest from all to whom his cave
Yielded enclosure deadly as the grave ;
But to all sad laments left her forlorn,   815
In which three watches she had nigh outworn.
   Fair silver-footed Thetis that time threw
Along the ocean with a beauteous crew
Of her attending sea-nymphs, Jove's bright lamps

805.—*Swarty*, sunburnt.   809.—*Hent*, took, seized.
812.—*Teen*, violence.

Guiding from rocks her chariot's hippocamps :*   820   * Sea-horses.
A journey only made unwares to spy
If any mighties of her empery
Oppress'd the least, and forc'd the weaker sort
To their designs by being great in court.
O ! should all potentates whose higher birth   825
Enrols their titles, other gods on earth,
Should they make private search, in veil of night,
For cruel wrongs done by each favourite ;
Here should they find a great one paling in
A mean man's land, which many years had been 830
His charge's life, and by the other's hest,
The poor must starve to feed a scurvy beast.
If any recompense drop from his fist,
His time's his own, the money what he list.
There should they see another that commands   835
His farmer's team from furrowing his lands,
To bring him stones to raise his building vast,
The while his tenant's sowing time is past.
Another (spending) doth his rents enhance,
Or gets by tricks the poor's inheritance.   840
But as a man whose age hath dimm'd his eyes,
Useth his spectacles, and as he prys
Through them all characters seem wondrous fair,
Yet when his glasses quite removed are,
Though with all careful heed he nearly look,   845
Cannot perceive one tittle in the book ;

831.—*Hest*, command.   845.—*Nearly*, closely.

So if a king behold such favourites,
Whose being great was being parasites,
With th' eyes of favour, all their actions are
To him appearing plain and regular :   850
But let him lay his sight of grace aside,
And see what men he hath so dignified,
They all would vanish, and not dare appear,
Who, atom-like, when their sun shined clear,
Danc'd in his beam ; but now his rays are gone, 855
Of many hundred we perceive not one.
Or as a man who, standing to descry
How great floods far off run, and valleys lie,
Taketh a glass prospective good and true,
By which things most remote are full in view :   860
If monarchs, so, would take an instrument
Of truth compos'd to spy their subjects drent
In foul oppression by those high in seat,
Who care not to be good but to be great,
In full aspect the wrongs of each degree   865
Would lie before them ; and they then would see
The devilish politician all convinces,
In murd'ring statesmen and in pois'ning princes ;
The prelate in pluralities asleep,
Whilst that the wolf lies preying on his sheep ; 870
The drowsy lawyer, and the false attorneys
Tire poor men's purses with their lifelong journeys ;
The country gentleman from 's neighbour's hand

862.—*Drent*, drowned.   867.—*Convinces*, overthrows.

Forceth th' inheritance, joins land to land,
And most insatiate seeks under his rent   875
To bring the world's most spacious continent ;
The fawning citizen (whose love's bought dearest)
Deceives his brother when the sun shines clearest,
Gets, borrows, breaks, lets in, and stops out light,
And lives a knave to leave his son a knight ;   880
The griping farmer hoards the seed of bread,
Whilst in the streets the poor lie famished :
And free there's none from all this worldly strife,
Except the shepherd's heaven-bless'd happy life. [885
　　But stay, sweet Muse, forbear this harsher strain !
Keep with the shepherds ; leave the satyrs' vein ;
Coop not with bears ; let Icarus alone
To scorch himself within the torrid zone :
Let Phaeton run on, Ixion fall,
And with an humble styled Pastoral   890
Tread through the valleys, dance about the streams.
The lowly dales will yield us anadems
To shade our temples, 'tis a worthy meed,
No better garland seeks mine oaten reed ;
Let others climb the hills, and to their praise,   895
Whilst I sit girt with flowers, be crown'd with bays.
　　Show now, fair Muse, what afterward became
Of great Achilles' mother ; she whose name
The mermaids sing, and tell the weeping strand
A braver lady never tripp'd on land,   900

892.—*Anadems*, garlands.

Except the ever-living Faëry Queen,
Whose virtues by her swain so written been,
That time shall call her high enhanced story
In his rare song, the Muses' chiefest glory.
　　So mainly Thetis drove her silver throne,　　905
Inlaid with pearls of price and precious stone,
For whose gay purchase she did often make
The scorched negro dive the briny lake,
That by the swiftness of her chariot wheels,
Scouring the main as well-built English keels,　　910
She of the new-found world all coasts had seen,
The shores of Thessaly, where she was queen,
Her brother Pontus' waves, embrac'd, with those
Mœotian fields and vales of Tenedos,　　　　[915
Strait Hellespont, whose high-brow'd cliffs yet sound
The mournful name of young Leander drown'd ;
Then with full speed her horses doth she guide
Through the Ægean Sea, that takes a pride
In making difference 'twixt the fruitful lands,
Europe and Asia almost joining hands,　　　　920
But that she thrusts her billows all afront
To stop their meeting through the Hellespont.
The Midland Sea so swiftly was she scouring,
The Adriatic gulf brave ships devouring.
To Padus' silver stream then glides she on,　　925
Enfamoused by reckless Phaeton,

Plin. lib. 3.
cap. 16.

902.—*Swain*, Spenser.
926.—*Enfamoused*, made famous.

Padus that doth beyond his limits rise,
When the hot dog-star rains his maladies,
And robs the high and air-invading Alps
Of all their winter-suits and snowy scalps,   930
To drown the levell'd lands along his shore,
And make him swell with pride.   By whom of yore
The sacred Heliconian damsels sat,
To whom was mighty Pindus consecrate,
And did decree, neglecting other men,   935
Their height of art should flow from Maro's pen ;
And prattling echoes evermore should long
For repetition of sweet Naso's song.
It was enacted here in after days
What wights should have their temples crown'd with
       bays ;   940
Learn'd Ariosto, holy Petrarch's quill,
And Tasso should ascend the Muses' hill.
Divinest Bartas, whose enriched soul
Proclaim'd his Maker's worth, should so enroll
His happy name in brass, that Time nor Fate   945
That swallow all, should ever ruinate :
Delightful Saluste, whose all-blessed lays
The shepherds make their hymns on holy-days ;
And truly say thou in one week hast penn'd
What time may ever study, ne'er amend.   950
Marot and Ronsard, Garnier's buskin'd Muse

947.—*Saluste*, Guillaume de Saluste du Bartas. *See* Note.
951.—*Garnier's buskin'd Muse*, the tragedies of Robert
Garnier, the French dramatist and poet (1545-1601).

Should spirit of life in very stones infuse ;
And many another swan whose powerful strain
Should raise the golden world to life again.
    But let us leave, fair Muse, the banks of Po ;   955
Thetis forsook his brave stream long ago,
And we must after.   See, in haste she sweeps
Along the Celtic shores ; th' Armorick deeps
She now is ent'ring : bear up then ahead,
And by that time she hath discovered   960
Our alablaster rocks, we may descry
And ken with her the coasts of Britany.
There will she anchor cast to hear the songs
Of English shepherds, whose all-tuneful tongues
So pleas'd the naiades, they did report   965
Their songs' perfection in great Nereus' court :
Which Thetis hearing, did appoint a day
When she would meet them in the British Sea,
And thither for each swain a dolphin bring
To ride with her, whilst she would hear him sing. 970
The time prefix'd was come ; and now the star
Of blissful light appear'd, when she her car
Stay'd in the Narrow Seas.   At Thames' fair port
The nymphs and shepherds of the Isle resort,
And thence did put to sea with mirthful rounds, 975
Whereat the billows dance above their bounds,
And bearded goats, that on the clouded head

958.—*Armorick deeps*, the sea sweeping the coast between
the Loire and the Seine.
973.—*Narrow Seas*, the Straits of Dover.

Of any sea-surveying mountain fed,
Leaving to crop the ivy, list'ning stood
At those sweet airs which did entrance the flood. 980
In jocund sort the goddess thus they met,
And after rev'rence done, all being set
Upon their finny coursers round her throne,
And she prepar'd to cut the wat'ry zone
Engirting Albion, all their pipes were still,   985
And Colin Clout began to tune his quill
With such deep art, that every one was given
To think Apollo, newly slid from heav'n,
Had ta'en a human shape to win his love,
Or with the Western swains for glory strove.   990
He sung th' heroic knights of fairyland
In lines so elegant, of such command,
That had the Thracian* play'd but half so well,   * Orpheus
He had not left Eurydice in hell.
But ere he ended his melodious song   995
An host of angels flew the clouds among,
And rapt this swan from his attentive mates
To make him one of their associates
In heaven's fair choir : where now he sings the praise
Of him that is the first and last of days.   1000
Divinest Spenser, heav'n-bred, happy Muse !
Would any power into my brain infuse
Thy worth, or all that poets had before,
I could not praise till thou deserv'st no more.

986.—*Colin Clout*, Spenser.   *Quill*, pipe.

A damp of wonder and amazement strook   1005
Thetis' attendants ; many a heavy look
Follow'd sweet Spenser, till the thick'ning air
Sight's further passage stopp'd.   A passionate tear
Fell from each nymph, no shepherd's cheek was dry,
A doleful dirge, and mournful elegy   1010
Flew to the shore ; when mighty Nereus' queen,
In memory of what was heard and seen,
Employ'd a factor, fitted well with store
Of richest gems, refined Indian ore,
To raise, in honour of his worthy name,   1015
A pyramis, whose head like winged Fame
Should pierce the clouds, yea, seem the stars to kiss,
And Mausolus' great tomb might shroud in his.
Her will had been performance, had not Fate,
That never knew how to commiserate,   1020
Suborn'd curs'd Avarice to lie in wait
For that rich prey—(gold is a taking bait)—
Who closely lurking like a subtle snake
Under the covert of a thorny brake,
Seiz'd on the factor by fair Thetis sent,   1025
And robb'd our Colin of his monument.
   Ye English shepherds, sons of Memory,
For satires change your pleasing melody ;
Scourge, rail and curse that sacrilegious hand,
That more than fiend of hell, that Stygian brand, 1030
All-guilty Avarice, that worst of evil,

1005.—*Damp*, dejection.

That gulf-devouring offspring of a devil :
Heap curse on curse so direful and so fell,
Their weight may press his damned soul to hell.
Is there a spirit so gentle can refrain   1035
To torture such ? O let a satyr's vein
Mix with that man ! to lash this hellish limb,
Or all our curses will descend on him.
   For mine own part, although I now commerce
With lowly shepherds in as low a verse,   1040
If of my days I shall not see an end
Till more years press me, some few hours I'll spend
In rough hewn satires, and my busied pen
Shall jerk to death this infamy of men.
And like a Fury glowing coulters bear,   1045
With which—But see how yonder fondlings tear
Their fleeces in the brakes ; I must go free
Them of their bonds ; rest you here merrily·
Till my return, when I will touch a string
Shall make the rivers dance and valleys ring.   1050

   1037.—*Limb*, a term of reproach, *e.g.* a limb of Satan.
   1044.—*Jerk*, beat.
   1045.—*Coulters*, ploughshares.
   1046.—*Fondlings*, lambs.

THE SECOND SONG.

—

THE ARGUMENT.

What shepherds on the sea were seen
To entertain the Ocean's Queen;
Remond in search of Fida gone,
And for his love young Doridon;
Their meeting with a woeful swain,
Mute, and not able to complain
His metamorphos'd mistress' wrong,
Is all the subject of this song.

—

THE Muses' friend (grey-eyed Aurora) yet
Held all the meadows in a cooling sweat,
The milk-white gossamers not upwards snow'd,
Nor was the sharp and useful-steering goad(
Laid on the strong-neck'd ox; no gentle bud   5
The sun had dried; the cattle chew'd the cud
Low levell'd on the grass; no fly's quick sting
Enforc'd the stonehorse in a furious ring
To tear the passive earth, nor lash his tail
About his buttocks broad; the slimy snail   10
Might on the wainscot, by his many mazes,
Winding meanders and self-knitting traces,

Be follow'd where he stuck, his glittering slime
Not yet wip'd off.   It was so early time,
The careful smith had in his sooty forge   15
Kindled no coal; nor did his hammers urge
His neighbours' patience : owls abroad did fly,
And day as then might plead his infancy.
Yet of fair Albion all the western swaines
Were long since up, attending on the plains   20
When Nereus' daughter with her mirthful host
Should summon them on their declining coast.
    But since her stay was long, for fear the sun
Should find them idle, some of them begun
To leap and wrestle, others threw the bar ;   25
Some from the company removed are
To meditate the songs they meant to play,
Or make a new round for next holiday.
Some tales of love their love-sick fellows told :
Others were seeking stakes to pitch their fold.   30
This, all alone was mending of his pipe :
That, for his lass sought fruits most sweet, most ripe.
Here from the rest a lovely shepherd's boy
Sits piping on a hill, as if his joy
Would still endure, or else that age's frost   35
Should never make him think what he had lost.
Yonder a shepherdess knits by the springs,
Her hands still keeping time to what she sings :
Or seeming, by her song, those fairest hands
Were comforted in working.   Near the sands   40
Of some sweet river sits a musing lad,

That moans the loss of what he sometime had,
IIis love by death bereft : when fast by him
An aged swain takes place, as near the brim
Of's grave as of the river, showing how   45
That as those floods, which pass along right now,
Are follow'd still by others from their spring,
And in the sea have all their burying :
Right so our times are known, our ages found,
(Nothing is permanent within this round,)   50
One age is now, another that succeeds,
Extirping all things which the former breeds :
Another follows that, doth new times raise,
New years, new months, new weeks, new hours, new
          days,
Mankind thus goes like rivers from their spring,   55
And in the earth have all their burying.
Thus sat the old man counselling the young ;
Whilst, underneath a tree which overhung
The silver stream (as some delight it took
To trim his thick boughs in the crystal brook)   60
Were set a jocund crew of youthful swains,
Wooing their sweetings with delicious strains.
Sportive Oreades the hills descended,
The Hamadryades their hunting ended,
And in the high woods left the long-liv'd harts   65
To feed in peace, free from their winged darts ;
Floods, mountains, valleys, woods, each vacant lies

50.—*Round,* globe, world.   62.—*Sweetings,* sweethearts.

Of nymphs that by them danc'd their haydigyes :
For all those powers were ready to embrace
The present means to give our shepherds grace.   70
And underneath this tree (till Thetis came)
Many resorted, where a swain of name
Less than of worth : (and we do never own
Nor apprehend him best that most is known).
Fame is uncertain, who so swiftly flies   75
By th' unregarded shed where Virtue lies ;
She, ill-inform'd of Virtue's worth, pursu'th
In haste Opinion for the simple truth.
True Fame is ever liken'd to our shade,
He soonest misseth her that most hath made   80
To overtake her ; whoso takes his wing,
Regardless of her, she'll be following :
Her true propriety she thus discovers,
"Loves her contemners, and contemns her lovers."
Th'applause of common people never yet   85
Pursu'd this swain ; he knew 't the counterfeit
Of settled praise, and therefore at his songs,
Though all the shepherds and the graceful throngs
Of semi-gods compar'd him with the best
That ever touch'd a reed, or was address'd   90
In shepherd's coat, he never would approve
Their attributes given in sincerest love ;
Except he truly knew them as his merit.
Fame gives a second life to such a spirit.

68.— *Haydigyes*, rural dances.

This swain, entreated by the mirthful rout,   95
That with entwined arms lay round about
The tree 'gainst which he lean'd, (so have I seen
Tom Piper stand upon our village green,
Back'd with the May-pole, whilst a jocund crew
In gentle motion circularly threw   100
Themselves about him), to his fairest ring
Thus 'gan in numbers well according sing :

   Venus by Adonis' side
   Crying kiss'd, and kissing cried,
   Wrung her hands and tore her hair   105
   For Adonis dying there.

   Stay (quoth she) O stay and live !
   Nature surely doth not give
   To the earth her sweetest flowers
   To be seen but some few hours.   110

   On his face, still as he bled
   For each drop a tear she shed,
   Which she kiss'd or wip'd away,
   Else had drown'd him where he lay.

   Fair Proserpina (quoth she)   115
   Shall not have thee yet from me ;
   Nor thy soul to fly begin
   While my lips can keep it in.

  98.—*Tom Piper*, one of the characters making up a morris
dance (BRAND, *Pop. Antiq.*, ed. Bohn, i. 266-7).

Here she clos'd again.   And some
Say Apollo would have come   120
To have cur'd his wounded limb,
But that she had smother'd him.

Look as a traveller in summer's day,
Nigh chok'd with dust and molt with Titan's ray,
Longs for a spring to cool his inward heat,   125
And to that end with vows doth Heaven entreat,
When going further finds an apple-tree,
Standing as did old Hospitality,
With ready arms to succour any needs :
Hence plucks an apple, tastes it, and it breeds   130
So great a liking in him for his thirst,
That up he climbs, and gathers to the first
A second, third ; nay, will not cease to pull
Till he have got his cap and pockets full :
" Things long desir'd so well esteemed are,   135
That when they come we hold them better far.
There is no mean 'twixt what we love and want,
Desire, in men, is so predominant : "
No less did all this quaint assembly long
Than doth the traveller : this shepherd's song   140
IIad so ensnar'd each acceptable ear,
That but a second, naught could bring them clear
From an affected snare ; had Orpheus been
Playing, some distance from them, he had seen
Not one to stir a foot for his rare strain,   145
But left the Thracian for the English swain.

Or had suspicious Juno (when her Jove

* Iö.   Into a cow transform'd his fairest love*)

Great Inachus' sweet stem in durance given

* Mercury.   To this young lad, the messenger of heaven,*   150

Fair Maia's offspring, with the depth of art

That ever Jove to Hermes might impart,

In fing'ring of a reed, had never won

Poor Iö's freedom.   And though Arctor's son,

Hundred-ey'd Argus, might be lull'd by him,   155

And loose his pris'ner, yet in every limb

That god of wit had felt this shepherd's skill,

And by his charms brought from the Muses' hill

Enforc'd to sleep ; then, robb'd of pipe and rod,

And vanquish'd so, turn swain, this swain a god. 160

Yet to this lad not wanted Envy's sting,

(" He's not worth aught that's not worth envying,")

Since many at his praise were seen to grutch.

For as a miller in his bolting-hutch

Drives out the pure meal nearly as he can,   165

And in his sifter leaves the coarser bran :

So doth the canker of a poet's name

Let slip such lines as might inherit fame,

And from a volume culls some small amiss

To fire such dogged spleens as mate with his.   170

Yet, as a man that by his art would bring

The ceaseless current of a crystal spring

To overlook the lowly flowing head,

163.—*Grutch*, grumble.   169.—*Amiss*, fault.

Sinks by degrees his soder'd pipes of lead
Beneath the fount, whereby the water goes   175
High, as a well that on a mountain flows :
So when detraction and a cynic's tongue
Have sunk desert unto the depth of wrong,
By that the eye of skill true worth shall see
To brave the stars, though low his passage
       be.   180
  But here I much digress, yet pardon, swains :
For as a maiden gath'ring on the plains
A scentful nosegay to set near her pap,
Or as a favour for her shepherd's cap,
Is seen far off to stray if she have spied   185
A flower that might increase her posy's pride :
So if to wander I am sometimes press'd,
'Tis for a strain that might adorn the rest.
  Requests, that with denial could not meet,
Flew to our shepherd, and the voices sweet   190
Of fairest nymphs entreating him to say
What wight he lov'd ; he thus began his lay :

    SHALL I tell you whom I love ?
      Hearken then awhile to me ;
    And if such a woman move,   195
      As I now shall versify ;
    Be assur'd, 'tis she, or none
    That I love, and love alone.

174.—*Soder'd*, soldered.

Nature did her so much right,
    As she scorns the help of Art ;   200
In as many virtues dight
    As e'er yet embrac'd a heart.
So much good so truly tried,
Some for less were deified.

Wit she hath without desire   205
    To make known how much she hath ;
And her anger flames no higher
    Than may fitly sweeten wrath.
Full of pity as may be,
Though perhaps not so to me.   210

Reason masters every sense,
    And her virtues grace her birth :
Lovely as all excellence,
    Modest in her most of mirth :
Likelihood enough to prove,   215
Only worth could kindle love.

Such she is: and if you know
    Such a one as I have sung ;
Be she brown, or fair, or so,
    That she be but somewhile young ;   220
Be assur'd, 'tis she, or none
That I love, and love alone.

* Eöus, Py-
roeis, Aethon,
and Phlegon,
were feigned
to be the
horses of the
Sun.

Eöus and his fellows in the team,*
(Who, since their wat'ring in the Western stream,

Had run a furious journey to appease   225
The night-sick eyes of our Antipodes,)
Now sweating were in our horizon seen
To drink the cold dew from each flow'ry green :
When Triton's trumpet with a shrill command
Told silver-footed Thetis was at hand.   230
　　As I have seen when on the breast of Thames
A heavenly bevy of sweet English dames,
In some calm ev'ning of delightful May,
With music give a farewell to the day,
Or as they would, with an admired tone,   235
Greet Night's ascension to her eben throne,
Rapt with their melody a thousand more
Run to be wafted from the bounding shore :
So ran the shepherds, and with hasty feet   [240
Strove which should first increase that happy fleet.
　　The true presagers of a coming storm,*   * Dolphins.
Teaching their fins to steer them to the form
Of Thetis' will, like boats at anchor stood,
As ready to convey the Muses' brood
Into the brackish lake that seem'd to swell   245
As proud so rich a burden on it fell.
　　Ere their arrival Astrophel had done
His shepherd's lay, yet equaliz'd of none.
Th' admired mirror, glory of our Isle,
Thou far-far-more than mortal man, whose style 250
Struck more men dumb to hearken to thy song,

247.—*Astrophel,* Sir Philip Sidney.

Than Orpheus' harp or Tully's golden tongue.
To him (as right) for wit's deep quintessence,
For honour, valour, virtue, excellence,
Be all the garlands, crown his tomb with bay,   255
Who spake as much as e'er our tongue can say.
    Happy Arcadia ! while such lovely strains
Sung of thy valleys, rivers, hills and plains ;
Yet most unhappy other joys among,
That never heard'st his music nor his song.   260
Deaf men are happy so, whose virtues' praise
(Unheard of them) are sung in tuneful lays.
And pardon me, ye sisters of the mountain,
Who wail his loss from the Pegasian fountain,
If, like a man for portraiture unable,   265
I set my pencil to Apelles' table ;
Or dare to draw his curtain, with a will
To show his true worth, when the artist's skill
Within that curtain fully doth express
His own art's-mast'ry, my unableness.   270
    He sweetly touched what I harshly hit,
Yet thus I glory in what I have writ ;
Sidney began (and if a wit so mean
May taste with him the dews of Hippocrene)
I sung the Past'ral next ; his Muse, my mover :   275
And on the plains full many a pensive lover
Shall sing us to their loves, and praising be
My humble lines the more for praising thee.

   266.—*Apelles' table*, a picture of Aphrodite left unfinished
at the painter's death.

Thus we shall live with them by rocks, by springs,
As well as Homer by the death of kings.   280
    Then in a strain beyond an oaten quill
The learned shepherd of fair Hitchin hill*   * M. Chap-
Sung the heroic deeds of Greece and Troy,   man.
In lines so worthy life, that I employ
My reed in vain to overtake his fame.   285
All praiseful tongues do wait upon that name.
    Our second Ovid, the most pleasing Muse
That Heav'n did e'er in mortal's brain infuse,
All-loved Drayton, in soul-raping strains,
A genuine note of all the nymphish trains   290
Began to tune ; on it all ears were hung
As sometime Dido's on Æneas' tongue.
    Jonson, whose full of merit to rehearse
Too copious is to be confin'd in verse ;
Yet therein only fittest to be known,   295
Could any write a line which he might own.
One so judicious, so well knowing, and
A man whose least worth is to understand ;
One so exact in all he doth prefer
To able censure ; for the theatre   300
Not Seneca transcends his worth of praise ;
Who writes him well shall well deserve the bays.
    Well-languag'd Daniel : Brooke, whose polish'd
        lines

282.—*Hitchin*, in Hertfordshire, the birthplace of George
Chapman, the translator of Homer's poems.
289.—*Soul-raping*, soul-ravishing.

Are fittest to accomplish high designs,
Whose pen (it seems) still young Apollo guides ; 305
Worthy the forked hill, for ever glides
Streams from thy brain, so fair, that time shall see
Thee honour'd by thy verse, and it by thee.
And when thy temple's well-deserving bays
Might imp a pride in thee to reach thy praise, 310
As in a crystal glass, fill'd to the ring
With the clear water of as clear a spring,
A steady hand may very safely drop
Some quantity of gold, yet o'er the top
Not force the liquor run, although before 315
The glass (of water) could contain no more :
Yet so, all-worthy Brooke, though all men sound
With plummets of just praise thy skill profound,
Thou in thy verse those attributes canst take,
And not apparent ostentation make, 320
That any second can thy virtues raise,
Striving as much to hide as merit praise.
   Davies and Wither, by whose Muses' power
A natural day to me seems but an hour,
And could I ever hear their learned lays, 325
Ages would turn to artificial days.
These sweetly chanted to the Queen of Waves,
She prais'd, and what she prais'd, no tongue depraves.
Then base contempt (unworthy our report)
Fly from the Muses and their fair resort, 330

310.—*Imp*, engraft, insert.
328.—*Depraves*, traduces, vilifies.

And exercise thy spleen on men like thee :
Such are more fit to be contemn'd than we.
·'Tis not the rancour of a canker'd heart
That can debase the excellence of Art ;
Nor great in titles make our worth obey,   335
Since we have lines far more esteem'd than they.
For there is hidden in a poet's name
A spell that can command the wings of Fame,
And maugre all Oblivion's hated birth,
Begin their immortality on earth ;   340
When he that 'gainst a Muse with hate combines,
May raise his tomb in vain to reach our lines.

  Thus Thetis rides along the Narrow Seas
Encompass'd round with lovely naiades,
With gaudy nymphs, and many a skilful swain,   345
Whose equals earth cannot produce again,
But leave the times and men that shall succeed them
Enough to praise that age which so did breed them.

  Two of the quaintest swains that yet have been
Fail'd their attendance on the Ocean's Queen,   350
Remond and Doridon, whose hapless fates
Late sever'd them from their more happy mates.
For, gentle swains, if you remember well,
When last I sung on brim of yonder dell,
And as I guess it was that sunny morn,   355
When in the grove there by my sheep were shorn,
I ween I told you, while the shepherds young
Were at their past'ral and their rural song,
The shrieks of some poor maid, fallen in mischance,

Invok'd their aid, and drew them from their dance :
Each ran a several way to help the maid ;   [360
Some tow'rds the valley, some the green wood st ray'd :
Here one the thicket beats, and there a swain
Enters the hidden caves ; but all in vain.   [365
Nor could they find the wight whose shrieks and cry
Flew through the gentle air so heavily,
Nor see or man or beast, whose cruel teen
Would wrong a maiden or in grave or green.
Back then return'd they all to end their sport
But Doridon and Remond, who resort   370
Back to those places which they erst had sought,
Nor could a thicket be by Nature wrought
In such a web, so intricate, and knit
So strong with briars, but they would enter it.
Remond his Fida calls ; Fida the woods   375
Resound again, and Fida speak the floods,
As if the rivers and the hills did frame
Themselves no small delight to hear her name.
Yet she appears not.   Doridon would now
Have call'd his love too, but he knew not how : 380
Much like a man who dreaming in his sleep
That he is falling from some mountain steep
Into a soundless lake, about whose brim
A thousand crocodiles do wait for him,   [385
And hangs but by one bough, and should that break
His life goes with it, yet to cry or speak,

367.— *Teen*, violence.

Though fain he would, can move nor voice nor
   tongue :
So when he Remond heard the woods among
Call for his Fida, he would gladly too
Have call'd his fairest love, but knew not who, 390
Or what to call ; poor lad, that canst not tell,
Nor speak the name of her thou lov'st so well.
 Remond by hap near to the arbour found,
Where late the hind was slain, the hurtless ground
Besmear'd with blood ; to Doridon he cried, 395
And tearing then his hair, O hapless tide
(Quoth he), behold ! some cursed hand hath ta'en
From Fida this ; O what infernal bane,
Or more than hellish fiend enforced this !
Pure as the stream of aged Simois, 400
And as the spotless lily was her soul !
Ye sacred Powers that round about the pole
Turn in your spheres ! O could you see this deed,
And keep your motion ?   If the eldest seed
Of chained Saturn hath so often been 405
In hunter's and in shepherd's habit seen
To trace our woods, and on our fertile plains
Woo shepherds' daughters with melodious strains,
Where was he now, or any other power ?
So many sev'ral lambs have I each hour, 410
And crooked horned rams brought to your shrines,

394.--*Hurtless*, innocent.
400.—*Simois*, the river in the plain of Troy.

And with perfumes clouded the sun that shines,
Yet now forsaken ? to an uncouth state
Must all things run, if such will be ingrate.   [415
     Cease, Remond, quoth the boy, no more complain,
Thy fairest Fida lives ; nor do thou stain
With vile reproaches any power above,
They all as much as thee have been in love :
Saturn his Rhea ; Jupiter had store,
As Iö, Leda, Europa, and more ;   420
Mars enter'd Vulcan's bed, partook his joy ;
* Hyacinth. Phœbus had Daphne, and the sweet-fac'd boy ;*
Venus, Adonis ; and the God of Wit
In chastest bonds was to the Muses knit,
And yet remains so, nor can any sever   425
His love, but brother-like affects them ever ;
Pale, changeful Cynthia her Endymion had,
And oft on Latmus sported with that lad :
If these were subject (as all mortal men)
Unto the golden shafts, they could not then   430
But by their own affections rightly guess
Her death would draw on thine ; thy wretchedness
Charge them respectless ; since no swain than thee
Hath offer'd more unto each deity.
But fear not, Remond, for those sacred Powers   435
Tread on oblivion ; no desert of ours
Can be entomb'd in their celestial breasts ;
They weigh our off'rings and our solemn feasts,
And they forget thee not : Fida (thy dear)   [440
Treads on the earth ; the blood that's sprinkled here

Ne'er fill'd her veins, the hind possess'd this gore ;
See where the collar lies she whilom wore.
Some dog hath slain her, or the griping carl
That spoils our plains in digging them for marl.
  Look, as two little brothers who address'd   445
To search the hedges for a thrush's nest,
And have no sooner got the leavy spring,
When mad in lust with fearful bellowing
A strong-neck'd bull pursues throughout the field,
One climbs a tree, and takes that for his shield,   450
Whence looking from one pasture to another,
What might betide to his much-loved brother,
Further than can his over-drowned eyes
Aright perceive, the furious beast he spies
Toss something on his horns, he knows not what, 455
But one thing fears, and therefore thinks it that ;
When coming nigher he doth well discern
It of the wondrous-one-night-seeding fern
Some bundle was : yet thence he homeward goes
Pensive and sad, nor can abridge the throes   460
His fear began, but still his mind doth move
Unto the worst : mistrust goes still with love.
So far'd it with our shepherd : though he saw
Not aught of Fida's raiment, which might draw
A more suspicion ; though the collar lay   465
There on the grass, yet goes he thence away
Full of mistrust, and vows to leave that plain,

444.—*Marl. See* Note.   447 —*Spring*, wood.

Till he embrace his chastest love again.
Love-wounded Doridon entreats him then
That he might be his partner, since no men   470
Had cases liker ; he with him would go,
Weep when he wept, and sigh when he did so.
I, quoth the boy, will sing thee songs of love,
And as we sit in some all-shady grove,
Where Philomela and such sweeten'd throats   475
Are for the mast'ry tuning various notes,
I'll strive with them, and tune so sad a verse,
That whilst to thee my fortunes I rehearse,
No bird but shall be mute, her note decline,
And cease her woe, to lend an ear to mine.   480
I'll tell thee tales of love, and show thee how
The gods have wander'd as we shepherds now,
And when thou plain'st thy Fida's loss, will I
Echo the same, and with mine own supply.
Know, Remond, I do love, but, well-a-day !   485
I know not whom ; but as the gladsome May
She's fair and lovely, as a goddess she
(If such as her's a goddess' beauty be)
First stood before me, and inquiring was
How to the marish she might soonest pass,   490
When rush'd a villain in, hell be his lot,
And drew her thence, since when I saw her not,
Nor know I where to search ; but if thou please
'Tis not a forest, mountain, rocks, or seas

490.—*Marish*, marsh.

Can in thy journey stop my going on.   495
Fate so may smile on hapless Doridon,
That he rebless'd may be with her fair sight,
Though thence his eyes possess eternal night.
    Remond agreed, and many weary days
They now had spent in unfrequented ways :   500
About the rivers, valleys, holts and crags,
Among the osiers and the waving flags
They nearly pry, if any dens there be,
Where from the sun might harbour cruelty :
Or if they could the bones of any spy,   505
Or torn by beasts, or human tyranny.
They close inquiry make in caverns blind,
Yet what they look for would be death to find.
Right as a curious man that would descry,
Led by the trembling hand of Jealousy,   510
If his fair wife have wrong'd his bed or no,
Meeteth his torment if he find her so.
    One ev'n, ere Phœbus near the golden shore
Of Tagus' stream his journey 'gan give o'er,
They had ascended up a woody hill,   515
Where oft the fauni with their bugles shrill
Waken'd the echo, and with many a shout
Follow'd the fearful deer the woods about,
Or through the brakes that hide the craggy rocks
Digg'd to the hole where lies the wily fox ;   520
Thence they beheld an underlying vale,

501.—*Holts*, woody hills.   503.—*Nearly*, closely.

Where Flora set her rarest flowers at sale,
Whither the thriving bee came oft to suck them,
And fairest nymphs to deck their hair did pluck
    them ;
Where oft the goddesses did run at base,   525
And on white harts began the wild-goose-chase :
Here various Nature seem'd adorning this,
In imitation of the fields of bliss ;
Or as she would entice the souls of men
To leave Elysium, and live here again.   530
Not Hybla mountain in the jocund prime
Upon her many bushes of sweet thyme
Shows greater number of industrious bees,
Than were the birds that sung there on the trees.
Like the trim windings of a wanton lake,   535
That doth his passage through a meadow make,
Ran the delightful valley 'tween two hills :
From whose rare trees the precious balm distils,
And hence Apollo had his simples good
That cur'd the gods hurt by the Earth's ill brood. 540
A crystal river on her bosom slid,
And passing seem'd in sullen mutt'rings chid
The artless songsters, that their music still
Should charm the sweet dale and the wistful hill :
Not suffering her shrill waters, as they run   544

525.—*Bas*, the game of prisoner's-bars.
526.—*Wild-goose-chase*, a game.
531.—*Prime*, spring.

Tun'd with a whistling gale in unison
To tell as high they priz'd the broider'd vale
As the quick linnet or sweet nightingale.
Down from a steep rock came the water first,
(Where lusty satyrs often quench'd their thirst)   550
And with no little speed seem'd all in haste,
Till it the lovely bottom had embrac'd :
Then as entranc'd to hear the sweet birds sing,
In curled whirlpools she her course doth bring,
As loath to leave the songs that lull'd the dale,   555
Or waiting time, when she and some soft gale
Should speak what true delight they did possess
Among the rare flowers which the valley dress.
But since those quaint musicians would not stay,
Nor suffer any to be heard but they :   560
Much like a little lad who gotten new
To play his part amongst a skilful crew
Of choice musicians on some softer string
That is not heard, the others' fingering
Drowning his art, the boy would gladly get   565
Applause with others that are of his set,
And therefore strikes a stroke loud as the best,
And often descants when his fellows rest ;
That to be heard (as usual singers do)
Spoils his own music and his partners' too :   570
So at the further end the waters fell
From off an high bank down a lowly dell,
As they had vow'd, ere passing from that ground,
The birds should be enforc'd to hear their sound.

No small delight the shepherds took to see   575
A coombe so dight in Flora's livery,*
Where fair Feronia* honour'd in the woods,
And all the deities that haunt the floods,
With powerful Nature strove to frame a plot,
Whose like the sweet Arcadia yielded not.   580
　　Down through the arched wood the shepherds wend,
And seek all places that might help their end,
When, coming near the bottom of the hill,
A deep-fetch'd sigh (which seem'd of power to kill
The breast that held it) pierc'd the list'ning wood; 585
Whereat the careful swains no longer stood
Where they were looking on a tree, whose rind
A love-knot held, which two join'd hearts entwin'd ;
But searching round, upon an aged root   [590
Thick lin'd with moss which (though to little boot)
Seem'd as a shelter it had lending been
Against cold winter's storms and wreakful teen :
Or clad the stock in summer with that hue
His wither'd branches not a long time knew :
For in his hollow trunk and perish'd grain   595
The cuckow now had many a winter lain,
And thriving pismires laid their eggs in store :
The dormouse slept there, and a many more—
Here sat the lad, of whom I think of old
Virgil's prophetic spirit had foretold,   600
Who whilst Dame Nature for her cunning's sake

* Valley.

* According to that of Silius, lib. 13. Punicor. —Itur in agros, Dives ubi ante omnes.colitur Feronia luco.

592.—*Teen,* violence.

A male or female doubted which to make,
And to adorn him more than all assay'd,
This pretty youth was almost made a maid.
Sadly he sat, and (as would Grief) alone,   605
As if the boy and tree had been but one,
Whilst down near boughs did drops of amber creep,
As if his sorrow made the trees to weep.
If ever this were true in Ovid's verse
That tears have power an adamant to pierce,   610
Or move things void of sense, 'twas here approv'd :
Things, vegetative once, his tears have mov'd.
Surely the stones might well be drawn in pity
To burst that he should moan, as for a ditty .
To come and range themselves in order all,   615
And of their own accord raise Thebes a wall.
Or else his tears (as did the other's song)
Might have th' attractive power to move the throng
Of all the forest's citizens and woods,
With ev'ry denizen of air and floods,   620
To sit by him and grieve : to leave their jars,
Their strifes, dissensions, and all civil wars ;
And though else disagreeing, in this one
Mourning for him should make an union.
For whom the heavens would wear a sable suit,   625
If men, beasts, fishes, birds, trees, stones were mute.
His eyes were fixed (rather fixed stars)
With whom it seem'd his tears had been in wars,

611.— *Approv'd*, proved.

The diff'rence this (a hard thing to descry)
Whether the drops were clearest, or his eye.   630
Tears fearing conquest to the eye might fall,
An inundation brought and drowned all.
Yet like true Virtue from the top of state,
Whose hopes vile Envy hath seen ruinate,
Being lowly cast, her goodness doth appear   635
(Uncloth'd of greatness) more apparent clear :
So though dejected, yet remain'd a feature,
Made sorrow sweet plac'd in so sweet a creature.
" The test of misery the truest is,
In that none hath but what is surely his."   640
His arms across, his sheep-hook lay beside him :
Had Venus pass'd this way, and chanc'd t' have spied
          him,
With open breast, locks on his shoulders spread,
She would have sworn (had she not seen him dead)
It was Adonis ; or if e'er there was   645
Held transmigration by Pythagoras
Of souls, that certain then her lost love's spirit
A fairer body never could inherit.
His pipe, which often wont upon the plain
To sound the Dorian, Phrygian, Lydian strain,   650
Lay from his hook and bag clean cast apart,
And almost broken like his master's heart.
Yet till the two kind shepherds near him stepp'd,
I find he nothing spake but that he wept.
    Cease, gentle lad (quoth Remond), let no tear   655
Cloud those sweet beauties in thy face appear ;

Why dost thou call on that which comes alone,
And will not leave thee till thyself art gone?
Thou may'st have grief, when other things are reft
       thee :
All else may slide away, this still is left thee ;   660
And when thou wantest other company,
Sorrow will ever be embracing thee.
But, fairest swain, what cause hast thou of woe?
Thou hast a well-fleec'd flock feed to and fro
(His sheep along the valley that time fed   665
Not far from him, although unfollowed).
What, do thy ewes abortives bring? or lambs
For want of milk seek to their fellows' dams?
No griping landlord hath enclos'd thy walks,
Nor toiling ploughman furrow'd them in balks.   670
Ver hath adorn'd thy pastures all in green
With clover-grass as fresh as may be seen :
Clear-gliding springs refresh thy meadows' heat,
Meads promise to thy charge their winter-meat,
And yet thou griev'st ! O ! had some swains thy
      store,   675
Their pipes should tell the woods they ask'd no more.
Or have the Parcæ with unpartial knife
Left some friend's body tenantless of life,
And thou bemoan'st that Fate in his youth's morn
O'ercast with clouds his light but newly born ?   680

670.—*Balks*, the ridge left by the plough between two
furrows.
677.—*Unpartial*, unkindly.

" Count not how many years he is bereav'd,
But those which he possess'd and had receiv'd ;
If I may tread no longer on this stage,
Though others think me young ; it is mine age :
For whoso hath his fate's full period told,   685
He full of years departs, and dieth old."
May be that avarice thy mind hath cross'd,
And so thy sighs are for some trifle lost.
Why shouldst thou hold that dear the world throws
          on thee ?   [690
" Think nothing good which may be taken from thee."
Look as some pond'rous weight or massy pack,
Laid to be carried on a porter's back,
Doth make his strong joints crack, and forceth him
(Maugre the help of every nerve and limb)
To straggle in his gait, and goeth double,   695
Bending to earth, such is his burden's trouble :
So any one by avarice engirt,
And press'd with wealth, lies grovelling in the dirt.
His wretched mind bends to no point but this,
That who hath most of wealth hath most of bliss. 700
Hence comes the world to seek such traffic forth
And passages through the congealed North,
Who when their hairs with icicles are hung,
And that their chatt'ring teeth confound their tongue,
Show them a glitt'ring stone, will straightways
          say,   ·   705
If pains thus prosper, oh, what fools would play ?
Yet I could tell them (as I now do thee)

." In getting wealth we lose our liberty.
Besides, it robs us of our better powers,
And we should be ourselves, were these not ours. 710
He is not poorest that hath least in store,
But he which hath enough, yet asketh more :
Nor is he rich by whom are all possess'd,
But he which nothing hath, yet asketh least.
If thou a life by Nature's leading pitch,   715
Thou never shalt be poor, nor ever rich
Led by Opinion ; for their states are such,
Nature but little seeks, Opinion much."
Amongst the many buds proclaiming May,
(Decking the fields in holy-day's array,   720
Striving who shall surpass in bravery)
Mark the fair blooming of the hawthorn-tree,
Who, finely clothed in a robe of white,
Feeds full the wanton eye with May's delight ;
Yet for the bravery that she is in   725
Doth neither handle card nor wheel to spin,
Nor changeth robes but twice : is never seen
In other colours than in white or green.
Learn then content, young shepherd, from this tree,
Whose greatest wealth is Nature's livery ;   730
And richest ingots never toil to find,
Nor care for poverty but of the mind.
     This spoke young Remond : yet the mournful lad

726.—*Doth neither handle card*, etc., Luke, c. xii. v. 27 ;
Spenser's *Faëry Queen*, b. 2. c. 6, st. 16, l. 8.
    732.—*Not care for poverty*, etc., Matt. c. 5, vv. 3, 6.

Not once replied ; but with a smile, though sad,
He shook his head, then cross'd his arms again,   735
And from his eyes did showers of salt tears rain ;
Which wrought so on the swains, they could not
          smother
Their sighs, but spent them freely as the other.
Tell us (quoth Doridon), thou fairer far
Than he whose chastity made him a star, *   740
More fit to throw the wounding shafts of Love
Than follow sheep, and pine here in a grove.
O do not hide thy sorrows, show them brief ;
" He oft finds aid that doth disclose his grief."
If thou wouldst it continue, thou dost wrong ;   745
" No man can sorrow very much and long : "
For thus much loving Nature hath dispos'd,
That 'mongst the woes that have us round enclos'd,
This comfort's left (and we should bless her for't)
That we may make our griefs be born, or short.   750
Believe me, shepherd, we are men no less
Free from the killing throes of heaviness
Than thou art here, and but this diff'rence sure,
That use hath made us apter to endure.
More he had spoke, but that a bugle shrill   755
Rung through the valley from the higher hill,
And as they turn'd them tow'rds the heart'ning sound,
A gallant stag, as if he scorn'd the ground,
Came running with the wind, and bore his head
As he had been the king of forests bred.   760
Not swifter comes the messenger of heaven,

* Hippoly-
tus.

Or winged vessel with a full gale driven,
Nor the swift swallow flying near the ground,
By which the air's distemp'rature is found :
Nor Myrrha's course, nor Daphne's speedy flight, 765
Shunning the daliiance of the God of light,
Than seem'd the stag, that had no sooner cross'd them,
But in a trice their eyes as quickly lost him.

   The weeping swain ne'er mov'd, but as his eyes
Were only given to show his miseries,   770
Attended those ; and could not once be won
To leave that object whence his tears begun.

   O had that man,* who (by a tyrant's hand)   * Phiton.
Seeing his children's bodies strew the sand,
And he next morn for torments press'd to go,   775
Yet from his eyes let no one small tear flow,
But being ask'd how well he bore their loss,
Like to a man affliction could not cross,
He stoutly answer'd : Happier sure are they
Than I shall be by space of one short day :   780
No more his grief was ; but had he been here,
He had been flint, had he not spent a tear.
For still that man the perfecter is known,
Who others' sorrows feels more than his own.

   Remond and Doridon were turning then   785
Unto the most disconsolate of men,
But that a gallant dame, fair as the morn
Or lovely blooms the peach-tree that adorn,
Clad in a changing silk, whose lustre shone
Like yellow flowers and grass far off in one,   790

Or like the mixture Nature doth display
Upon the quaint wings of the popinjay :
Her horn about her neck with silver tip,
Too hard a metal for so soft a lip,
Which it no oft'ner kiss'd than Jove did frown,   795
And in a mortal's shape would fain come down
To feed upon those dainties, had not he
Been still kept back by Juno's jealousy.
An ivory dart she held of good command,
White was the bone, but whiter was her hand ;   800
Of many pieces was it neatly fram'd,
But more the hearts were that her eyes inflam'd.
Upon her head a green light silken cap :
A piece of white lawn shadow'd either pap,
Between which hillocks many Cupids lay,   805
Where with her neck or with her teats they play,
Whilst her quick heart will not with them dispense,
But heaves her breasts as it would beat them thence :
Who, fearing much to lose so sweet repair,
Take faster hold by her dishevell'd hair.   810
Swiftly she ran ; the sweet briars to receive her
Slipp'd their embracements, and (as loath to leave her)
Stretch'd themselves to their length ; yet on she
      goes.
So great Diana frays a herd of roes
And speedy follows : Arethusa fled   815
Alpheus.   So from the river that her ravished.

792.—*Popinjay*, parrot.   814.—*Frays*, affrights.

When this brave huntress near the shepherds drew
Her lily arm in full extent she threw
To pluck a little bough to fan her face
From off a thick-leav'd ash (no tree did grace   820
The low grove as did this, the branches spread
Like Neptune's trident upwards from the head).
No sooner did the grieved shepherd see
The nymph's white hand extended tow'rds the tree,
But rose and to her ran, yet she had done   825
Ere he came near, and to the wood was gone ;
Yet now approach'd the bough the huntress tore,
He suck'd it with his mouth, and kiss'd it o'er
A hundred times, and softly 'gan it bind
With dock-leaves and a slip of willow rind.   830
Then round the trunk he wreathes his weaken'd arms,
And with his scalding tears the smooth bark warms,
Sighing and groaning, that the shepherds by
Forgot to help him, and lay down to cry :
"For 'tis impossible a man should be   835
Griev'd to himself, or fail of company."
Much the two swains admir'd, but pitied more
That he no power of words had to deplore
Or show what sad misfortune 'twas befell
To him, whom Nature (seem'd) regarded well.   840
    As thus they lay, and while the speechless swain
His tears and sighs spent to the woods in vain,
One like a wild man overgrown with hair,

837.—*Admir'd*, wondered.

His nails long grown, and all his body bare,
Save that a wreath of ivy twist did hide   845
Those parts which Nature would not have descried,
And the long hair that curled from his head
A grassy garland rudely covered——
    But, shepherds, I have wrong'd you ; 'tis now late,
For see our maid stands hollowing on yond gate. 850
'Tis supper-time withal, and we had need
Make haste away unless we mean to speed
With those that kiss the hare's foot : rheums are bred,
Some say, by going supperless to bed,
And those I love not ; therefore cease my rhyme, 855
And put my pipes up till another time.

853.—*Kiss the hare's foot*, a proverbial expression signifying
to be too late for anything.

THE THIRD SONG.

———

The Argument.

A redbreast doth from pining save
Marina shut in Famine's Cave.
The golden age described plain,
And Limos by the shepherds slain,
Do give me leave awhile to move
My pipe of 'Tavy and his love.

———

ALAS that I have done so great a wrong
Unto the fairest maiden of my song,
Divine Marina, who in Limos' cave
Lies ever fearful of a living grave,
And night and day upon the harden'd stones   5
Rests, if a rest can be amongst the moans
Of dying wretches ; where each minute all
Stand still afraid to hear the death's-man call.
  Thrice had the golden sun his hot steeds wash'd
In the west main, and thrice them smartly lash'd   10
Out of the balmy east, since the sweet maid
Had in that dismal cave been sadly laid.
Where hunger pinch'd her so, she need not stand

In fear of murd'ring by a second hand :
For through her tender sides such darts might pass 15
'Gainst which strong walls of stone, thick gates of
       brass,
Deny no entrance, nor the camps of kings,
Since soonest there they bend their flaggy wings.
   But Heaven that stands still for the best's avail,
Lendeth his hand when human helpings fail ;   20
For 'twere impossible that such as she
Should be forgotten of the Deity ;
Since in the spacious orb could no man find
A fairer face match'd with a fairer mind.
   A little robin-redbreast, one clear morn,   25
Sat sweetly singing on a well-leav'd thorn :
Whereat Marina rose, and did admire
He durst approach from whence all else retire :
And pitying the sweet bird what in her lay,
She fully strove to fright him thence away.   30
Poor harmless wretch, quoth she, go, seek some
       spring,
And to her sweet fall with thy fellows sing ;
Fly to the well-replenish'd groves, and there
Do entertain each swain's harmonious ear ;
Traverse the winding branches ; chant so free,   35
That every lover fall in love with thee ;
And if thou chance to see that lovely boy
(To look on whom the sylvans count a joy) :

27.—*Admire*, wonder.

He whom I lov'd no sooner than I lost,
Whose body all the Graces hath engross'd,   40
To him unfold (if that thou dar'st to be
So near a neighbour to my tragedy)
As far as can thy voice (in plaints so sad,
And in so many mournful accents clad,
That as thou sing'st upon a tree there by   45
He may some small time weep, yet know not why),
How I in death was his, though Powers divine
Will not permit that he in life be mine.
Do this, thou loving bird ; and haste away
Into the woods : but if so be thou stay   50
To do a deed of charity on me,
When my pure soul shall leave mortality,
By cov'ring this poor body with a sheet
Of green leaves, gather'd from a valley sweet ;
It is in vain : these harmless limbs must have   55
Than in the caitiff's womb no other grave.
Hence then, sweet robin ; lest in staying long
At once thou chance forego both life and song.
With this she hush'd him thence ; he sung no more,
But ('fraid the second time) flew tow'rds the shore. 60
    Within as short time as the swiftest swain
Can to our May-pole run and come again,
The little redbreast to the prickled thorn
Return'd, and sung there as he had beforn :
And fair Marina to the loophole went,   65
Pitying the pretty bird, whose punishment
Limos would not defer if he were spied.

No sooner had the bird the maiden eyed,
But leaping on the rock, down from a bough,
He takes a cherry up (which he but now   70
Had thither brought, and in that place had laid
Till to the cleft his song had drawn the maid),
And flying with the small stem in his bill,
(A choicer fruit than hangs on Bacchus' hill,)*
In fair Marina's bosom took his rest,   75
A heavenly seat fit for so sweet a guest :
Where Cytherea's doves might billing sit,
And gods and men with envy look on it ;
Where rose two mountains, whose rare sweets to crop
Was harder than to reach Olympus' top :   80
For those the gods can ; but to climb these hills
Their powers no other were than mortal wills.
Here left the bird the cherry, and anon
Forsook her bosom, and for more is gone,
Making such speedy flights into the thick,   85
That she admir'd he went and came so quick.
Then lest his many cherries should distaste,
Some other fruit he brings than he brought last.
Sometime of strawberries a little stem,
Oft changing colours as he gather'd them :   90
Some green, some white, some red on them infus'd,
These lov'd, those fear'd, they blush'd to be so us'd.
The peascod green oft with no little toil
He'd seek for in the fattest, fertil'st soil,

* Cithæron in Bœotia.

85.—*Thick*, thicket.   86.—*Admir'd*, wondered.

And rend it from the stalk to bring it to her,   95
And in her bosom for acceptance woo her.
No berry in the grove or forest grew,
That fit for nourishment the kind bird knew,
Nor any powerful herb in open field
To serve her brood the teeming earth did yield,   100
But with his utmost industry he sought it,
And to the cave for chaste Marina brought it.
So from one well-stor'd garden to another, ·
To gather simples runs a careful mother,
Whose only child lies on the shaking bed   105
Grip'd with a fever (sometime honoured
In Rome as if a god*), nor is she bent
To other herbs than those for which she went.
    The feather'd hours five times were overtold,
And twice as many floods and ebbs had roll'd   110
The small sands out and in, since fair Marine
(For whose long loss a hundred shepherds pine)
Was by the charitable robin fed :
For whom (had she not so been nourished)
A hundred doves would search the sunburnt hills,   115
Or fruitful valleys lac'd with silver rills,
To bring her olives.   Th' eagle strong of sight
To countries far remote would bend her flight,
And with unwearied wing strip through the sky
To the choice plots of Gaul and Italy,   120
And never lin till homeward she escape

* Febrem ad minus nocendum templis colebant, ait Val. Maximus.   Vide Tullium in tertio de Nat. Deorum, et secundo de Legibus.

119.—*Strip*, fly rapidly.   121.—*Lin*, cease.

With the pomegranate, lemon, orange, grape,
Or the lov'd citron, and attain'd the cave.
The well-plum'd goshawk (by th' Egyptians grave
Us'd in their mystic characters for speed)   125
Would not be wanting at so great a need,
But from the well-stor'd orchards of the land
Brought the sweet pear, once by a cursed hand
At Swinsted* us'd with poison for the fall
Of one who on these plains rul'd lord of all.   130
The scentful osprey by the rock had fish'd,
And many a pretty shrimp in scallops dish'd,
Some way convey'd her ; no one of the shoal
That haunt the waves, but from his lurking hole
Had pull'd the crayfish, and with much ado   135
Brought that the maid, and periwinkles too.
But these for others might their labours spare,
And not with robin for their merits share.
Yet as a herdess in a summer's day,
Heat with the glorious sun's all-purging ray,   140
In the calm evening, leaving her fair flock,
Betakes herself unto a froth-girt rock,
On which the headlong Tavy throws his waves,
And foams to see the stones neglect his braves :
Where sitting to undo her buskins white,   145
And wash her neat legs, as her use each night,
Th' enamour'd flood, before she can unlace them,
Rolls up his waves as hast'ning to embrace them,

* One writes that K. John was poison'd at Swinsted, with a dish of pears : others, there, in a cup of wine : some that he died at Newark of the flux. A fourth by the distemperature of peaches eaten in his fit of an ague. Among so many doubts, I leave you to believe the author most in credit with our best of antiquaries.

144.—*Braves*, boasts, vauntings.

And though to help them some small gale do blow,
And one of twenty can but reach her so ;   150
Yet will a many little surges be
Flashing upon the rock full busily,
And do the best they can to kiss her feet,
But that their power and will not equal meet :
So as she for her nurse look'd tow'rds the land,   155
And now beholds the trees that grace the strand,
Then looks upon a hill whose sliding sides
A goodly flock like winter's cov'ring hides,
And higher on some stone that jutteth out, '
Their careful master guiding his trim rout   160
By sending forth his dog as shepherds do,
Or piping sat, or clouting of his shoe ;
Whence, nearer hand drawing her wand'ring sight,
So from the earth steals the all-quick'ning light,
Beneath the rock, the waters high, but late,   165
(I know not by what sluice or empting gate)
Were at a low ebb ; on the sand she spies
A busy bird that to and fro still flies,
Till pitching where a heatful oyster lay,
Opening his close jaws, closer none than they   170
Unless the griping fist, or cherry lips
Of happy lovers in their melting sips,
Since the decreasing waves had left him there
Gaping for thirst, yet meets with nought but air,
And that so hot, ere the returning tide,   175

162.—*Clouting*, patching.

He in his shell is likely to be fried ;
The wary bird a pretty pebble takes
And claps it 'twixt the two pearl-hiding flakes
Of the broad-yawning oyster, and she then
Securely picks the fish out (as some men   180
A trick of policy thrust 'tween two friends,
Sever their powers), and his intention ends.
The bird thus getting that for which she strove,
Brought it to her : to whom the Queen of Love
Serv'd as a foil, and Cupid could no other,   185
But fly to her mistaken for his mother.
Marina from the kind bird took the meat,
And (looking down) she saw a number great
Of birds, each one a pebble in his bill,
Would do the like, but that they wanted skill :   190
Some threw it in too far, and some too short ;
This could not bear a stone fit for such sport,
But, harmless wretch, putting in one too small,
The oyster shuts and takes his head withal.
Another bringing one too smooth and round,   195
(Unhappy bird that thine own death hast found)
Lays it so little way in his hard lips,
That with their sudden close, the pebble slips
So strongly forth (as when your little ones
Do 'twixt their fingers slip their cherry-stones),   200
That it in passage meets the breast or head
Of the poor wretch, and lays him there for dead.
A many striv'd, and gladly would have done
As much or more than he which first begun,

But all in vain : scarce one of twenty could   205
Perform the deed, which they full gladly would.
For this not quick is to that act he go'th,
That wanteth skill, this cunning, and some both :
Yet none a will, for from the cave she sees
Not in all-lovely May th' industrious bees   210
More busy with the flowers could be, than these
Among the shell-fish of the working seas.
   Limos had all this while been wanting thence,
And but just Heav'n preserv'd pure innocence
By the two birds, her life to air had flit,   215
Ere the curst caitiff should have forced it.
   The first night that he left her in his den,
He got to shore, and near th' abodes of men
That live as we by tending of their flocks,
To interchange for Ceres' golden locks,   220
Or with the neatherd for his milk and cream,
Things we respect more than the diadem
His choice made-dishes.   O ! the golden age
Met all contentment in no surplusage
Of dainty viands, but, as we do still,   225
Drank the pure water of the crystal rill,
Fed on no other meats than those they fed,
Labour the salad that their stomachs bred.
Nor sought they for the down of silver swans,
Nor those sow-thistle locks each small gale fans, 230
But hides of beasts, which when they liv'd they kept,

222.—*Diadem.* monarch.
224.—*Surplusage,* excess.

Serv'd them for bed and cov'ring when they slept.
If any softer lay, 'twas (by the loss
Of some rock's warmth) on thick and spongy moss,
Or on the ground : some simple wall of clay   235
Parting their beds from where their cattle lay.
And on such pallets one man clipped then
More golden slumbers than this age again.
That time physicians thriv'd not : or, if any,
I dare say all : yet then were thrice as many   240
As now profess't, and more ; for every man
Was his own patient and physician.
None had a body then so weak and thin,
Bankrupt of nature's store, to feed the sin
Of an insatiate female, in whose womb   245
Could nature all hers past, and all to come
Infuse, with virtue of all drugs beside,
She might be tir'd, but never satisfied.
To please which ork her husband's weaken'd piece
Must have his cullis mix'd with ambergris ;   250
Pheasant and partridge into jelly turn'd,
Grated with gold, seven times refin'd and burn'd
With dust of Orient pearl, richer the East
Yet ne'er beheld : (O Epicurean feast !)
This is his breakfast ; and his meal at night   255
Possets no less provoking appetite,

237.—*Clipped*, embraced.
249.—*Ork*, a sea-monster : here employed to signify a prodigy of lust.
250. – *Cullis*, broth.

Whose dear ingredients valu'd are at more
Than all his ancestors were worth before.
When such as we by poor and simple fare
More able liv'd, and died not without heir,   260
Sprung from our own loins, and a spotless bed
Of any other power unseconded :
When th' other's issue, like a man fall'n sick,
Or through the fever, gout, or lunatic,
Changing his doctors oft, each as his notion   265
Prescribes a sev'ral diet, sev'ral potion,
Meeting his friend (who meet we nowadays
That hath not some receipt for each disease ?)
He tells him of a plaister, which he takes ;
And finding after that, his torment slakes,   270
(Whether because the humour is out-wrought,
Or by the skill which his physician brought,
It makes no matter :) for he surely thinks
None of their purges nor their diet drinks
Have made him sound ; but his belief is fast   275
That med'cine was his health which he took last :
So by a mother being taught to call
One for his father, though a son to all,
His mother's often 'scapes, though truly known,
Cannot divert him ; but will ever own   280
For his begetter him, whose name and rents
He must inherit.   Such are the descents
Of these men ; to make up whose limber heir

283.—*Limber,* flabby.

As many as in him must have a share ;
When he that keeps the last yet least ado,   285
Father the people's child, and gladly too.
   Happier those times were when the flaxen clew
By fair Arachne's hand the Lydians knew,
And sought not to the worm for silken threads,
To roll their bodies in, or dress their heads.   290
When wise Minerva did th' Athenians learn
To draw their milk-white fleeces into yarn ;
And knowing not the mixtures which began
(Of colours) from the Babylonian,
Nor wool in Sardis dyed, more various known   295
By hues, than Iris to the world hath shown :
The bowels of our mother were not ripp'd
For madder-pits, nor the sweet meadows stripp'd
Of their choice beauties, nor for Ceres' load
The fertile lands burden'd with needless woad.   300
Through the wide seas no winged pine did go
To lands unknown for staining indico ;
Nor men in scorching climates moor'd their keel
To traffic for the costly cochineal.
Unknown was then the Phrygian broidery,   305
The Tyrian purple, and the scarlet dye,
Such as their sheep clad, such they wove and wore,
Russet or white, or those mix'd, and no more :
Except sometimes (to bravery inclin'd)
They dyed them yellow caps with alder rind.   310

   287.—*Clew*, thread.   302.—*Indico*, indigo.

The Grecian mantle, Tuscan robes of state,
Tissue, nor cloth of gold of highest rate,
They never saw ; only in pleasant woods,
Or by th' embroidered margin of the floods,
The dainty nymphs they often did behold   315
Clad in their light silk robes, stitch'd oft with gold.
The arras hangings round their comely halls
Wanted the cerite's web and minerals :
Green boughs of trees which fatt'ning acorns lade,
Hung full with flowers and garlands quaintly
            made,   320
Their homely cotes deck'd trim in low degree,
As now the court with richest tapestry.
Instead of cushions wrought in windows lain,
They pick'd the cockle from their fields of grain,
Sleep-bringing poppy, by the ploughmen late   325
Not without cause to Ceres consecrate,
For being round and full at his half birth
It signified the perfect orb of earth ;
And by his inequalities when blown,   [330
The earth's low vales and higher hills were shown.
By multitude of grains it held within,
Of men and beasts the number noted been ;
And she since taking care all earth to please,
Had in her Thesmophoria* offer'd these.
Or cause that seed our elders us'd to eat,   335

318.—*Cerite*, a rare mineral of a pale rose-red colour, with a
tinge of yellow.

321.—*Cotes*, cottages.

* Θεσμοφό-
ρια and Δη-
μήτρια were
sacrifices
peculiar to
Ceres, the
one for being
a lawgiver,
the other as
goddess of
the grounds.

With honey mix'd, and was their after meat,
Or since her daughter that she lov'd so well
By him that in th' infernal shades doth dwell,
And on the Stygian banks for ever reigns,
Troubled with horrid cries and noise of chains,   340
Fairest Proserpina, was rapt away ;
And she in plaints the night, in tears the day
Had long time spent, when no high Power could
          give her
Any redress ; the poppy* did relieve her :
For eating of the seeds they sleep procur'd,   345
And so beguil'd those griefs she long endur'd.
Or rather since her love, then happy man,
Micon ycleep'd, the brave Athenian,
Had been transform'd into this gentle flower,
And his protection kept from Flora's power.   350
The daisy scatter'd on each mead and down,
A golden tuft within a silver crown ;
(Fair fall that dainty flower ! and may there be
No shepherd grac'd that doth not honour thee !)
The primrose, when with six leaves gotten grace   355
Maids as a true-love in their bosoms place ;
The spotless lily, by whose pure leaves be
Noted the chaste thoughts of virginity ;
Carnations sweet with colour like the fire,
The fit impresas for inflam'd desire ;   360
The harebell for her stainless azur'd hue

348.—*Ycleep'd*, called.   360.—*Impresas*, devices.

Claims to be worn of none but those are true;
The rose, like ready youth, enticing stands,
And would be cropp'd if it might choose the hands.
The yellow kingcup Flora them assign'd   365
To be the badges of a jealous mind ;
The orange-tawny marigold : the night
Hides not her colour from a searching sight.
To thee then, dearest friend (my song's chief mate),
This colour chiefly I appropriate,   370
That spite of all the mists oblivion can
Or envious frettings of a guilty man,
Retain'st thy worth ; nay, mak'st it more in price,
Like tennis-balls, thrown down hard, highest rise.
The columbine in tawny often taken,   375
Is then ascrib'd to such as are forsaken ;
Flora's choice buttons of a russet dye
Is hope even in the depth of misery.
The pansy, thistle, all with prickles set,
The cowslip, honeysuckle, violet,   380
And many hundreds more that grac'd the meads,
Gardens and groves, where beauteous Flora treads,
Were by the shepherds' daughters (as yet are
Us'd in our cotes) brought home with special care :
For bruising them they not alone would quell   385
But rot the rest, and spoil their pleasing smell.
Much like a lad, who, in his tender prime,
Sent from his friends to learn the use of time,
As are his mates or good or bad, so he
Thrives to the world, and such his actions be.   390

T 2

As in the rainbow's many-colour'd hue,
Here see we watchet deepen'd with a blue :
There a dark tawny with a purple mix'd,
Yellow and flame, with streaks of green betwixt,
A bloody stream into a blushing run,   395
And ends still with the colour which begun ;
Drawing the deeper to a lighter stain,
Bringing the lightest to the deep'st again,
With such rare art each mingleth with his fellow,
The blue with watchet, green and red with yellow ;
Like to the changes which we daily see   · [400
About the dove's neck with variety,
Where none can say (though he it strict attends)
Here one begins, and there the other ends :
So did the maidens with their various flowers   405
Deck up their windows, and make neat their bowers :
Using such cunning as they did dispose
The ruddy piny with the lighter rose,
The monkshood with the bugloss, and entwine
The white, the blue, the flesh-like columbine   410
With pinks, sweet-williams : that far off the eye
Could not the manner of their mixtures spy.
    Then with those flowers they most of all did
            prize,
With all their skill, and in most curious wise
On tufts of herbs and rushes, would they frame   415
A dainty border round their shepherd's name.

392.—*Watchet*, pale blue.   407.—*Piny*, peony.

Or posies make, so quaint, so apt, so rare,
As if the Muses only lived there :
And that the after world should strive in vain
What they then did, to counterfeit again.   420
Nor will the needle nor the loom e'er be
So perfect in their best embroidery,
Nor such composures make of silk and gold,
As theirs, when Nature all her cunning told.

The word of mine did no man then bewitch,   425
They thought none could be fortunate if rich.
And to the covetous did wish no wrong
But what himself desir'd : to live here long.

As of their songs, so of their lives they deem'd :
Not of the long'st, but best perform'd, esteem'd. 430
They thought that Heaven to him no life did
       give,
Who only thought upon the means to live.
Nor wish'd they 'twere ordain'd to live here ever,
But as life was ordain'd they might persever.

O happy men ! you ever did possess   435
No wisdom but was mix'd with simpleness ;
So wanting malice and from folly free,
Since reason went with your simplicity,
You search'd yourselves if all within were fair,
And did not learn of others what you were.   440
Your lives the patterns of those virtues gave,
Which adulation tells men now they have.

With poverty in love we only close,
Because our lovers it most truly shows :

When they who in that blessed age did move,   445
Knew neither poverty nor want of love.
  The hatred which they bore was only this,
That every one did hate to do amiss.
Their fortune still was subject to their will :
Their want (O happy !) was the want of ill.   450
  Ye truest, fairest, loveliest nymphs that can
Out of your eyes lend fire Promethean,
All-beauteous ladies, love-alluring dames,
That on the banks of Isca, Humber, Thames,
By your encouragement can make a swain   455
Climb by his song where none but souls attain :
And by the graceful reading of our lines
Renew our heat to further brave designs :
You, by whose means my Muse thus boldly says :
Though she do sing of shepherds' loves and lays,
And flagging weakly low gets not on wing   [460
To second that of Helen's ravishing :
Nor hath the love nor beauty of a queen
My subject grac'd, as other works have been ;
Yet not to do their age nor ours a wrong,   465
Though queens, nay, goddesses, fam'd Homer's
          song :
Mine hath been tun'd and heard by beauties more
Than all the poets that have liv'd before.
Not 'cause it is more worth, but it doth fall
That Nature now is turn'd a prodigal,   470

451.—*Isca*, the river Exe.   466.—*Fam'd*, made famous.

And on this age so much perfection spends,
That to her last of treasure it extends ;
For all the ages that are slid away
Had not so many beauties as this day.
  O what a rapture have I gotten now !   475
That age of gold, this of the lovely brow
Have drawn me from my song ! I onward run
Clean from the end to which I first begun.
But ye, the heavenly creatures of the West,
In whom the virtues and the graces rest,   480
Pardon ! that I have run astray so long,
And grow so tedious in so rude a song,
If you yourselves should come to add one grace
Unto a pleasant grove or such like place,
Where here the curious cutting of a hedge :   485
There, by a pond, the trimming of the sedge :
Here the fine setting of well-shading trees :
The walks there mounting up by small degrees,
The gravel and the green so equal lie,
It, with the rest, draws on your ling'ring eye :   490
Here the sweet smells that do perfume the air,
Arising from the infinite repair
Of odoriferous buds and herbs of price,
(As if it were another Paradise)
So please the smelling sense, that you are fain   495
Where last you walk'd to turn and walk again.
There the small birds with their harmonious notes

492.—*Repair*, resort.

Sing to a spring that smileth as she floats :
For in her face a many dimples show,
And often skips as it did dancing go :   500
Here further down an over-arched alley,
That from a hill goes winding in a valley,
You spy at end thereof a standing lake,
Where some ingenious artist strives to make
The water (brought in turning pipes of lead   505
Through birds of earth most lively fashioned)
To counterfeit and mock the sylvans all,
In singing well their own set madrigal.
This with no small delight retains your ear,
And makes you think none blest but who live
        there.   510
Then in another place the fruits that be
In gallant clusters decking each good tree,
Invite your hand to crop some from the stem,
And liking one, taste every sort of them :
Then to the arbours walk, then to the bowers,   515
Thence to the walks again, thence to the flowers,
Then to the birds, and to the clear spring thence,
Now pleasing one, and then another sense.
Here one walks oft, and yet anew begin'th,
As if it were some hidden labyrinth ;   520
So loath to part, and so content to stay,
That when the gard'ner knocks for you away,
It grieves you so to leave the pleasures in it,
That you could wish that you had never seen it :
Blame me not then, if while to you I told   525

The happiness our fathers clipt of old,
The mere imagination of their bliss
So rapt my thoughts, and made me sing amiss.
And still the more they ran on those days' worth,
The more unwilling was I to come forth.   530
Oh ! if the apprehension joy us so,
What would the action in a human show ?
Such were the shepherds (to all goodness bent)
About whose thorps* that night curs'd Limos went ;   * Villages.
Where he had learn'd that next day all the swains,
That any sheep fed on the fertile plains,   [535
The feast of Pales, goddess of their grounds,
Did mean to celebrate.   Fitly this sounds,
He thought, to what he formerly intended,
His stealth should by their absence be befriended: 540
For whilst they in their off'rings busied were,
He 'mongst the flocks might range with lesser fear.
How to contrive his stealth he spent the night.

   The morning now in colours richly dight
Stepp'd o'er the Eastern thresholds, and no lad   545
That joy'd to see his pastures freshly clad,
But for the holy rites himself address'd
With necessaries proper to that feast.
   The altars everywhere now smoking be
With bean-stalks, savin, laurel, rosemary,   550
Their cakes of grummell-seed they did prefer,

537.—*Pales*, the goddess of sheepfolds.
550.—*Savin*, a species of juniper.
551.--*Grummell*, more usually gromwell.

And pails of milk in sacrifice to her.
Then hymns of praise they all devoutly sung
In those Palilia for increase of young.
But ere the ceremonies were half past   555
One of their boys came down the hill in haste,
And told them Limos was among their sheep;
That he, his fellows, nor their dogs could keep
The rav'ner from their flocks; great store were kill'd,
Whose blood he suck'd, and yet his paunch not
        fill'd.   560
O hasten then away ! for in an hour
He will the chiefest of your fold devour. ˙
  With this most ran (leaving behind some few
To finish what was to fair Pales due),
And as they had ascended up the hill,   565
Limos they met, with no mean pace and skill
Following a well-fed lamb ; with many a shout
They then pursu'd him all the plain about.
And either with fore-laying of his way,
Or he full gorg'd ran not so swift as they,   570
Before he could recover down the strand,
No swain but on him had a fasten'd hand.
  Rejoicing then (the worst wolf to their flock
Lay in their powers), they bound him to a rock
With chains ta'en from the plough, and leaving
        him   575
Return'd back to their feast.   His eyes late dim

554.—*Palilia*, the festival or rites of Pales.

Now sparkle forth in flames, he grinds his teeth,
And strives to catch at everything he seeth ;
But to no purpose : all the hope of food
Was ta'en away ; his little flesh, less blood,   580
He suck'd and tore at last, and that denied,
With fearful shrieks most miserably died.
   Unfortunate Marina, thou art free
From his jaws now, though not from misery.
Within the cave thou likely art to pine,   585
If (O may never) fail a help divine,
And though such aid thy wants do still supply,
Yet in a prison thou must ever lie.
But Heav'n, that fed thee, will not long defer
To send thee thither some deliverer :   590
For than to spend thy sighs there to the main
Thou fitter wert to honour Thetis' train :
Who so far now with her harmonious crew
Scour'd through the seas (O who yet ever knew
So rare a concert ?) she had left behind   595
The Kentish, Sussex shores, the Isle* assigned
To brave Vespasian's conquest, and was come
Where the shrill trumpet and the rattling drum
Made the waves tremble (ere befell this chance)
And to no softer music us'd to dance.   600
   Hail, thou my native soil ! thou blessed plot
Whose equal all the world affordeth not !
Show me who can so many crystal rills,

* Vecta quam Vespasianus a Claudio missus subjugavit. *Vide* Bed. in Hist. Ecc. lib. i. ca. 3.

596.—*The Isle*, Isle of Wight.

Such sweet-cloth'd valleys or aspiring hills ; [605
Such wood-ground, pastures, quarries, wealthy mines ;
Such rocks in whom the diamond fairly shines ;
And if the earth can show the like again,
Yet will she fail in her sea-ruling men.
Time never can produce men to o'ertake
The fames of Grenville, Davies, Gilbert, Drake, 610
Or worthy Hawkins, or of thousands more
That by their power made the Devonian shore
Mock the proud Tagus ; for whose richest spoil
The boasting Spaniard left the Indian soil
Bankrupt of store, knowing it would quit cost 615
By winning this, though all the rest were lost.
   As oft the sea-nymphs on her strand have set,
Learning of fishermen to knit a net,
Wherein to wind up their dishevell'd hairs,
They have beheld the frolic mariners 620
For exercise (got early from their beds)
Pitch bars of silver, and cast golden sleds.
   At Exe a lovely nymph with Thetis met :
She singing came, and was all round beset
With other wat'ry powers, which by her song 625
She had allur'd to float with her along.
The lay she chanted she had learn'd of yore,
Taught by a skilful swain,* who on her shore
Fed his fair flock : a work renown'd as far
As his brave subject of the Trojan war. 630

* Joseph of Exeter wrote a poem of the Trojan War according to Dares the Phrygian's story, but falsely attributed to Cornelius Nepos, as it is printed. He lived in the time of Hen. 2, and Rich. 1. See the illustrations of my most worthy friend, M. Selden, upon M. Drayton's Polyolbion, p. 98.

622.—*Sleds*, sledge-hammers.

When she had done, a pretty shepherd's boy
That from the near Downs came (though he small joy
Took in his tuneful reed, since dire neglect
Crept to the breast of her he did affect,
And that an ever-busy-watchful eye   635
Stood as a bar to his felicity),
Being with great entreaties of the swains,
And by the fair queen of the liquid plains
Woo'd to his pipe, and bade to lay aside
All troubled thoughts, as others at that tide,   640
And that he now some merry note should raise,
To equal others which had sung their lays :
He shook his head, and knowing that his tongue
Could not belie his heart, thus sadly sung :

As new-born babes salute their ages' morn   645
With cries unto their woful mother hurl'd :
My infant Muse, that was but lately born,
Began with wat'ry eyes to woo the world.
She knows not how to speak, and therefore weeps
   Her woe's excess,   650
And strives to move the heart that senseless sleeps,
   To heaviness ;
  Her eyes enveil'd with sorrow's clouds
   Scarce see the light,
  Disdain hath wrapt her in the shrouds   655
   Of loathed night.
How should she move then her grief-laden wing,
Or leave my sad complaints, and pæans sing ?

Six Pleiads live in light, in darkness one.
Sing, mirthful swains, but let me sigh alone.   66o

It is enough that I in silence sit,
And bend my skill to learn your lays aright ;
Nor strive with you in ready strains of wit,
Nor move my hearers with so true delight.
But if for heavy plaints and notes of woe   665
        Your ears are prest ;
No shepherd lives that can my pipe outgo
        In such unrest.
    I have not known so many years
        As chances wrong,   67o
    Nor have they known more floods of tears
        From one so young.
Fain would I tune to please as others do,
Were't not for feigning song and numbers too.
Then (since not fitting now are songs of moan) 675
Sing, mirthful swains, but let me sigh alone.

The nymphs that float upon these wat'ry plains
Have oft been drawn to listen to my song,
And sirens left to tune dissembling strains
In true bewailing of my sorrows long.   68o

659.—*In darkness one*, Electra.

666.—*Prest*, ready.

Upon the waves of late a silver swan
    By me did ride ;
And thrilled with my woes forthwith began
    To sing, and died.
    Yet where they should, they cannot move. 685
      O hapless verse !
    That fitter than to win a love
      Art for a hearse.
Henceforward silent be ; and ye my cares
Be known but to myself, or who despairs ;   690
Since pity now lies turned to a stone.
Sing, mirthful swains, but let me sigh alone.

The fitting accent of his mournful lay
So pleas'd the pow'rful Lady of the Sea,
That she entreated him to sing again ;   695
And he obeying tun'd this second strain :

Born to no other comfort than my tears,
Yet robb'd of them by griefs too inly deep,
I cannot rightly wail my hapless years,
Nor move a passion that for me might weep.   700
    Nature, alas ! too short hath knit
      My tongue to reach my woe :
    Nor have I skill sad notes to fit
      That might my sorrow show.
And to increase my torments' ceaseless sting, 705

698.—*Inly*, inwardly.

There's no way left to show my pains,
But by my pen in mournful strains,
Which others may perhaps take joy to sing.

As (woo'd by May's delights) I have been borne
To take the kind air of a wistful morn   710
Near Tavy's voiceful stream (to whom I owe
More strains than from my pipe can ever flow),
Here have I heard a sweet bird never lin
To chide the river for his clam'rous din;
There seem'd another in his song to tell,   715
That what the fair stream did he liked well;
And going further heard another too,
All varying still in what the others do;
A little thence, a fourth with little pain
Conn'd all their lessons, and them sung again;   720
So numberless the songsters are that sing
In the sweet groves of the too-careless spring,
That I no sooner could the hearing lose
Of one of them, but straight another rose,
And perching deftly on a quaking spray,   725
Nigh tir'd herself to make her hearer stay;
Whilst in a bush two nightingales together
Show'd the best skill they had to draw me thither:
So (as bright Thetis pass'd our cleeves along)
This shepherd's lay pursu'd the others' song,   730
And scarce one ended had his skilful stripe,
But straight another took him to his pipe.

713.—*Lin*, cease.   729.—*Cleeves*, cliffs.   731.—*Stripe*, strain.

By that the younger swain had fully done,
Thetis with her brave company had won
The   mouth   of   Dart,   and   whilst   the   Tritons
        charm   735
The dancing waves, passing the crystal Earme,
Sweet Yealm and Plym, arriv'd where Tamar pays
Her daily tribute to the western seas.
Here sent she up her dolphins, and they plied
So busily their fares on every side,   740
They made a quick return, and brought her down
A many homagers to Tamar's crown,
Who in themselves were of as great command
As any meaner rivers of the land.
With every nymph the swain of most account   745
That fed his white sheep by her clearer fount :
And every one to Thetis sweetly sung.
   Among the rest a shepherd (though but young,
Yet hearten'd to his pipe) with all the skill
His few years could, began to fit his quill.   750
By Tavy's speedy stream he fed his flock,
Where when he sat to sport him on a rock,
The water-nymphs would often come unto him,
And for a dance with many gay gifts woo him.
Now posies of this flower, and then of that ;   755
Now with fine shells, then with a rushy hat.
With coral or red stones brought from the deep
To make him bracelets, or to mark his sheep :

749.—*Hearten'd*, wedded or attached heartily.

Willy he hight.   Who by the ocean's queen
More cheer'd to sing than such young lads had
      been,   760
Took his best framed pipe, and thus 'gan move
His voice of Walla, Tavy's fairest love :

Fair was the day, but fairer was the maid
Who that day's morn into the greenwoods stray'd.
Sweet was the air, but sweeter was her breath-
      ing,   765
Such rare perfumes the roses are bequeathing.
Bright shone the sun, but brighter were her eyes,
Such are the lamps that guide the deities ;
Nay such the fire is, whence the Pythian knight
Borrows his beams, and lends his sister light.   770
Not Pelops' shoulder whiter than her hands,
Nor snowy swans that jet on Isca's sands.
Sweet Flora, as if ravish'd with their sight,
In emulation made all lilies white :
For as I oft have heard the wood-nymphs say,   775
The dancing fairies, when they left to play,
Then back did pull them, and in holes of trees
Stole the sweet honey from the painful bees ;
Which in the flower to put they oft were seen,
And for a banquet brought it to their queen.   780

762.—*Walla. See* Note.
772 —*Jet*, strut.   *Isca*, the river Exe.
776.—*Left to play*, ceased playing.

But she that is the goddess of the flowers
(Invited to their groves and shady bowers)
Mislik'd   their   choice.   They said   that   all   the
         field
No other flower did for that purpose yield;
But quoth a nimble fay that by did stand :   785
If you could give 't the colour of yond hand,
(Walla by chance was in a meadow by
Learning to sample earth's embroidery.)
It were a gift would Flora well befit,
And our great queen the more would honour it.   790
She gave consent ; and by some other power
Made Venus' doves be equall'd by the flower,
But not her hand ; for Nature this prefers :
All other whites but shadowings to hers.
Her hair was roll'd in many a curious fret,   795
Much like a rich and artful coronet,
Upon whose arches twenty Cupids lay,
And were or tied, or loath to fly away.
Upon her bright eyes Phœbus his inclin'd,
And by their radiance was the god struck blind, 800
That clean awry th' ecliptic then he stripp'd
And from the milky way his horses whipp'd ;
So that the Eastern world to fear begun
Some stranger drove the chariot of the sun.
And never but that once did heaven's bright eye 805
Bestow one look on the Cimmerii.
A green silk frock her comely shoulders clad,
And took delight that such a seat it had,

u 2

Which at her middle gather'd up in pleats,
A love-knot girdle willing bondage threats.   810
Not Venus' ceston held a braver piece,
Nor that which girt the fairest flower of Greece.
Down from her waist her mantle loose did fall,
Which Zephyr (as afraid) still play'd withal,
And then tuck'd up somewhat below the knee   815
Show'd searching eyes where Cupid's columns be.
The inside lin'd with rich carnation silk,
And in the midst of both, lawn white as milk,
Which white beneath the red did seem to shroud,
As Cynthia's beauty through a blushing cloud.   820
About the edges curious to behold
A deep fringe hung of rich and twisted gold,
So on the green marge of a crystal brook
A thousand yellow flowers at fishes look ;
And such the beams are of the glorious sun,   825
That through a tuft of grass dispersed run.
Upon her leg a pair of buskins white,
Studded with orient pearl and chrysolite,
And like her mantle stitch'd with gold and green,
(Fairer yet never wore the forest's queen)   830
Knit close with ribbons of a party hue,
A knot of crimson and a tuft of blue ;
Nor can the peacock in his spotted train

811.—*Ceston*, cestus, a studded girdle.
812.—*Fairest flower of Greece*, Helen.
828.—*Chrysolite*, a stone of a green colour.

So many pleasing colours show again ;
Nor could there be a mixture with more grace,   835
Except the heav'nly roses in her face.
A silver quiver at her back she wore,
With darts and arrows for the stag and boar,
But in her eyes she had such darts again   [840
Could conquer gods, and wound the hearts of
        men.
Her left hand held a knotty Brazil bow,
Whose strength with tears she made the red deer
        know.
So clad, so arm'd, so dress'd to win her will
Diana never trod on Latmus' hill.
Walla, the fairest nymph that haunts the woods, 845
Walla, belov'd of shepherds, fawns, and floods,
Walla, for whom the frolic satyrs pine,
Walla, with whose fine foot the flow'rets twine,
Walla, of whom sweet birds their ditties move,
Walla, the earth's delight, and Tavy's love.   850
    This fairest nymph, when Tavy first prevail'd
And won affection where the sylvans fail'd,
Had promis'd (as a favour to his stream)
Each week to crown it with an anadem :
And now Hyperion from his glitt'ring throne   855
Sev'n times his quick'ning rays had bravely shown
Unto the other world, since Walla last
Had on her Tavy's head the garland plac'd ;

854.—*Anadem*, garland.

And this day (as of right) she wends abroad
To ease the meadows of their willing load.   860
Flora, as if to welcome her, those hours
Had been most lavish of her choicest flowers,
Spreading more beauties to entice that morn
Than she had done in many days beforn.

   Look as a maiden sitting in the shade   865
Of some close arbour by the woodbind made,
Withdrawn alone where undescri'd she may
By her most curious needle give assay
Unto some purse (if so her fancy move)
Or other token for her truest love ;   870
Variety of silk about her pap,
Or in a box she takes upon her lap,
Whose pleasing colours wooing her quick eye,
Now this she thinks the ground would beautify,
And that, to flourish with, she deemeth best ;   875
When spying others, she is straight possess'd
Those fittest are ; yet from that choice doth fall,
And she resolves at last to use them all :
So Walla, which to gather long time stood,
Whether those of the field, or of the wood,   880
Or those that 'mong the springs and marish lay ;
But then the blossoms which enrich'd each spray
Allur'd her look ; whose many-colour'd graces
Did in her garland challenge no mean places :
And therefore she (not to be poor in plenty)   885

881.—*Marish,* marsh.

From meadows, springs, woods, sprays, culls some
   one dainty,
Which in a scarf she put, and onwards set
To find a place to dress her coronet.
 A little grove is seated on the marge
Of Tavy's stream, not over-thick nor large,   890
Where every morn a choir of sylvans sung,
And leaves to chatt'ring winds serv'd as a tongue,
By whom the water turns in many a ring,
As if it fain would stay to hear them sing;
And on the top a thousand young birds fly,   895
To be instructed in their harmony.
Near to the end of this all-joysome grove
A dainty circled plot seem'd as it strove
To keep all briars and bushes from invading
Her pleasing compass by their needless shading, 900
Since it was not so large, but that the store
Of trees around could shade her breast and more.
In midst thereof a little swelling hill,
Gently disburden'd of a crystal rill
Which from the greenside of the flow'ry bank 905
Ate down a channel; here the wood-nymphs drank,
And great Diana having slain the deer,
Did often use to come and bathe her here.
Here talk'd they of their chase, and where next day
They meant to hunt; here did the shepherds play, 910
And many a gaudy nymph was often seen

911.—*Gaudy,* gay.

Embracing shepherds' boys upon this green.
From hence the spring hastes down to Tavy's brim,
And pays a tribute of his drops to him.
　　Here Walla rests the rising mount upon,　　915
That seem'd to swell more since she sat thereon,
And from her scarf upon the grass shook down
The smelling flowers that should her river crown :
The scarf (in shaking it) she brushed oft,
Whereon were flowers so fresh and lively wrought, 920
That her own cunning was her own deceit,
Thinking those true which were but counterfeit.
　　Under an alder on his sandy marge
Was Tavy set to view his nimble charge,
And there his love he long time had expected :　925
While many a rose-cheek'd nymph no wile neglected
To woo him to embraces ; which he scorn'd,
As valuing more the beauties which adorn'd
His fairest Walla, than all Nature's pride
Spent on the cheeks of all her sex beside.　　930
Now would they tempt him with their open breasts,
And swear their lips were love's assured tests :
That Walla sure would give him the denial
Till she had known him true by such a trial.
Then comes another, and her hand bereaves　935
The soon slipp'd alder of two clammy leaves,
And clapping them together, bids him see
And learn of love the hidden mystery.
Brave flood (quoth she) that hold'st us in suspense,
And show'st a godlike power in abstinence,　　940

At this thy coldness we do nothing wonder,
These leaves did so, when once they grew asunder;
But since the one did taste the other's bliss,
And felt his partner's kind partake with his,
Behold how close they join; and had they power 945
To speak their now content, as we can our,
They would on Nature lay a heinous crime
For keeping close such sweets until this time.
Is there to such men ought of merit due,
That do abstain from what they never knew?   950
No: then as well we may account him wise
For speaking nought, who wants those faculties.
Taste thou our sweets; come here and freely sip
Divinest nectar from my melting lip;
Gaze on mine eyes, whose life-infusing beams   955
Have power to melt the icy northern streams,
And so inflame the gods of those bound seas
They should unchain their virgin passages,
And teach our mariners from day to day
To bring us jewels by a nearer way.   960
Twine thy long fingers in my shining hair,
And think it no disgrace to hide them there;
For I could tell thee how the Paphian queen
Met me one day upon yond pleasant green,
And did entreat a slip (though I was coy)   965
Wherewith to fetter her lascivious boy.
Play with my teats that swell to have impression;
And if thou please from thence to make digression,
Pass thou that milky way where great Apollo

And higher powers than he would gladly follow. 970
When to the full of these thou shalt attain,
It were some mast'ry for thee to refrain;
But since thou know'st not what such pleasures be
The world will not commend but laugh at thee.
But thou wilt say, thy Walla yields such store   975
Of joys, that no one love can raise thee more;
Admit it so, as who but thinks it strange?
Yet shalt thou find a pleasure more, in change.
If that thou lik'st not, gentle flood, but hear:
To prove that state the best I never fear.   980
Tell me wherein the state and glory is
Of thee, of Avon, or brave Thamesis?
In your own springs? or by the flowing head
Of some such river only seconded?
Or is it through the multitude that do   985
Send down their waters to attend on you?
Your mixture with less brooks adds to your fames,
So long as they in you do lose their names:
And coming to the ocean, thou dost see,
It takes in other floods as well as thee;   990
It were no sport to us that hunting love
If we were still confin'd to one large grove.
The water which in one pool hath abiding
Is not so sweet as rillets ever gliding.
Nor would the brackish waves in whom you
      meet   995
Contain that state it doth, but be less sweet,
And with contagious streams all mortals smother,

But that it moves from this shore to the other.
There's no one season such delight can bring,
As summer, autumn, winter, and the spring.   1000
Nor the best flower that doth on earth appear
Could by itself content us all the year.
The salmons, and some more as well as they,
Now love the freshet, and then love the sea.
The flitting fowls not in one coast do tarry,   1005
But with the year their habitation vary.
What music is there in a shepherd's quill
(Play'd on by him that hath the greatest skill)
If but a stop or two thereon we spy?
Music is best in her variety.   1010
So is discourse, so joys ; and why not then
As well the lives and loves of gods as men?
   More she had spoke, but that the gallant flood
Replied : ye wanton rangers of the wood,
Leave your allurements ; hie ye to your chase ;   1015
See where Diana with a nimble pace
Follows a struck deer : if you longer stay
Her frown will bend to me another day.
Hark how she winds her horn ; she some doth
         call,
Perhaps for you, to make into the fall.   1020
   With this they left him. Now he wonders
         much
Why at this time his Walla's stay was such,
And could have wish'd the nymphs back, but for
         fear

IIis love might come and chance to find them
    there.
To pass the time at last he thus began   1025
(Unto a pipe join'd by the art of Pan)
To praise his love : his hasty waves among
The frothed rocks, bearing the under-song :

As careful merchants do expecting stand,
After long time and merry gales of wind,   1030
Upon the place where their brave ship must land :
So wait I for the vessel of my mind.

Upon a great adventure is it bound,
Whose safe return will valu'd be at more   [1035
Than all the wealthy prizes which have crown'd
The golden wishes of an age before.

Out of the East jewels of worth she brings ;
Th' unvalu'd diamond of her sparkling eye
Wants in the treasures of all Europe's kings ;
And were it mine they nor their crowns should
    buy.   1040

The sapphires ringed on her panting breast
Run as rich veins of ore about the mould,
And are in sickness with a pale possess'd,
So true ; for them I should disvalue gold.

1023.—*Under-song*, burden.

The melting rubies on her cherry lip   1045
Are of such power to hold, that as one day
Cupid flew thirsty by, he stoop'd to sip,
And fasten'd there could never get away.

The sweets of Candy are no sweets to me
When hers I taste ; nor the perfumes of price 1050
Robb'd from the happy shrubs of Araby,
As her sweet breath, so powerful to entice.

O hasten then ! and if thou be not gone
Unto that wished traffic through the main,
My powerful sighs shall quickly drive thee on, 1055
And then begin to draw thee back again.

If in the mean rude waves have it oppress'd,
It shall suffice I ventur'd at the best.

Scarce had he given a period to his lay
When from a wood (wherein the eye of day   1060
Had long a stranger been, and Phœbe's light
Vainly contended with the shades of night,)
One of those wanton nymphs that woo'd him
          late
Came crying tow'rds him ; O thou most ingrate,
Respectless flood ! canst thou here idly sit,   1065
And loose desires to looser numbers fit ?
Teaching the air to court thy careless brook,
Whilst thy poor Walla's cries the hills have shook

With an amazed terror : hear ! O hear !
A hundred echoes shrieking everywhere !   1070
See how the frightful herds run from the wood !
Walla, alas ! as she, to crown her flood,
Attended the composure of sweet flowers,
Was by a lust-fir'd satyr 'mong our bowers
Well-near surpris'd, but that she him descri'd   1075
Before his rude embracement could betide.
Now but her feet no help, unless her cries
A needful aid draw from the deities.
  It needless was to bid the flood pursue :
Anger gave wings ; ways that he never knew   1080
Till now, he treads ; through dells and hidden brakes
Flies through the meadows, each where overtakes
Streams swiftly gliding, and them brings along
To further just revenge for so great wrong.
His current till that day was never known,   1085
But as a mead in July, which unmown
Bears in an equal height each bent and stem,
Unless some gentle gale do play with them.
Now runs it with such fury and such rage,
That mighty rocks opposing vassalage   1090
Are from the firm earth rent and overborne
In fords where pebbles lay secure beforn.
Lo'd cataracts, and fearful roarings now
Affright the passenger ; upon his brow
Continual bubbles like compelled drops,   1095

1071.—*Frightful,* frightened.

And where (as now and then) he makes short
    stops
In little pools drowning his voice too high,
'Tis where he thinks he hears his Walla cry.
Yet vain was all his haste, bending away,
Too much declining to the Southern Sea,   1100
Since she had turned thence, and now begun
To cross the brave path of the glorious sun.
    There lies a vale extended to the north
Of Tavy's stream, which (prodigal) sends forth
In autumn more rare fruits than have been spent 1105
In any greater plot of fruitful Kent.
Two high-brow'd rocks on either side begin,
As with an arch to close the valley in :
Upon their rugged fronts short writhen oaks
Untouch'd of any feller's baneful strokes :   1110
The ivy twisting round their barks hath fed
Past time wild goats which no man followed.
Low in the valley some small herds of deer,
For head and footmanship withouten peer,   [1115
Fed undisturb'd.   The swains that thereby thriv'd
By the tradition from their sires deriv'd,
Call'd it sweet Ina's Coombe : but whether she
Were of the earth or greater progeny,
Judge by her deeds ; once this is truly known
She many a time hath on a bugle blown,   1120

1109.—*Writhen*, twisted.

1117.—*Ina's Coombe*, Inexcombe, or Inscoombe, about a mile
and a half from Tavistock.

And through the dale pursu'd the jolly chase,
As she had bid the winged winds a base.
  Pale and distracted hither Walla runs,
As closely follow'd as she hardly shuns ;
Her mantle off, her hair now too unkind   1125
Almost betray'd her with the wanton wind.
Breathless and faint she now some drops discloses,
As in a limbeck the kind sweat of roses,
Such hang upon her breast, and on her cheeks ;[1130
Or like the pearls which the tann'd Æthiop seeks.
The satyr (spurr'd with lust) still getteth ground,
And longs to see his damn'd intention crown'd.
  As when a greyhound of the rightest strain
Let slip to some poor hare upon the plain,
He for his prey strives, th' other for her life,   1135
And one of these or none must end the strife ;
Now seems the dog by speed and good at bearing
To have her sure ; the other ever fearing
Maketh a sudden turn, and doth defer
The hound a while from so near reaching her :   1140
Yet being fetch'd again and almost ta'en,
Doubting (since touch'd of him) she 'scapes her bane :
So of these two the minded races were,
For hope the one made swift, the other fear.
  O if there be a power (quoth Walla then,   1145
Keeping her earnest course) o'erswaying men

1122.—*Base*, the game of prisoner's bars.
1128.—*Limbeck*, still.
1142.—*Bane*, doom.

And their desires ! O let it now be shown
Upon this satyr half part earthly known.
What I have hitherto with so much care
Kept undefiled, spotless, white and fair,   1150
What in all speech of love I still reserv'd,
And from its hazard ever gladly swerv'd ;
O be it now untouch'd ! and may no force
That happy jewel from myself divorce !
I that have ever held all women be   1155
Void of all worth if wanting chastity ;
And whoso any lets that best flower pull,
She might be fair, but never beautiful :
O let me not forgo it ! strike me dead !
Let on these rocks my limbs be scattered !   1160
Burn me to ashes with some powerful flame,
And in mine own dust bury mine own name,
Rather than let me live and be defil'd.
   Chastest Diana ! in the deserts wild,
Have I so long thy truest handmaid been ?   1165
Upon the rough rock-ground thine arrows keen,
Have I (to make thee crowns) been gath'ring still
Fair-cheek'd Etesia's yellow camomile ?
And sitting by thee on our flow'ry beds   [1170
Knit thy torn buckstalls with well-twisted threads,
To be forsaken ? O now present be,
If not to save, yet help to ruin me !
   If pure virginity have heretofore

1170.—*Buckstalls*, nets for catching deer.

By the Olympic powers been honour'd more
Than other states; and gods have been dis-
      pos'd   1175
To make them known to us, and still disclos'd
To the chaste hearing of such nymphs as we
Many a secret and deep mystery;
If none can lead without celestial aid
Th' immaculate and pure life of a maid,   1180
O let not then the Powers all-good, divine,
Permit vile lust to soil this breast of mine!
   Thus cried she as she ran: and looking back
Whether her hot pursuer did ought slack
His former speed, she spies him not at all,   1185
And somewhat thereby cheer'd 'gan to recall
Her nigh-fled hopes: yet fearing he might lie
Near some cross path to work his villainy,
And being weary, knowing it was vain
To hope for safety by her feet again,   1190
She sought about where she herself might hide.
   A hollow vaulted rock at last she spied,
About whose sides so many bushes were,
She thought securely she might rest her there.
Far under it a cave, whose entrance straight   1195
Clos'd with a stone-wrought door of no mean
      weight;
Yet from itself the gemels beaten so
That little strength could thrust it to and fro.

1197.—*Gemels*, hinges.

Thither she came, and being gotten in
Barr'd fast the dark cave with an iron pin.   1200
  The satyr follow'd, for his cause of stay
Was not a mind to leave her, but the way
Sharp-ston'd and thorny, where he pass'd of late,
Had cut his cloven foot, and now his gait
Was not so speedy, yet by chance he sees   1205
Through some small glade that ran between the
          trees
Where Walla went, and with a slower pace,
Fir'd with hot blood, at last attain'd the place.
  When like a fearful hare within her form,   [1210
Hearing the hounds come like a threat'ning storm,
In full cry on the walk where last she trod,
Doubts to stay there, yet dreads to go abroad :
So Walla far'd.   But since he was come nigh,
And by an able strength and industry
Sought to break in, with tears anew she fell   1215
To urge the Powers that on Olympus dwell.
And then to Ina call'd : O if the rooms,
The walks and arbours in these fruitful coombes
Have famous been through all the Western plains
In being guiltless of the lasting stains   1220
Pour'd on by lust and murder : keep them free !
Turn me to stone, or to a barked tree,
Unto a bird, or flower, or ought forlorn ;   ·
So I may die as pure as I was born.
" Swift are the prayers and of speedy haste,   1225
That take their wing from hearts so pure and chaste.

And what we ask of Heaven it still appears
More plain to it in mirrors of our tears."
Approv'd in Walla.   When the satyr rude
Had broke the door in two, and 'gan intrude   1230
With steps profane into that sacred cell,
Where oft (as I have heard our shepherds tell)
Fair Ina us'd to rest from Phœbus' ray :
She or some other having heard her pray,
Into a fountain turn'd her ; and now rise   1235
Such streams out of the cave, that they surprise
The satyr with such force and so great din,
That quenching his life's flame as well as sin,
They roll'd him through the dale with mighty roar
And made him fly that did pursue before.   1240
    Not far beneath i' the valley as she trends
Her silver stream, some wood-nymphs and her friends
That follow'd to her aid, beholding how
A brook came gliding, where they saw but now
Some herds were feeding, wond'ring whence it
      came :   1245
Until a nymph that did attend the game
In that sweet valley, all the process told,
Which from a thick-leav'd tree she did behold :
See, quoth the nymph, where the rude satyr lies
Cast on the grass, as if she did despise   1250
To have her pure waves soil'd with such as he :
Retaining still the love of purity.

1241.—*Trends*, bends, an uncommon word even in Devonshire.

To Tavy's crystal stream her waters go,
As if some secret power ordained so,
And as a maid she lov'd him, so a brook   1255
To his embracements only her betook.
Where growing on with him, attain'd the state
Which none but Hymen's bonds can imitate.
  On Walla's brook her sisters now bewail,
For whom the rocks spend tears when others fail, 1260
And all the woods ring with their piteous moans :
Which Tavy hearing as he chid the stones,
That stopp'd his speedy course, raising his head
Inquir'd the cause, and thus was answered :
Walla is now no more.   Nor from the hill   1265
Will she more pluck for thee the daffodil,
Nor make sweet anadems to gird thy brow,
Yet in the groves she runs, a river now.
  Look as the feeling plant* (which learned swains   * Sentida.
Relate to grow on the East Indian plains)   1270
Shrinks up his dainty leaves, if any sand
You throw thereon, or touch it with your hand :
So with the chance the heavy wood-nymphs told,
The river (inly touch'd) began to fold
His arms across, and while the torrent raves,   1275
Shrunk his grave head beneath his silver waves.
  Since when he never on his banks appears
But as one frantic : when the clouds spend tears

1269.—*Feeling plant*, sensitive plant.
1273.—*Chance*, mishap.
1274.—*Inly*, inwardly, to the very depths.

He thinks they of his woes compassion take,
(And not a spring but weeps for Walla's sake)   1280
And then he often, to bemoan her lack,
Like to a mourner goes, his waters black,
And every brook attending in his way,
For that time meets him in the like array.
    Here Willy that time ceas'd ; and I a while :   1285
For yonder's Roget coming o'er the stile ;
'Tis two days since I saw him (and you wonder,
You'll say, that we have been so long asunder).
I think the lovely herdess of the dell
That to an oaten quill can sing so well,   1290
Is she that's with him : I must needs go meet them,
And if some other of you rise to greet them
'Twere not amiss, the day is now so long
That I ere night may end another song.

1290.—Quill, pipe.

THE FOURTH SONG.

———

THE ARGUMENT.

The Cornish swains and British bard
Thetis hath with attention heard.
And after meets an aged man
That tells the hapless love of Pan:
And why the flocks do live so free
From wolves within rich Britanny.

———

LOOK as a lover with a ling'ring kiss
About to part with the best half that's his,
Fain would he stay but that he fears to do it,
And curseth time for so fast hast'ning to it :
Now takes his leave, and yet begins anew   5
To make less vows than are esteemed true :
Then says he must be gone, and then doth find
Something he should have spoke that's out of mind ;
And whilst he stands to look for't in her eyes,
Their sad-sweet glance so tie his faculties   10
To think from what he parts, that he is now
As far from leaving her, or knowing how,

As when he came ; begins his former strain,
To kiss, to vow, and take his leave again :
Then turns, comes back, sighs, parts, and yet doth
    go,   15
Apt to retire, and loath to leave her sc.
Brave stream, so part I from thy flow'ry bank,
Where first I breath'd, and, though unworthy, drank
Those sacred waters which the Muses bring
To woo Britannia to their ceaseless spring.   20

Vide de amœ- Now would I on, but that the crystal wells,
nitate loci.
Malmesb. 2. The fertile meadows and their pleasing smells,
lib. de gest. The woods delightful and the scatter'd groves,
Pontif. fo.
146. Where many nymphs walk with their chaster loves,

* Ordulphus. Soon make me stay : and think that Ordgar's* son, 25
Admonish'd by a heavenly vision,
Not without cause did that apt fabric rear,
Wherein we nothing now but echoes hear
That wont with heavenly anthems daily ring
And duest praises to the greatest King,   30
In this choice plot, since he could light upon
No place so fit for contemplation.
Though I awhile must leave this happy soil,
And follow Thetis in a pleasing toil,
Yet when I shall return, I'll strive to draw   35
The nymphs by Tamar, Tavy, Exe and Taw,
By Turridge, Otter, Ock, by Dart and Plym,
With all the naiades that fish and swim

27.—*That apt fabric*, Tavistock Abbey. *See* Note.

In their clear streams, to these our rising Downs,
Where while they make us chaplets, wreaths and
    crowns,   40
I'll tune my reed unto a higher key,
And have already conn'd some of the lay,
Wherein, as Mantua by her Virgil's birth,
And Thames by him that sung her nuptial mirth,
You may be known, though not in equal pride,   45
As far as Tiber throws his swelling tide.
And by a shepherd, feeding on your plains,
In humble, lowly, plain, and ruder strains,
Hear your worths challenge other floods among,
To have a period equal with their song.   50
    Where Plym and Tamar with embraces meet,
Thetis weighs anchor now, and all her fleet :
Leaving that spacious sound,* within whose arms * Plym
I have those vessels seen, whose hot alarms   mouth.
Have made Iberia tremble, and her towers   55
Prostrate themselves before our iron showers ;
While their proud builders' hearts have been
    inclin'd
To shake, as our brave ensigns, with the wind.
For as an eyerie from their siege's wood
Led o'er the plains and taught to get their food 60
By seeing how their breeder takes his prey ;

44.—*Him that sung*, Spenser, in the *Faëry Queen*, B. iv. c. 11.
55.—*Iberia*, Spain.
58.—*Ensigns*, flags.
59.—*Eyerie*, young brood.   *Siege*, a company of herons.

Now from an orchard do they scare the jay,
Then o'er the cornfields as they swiftly fly,
Where many thousand hurtful sparrows lie
Beating the ripe grain from the bearded ear,   65
At their approach all (overgone with fear)
Seek for their safety : some into the dike,
Some in the hedges drop, and others like
The thick-grown corn as for their hiding best,
And under turfs or grass most of the rest ;   70
That of a flight which cover'd all the grain,
Not one appears, but all or hid, or slain :
So by heröes were we led of yore,
And by our drums that thunder'd on each shore,
Struck with amazement countries far and near ; 75
Whilst their inhabitants, like herds of deer
By kingly lions chas'd, fled from our arms.
If any did oppose instructed swarms
Of men immail'd, Fate drew them on to be
A greater fame to our got victory.   80
   But now our leaders want ; those vessels lie
Rotting, like houses through ill husbandry ;
And on their masts, where oft the ship-boy stood,
Or silver trumpets charm'd the brackish flood,
Some wearied crow is set ; and daily seen   85
Their sides instead of pitch caulk'd o'er with
       green :
Ill hap (alas) have you that once were known
By reaping what was by Iberia sown,
By bringing yellow sheaves from out their plain,

Making our barns the storehouse for their grain : 90
When now as if we wanted land to till,
Wherewith we might our useless soldiers fill :
Upon their hatches where half-pikes were borne,
In every chink rise stems of bearded corn :
Mocking our idle times that so have wrought us, 95
Or putting us in mind what once they brought
       us.
Bear with me, shepherds, if I do digress,
And speak of what ourselves do not profess.
Can I behold a man that in the field,
Or at a breach hath taken on his shield   100
More darts than ever Roman* ; that hath spent   * M. Scæva.
Many a cold December in no tent
But such as earth and heaven make ; that hath been
Except in iron plates not long time seen ;
Upon whose body may be plainly told   105
More wounds than his lank purse doth almsdeeds
      hold ;
O ! can I see this man, advent'ring all,
Be only grac'd with some poor hospital,
Or may be worse, entreating at his door
For some relief whom he secur'd before,   110
And yet not show my grief ? First may I learn
To see, and yet forget how to discern ;
My hands neglectful be at any need,
Or to defend my body, or to feed,

106.—*Almsdeeds*, money bestowed in charity.

Ere I respect those times that rather give him   115
Hundreds to punish than one to relieve him.
As in an evening when the gentle air
Breathes to the sullen night a soft repair,
I oft have sat on Thames' sweet bank to hear   [120
My friend with his sweet touch to charm mine
        ear,
When he hath play'd, as well he can, some strain
That likes me, straight I ask the same again ;
And he as gladly granting, strikes it o'er
With some sweet relish was forgot before,
I would have been content if he would play   125
In that one strain to pass the night away ;
But fearing much to do his patience wrong,
Unwillingly have ask'd some other song :
So in this diff'ring key, though I could well
A many hours but as few minutes tell,   130
Yet lest mine own delight might injure you,
Though loath so soon, I take my song anew.
    Yet as when I with other swains have been
Invited by the maidens of our green
To wend to yonder wood, in time of year   135
When cherry-trees enticing burdens bear,
He that with wreathed legs doth upwards go,
Plucks not alone for those which stand below ;
But now and then is seen to pick a few
To please himself as well as all his crew :   140

118.—*Repair*, salute.

Or if from where he is he do espy
Some apricock upon a bough thereby,
Which overhangs the tree on which he stands,
Climbs up and strives to take it with his hands :
So if to please myself I somewhat sing,   145
Let it not be to you less pleasuring.
No thirst of glory tempts me : for my strains
Befit poor shepherds on the lowly plains ;
The hope of riches cannot draw from me
One line that tends to servile flattery,   150
Nor shall the most in titles on the earth
Blemish my Muse with an adulterate birth,
Nor make me lay pure colours on a ground
Where nought substantial can be ever found.
No ; such as sooth a base and dunghill spirit,   155
With attributes fit for the most of merit,
Cloud their free Muse ; as when the sun doth
       shine
On straw and dirt mix'd by the sweating hyne,
It nothing gets from heaps so much impure
But noisome steams that do his light obscure.   160
  My freeborn Muse will not like Danae be,
Won with base dross to clip with slavery ;
Nor lend her choicer balm to worthless men,
Whose names would die but for some hired pen.
No ; if I praise, virtue shall draw me to it,   165
And not a base procurement make me do it.

158.—*Hyne,* or hind, farm-servant.

What now I sing is but to pass away
A tedious hour, as some musicians play ;
Or make another my own griefs bemoan ;
Or to be least alone when most alone.   170
In this can I as oft as I will choose,
Hug sweet content by my retired Muse,
And in a study find as much to please
As others in the greatest palaces.
Each man that lives, according to his power,   175
On what he loves bestows an idle hour.
Instead of hounds that make the wooded hills
Talk in a hundred voices to the rills,
I like the pleasing cadence of a line
Struck by the consort of the sacred Nine.   180
In lieu of hawks, the raptures of my soul
Transcend their pitch and baser earth's control.
For running horses, Contemplation flies
With quickest speed to win the greatest prize.
For courtly dancing, I can take more pleasure   185
To hear a verse keep time and equal measure.
For winning riches, seek the best directions
How I may well subdue mine own affections.
For raising stately piles for heirs to come,
Here in this poem I erect my tomb.   190
And Time may be so kind in these weak lines
To keep my name enroll'd past his that shines
In gilded marble, or in brazen leaves :
Since verse preserves, when stone and brass de-
      ceives.

Or if (as worthless) Time not lets it live   195
To those full days which others' Muses give,
Yet I am sure I shall be heard and sung
Of most severest eld and kinder young
Beyond my days ; and, maugre Envy's strife,
Add to my name some hours beyond my life.   200
   Such of the Muses are the able powers,
And since with them I spent my vacant hours,
I find nor hawk, nor hound, nor other thing,
Tourneys nor revels, pleasures for a king,
Yield more delight : for I have oft possess'd   205
As much in this as all in all the rest,
And that without expense, when others oft
With their undoings have their pleasures bought.
   On now, my loved Muse, and let us bring
Thetis to hear the Cornish Michael sing ;   210
And after him to see a swain unfold
The tragedy of Drake in leaves of gold.
Then hear another Grenville's name relate,
Which times succeeding shall perpetuate,
And make those two the pillars great of fame,   215
Beyond whose worths shall never sound a name,
Nor Honour in her everlasting story
More deeper grave for all ensuing glory.
   Now Thetis stays to hear the shepherds tell
Where Arthur met his death, and Mordred fell :   220
Of holy Ursula, that fam'd her age,
With other virgins in her pilgrimage :
And as she forwards steers is shown the rock

Main-Amber, to be shook with weakest shock,
So equal is it pois'd ; but to remove   225
All strength would fail, and but an infant's prove.
Thus while to please her some new songs devise,
And others diamonds (shaped angle-wise,
And smooth'd by Nature, as she did impart
Some willing time to trim herself by art,)   230
Sought to present her and her happy crew ;
She of the Gulf and Scillies took a view,
And doubling then the Point, made on away
Tow'rds goodly Severn and the Irish Sea ;
There meets a shepherd that began sing o'er   235
The lay which aged Robert* sung of yore,
In praise of England and the deeds of swains
That whilom fed and rul'd upon our plains.
The British bards then were not long time mute,
But to their sweet harps sung their famous Brute: 240
Striving in spite of all the mists of eld,
To have his story more authentic held.
   Why should we envy them those wreaths of fame :
Being as proper to the Trojan name,
As are the dainty flowers which Flora spreads   245
Unto the spring in the discolour'd meads ?
Rather afford them all the worth we may,

*Robert of
Gloucester.

224.—*The Rock Main-Amber*, probably the Logan Rock
near Land's End.
232.—*The Gulf*, Mount's Bay.
233.—*The Point*, Lizard Point.
246.—*Discolour'd*, variously coloured.

For what we give to them adds to our ray.
And, Britons, think not that your glories fall,
Derived from a mean original;   .   250
Since lights that may have power to check the
            dark,
Can have their lustre from the smallest spark.
"Not from nobility doth virtue spring,
But virtue makes fit nobles for a king.
From highest nests are croaking ravens born,   255
When sweetest nightingales sit in the thorn."
From what low fount soe'er your beings are,
In softer peace and mighty brunts of war,
Your own worths challenge as triumphant bays
As ever Trojan hand had power to raise.   260
And when I leave my music's plainer ground,
The world shall know it from Bellona's sound.
Nor shall I err from truth; for what I write
She doth peruse, and helps me to indite.
The small converse which I have had with some, 265
Branches which from those gallant trees have come,
Doth what I sing in all their acts approve,
And with more days increase a further love.
    As I have seen the Lady of the May
Set in an arbour, on a holiday,   270
Built by the May-pole, where the jocund swains
Dance with the maidens to the bagpipe's strains,
When envious night commands them to be gone,
Call for the merry youngsters one by one,
And for their well performance soon disposes: 275

To this a garland interwove with roses,
To that a carved hook or well-wrought scrip,
Gracing another with her cherry lip ;
To one her garter, to another then
A handkerchief cast o'er and o'er again ;   280
And none returneth empty that hath spent
His pains to fill their rural merriment :
So Nereus' daughter, when the swains had done,
With an unsparing, liberal hand begun
To give to every one that sung before,   285
Rich orient pearls brought from her hidden store,
Red branching coral, and as precious gems
As ever beautified the diadems :
That they might live what chance their sheep betide,
On her reward, yet leave their heirs beside.   290
Since when I think the world doth nothing give
          them,
As weening Thetis ever should relieve them ;
And poets freely spend a golden shower,
As they expected her again each hour.
    Then with her thanks and praises for their skill 295
In tuning numbers of the sacred hill,
She them dismiss'd to their contented cotes ;
And every swain a several passage floats
Upon his dolphin.   Since whose safe repair,
Those fishes like a well-composed air ;   300
And (as in love to men) are ever seen

299.—*Repair*, resort.

Before a tempest's rough regardless teen,
To swim high on the waves, as none should dare,
Excepting fishes, to adventure there.
   When these had left her, she drave on in pride 305
Her prouder coursers through the swelling tide,
To view the Cambrian cliffs, and had not gone
An hour's full speed, but near a rock (whereon
Congealed frost and snow in summer lay,
Seldom dissolved by Hyperion's ray,)   310
She saw a troop of people take their seat,
Whereof some wrung their hands, and some did
     beat
Their troubled breasts, in sign of mickle woe,
For those are actions grief enforceth to.
Willing to know the cause, somewhat near hand 315
She spies an aged man sit by the strand,
Upon a green hillside, not meanly crown'd
With golden flowers, as chief of all the ground :
By him a little lad, his cunning heir,
Tracing green rushes for a winter chair.   320
The old man while his son full neatly knits them
Unto his work begun, as trimly fits them.
Both so intending what they first propounded,
As all their thoughts by what they wrought were
    bounded.
   To them she came, and kindly thus bespake : 325

302.—*Teen*, violence.   319.—*Cunning*, skilful.
320.—*Tracing*, plaiting.

Ye happy creatures, that your pleasures take
In what your needs enforce, and never aim
A limitless desire to what may maim
The settled quiet of a peaceful state,
Patience attend your labours !   And when Fate   330
Brings on the restful night to your long days,
Wend to the fields of bliss !   Thus Thetis prays.
　　Fair queen, to whom all duteous praise we owe,
Since from thy spacious cistern daily flow
(Replied the swain) refreshing streams that fill   335
Earth's dugs, the hillocks, so preserving still
The infant grass, when else our lambs might bleat
In vain for suck, whose dams have nought to eat :
For these thy prayers we are doubly bound,   [340
And that these cleeves should know ; but, O, to
　　　　sound
My often mended pipe presumption were,
Since Pan would play if thou wouldst please to hear.
The louder blasts which I was wont to blow
Are now but faint, nor do my fingers know
To touch half part those merry tunes I had.   345
Yet if thou please to grace my little lad
With thy attention, he may somewhat strike
Which thou from one so young may'st chance to like.
With that the little shepherd left his task,
And with a blush, the roses' only mask,   350
Denied to sing.   Ah father, quoth the boy,

340.—*Cleeves*, cliffs.

How can I tune a seeming note of joy?
The work which you command me, I intend
Scarce with a half-bent mind, and therefore spend
In doing little, now, an hour or two,   355
Which I in lesser time could neater do.
As oft as I with my more nimble joints
Trace the sharp rushes' ends, I mind the points
Which Philocel did give ; and when I brush
The pretty tuft that grows beside the rush,   360
I never can forget in yonder lair
How Philocel was wont to stroke my hair.
No more shall I be ta'en unto the wake,
Nor wend a-fishing to the winding lake ;
No more shall I be taught on silver strings   365
To learn the measures of our banquetings ;
The twisted collars and the ringing bells,
The morris scarves and cleanest drinking shells
Will never be renew'd by any one ;
Nor shall I care for more when he is gone.   370
See ! yonder hill where he was wont to sit,
A cloud doth keep the golden sun from it,
And for his seat, as teaching us, hath made
A mourning covering with a scowling shade.
The dew on every flower this morn hath lain   375
Longer than it was wont this side the plain ;
Belike they mean, since my best friend must die,
To shed their silver drops as he goes by.

361.—*Lair*, pasture, or plain.

Not all this day here, nor in coming hither,   [380
Heard I the sweet birds tune their songs together,
Except one nightingale in yonder dell
Sigh'd a sad elegy for Philocel ;
Near whom a wood-dove kept no small ado
To bid me in her language " Do so too."
The wether's bell that leads our flock around   385
Yields, as methinks, this day a deader sound.
The little sparrows which in hedges creep,
Ere I was up did seem to bid me weep.
If these do so, can I have feeling less,
That am more apt to take and to express?   390
No ; let my own tunes be the mandrake's groan,
If now they tend to mirth when all have none.
    My pretty lad, quoth Thetis, thou dost well
To fear the loss of thy dear Philocel.
But tell me, sire, what may that shepherd be?   395
Or if it lie in us to set him free,
Or if with you yond people touch'd with woe
Under the self-same load of sorrow go.
    Fair queen, replied the swain, one is the cause
That moves our grief, and those kind shepherds
        draws   400
To yonder rock.   Thy more than mortal spirit
May give a good beyond our power to merit ;
And therefore please to hear while I shall tell
The hapless fate of hopeless Philocel.
    Whilom great Pan, the father of our flocks,   405
Lov'd a fair lass so famous for her locks,

That in her time all women first begun
To lay their looser tresses to the sun ;
And theirs whose hue to hers was not agreeing,
Were still roll'd up as hardly worth the seeing.   410
Fondly have some been led to think that man
Music's invention first of all began
From the dull hammer's stroke ; since well we know
From sure tradition that hath taught us so,
Pan, sitting once to sport him with his fair,   415
Mark'd the intention of the gentle air,
In the sweet sound her chaste words brought along,
Fram'd by the repercussion of her tongue :
And from that harmony begun the art
Which others (though unjustly) do impart   420
To bright Apollo from a meaner ground :
A sledge or parched nerves ; mean things to found
So rare an art on ; when there might be given
All earth for matter with the gyre of heaven.
To keep her slender fingers from the sun,   425
Pan through the pastures oftentimes hath run
To pluck the speckled foxgloves from their stem,
And on those fingers neatly placed them.
The honeysuckles would he often strip,
And lay their sweetness on her sweeter lip,   430
And then, as in reward of such his pain,
Sip from those cherries some of it again.

411.—*Fondly*, foolishly.   422.—*Sledge*, hammer.
424.—*Gyre*, circle.

Some say that Nature, while this lovely maid
Liv'd on our plains, the teeming earth array'd
With damask roses in each pleasant place,   435
That men might liken somewhat to her face.
Others report : Venus, afraid her son
Might love a mortal as he once had done,
Preferr'd an earnest suit to highest Jove,
That he which bore the winged shafts of love,   440
Might be debarr'd his sight, which suit was sign'd,
And ever since the god of love is blind.
Hence is't he shoots his shafts so clean awry,
Men learn to love when they should learn to die ;
And women, which before to love began   445
Man without wealth, love wealth without a man.
     Great Pan of his kind nymph had the embrac-
          ing
Long, yet too short a time.   For as in tracing
These pithful rushes, such as are aloft
By those that rais'd them presently are brought   450
Beneath unseen : so in the love of Pan
(For gods in love do undergo as man),
She whose affection made him raise his song,
And, for her sport, the satyrs rude among
Tread wilder measures than the frolic guests,   455
That lift their light heels at Lyæus' feasts :
She by the light of whose quick-turning eye
He never read but of felicity :
She whose assurance made him more than Pan,
Now makes him far more wretched than a man.   460

For mortals in their loss have death a friend,
When gods have losses, but their loss no end.
  It chanc'd one morn, clad in a robe of grey,
And blushing oft as rising to betray,
Entic'd this lovely maiden from her bed   465
(So when the roses have discovered
Their taintless beauties, flies the early bee
About the winding alleys merrily)
Into the wood, and 'twas her usual sport,
Sitting where most harmonious birds resort,   470
To imitate their warbling in a quill
Wrought by the hand of Pan, which she did fill
Half full with water : and with it hath made
The nightingale, beneath a sullen shade,
To chant her utmost lay, nay, to invent   475
New notes to pass the other's instrument,
And, harmless soul, ere she would leave that strife,
Sung her last song, and ended with her life ;
So gladly choosing, as do other some,
Rather to die than live and be o'ercome.   480
  But as in autumn (when birds cease their notes,
And stately forests don their yellow coats ;
When Ceres' golden locks are nearly shorn,
And mellow fruit from trees are roughly torn),
A little lad set on a bank to shale   485
The ripen'd nuts pluck'd in a woody vale,
Is frighted thence, of his dear life afeard,

485.—*Shale*, shell.

By some wild bull loud bellowing for the herd :
So while the nymph did earnestly contest
Whether the birds or she recorded best,   490
A ravenous wolf, bent eager to his prey,
Rush'd from a thievish brake ; and making way,
The twined thorns did crackle one by one,
As if they gave her warning to be gone.
A rougher gale bent down the lashing boughs,   495
To beat the beast from what his hunger vows.
When she (amaz'd) rose from her hapless seat
(Small is resistance where the fear is great),
And striving to be gone, with gaping jaws
The wolf pursues, and as his rending paws   500
Were like to seize, a holly bent between ;
For which good deed his leaves are ever green.
    Saw you a lusty mastive at the stake,
Thrown from a cunning bull, more fiercely make
A quick return ? yet to prevent the gore   505
Or deadly bruise which he escap'd before,
Wind here and there, nay creep if rightly bred,
And proff'ring otherwhere, fight still at head :
So though the stubborn boughs did thrust him back,
(For Nature, loath so rare a jewel's wrack,   510
Seem'd as she here and there had plash'd a tree,
If possible to hinder destiny,)
The savage beast foaming with anger flies

492.—*Thievish brake*, a thicket that might harbour thieves.
511.—*Plash'd*, had bent down and interwoven the branches
or twigs.

More fiercely than before, and now he tries
By sleights to take the maid ; as I have seen   515
A nimble tumbler on a burrow'd green,
Bend clean awry his course, yet give a check
And throw himself upon a rabbit's neck.
For as he hotly chas'd the love of Pan,
A herd of deer out of a thicket ran,   520
To whom he quickly turn'd, as if he meant
To leave the maid, but when she swiftly bent
Her race down to the plain, the swifter deer
He soon forsook ; and now was got so near
That, all in vain, she turned to and fro   525
As well she could, but not prevailing so,
Breathless and weary calling on her love
With fearful shrieks that all the echoes move
To call him too, she fell down deadly wan,
And ends her sweet life with the name of Pan.   530
　　A youthful shepherd of the neighbour wold,
Missing that morn a sheep out of his fold,
Carefully seeking round to find his stray,
Came on the instant where this damsel lay.
Anger and pity in his manly breast   535
Urge yet restrain his tears. Sweet maid, possess'd
(Quoth he) with lasting sleep, accept from me
His end, who ended thy hard destiny !
With that his strong dog, of no dastard kind,
Swift as the foals conceived by the wind,   540

516.—*Tumbler*, a rabbit-dog.

He sets upon the wolf, that now with speed
Flies to the neighbour-wood ; and lest a deed
So full of ruth should unrevenged be,
The shepherd follows too, so earnestly
Cheering his dog. that he ne'er turn'd again   545
Till the curst wolf lay strangled on the plain.
   The ruin'd temple of her purer soul
The shepherd buries.   All the nymphs condole
So great a loss, while on a cypress' graff
Near to her grave they hung this epitaph :   550

    Lest loathed age might spoil the work in whom
    All earth delighted, Nature took it home ;
    Or angry all hers else were careless deem'd,
    Here did her best to have the rest esteem'd ;
    For fear men might not think the Fates so cross, 555
    But by their rigour in as great a loss.
    If to the grave there ever was assign'd
    One like this nymph in body and in mind,
    We wish her here in balm not vainly spent,
    To fit this maiden with a monument.   560
    For brass and marble were they seated here
    Would fret or melt in tears to lie so near.

Now Pan may sit and tune his pipe alone
Among the wished shades, since she is gone,
Whose willing ear allur'd him more to play,   565
Than if to hear him should Apollo stay.

549.—*Graff,* shoot.

Yet happy Pan ! and in thy love more blest,
Whom none but only death hath dispossess'd ;
While others love as well, yet live to be
Less wrong'd by Fate than by inconstancy.   570
　　The sable mantle of the silent night
Shut from the world the ever-joysome light ;
Care fled away, and softest slumbers please
To leave the court for lowly cottages ;
Wild beasts forsook their dens on woody hills,   575
And sleightful otters left the purling rills ;
Rooks to their nests in high woods now were flung,
And with their spread wings shield their naked
　　　　young ;
When thieves from thickets to the cross-ways stir,
And terror frights the lonely passenger ;   580
When nought was heard but now and then the howl
Of some vild cur, or whooping of the owl ;
Pan, that the day before was far away
At shepherds' sports, return'd ; and as he lay
Within the bower wherein he most delighted,   585
Was by a ghastly vision thus affrighted :
Heart-thrilling groans first heard he round his bower,
And then the screech-owl with her utmost power
Labour'd her loathed note, the forests bending
With winds, as Hecate had been ascending.   590
Hereat his curled hairs on end do rise,
And chilly drops trill o'er his staring eyes.

576.—*Sleightful*, cunning, sly.

Fain would he call, but knew not who, nor why,
Yet getting heart at last would up and try
If any devilish hag were come abroad   595
With some kind mother's late deliver'd load,
A ruthless bloody sacrifice to make
To those infernal powers that by the lake
Of mighty Styx and black Cocytus dwell,
Aiding each witch's charm and mystic spell.   600
But as he rais'd himself within his bed,
A sudden light about his lodging spread,
And therewithal his love, all ashy pale
As evening mist from up a wat'ry vale,
Appear'd, and weakly near his bed she press'd.   605
A ravell'd wound distain'd her purer breast,
Breasts softer far than tufts of unwrought silk,
Whence had she liv'd to give an infant milk,
The virtue of that liquor, without odds,
Had made her babe immortal as the gods.   610
Pan would have spoke, but him she thus prevents :
Wonder not that the troubled elements
Speak my approach ; I draw no longer breath,
But am enforced to the shades of death.
My exequies are done, and yet before   615
I take my turn to be transported o'er
The nether floods among the shades of Dis,
To end my journey in the fields of bliss,
I come to tell thee that no human hand
Made me seek waftage on the Stygian strand ;   620
It was an hungry wolf that did imbrue

Himself in my last blood.   And now I sue
In hate to all that kind, and shepherds' good,
To be revenged on that cursed brood.   [625
Pan vow'd, and would have clipp'd her, but she fled,
And as she came, so quickly vanished.
  Look as a well-grown, stately-headed buck,
But lately by the woodman's arrow struck,
Runs gadding o'er the lawns, or nimbly strays
Among the cumbrous brakes a thousand ways,   630
Now through the high-wood scours, then by the
          brooks,
On every hillside, and each vale he looks,
If 'mongst their store of simples may be found
An herb to draw and heal his smarting wound,
But when he long hath sought, and all in vain,   635
Steals to the covert closely back again,
Where round engirt with fern more highly sprung,
Strives to appease the raging with his tongue,
And from the speckled herd absents him till
He be recover'd somewhat of his ill :   640
So wounded Pan turns in his restless bed,
But finding thence all ease abandoned,
He rose, and through the wood distracted runs :
Yet carries with him what in vain he shuns.
Now he exclaim'd on Fate, and wish'd he ne'er   645
Had mortal lov'd, or that he mortal were.
And sitting lastly on an oak's bare trunk,
Where rain in winter stood long time unsunk,
His plaints he 'gan renew, but then the light

That through the boughs flew from the Queen of
    Night,   650
As giving him occasion to repine,
Bewray'd an elm embraced by a vine,
Clipping so strictly that they seem'd to be
One in their growth, one shade, one fruit, one tree,
Her boughs his arms, his leaves so mix'd with hers,
That with no wind he mov'd but straight she stirs,[655
As showing all should be, whom love combin'd :
In motion one, and only two in kind.
This more afflicts him while he thinketh most
Not on his loss, but on the substance lost.   660
O hapless Pan, had there but been one by
To tell thee, though as poor a swain as I,
Though, whether casual means or death do move,
" We part not without grief things held with love :
Yet in their loss some comfort may be got   665
If we do mind the time we had them not."
This might have lessen'd somewhat of thy pain,
Or made thee love as thou might'st lose again.
If thou the best of women didst forego,   [670
Weigh if thou found'st her, or didst make her so ;
If she were found so, know there's more than one ;
If made, the workman lives, though she be gone.
Should from mine eyes the light be ta'en away,
Yet night her pleasures hath as well as day ;
And my desires to Heaven yield less offence,   675
Since blindness is a part of innocence.
So though thy love sleep in eternal night,

Yet there's in loneness somewhat may delight.
Instead of dalliance, partnership in woes
It wants, the care to keep, and fear to lose.   680
For jealousies and fortune's baser pelf,
He rest enjoys that well enjoys himself.
   Had some one told thee thus, or thou bethought
      thee
Of inward help, thy sorrow had not brought thee
To weigh misfortune by another's good :   685
Nor leave thy seat to range about the wood.
Stay where thou art, turn where thou wert before,
Light yields small comfort, nor hath darkness
      more.
   A woody hill there stood, at whose low feet
Two goodly streams in one broad channel meet, 690
Whose fretful waves beating against the hill,
Did all the bottom with soft mutt'rings fill.
Here in a nook made by another mount,
(Whose stately oaks are in no less account
For height or spreading, than the proudest be   695
That from Oëta look on Thessaly,)
Rudely o'erhung there is a vaulted cave,
That in the day as sullen shadows gave,
As evening to the woods.   An uncouth place,
(Where hags and goblins might retire a space,)   700
And hated now of shepherds, since there lies
The corpse of one, less loving deities
Than we affected him, that never lent
His hand to ought but to our detriment.

A man that only liv'd to live no more,   705
And died still to be dying ; whose chief store
Of virtue was, his hate did not pursue her,
Because he only heard of her, not knew her ;
That knew no good, but only that his sight
Saw everything had still his opposite ;   710
And ever this his apprehension caught,
That what he did was best, the other naught ;
That always lov'd the man that never lov'd ;
And hated him whose hate no death had mov'd ;
That (politic) at fitting time and season   715
Could hate the traitor,. and yet love the treason ;
That many a woful heart (ere his decease)
In pieces tore to purchase his own peace ;
Who never gave his alms but in this fashion,
To salve his credit more than for salvation ;   720
Who on the names of good men ever fed,
And (most accursed) sold the poor for bread.
Right like the pitch-tree, from whose any limb
Comes never twig, shall be the seed of him.
The Muses scorn'd by him, laugh at his fame,   725
And never will vouchsafe to speak his name.
Let no man for his loss one tear let fall,
But perish with him his memorial !

   Into this cave the god of shepherds went ;
The trees in groans, the rocks in tears lament   730
His fatal chance : the brooks that whilom leapt
To hear him play while his fair mistress slept,
Now left their eddies and such wanton moods,

And   with loud clamours fill'd   the neighb'ring
      woods.
There spent he most of night ; but when the day
Drew from the earth her pitchy veil away,   [735
When all the flow'ry plains with carols rung
That by the mounting lark were shrilly sung,
When dusky mists rose from the crystal floods,
And darkness nowhere reign'd but in the woods, 740
Pan left the cave, and now intends to find
The sacred place where lay his love enshrin'd :
A plot of earth, in whose chill arms was laid
As much perfection as had ever maid ;
If curious Nature had but taken care   745
To make more lasting what she made so fair.
   Now wanders Pan the arched groves, and hills
Where fairies often danc'd, and shepherds' quills
In sweet contentions pass'd the tedious day :
Yet, being early, in his unknown way   750
Met not a shepherd, nor on all the plain
A flock then feeding saw, nor of his train
One jolly satyr stirring yet abroad,
Of whom he might inquire ; this to the load
Of his affliction adds.   Now he invokes   755
Those nymphs* in mighty forests that with oaks   * Hamadry-
Have equal fates, each with her several tree   ades.
Receiving birth and ending destiny :
Calls on all powers, entreats that he might have
But for his love the knowledge of her grave ;   760
That since the fates had ta'en the gem away,

z 2

He might but see the cark'net where it lay,
To do fit right to such a part of mould,
Covering so rare a piece that all the gold
Or diamond earth can yield, for value ne'er   765
Shall match the treasure which was hidden there !
  A hunting nymph awaken'd with his moan,
(That in a bower near hand lay all alone,
Twining her small arms round her slender waist,
That by no others us'd to be embrac'd,)   770
Got up, and knowing what the day before
Was guilty of, she adds not to his store
As many simply do, whose friends so cross'd
They more afflict by showing what is lost,
But bade him follow her.   He, as she leads,   775
Urgeth her haste.   So a kind mother treads
Earnest, distracted, where with blood defil'd
She hears lies dead her dear and only child.
Mistrust now wing'd his feet, then raging ire,
" For speed comes ever lamely to desire."   780
  Delays, the stones that waiting suitors grind,
By whom at court the poor man's cause is sign'd,
Who to dispatch a suit will not defer
To take death for a joint commissioner ;
Delay, the wooer's bane, revenge's hate,   785
The plague to creditors' decay'd estate,
The test of patience, of our hopes the rack,

762.—*Cark'net*, carkanet, a necklace, but possibly ' casknet,'
a casket, should be read.

That draws them forth so long until they crack ;
Virtue's best benefactor in our times,
One that is set to punish great men's crimes,   790
She that had hinder'd mighty Pan a while,
Now steps aside : and as o'erflowing Nile
Hid from Clymene's son his reeking head,
So from his rage all opposition fled,
Giving him way to reach the timeless tomb   795
Of Nature's glory, for whose ruthless doom
(When all the Graces did for mercy plead,
And youth and goodness both did intercede,)
The sons of earth, if living, had been driven
To heap on hills, and war anew with Heaven.   800
The shepherds which he miss'd upon the downs
Here meets he with : for from the neighb'ring towns
Maidens and men resorted to the grave
To see a wonder more than time e'er gave.

    The holy priests had told them long agone   805
Amongst the learned shepherds there was one
So given to piety, and did adore
So much the name of Pan, that when no more
He breath'd, those that to ope his heart began,
Found written there with gold the name of Pan. 810
Which unbelieving man that is not mov'd
To credit ought, if not by reason prov'd,
And ties the overworking power to do
Nought otherwise than Nature reacheth to,

793.—*Clymene's son*, Phaeton.

Held as most fabulous : not inly seeing,   815
The hand by whom we live, and all have being,
No work for admirable doth intend,
Which reason hath the power to comprehend,
And faith no merit hath from heaven lent
Where human reason yields experiment.   820
Till now they durst not trust the legend old,
Esteeming all not true their elders told,
And had not this last accident made good
The former, most in unbelief had stood.   [825
   But Fame, that spread the bruit of such a wonder,
Bringing the swain[s] of places far asunder
To this selected plot (now famous more
Than any grove, mount, plain, had been before
By relic, vision, burial, or birth
Of anchoress, or hermit yet on earth),   830
Out of the maiden's bed of endless rest
Shows them a tree new grown, so fairly dress'd
With spreading arms and curled top that Jove
Ne'er braver saw in his Dodonian grove ;
The heart-like leaves oft each with other pile, 835
As do the hard scales of the crocodile ;
And none on all the tree was seen but bore
Written thereon in rich and purest ore
The name of Pan ; whose lustre far beyond
Sparkled, as by a torch the diamond ;   840
Or those bright spangles which, fair goddess, do

815.—*Inly,* inwardly.

Shine in the hair of these which follow you.
The shepherds by direction of great Pan
Search'd for the root, and finding it began
In her true heart, bids them again enclose   845
What now his eyes for ever, ever lose.
Now in the self-same sphere his thoughts must move
With him* that did the shady plane-tree love.   * Xerxes
Yet though no issue from her loins shall be
To draw from Pan a noble pedigree,   850
And Pan shall not, as other gods have done,
Glory in deeds of an heroic son,
Nor have his name in countries near and far
Proclaim'd, as by his child the Thunderer;
If Phœbus on this tree spread warming rays,   855
And northern blasts kill not her tender sprays,
His love shall make him famous in repute,
And still increase his name, yet bear no fruit.

   To make this sure, the god of shepherds last,
When other ceremonies were o'erpast,   860
And to perform what he before had vow'd
To dire revenge, thus spake unto the crowd :
What I have lost, kind shepherds, all you know,
And to recount it were to dwell in woe :
To show my passion in a funeral song,   865
And with my sorrow draw your sighs along,
Words, then, well plac'd might challenge somewhat
     due,
And not the cause alone, win tears from you.
This to prevent, I set orations by,

" For passion seldom loves formality."   870
What profits it a prisoner at the bar,
To have his judgment spoken regular ?
Or in the prison hear it often read,
When he at first knew what was forfeited ?
Our griefs in others' tears, like plates in water,   875
Seem more in quantity.   To be relator
Of my mishaps, speaks weakness, and that I
Have in myself no power of remedy.
    Once (yet that once too often) heretofore
The silver Ladon on his sandy shore   880
Heard my complaints, and those cool groves that be
Shading the breast of lovely Arcady
Witnesse[d] the tears which I for Syrinx spent :
Syrinx the fair, from whom the instrument   [885
That fills your feasts with joy (which when I blow
Draws to the sagging dug milk white as snow),
Had his beginning.   This enough had been
To show the Fates, my deemed sisters,* teen.
Here had they stay'd, this adage had been none :
" That our disasters never come alone."   890
What boot is it though I am said to be
The worthy son of winged Mercury ?
That I with gentle nymphs in forests high
Kiss'd out the sweet time of my infancy ?
And when more years had made me able grown, 895

* Pronapis
in suo Proto-
cosmo.

886.—*Sagging*, drooping.
888.—*Teen*, violence.

Was through the mountains for their leader known?
That high-brow'd Mænalus where I was bred,
And stony hills not few have honoured
Me as protector by the hands of swains,
Whose sheep retire there from the open plains?   900
That I in shepherds' cups (rejecting gold*)
Of milk and honey measures eight times told
Have offer'd to me, and the ruddy wine
Fresh and new pressed from the bleeding vine?
That gleesome hunters, pleased with their sport,   905
With sacrifices due have thank'd me for't?
That patient anglers standing all the day
Near to some shallow stickle or deep bay,
And fishermen whose nets have drawn to land
A shoal so great it well-nigh hides the sand,   910
For such success some promontory's head
Thrust at by waves, hath known me worshipped?
But to increase my grief, what profits this,
"Since still the loss is as the loser is?"
      The many-kernel-bearing pine of late   915
From all trees else to me was consecrate,
But now behold a root more worth my love,
Equal to that which in an obscure grove
Infernal Juno proper takes to her:
Whose golden slip the Trojan wanderer,   920

* Apollonius
Smyrnæus.

908.—*Stickle*, a run or swift part of a river; a word still used
in Devonshire.
920.—*The Trojan wanderer*, Æneas (Virgil, *Æn.* vi. 136
et seq.)

By sage Cumæan Sybil taught, did bring,
By Fates decreed, to be the warranting
Of his free passage, and a safe repair
Through dark Avernus to the upper air.
This must I succour, this must I defend,   925
And from the wild boars' rooting ever shend.
Here shall the woodpecker no entrance find,
Nor Tavy's beavers gnaw the clothing rind,
Lambeder's herds, nor Radnor's goodly deer
Shall never once be seen a-browsing here.   930
And now, ye British swains, whose harmless sheep
Than all the world's besides I joy to keep,
Which spread on every plain and hilly wold
Fleeces no less esteem'd than that of gold,
For whose exchange one Indy gems of price,   935
The other gives you of her choicest spice,
And well she may ; but we unwise the while
Lessen the glory of our fruitful Isle,
Making those nations think we foolish are
For baser drugs to vent our richer ware,   940
Which, save the bringer, never profit man
Except the sexton and physician ;
And whether change of climes or what it be
That proves our mariners' mortality,
Such expert men are spent for such bad fares   945
As might have made us lords of what is theirs—

926.—*Shend*, defend.
929.—*Lambeder*, Llanbedr in Radnorshire.

Stay, stay at home, ye nobler spirits, and prize
Your lives more high than such base trumperies :
Forbear to fetch, and they'll go near to sue,
And at your own doors offer them to you ;   950
Or have their woods and plains so overgrown
With pois'nous weeds, roots, gums and seeds un-
   known,
That they would hire such weeders as you be
To free their land from such fertility ?
Their spices hot their nature best endures,   955
But 'twill impair and much distemper yours.
What our own soil affords befits us best,
And long, and long, for ever, may we rest
Needless of help ! and may this Isle alone
Furnish all other lands, and this·land none !   960
 Excuse me, Thetis, quoth the aged man,
If passion drew me from the words of Pan,
Which thus I follow : you whose flocks, quoth he,
By my protection quit your industry,
For all the good I have and yet may give   965
To such as on the plains hereafter live,
I do entreat what is not hard to grant,
That not a hand rend from this holy plant
The smallest branch ; and whoso cutteth this
Die for th' offence ; to me so heinous 'tis.   970
And by the floods infernal here I swear,
(An oath whose breach the greatest gods forbear,)

964.—*Quit*, requite.

Ere Phœbe thrice twelve times shall fill her horns
No furzy tuft, thick wood, nor brake of thorns
Shall harbour wolf, nor in this Isle shall breed, 975
Nor live one of that kind, if what's decreed
You keep inviolate.   To this they swore :
And since those beasts have frighted us no more.
But swain, quoth Thetis, what is this you tell,
To what you fear shall fall on Philocel ? 980
   Fair queen, attend ; but oh I fear, quoth he,
Ere I have ended my sad history,
Unstaying time may bring on his last hour,
And so defraud us of thy wished pow'r.
Yond goes a shepherd : give me leave to run 985
And know the time of execution.
Mine aged limbs I can a little strain,
And quickly come, to end the rest, again.

THE FIFTH SONG.

THE ARGUMENT.

Within this Song my Muse doth tell
The worthy fact* of Philocel,
And how his Love and he in thrall
To death depriv'd of funeral
The Queen of Waves doth gladly save,
And frees Marina from the cave.

So soon as can a martin from our town
Fly to the river underneath the down,
And back return with mortar in her bill,
Some little cranny in her nest to fill,
The shepherd came, and thus began anew :   5
Two hours, alas, only two hours are due
From time to him, 'tis sentenc'd so of those
That here on earth as Destinies dispose
The lives and deaths of men ; and that time past
He yields his judgment leave and breathes his last. 10
　　But to the cause.   Great goddess, understand
In Mona-Isle thrust from the British land,

* *Fact*, deed.

As (since it needed nought of others' store)
It would entire be and a part no more,
There liv'd a maid so fair, that for her sake   15
Since she was born the Isle had never snake,
Nor were it fit a deadly sting should be
To hazard such admired symmetry:
So many beauties so commix'd in one,
That all delight were dead if she were gone.   20
Shepherds that in her clear eyes did delight,
Whilst they were open never held it night;
And were they shut, although the morning grey
Call'd up the sun, they hardly thought it day;
Or if they call'd it so, they did not pass   25
Withal to say that it eclipsed was.
The roses on her cheeks, such as each turn,
Phœbus might kiss, but had no pow'r to burn.
From her sweet lips distil sweets sweeter do,
Than from a cherry half way cut in two;   30
Whose yielding touch would, as Promethean fire,
Lumps truly senseless with a Muse inspire;
Who praising her would youth's desire so stir,
Each man in mind should be a ravisher.
Some say the nimble-witted Mercury   35
Went late disguis'd professing palmistry,
And milkmaids' fortunes told about the land,
Only to get a touch of her soft hand;
And that a shepherd walking on the brim

25.—*Pass,* hesitate.

Of a·clear stream where she did use to swim,   40
Saw her by chance, and thinking she had been
Of chastity the pure and fairest queen,
Stole thence dismay'd, lest he by her decree
Might undergo Actæon's destiny.
Did youth's kind heat inflame me (but the snow   45
Upon my head shows it cool'd long ago),
I then could give, fitting so fair a feature,
Right to her fame, and fame to such a creature.
When now much like a man the palsy shakes
And spectacles befriend, yet undertakes   50
To limn a lady, to whose red and white
Apelles' curious hand would owe some right :
His too unsteady pencil shadows here
Somewhat too much, and gives not overclear ;
His eye deceiv'd mingles his colours wrong,   55
There strikes too little, and here·stays too long,
Does and undoes, takes off, puts on (in vain)
Now too much white, then too much red again ;
And thinking then to give some special grace,
He works it ill, or so mistakes the place,   60
That she which sits were better pay for nought,
Than have it ended, and so lamely wrought :
So do I in this weak description err,
And striving more to grace, more injure her ;
For ever where true worth for praise doth call,   65
He rightly nothing gives that gives not all ;
But as a lad who learning to divide,

42.—Queen, Diana.

By one small miss the whole hath falsified.
Cælia men call'd, and rightly call'd her so :
Whom Philocel (of all the swains I know   70
Most worthy) lov'd : alas ! that love should be
Subject to fortune's mutability !
Whatever learned bards tofore have sung,
Or on the plains shepherds and maidens young,
Of sad mishaps in love are set to tell,   75
Comes short to match the fate of Philocel.
　For as a labourer toiling at a bay
To force some clear stream from his wonted way,
Working on this side sees the water run
Where he wrought last and thought it firmly done ; 80
And that leak stopp'd, hears it come breaking out
Another where, in a far greater spout,
Which mended too, and with a turf made trim,
The brook is ready to o'erflow the brim ;
Or in the bank the water having got,   85
Some mole-hole, runs where he expected not ;
And when all's done, still fears lest some great rain
Might bring a flood and throw all down again :
So in our shepherd's love : one hazard gone,
Another still as bad was coming on :   90
This danger past, another doth begin,
And one mishap thrust out lets twenty in.
For he that loves, and in it hath no stay,
Limits his bliss seld' past the marriage-day.
　But Philocel's, alas, and Cælia's too   95

70.—*Philocel*, perhaps Philo-Cælia.

Must ne'er attain so far as others do ;
Else Fortune in them from her course should swerve,
Who most afflicts those that most good deserve.
   Twice had the glorious sun run through the signs,
And with his kindly heat improv'd the mines,   100
(As such affirm with certain hopes that try
The vain and fruitless art of alchemy,)
Since our swain lov'd : and twice had Phœbus been
In horned Aries taking up his inn,
Ere he of Cælia's heart possession won ;   105
And since that time all his intentions done
Nothing to bring her thence.   All eyes upon her
Watchful, as Virtue's are on truest honour :
Kept on the Isle as carefully of some,
As by the Trojans their Palladium.   110
   But where's the fortress that can Love debar ?
The forces to oppose when he makes war ?
The watch which he shall never find asleep ?
The spy that shall disclose his counsels deep?   [115
That fort, that force, that watch, that spy would be
A lasting stop to a fifth empery ;
But we as well may keep the heat from fire
As sever hearts whom love hath made entire.
   In lovely May when Titan's golden rays   [120
Make odds in hours between the nights and days,

110.—*Palladium*, the image or statue of Pallas, which, in
the reign of Ilus, fell from heaven at Troy, and upon the
possession of which depended the fate of the city (Virgil,
Æneid, ii. 166).

And weigheth almost down the once-even scale
Where night and day by th' Equinoctial
Were laid in balance, as his pow'r he bent
To banish Cynthia from her regiment
To Latmus' stately hill, and with his light   125
To rule the upper world both day and night :
Making the poor Antipodes to fear
A like conjunction 'twixt great Jupiter
And some Alcmena new, or that the sun
From their horizon did obliquely run :   130
This time the swains and maidens of the Isle
The day with sportive dances do beguile,
And every valley rings with shepherds' songs,
And every echo each sweet note prolongs,
And every river with unusual pride   135
And dimpled cheek rolls sleeping to the tide ;
And lesser springs, which aërie-breeding woods
Prefer as handmaids to the mighty floods,
Scarce fill up half their channels, making haste
(In fear, as boys) lest all the sport be past.   140
    Now was the Lord and Lady of the May
Meeting the May-pole at the break of day,
And Cælia, as the fairest on the green,
Not without some maids' envy chosen queen.
Now was the time com'n, when our gentle swain 145
Must in his harvest or lose all again.

137.—*Aërie-breeding woods,* woods chosen by hawks to rear
their young, hence well-grown, lofty
  146.—*In,* gather in.

Now must he pluck the rose lest other hands,
Or tempests, blemish what so fairly stands :
And therefore, as they had before decreed,
Our shepherd gets a boat, and with ail speed   150
In night, that doth on lovers' actions smile,
Arrived safe on Mona's fruitful isle.
  Between two rocks (immortal, without mother,)
That stand as if out-facing one another,
There ran a creek up, intricate and blind,   155
As if the waters hid them from the wind ;
Which never wash'd but at a higher tide
The frizzled coats which do the mountains hide ;
Where never gale was longer known to stay
Than from the smooth wave it had swept away   160
The new divorced leaves, that from each side
Left the thick boughs to dance out with the tide.
At further end the creek a stately wood
Gave a kind shadow to the brackish flood
Made up of trees, not less kenn'd by each skiff   165
Than that sky-scaling Peak of Teneriffe,
Upon whose tops the hernshaw bred her young,
And hoary moss upon their branches hung;
Whose rugged rinds sufficient were to show,   [170
Without their height, what time they 'gan to grow ;
And if dry eld by wrinkled skin appears,
None could allot them less than Nestor's years.
As under their command the thronged creek

167.—*Hernshaw*, heron.

Ran lessen'd up.   Here did the shepherd seek
Where he his little boat might safely hide,   175
Till it was fraught with what the world beside
Could not outvalue ; nor give equal weight
Though in the time when Greece was at her height.
    The ruddy horses of the rosy Morn
Out of the Eastern gates had newly borne   180
Their blushing mistress in her golden chair,
Spreading new light throughout our hemisphere,
When fairest Cælia with a lovelier crew
Of damsels than brave Latmus ever knew   [185
Came forth to meet the youngsters, who had here
Cut down an oak that long withouten peer
Bore his round head imperiously above
His other mates there, consecrate to Jove.
The wished time drew on : and Cælia now,
That had the fame for her white arched brow,   190
While all her lovely fellows busied were
In picking off the gems from Tellus' hair,
Made tow'rds the creek, where Philocel unspied
Of maid or shepherd that their May-games plied,
Receiv'd his wish'd-for Cælia, and begun   195
To steer his boat contrary to the sun,
Who could have wish'd another in his place
To guide the car of light, or that his race
Were to have end (so he might bless his hap)

184.—*Latmus,* a mountain in Caria, where Artemis (Luna)
kissed the sleeping Endymion.

In Cælia's bosom, not in Thetis' lap.   200
The boat oft danc'd for joy of what it held :
The hoist-up sail not quick but gently swell'd,
And often shook, as fearing what might fall,
Ere she deliver'd what she went withal.
Winged Argestes,* fair Aurora's son,   205
Licens'd that day to leave his dungeon,
Meekly attended and did never err,
Till Cælia grac'd our land, and our land her.
As through the waves their love-fraught wherry ran,
A many Cupids, each set on his swan,   210
Guided with reins of gold and silver twist
The spotless birds about them as they list :
Which would have sung a song (ere they were gone),
Had unkind Nature given them more than one ;
Or in bestowing that had not done wrong,   215
And made their sweet lives forfeit one sad song.
  Yet that their happy voyage might not be
Without time's short'ner, heaven-taught melody
(Music that lent feet to the stable woods,
And in their currents turn'd the mighty floods :   220
Sorrow's sweet nurse, yet keeping joy alive :
Sad discontent's most welcome corrosive :
The soul of Art, best lov'd when Love is by :
The kind inspirer of sweet Poesy,   [225
Lest thou shouldst wanting be, when swans would fain
Have sung one song, and never sung again,)
The gentle shepherd hasting to the shore
Began this lay, and tim'd it with his oar :

* The western wind. And supposed (with the stars) the birth of Aurora by Astræus as Apollodorus : Ἠοῦς δὲ καὶ Ἀστραίου ὄνεμοι καὶ ἄστρα.

Never more let holy Dee
  O'er other rivers brave,   230
Or boast how (in his jollity)
  Kings row'd upon his wave ;
But silent be, and ever know
That Neptune for my fare would row.

Those were captives. If he say   235
  That now I am no other,
Yet she that bears my prison's key
  Is fairer than Love's mother.
A god took me, those, one less high :
They wore their bonds, so do not I.   240

Swell then, gently swell, ye floods,
  As proud of what ye bear,
And nymphs, that in low coral woods
  String pearls upon your hair,
Ascend : and tell if ere this day   245
A fairer prize was seen at sea.

See, the salmons leap and bound
  To please us as we pass;
Each mermaid on the rocks around,
  Lets fall her brittle glass,   250

232.—*Kings, i.e.*, of the Scots, of Cumberland, and of the
Isles, and five Welsh princes, who declared their vassalage to
Eadgar, king of the English, by rowing him in a boat which
he himself steered at his coronation in 973.

As they their beauties did despise,
And lov'd no mirror but your eyes.

Blow, but gently blow, fair wind,
    From the forsaken shore,
And be as to the Halcyon kind,   255
    Till we have ferried o'er :
So may'st thou still have leave to blow,
And fan the way where she shall go.

Floods, and nymphs, and winds, and all
    That see us both together,   260
Into a disputation fall,
    And then resolve me whether
The greatest kindness each can show
Will quit our trust of you or no.

Thus as a merry milkmaid, neat and fine,   265
Returning late from milking of her kine,
Shortens the dew'd way which she treads along
With some self-pleasing-since-new-gotten song,
The shepherd did their passage well beguile.
And now the horned flood bore to our Isle 270
His head more high than he had us'd to do,
Except by Cynthia's newness forced to.
Not January's snow dissolv'd in floods
Makes Tamar more intrude on Blanchden Woods,

274.—*Blanchden*, or *Blanchdown Woods*, on the east bank
of the Tamar, about four miles west of Tavistock.

Nor the concourse of waters where they fleet   275
After a long rain, and in Severn meet,
Rais'th her enraged head to root fair plants,
Or more affright her nigh inhabitants,
(When they behold the waters ruefully,
And save the waters nothing else can see,)   280
Than Neptune's subject now, more than of yore :
As loath to set his burden soon on shore.

   O Neptune ! hadst thou kept them still with thee,
Though both were lost to us and such as we,   [285
And with those beauteous birds which on thy breast
Get and bring up, afforded them a rest,
Delos, that long time wand'ring piece of earth,
Had not been fam'd more for Diana's birth,
Than those few planks that bore them on the seas,
By the blest issue of two such as these.   290

   But they were landed : so are not our woes,
Nor ever shall, whilst from an eye there flows
One drop of moisture ; to these present times
We will relate, and some sad shepherd's rhymes
To after ages may their fates make known,   295
And in their depth of sorrow drown his own.
So our relation and his mournful verse
Of tears shall force such tribute to their hearse,
That not a private grief shall ever thrive
But in that deluge fall, yet this survive.   300

   Two furlongs from the shore they had not gone,
When from a low-cast valley (having on
Each hand a woody hill, whose boughs unlopp'd

Have not alone at all time sadly dropp'd,
And turn'd their storms on her dejected breast,   305
But when the fire of heaven is ready prest
To warm and further what it should bring forth,
For lowly dales mate mountains in their worth,
The trees (as screenlike greatness) shade his ray,
As it should shine on none but such as they)—   310
Came, and full sadly came, a hapless wretch,
Whose walks and pastures once were known to stretch
From east to west so far that no dike ran
For noted bounds, but where the ocean
His wrathful billows thrust, and grew as great   315
In shoals of fish as were the other's neat :
Who now dejected and depriv'd of all,
Longs, and hath done so long, for funeral.
   For as with hanging head I have beheld
A widow vine stand in a naked field,   320
Unhusbanded, neglected, all forlorn,
Brows'd on by deer, by cattle cropp'd and torn ;
Unpropp'd, unsuccoured by stake or tree
From wreakful storms' impetuous tyranny,
When, had a willing hand lent kind redress,   325
Her pregnant bunches might from out the press
Have sent a liquor both for taste and show
No less divine than those of Malligo :
Such was this wight, and such she might have been.

316.—*Neat*, oxen.
328.—*Malligo*, a corruption of Malaga, famous for its wine.

She both th' extremes hath felt of Fortune's teen, 330
For never have we heard from times of yore,
One sometime envied and now pitied more.
Her object, as her state, is low as earth ;
Privation her companion ; thoughts of mirth
Irksome ; and in one self-same circle turning,   335
With sudden sports brought to a house of mourning.
Of others' good her best belief is still
And constant to her own in nought but ill.
The only enemy and friend she knows
Is Death, who, though defers, must end her woes; 340
Her contemplation frightful as the night ;
She never looks on any living wight
Without comparison ; and as the day
Gives us, but takes the glowworm's light away :
So the least ray of bliss on others thrown   345
Deprives and blinds all knowledge of her own.
Her comfort is (if for her any be)
That none can show more cause of grief than she.
Yet somewhat she of adverse Fate hath won,
Who had undone her were she not undone.   350
For those that on the sea of greatness ride
Far from the quiet shore, and where the tide
In ebbs and floods is guess'd, not truly known ;
Expert of all estates except their own ;
Keeping their station at the helm of State   355
Not by their virtues but auspicious fate ;

330.—*Teen*, violence.

Subject to calms of favour, storms of rage,
Their actions noted as the common stage ;
Who, like a man born blind that cannot be
By demonstration shown what 'tis to see,   360
Live still in ignorance of what they want,
Till misery become the adamant,
And touch them for that point, to which with speed
None comes so sure as by the hand of Need.
A mirror strange she in her right hand bore,   365
By which her friends from flatterers heretofore
She could distinguish well ; and by her side,
As in her full of happiness, untied
Unforc'd and uncompell'd did sadly go,
As if partaker of his mistress' woe,   370
A loving spaniel, from whose rugged back,
The only thing but death she moans to lack,
She plucks the hair, and working them in pleats
Furthers the suit which modesty entreats.
Men call her Athliot : who cannot be   375
More wretched made by infelicity,
Unless she here had an immortal breath,
Or living thus, liv'd timorous of death.
   Out of her lowly and forsaken dell
She running came, and cried to Philocel :   380
Help ! help ! kind shepherd, help ! see yonder, where
A lovely lady hung up by the hair
Struggles, but mildly struggles, with the Fates,

375.—*Athliot*, Gr. ἀθλιότης, wretchedness.

Whose thread of life, spun to a thread that mates
Dame Nature's in her hair, stays them to wonder, 385
While too fine twisting makes it break in sunder.
So shrinks the rose that with the flames doth meet ;
So gently bows the virgin parchment sheet ;
So roll the waves up and fall out again,
As all her beauteous parts, and all in vain.   390
Far, far, above my help or hope in trying,
Unknown, and so more miserably dying,
Smoth'ring her torments in her panting breast,
She meekly waits the time of her long rest.
Hasten ! O hasten then ! kind shepherd, haste. 395
    He went with her, and Cælia, that had grac'd
Him past the world besides, seeing the way
He had to go, not far, rests on the lay.
    'Twas near the place where Pan's transformed love
Her gilded leaves display'd, and boldly strove   400
For lustre with the sun : a sacred tree,
Pal'd round and kept from violation free :
Whose smallest spray rent off we never prize
At less than life.   Here, though her heavenly eyes
From him she lov'd could scarce afford a sight,   405
As if for him they only had their light,
Those kind and brighter stars were known to err
And to all misery betrayed her.
For turning them aside, she (hapless) spies
The holy tree, and (as all novelties   410

398.—*Lay*, lea, pasture.

In tempting women have small labour lost
Whether for value nought, or of more cost,)
Led by the hand of uncontroll'd desire
She rose, and thither went.   A wrested briar
Only kept close the gate which led into it,   415
(Easy for any all times to undo it,
That with a pious hand hung on the tree
Garlands or raptures of sweet poesy,)
Which by her opened, with unweeting hand
A little spray she pluck'd, whose rich leaves fann'd 420
And chatter'd with the air, as who should say :
Do not for once, O do not this bewray !
Nor give sound to a tongue for that intent !
" Who ignorantly sins, dies innocent."
By this was Philocel returning back,   425
And in his hand the lady ; for whose wrack
Nature had clean foresworn to frame a wight
So wholly pure, so truly exquisite ;
But more deform'd and from a rough-hewn mould,
Since what is best lives seldom to be old.   430
Within their sight was fairest Cælia now ;
Who drawing near, the life-priz'd golden bough
Her love beheld.   And as a mother kind
What time the new-cloth'd trees by gusts of wind
Unmov'd, stand wistly list'ning to those lays   435
The feather'd quiristers upon their sprays
Chant to the merry Spring, and in the even

426.—*Wrack*, destruction.

She with her little son for pleasure given,
To tread the fring'd banks of an amorous flood,
That with her music courts a sullen wood,   440
Where ever talking with her only bliss,
That now before and then behind her is,
She stoops for flow'rs the choicest may be had,
And bringing them to please her pretty lad,
Spies in his hand some baneful flow'r or weed,   445
Whereon he 'gins to smell, perhaps to feed,
With a more earnest haste she runs unto him,
And pulls that from him which might else undo him :
So to his Cælia hasten'd Philocel,
And raught the bough away : hid it : and fell   450
To question if she broke it, or if then
An eye beheld her.   Of the race of men,
Replied she, when I took it from the tree
Assure yourself was none to testify,
But what hath past since in your hand, behold,   455
A fellow running yonder o'er the wold
Is well inform'd of.   Can there, love, ensue,
Tell me ! oh tell me ! any wrong to you
By what my hand hath ignorantly done ?
(Quoth fearful Cælia) Philocel ! be won   460
By these unfeigned tears, as I by thine,
To make thy greatest sorrows partly mine !
Clear up these showers, my Sun, quoth Philocel,
The ground it needs not.   Nought is so from well

450.– *Raught*, snatched.

But that reward and kind entreaties may   465
Make smooth the front of wrath, and this allay.
Thus wisely he suppress'd his height of woe,
And did resolve, since none but they did know
Truly who rent it, and the hateful swain
That lately pass'd by them upon the plain   470
(Whom well he knew did bear to him a hate,
Though undeserved, so inveterate
That to his utmost pow'r he would assay
To make his life have ended with that day)
Except in his had seen it in no hand,   475
That he against all throes of Fate would stand,
Acknowledge it his deed, and so afford
A passage to his heart for Justice' sword,
Rather than by her loss the world should be
Despis'd and scorn'd for losing such as she.   480
    Now, with a vow of secrecy from both,
Enforcing mirth, he with them homewards go'th ;
And by the time the shades of mighty woods
Began to turn them to the eastern floods,
They thither got : where with undaunted heart   485
He welcomes both, and freely doth impart
Such dainties as a shepherd's cottage yields,
Ta'en from the fruitful woods and fertile fields :
No way distracted nor disturb'd at all.
And to prevent what likely might befall   490
His truest Cælia, in his apprehending,
Thus to all future care gave final ending :
Into their cup (wherein for such sweet girls

Nature would myriads of richest pearls
Dissolve, and by her pow'rful simples strive   495
To keep them still on earth, and still alive),
Our swain infus'd a powder which they drank :
And to a pleasant room, set on a bank
Near to his coat, where he did often use
At vacant hours to entertain his Muse,   500
Brought them and seated on a curious bed,
Till what he gave in operation sped,
And robb'd them of his sight, and him of theirs,
Whose new enlight'ning will be quench'd with tears.
    The glass of Time had well-nigh spent the sand 505
It had to run ere with impartial hand
Justice must to her upright balance take him :
Which he (afraid it might too soon forsake him)
Began to use as quickly as perceive,
And of his love thus took his latest leave :   510
    Cælia ! thou fairest creature ever eye
Beheld, or yet put on mortality !
Cælia, that hast but just so much of earth,
As makes thee capable of death !   Thou birth
Of every virtue, life of every good !   515
Whose chastest sports and daily taking food
Is imitation of the highest pow'rs
Who to the earth lend seasonable show'rs;
That it may bear, we to their altars bring
Things worthy their accept, our offering.   520

499.—*Coat,* cote, a cottage.

I the most wretched creature ever eye
Beheld, or yet put on mortality,
Unhappy Philocel, that have of earth
Too much to give my sorrows endless birth,
The spring of sad misfortunes ; in whom lies   525
No bliss that with thy worth can sympathize,
Clouded with woe that hence will never flit,
Till death's eternal night grow one with it :
I as a dying swan that sadly sings
Her moanful dirge unto the silver springs,   530
Which careless of her song glide sleeping by
Without one murmur of kind elegy,
Now stand by thee ; and as a turtle's mate,
With lamentations inarticulate,
The near departure from her love bemoans,   535
Spend these my bootless sighs and killing groans.
Here as a man (by Justice' doom) exil'd
To coasts unknown, to deserts rough and wild,
Stand I to take my latest leave of thee :
Whose happy and heaven-making company   540
Might I enjoy in Libya's continent,
Were blest fruition and not banishment.
First of those eyes that have already ta'en
Their leave of me : lamps fitting for the fane
Of heaven's most pow'r, and which might ne'er
         expire   545
But be as sacred as the vestal fire :

541.—*Libya's continent*, Africa.

Then of those plots, where half-ros'd lilies be,
Not one by Art but Nature's industry,
From which I go as one excluded from
The taintless flow'rs of blest Elysium :   550
Next from those lips I part, and may there be
No one that shall hereafter second me !
Guiltless of any kisses but their own,
Their sweets but to themselves to all unknown :
For should our swains divulge what sweets there
          be   555
Within the sea-clipt bounds of Britany,
We should not from invasions be exempted,
But with that prize would all the world be tempted.
Then from her heart : O no ! let that be never,
For if I part from thence I die for ever.   560
Be that the record of my love and name !
Be that to me as is the Phœnix' flame !
Creating still anew what Justice' doom
Must yield to dust and a forgotten tomb.
Let thy chaste love to me (as shadows run   565
In full extent unto the setting sun)
Meet with my fall ; and when that I am gone,
Back to thyself retire, and there grow one.
If to a second light thy shadow be,
Let him still have his ray of love from me ;   570
And if, as I, that likewise do decline,
Be mine or his, or else be his and mine.
But know no other, nor again be sped,
" She dies a virgin that but knows one bed."

And now from all at once my leave I take   575
With this petition, that when thou shalt wake,
My tears already spent may serve for thine,
And all thy sorrows be excus'd by mine !
Yea, rather than my loss should draw on hers,   [580
(Hear, Heaven, the suit which my sad soul prefers !)
Let this her slumber, like Oblivion's stream,
Make her believe our love was but a dream !
Let me be dead in her as to the earth,
Ere Nature lose the grace of such a birth.
Sleep thou, sweet soul, from all disquiet free,   585
And since I now beguile thy destiny,
Let after patience in thy breast arise,
To give his name a life who for thee dies.
He dies for thee that worthy is to die,
Since now in leaving that sweet harmony   590
Which Nature wrought in thee, he draws not to him
Enough of sorrow that might straight undo him ;
And have for means of death his parting hence,
So keeping Justice still in innocence.

Here stay'd his tongue, and tears anew began : 595
"Parting knows more of grief than absence can."
And with a backward pace and ling'ring eye
Left, and for ever left, their company.

By this the curs'd informer of the deed   [600
With wings of mischief (and those have most speed)
Unto the priests of Pan had made it known ;
And, though with grief enough, were thither flown
With strict command the officers that be

As hands of Justice in her each decree.   [605
Those unto judgment brought him : where, accus'd
That with unhappy hand he had abus'd
The holy tree, and by the oath of him
Whose eye beheld the separated limb,
All doubts dissolv'd, quick judgment was awarded,
And but last night, that hither strongly guarded 610
This morn he should be brought, and from yond rock,
Where every hour new store of mourners flock,
He should be headlong thrown, too hard a doom,
To be depriv'd of life, and dead, of tomb.

    This is the cause, fair goddess, that appears   615
Before you now clad in an old man's tears,
Which willingly flow out, and shall do more
Than many winters have seen heretofore.

    But father, quoth she, let me understand
How you are sure that it was Cælia's hand   620
Which rent the branch ; and then (if you can) tell
What nymph it was which near the lonely dell
Your shepherd succour'd.   Quoth the good old man :
The last time in her orb pale Cynthia ran,
I to the prison went, and from him knew   625·
(Upon my vow) what now is known to you ;
And that the lady which he found distress'd,
Is Fida call'd, a maid not meanly bless'd
By heaven's endowments, and—Alas ! but see,
Kind Philocel, engirt with misery   630
More strong than by his bonds, is drawing nigh
The place appointed for his tragedy !

You may walk thither and behold his fall ;
While I come near enough, yet not at all.
Nor shall it need I to my sorrow knit   635
The grief of knowing with beholding it.
    The goddess went—(but ere she came did shroud
Herself from every eye within a cloud)—
Where she beheld the shepherd on his way,
Much like a bridegroom on his marriage-day,   640
Increasing not his misery with fear :
Others for him, but he shed not a tear.
His knitting sinews did not tremble ought,
Nor to unusual palpitation brought
Was or his heart or liver : nor his eye,   645
Nor tongue, nor colour show'd a dread to die.
His resolution keeping with his spirit,
Both worthy him that did them both inherit,
Held in subjection every thought of fear,
Scorning so base an executioner.   650
    Some time he spent in speech, and then began
Submissly prayen to the name of Pan,
When suddenly this cry came from the plains :
From guiltless blood be free, ye British swains ! [655
Mine be those bonds, and mine the death appointed !
Let me be headlong thrown, these limbs disjointed !
Or if you needs must hurl him from that brim,
Except I die there dies but part of him.
Do then right, Justice, and perform your oath,
Which cannot be without the death of both !   660
    Wonder drew thitherward their drowned eyes,

And sorrow Philocel's.   Where he espies,
What he did only fear, the beauteous maid,
His woful Cælia, whom (ere night array'd
Last time the world in suit of mournful black,   665
More dark than use, as to bemoan their wrack)
He at his cottage left in sleep's soft arms
By pow'r of simples and the force of charms :
Which time had now dissolv'd, and made her know
For what intent her love had left her so.   670
She stay'd not to awake her mate in sleep,
Nor to bemoan her fate.   She scorn'd to weep,
Or have the passion that within her lies
So distant from her heart as in her eyes.
But rending of her hair, her throbbing breast   675
Beating with ruthless strokes, she onward press'd
As an enraged furious lioness,
Through uncouth treadings of the wilderness,
In hot pursuit of her late missed brood.
The name of Philocel speaks every wood,   680
And she begins to still and still her pace :
Her face deck'd anger, anger deck'd her face.
So ran distracted Hecuba along
The streets of Troy.   So did the people throng
With helpless hands and heavy hearts to see   685
Their woful ruin in her progeny.
And harmless flocks of sheep that nearly fed
Upon the open plains wide scattered,

666.—Wrack, destruction.   681.—Still, slacken.

Ran all afront, and gaz'd with earnest eye
(Not without tears) while thus she passed by.   690
Springs that long time before had held no drop,
Now welled forth and over-went the top :
Birds left to pay the spring their wonted vows,
And all forlorn sat drooping on the boughs :   [695
Sheep, springs and birds, nay trees' unwonted groans
Bewail'd her chance, and forc'd it from the stones.

  Thus came she to the place (where aged men,
Maidens and wives, and youth and childeren   .
That had but newly learnt their mothers' name,
Had almost spent their tears before she came,)   700
And those her earnest and related words
Threw from her breast ; and unto them affords
These as the means to further her pretence :
Receive not on your souls, by innocence   [705
Wrong'd, lasting stains which from a sluice the sea
May still wash o'er, but never wash away.
Turn all your wraths on me : for here behold
The hand that tore your sacred tree of gold ;
These are the feet that led to that intent ;
Mine was th' offence, be mine the punishment.   710
Long hath he liv'd among you, and he knew
The danger imminent that would ensue ;
His virtuous life speaks for him, hear it then !
And cast not hence the miracle of men !
What now he doth is through some discontent :   715
Mine was the fact, be mine the punishment !

716. - Fact, crime.

What certain death could never make him do
(With Cælia's loss), her presence forc'd him to.
She that could clear his greatest clouds of woes,
Some part of woman made him now disclose,   720
And show'd him all in tears : and for a while
Out of his heart unable to exile
His troubling thoughts in words to be conceiv'd ;
But weighing what the world should be bereav'd,
He of his sighs and throbs some license wan,   725
And to the sad spectators thus began :
Hasten ! O haste ! the hour's already gone,
Do not defer the execution !
Nor make my patience suffer ought of wrong !
'Tis nought to die, but to be dying long !   730
Some fit of frenzy hath possess'd the maid :
She could not do it, though she had assay'd ;
No bough grows in her reach ; nor hath the tree
A spray so weak to yield to such as she.
To win her love I broke it, but unknown   735
And undesir'd of her ; then let her own
No touch of prejudice without consent.
Mine was the fact, be mine the punishment !
   O ! who did ever such contention see
Where death stood for the prize of victory ?   740
Where love and strife were firm and truly known,
And where the victor must be overthrown ?
Where both pursu'd, and both held equal strife
That life should further death, death further life.
   Amazement struck the multitude ; and now   745

They knew not which way to perform their vow.
If only one should be depriv'd of breath,
They were not certain of th' offender's death ;
If both of them should die for that offence,
They certainly should murder innocence ;   750
If none did suffer for it, then there ran
Upon their heads the wrath and curse of Pan.
This much perplex'd and made them to defer
The deadly hand of th' executioner,
Till they had sent an officer to know   755
The judges' wills (and those with Fate's do go) :
Who back return'd, and thus with tears began :
The substitutes on earth of mighty Pan
Have thus decreed (although the one be free)
To clear themselves from all impunity,   760
If, who the offender is, no means procure,
Th' offence is certain, be their death as sure.
This is their doom (which may all plagues prevent)
To have the guilty kill the innocent.   [765
    Look as two little lads, their parents' treasure,
Under a tutor strictly kept from pleasure,
While they their new-given lesson closely scan,
Hear of a message by their father's man,
That one of them, but which he hath forgot,
Must come along and walk to some fair plot ;   770
Both have a hope : their careful tutor loath
To hinder either, or to license both,
Sends back the messenger that he may know
His master's pleasure which of them must go :

While both his scholars stand alike in fear   775
Both of their freedom and abiding there,
The servant comes and says that for that day
Their father wills to have them both away.
Such was the fear these loving souls were in
That time the messenger had absent been.   780
But far more was their joy 'twixt one another,
In hearing neither should outlive the other.
    Now both entwin'd, because no conquest won
Yet either ruined, Philocel begun
To arm his love for death : a robe unfit   785
Till Hymen's saffron'd weed had usher'd it.
My fairest Cælia ! come ; let thou and I,
That long have learn'd to love, now learn to die ;
It is a lesson hard if we discern it,
Yet none is born so soon as bound to learn it.   790
Unpartial fate lays ope the book to us,
And let[s] us con it still embracing thus ;
We may it perfect have, and go before
Those that have longer time to read it o'er ;
And we had need begin and not delay,   795
For 'tis our turn to read it first to-day.
Help when I miss, and when thou art in doubt
I'll be thy prompter, and will help thee out.
But see how much I err : vain metaphor
And elocution destinies abhor.   800
Could death be stay'd with words, or won with tears,
Or mov'd with beauty, or with unripe years,
Sure thou couldst do't ; this rose, this sun-like eye

Should not so soon be quell'd, so quickly die.
But we must die, my love ; not thou alone,   805
Nor only I, but both ; and yet but one.
Nor let us grieve ; for we are married thus,
And have by death what life denied us.
It is a comfort from him more than due ;
" Death severs many, but he couples few."   810
Life is a flood that keeps us from our bliss,
The ferryman to waft us thither is
Death, and none else ; the sooner we get o'er
Should we not thank the ferryman the more?
Others entreat him for a passage hence,   815
And groan beneath their griefs and impotence,
Yet (merciless) he lets those longer stay,
And sooner takes the happy man away.
Some little happiness have thou and I,
Since we shall die before we wish to die.   820
Should we here longer live, and have our days
As full in number as the most of these,
And in them meet all pleasures may betide,
We gladly might have liv'd and patient died.
When now our fewer years, made long by cares,   825
That without age can snow down silver hairs,
Make all affirm which do our griefs descry
We patiently did live, and gladly die.
The difference, my love, that doth appear
Betwixt our fates and theirs that see us here,   830
Is only this : the high all-knowing Pow'r
Conceals from them, but tells us our last hour.

For which to Heaven we far-far more are bound
Since in the hour of death we may be found,
By its prescience, ready for the hand   835
That shall conduct us to the holy land.
When those, from whom that hour conceal'd is, may
Even in their height of sin be ta'en away.
Besides, to us Justice a friend is known,
Which neither lets us die nor live alone.   840
That we are forc'd to it cannot be held ;
" Who fears not death, denies to be compell'd."
    O that thou wert no actor in this play,
My sweetest Cælia ! or divorc'd away
From me in this : O Nature ! I confess   845
I cannot look upon her heaviness
Without betraying that infirmity
Which at my birth thy hand bestow'd on me.
Would I had died when I receiv'd my birth !
Or known the grave before I knew the earth !   850
Heavens ! I but one life did receive from you,
And must so short a loan be paid with two ?
Cannot I die but like that brutish stem
Which have their best belov'd to die with them ?
O let her live ! some bless'd power hear my cry! 855
Let Cælia live and I contented die.
    My Philocel (quoth she) neglect these throes !
Ask not for me, nor add not to my woes !
Can there be any life when thou art gone ?

853.—Stem, race, nation.

Nay, can there be but desolation ?   860
Art thou so cruel as to wish my stay,
To wait a passage at an unknown day ?
Or have me dwell within this vale of woe,
Excluded from those joys which thou shalt know ?
Envy not me that bliss ! I will assay it,   865
My love deserves it, and thou canst not stay it.
Justice ! then take thy doom ; for we intend,
Except both live, no life : one love, one end.

Thus with embraces and exhorting other :   [870
With tear-dew'd kisses that had pow'r to smother
Their soft and ruddy lips close join'd with either,
That in their deaths their souls might meet together :
With prayers as hopeful as sincerely good,
Expecting death they on the cliff's edge stood,
And lastly were (by one oft forcing breath)   875
Thrown from the rock into the arms of death.

Fair Thetis, whose command the waves obey,
Loathing the loss of so much worth as they,
Was gone before their fall ; and by her pow'r
The billows (merciless, us'd to devour,   880
And not to save,) she made to swell up high,
Even at the instant when the tragedy
Of those kind souls should end : so to receive them,
And keep what cruelty would fain bereave them.
Her hest was soon perform'd : and now they lay 885
Embracing on the surface of the sea,

885.—*Hest*, behest, command.

Void of all sense ; a spectacle so sad
That Thetis, nor no nymph which there she had,
Touch'd with their woes, could for a while refrain,
But from their heavenly eyes did sadly rain   890
Such show'rs of tears (so pow'rful, since divine)
That ever since the sea doth taste of brine.
With tears, thus to make good her first intent,
She both the lovers to her chariot hent :
Recalling life that had not clearly ta'en   895
Full leave of his or her more curious fane,
And with her praise sung by these thankful pair
Steer'd on her coursers, swift as fleeting air,
Towards her palace built beneath the seas,
Proud of her journey, but more proud of these. 900
  By that time Night had newly spread her robe
Over our half-part of this massy globe,
She won that famous Isle which Jove did please
To honour with the holy Druidës ;
And as the western side she stript along,   905
Heard, and so stay'd to hear, this heavy song :

O Heaven ! what may I hope for in this cave ?
                              A Grave.
But who to me this last of helps shall retch ?
                              A Wretch.   910
Shall none be by pitying so sad a wight ?
                              Yes : Night.

894.—*Hent*, took.   903.—*Isle*, Anglesea.
905.—*Stript*, moved rapidly.   909.—*Retch*, reach.

Small comfort can befall in heavy plight
To me, poor maid, in whose distresses be
Nor hope, nor help, nor one to pity me,   915
But a cold Grave, a Wretch, and darksome Night.

To dig that grave what fatal things appears?
                              Thy Tears.
What bell shall ring me to that bed of ease?
                              Rough Seas.   920
And who for mourners hath my Fate assign'd?
                              Each Wind.
Can any be debarr'd from such I find?
When to my last rites gods no other send   [925
To make my grave, for knell, or mourning friend,
Than mine own Tears, rough Seas, and gusts of
        Wind.

Tears must my grave dig : but who bringeth those?
                              Thy Woes.
What monument will Heaven my body spare?
                              The Air.   930
And what the epitaph when I am gone?
                              Oblivion.
Most miserable I, and like me none
Both dying, and in death, to whom is lent
Nor spade, nor epitaph, nor monument,   935
Excepting Woes, Air, and Oblivion.

The end of this gave life unto a groan,
As if her life and it had been but one ;

Yet she as careless of reserving either,
If possible would leave them both together.   940
It was the fair Marina, almost spent
With grief and fear of future famishment.
For (hapless chance) but the last rosy morn
The willing redbreast, flying through a thorn,
Against a prickle gor'd his tender side,   945
And in an instant so, poor creature, died.
   Thetis, much mov'd with those sad notes she heard,
Her freeing thence to Triton soon referr'd ;
Who found the cave as soon as set on shore,
And by his strength removing from the door   950
A weighty stone, brought forth the fearful maid,
Which kindly led where his fair mistress stay'd,
Was entertain'd as well became her sort,
And with the rest steer'd on to Thetis' court,
For whose release from imminent decay   955
My Muse awhile will here keep holiday.

THE END OF THE SECOND BOOK.

THE END OF VOL. I.